Above Scandal

Joan Leacott

For Jackie
Welcome to the streets
of Clarence Bay
Joan Leacott

Woven Red Productions
Toronto, Canada

Woven Red Productions
19 Watford Avenue
Toronto, Ontario, Canada M6C 1G4
wovenred@gmail.com

Cover by Kim Killion, TheKillionGroupInc.com
Edited by Kristin Anders, TheRomanticEditor.com
Formatted by Amy Atwell, AuthorEMS.com

Above Scandal/Joan Leacott—1st edition
ISBN 978-0-9920028-0-0

All my love to my Victor; husband, supporter, and best friend. I don't know what I'd do without you.

Clarence (Cal) F. Armstrong, 1923-2004
"It's refreshing!"

Acknowledgements

This story could not have come alive without the dedication, patience and skill of
Helen Scott Taylor,
Mona Risk and
Gina Grant.

Donating additional brain power were
Tina Everitt, Kate Freiman,
Irene Jorgensen, and Bonnie Staring.

Making sure I got the Italian phrases just right is my friend and translator,
Luisa Giacometti.

Much appreciation goes to my publishing team;
Editor Kristin Anders who makes me sound so good,
Cover Designer Kim Killion who makes me look so good
and
Amy Atwell who's good for whatever ails a writer.

Thank you all!

"'Books are people,' smiled Miss Marks, 'In every book worth reading, the author is there to meet you, to establish contact with you. He takes you into his confidence and reveals his thoughts to you.'"

The Four Graces
D.E. Stevenson

Table of Contents

Chapter 1
Homecoming 15

Chapter 2
Seeing Is Believing 33

Chapter 3
Stay or Go 55

Chapter 4
New Friends 72

Chapter 5
Truth and Lies 88

Chapter 6
Proposals 101

Chapter 7
Name Calling 115

Chapter 8
Sorting Things Out 134

Chapter 9
Wishes and Words 155

Chapter 10
Photograph and Memory 172

Chapter 11
Secrets and Bargains 192

Chapter 12
Revelations 216

Chapter 13
Reunion 245

Chapter 14
A Funeral 266

Chapter 15
Choices 286

Chapter 16
Election Results 314

Chapter 17
Mother and Daughter 326

Chapter 18
Third Time Lucky 346

Epilogue 360

Meet Joan 367

Other Books by Joan Leacott 369

CHAPTER 1

Homecoming

Home. Memories of screaming matches, slamming doors, and bitter tears rose on a sour wave of bile.

Stopped in the driveway of the big red brick house, Cathy unglued her fingers one at a time from the steering wheel and put the idling Lexus in reverse.

"Mom, is this Nonna's house?" ten-year-old Hayley asked.

Cathy nodded.

"Mo-om, are you okay?"

Maybe. If they let us in.

"Just nervous, Hayley sweetie. It's been a while." Eleven years since life had driven Cathy away. Now death drew her back.

Through the rear-view mirror, she glimpsed Ryan's house across the street. Did he still live there?

Low pewter clouds bustled overhead. If only her memory could be cleansed as easily as the rain washed the dusty roads and sidewalks of Clarence Bay.

Sighing hard and deep, Cathy put her car in park and turned off the engine. She climbed out, smoothed her sleeveless pink blouse over her black jeans, and pushed her eyeglasses up her nose. A chilly raindrop splat on her shoulder and ran down her pristine front. She shivered and groaned at the mess.

Hayley giggled. "Better'n bird poop."

Cathy's tension eased just enough to permit a wry huff before snapping back like a hard rubber band. Holding hands, they walked up the front path to the deep porch.

"Well, here goes nothing." Cathy pressed the doorbell with a trembling finger.

"Don't worry, Mom. It'll work itself out."

Cathy's jumpy gaze skittered over the old house and its property—the neatly mown lawn, the freshly dug garden without a weed in sight, the sparkling windows. Somebody had a great way with yard tools.

The screen door rattled as the inside door opened. Zia Yola, grown softer and rounder in Cathy's absence, stood gaping at them.

"*Ciao*, Zia Yola," Cathy said in Italian and held her breath for her aunt's reaction.

Zia Yola's hands fluttered to her pale cheeks, her dark eyes huge above her stubby nails. Her gaze bounced between Cathy and Hayley as if she didn't quite believe her own sight.

"Are you my grandmother?" Hayley asked.

Zia Yola's fingers slid to cover her mouth and fisted there. She blinked rapidly and a few tears trickled down her cheeks. After several minutes of struggle, she released a shuddering breath. "No, I am nobody's *nonna*. I am your *prozia*, your great-aunt Yolanda. *Sì*, Caterina?"

Cathy nodded, distracted by the current of sadness running under Zia Yola's words. Nobody's grandmother. How much had her tender-hearted aunt sacrificed to help raise her?

Zia Yola shook herself. "*Santo cielo*, what am I doing keeping you on the doorstep? Come in, come in." She stepped back and opened the door wide.

Cathy followed Hayley into the square front hall that seemed smaller and darker than she remembered. The scent of sautéed garlic, ripe tomatoes, and fresh basil hadn't changed. Here, the upkeep was just as obvious as outside, but not as surprising. No self-respecting Italian homemaker allowed her home to become dirty, no matter the state of her health.

Hayley crossed her legs tightly. "Mom, I need to pee so bad," she whispered behind her hand.

Cathy pointed down the hall. "The washroom is through the kitchen and on your left." Hayley's jean-clad little butt disappeared before Cathy confirmed the location with her aunt.

"*Sì*, it's still in the same place." Zia Yola scrutinized Cathy from head to toe, then crossed an arm over her waist and propped the other akimbo in her characteristic stance showing both her strength and her indecision.

"You look well, Caterina. I—we missed you."

"I—um—I missed you, too." As she said the words, Cathy acknowledged the truth. She had missed her aunt. Her nerves twisted in sharp anxiety. Afraid to ask, she needed to know. "How's Mamma?"

Zia Yola shook her head. "As well as can be expected. The cancer is gone, but the chemotherapy wore her out. She is very weak, very tired, always sleeping. And her hair—" Zia Yola ran a jittery hand over her own thick waves and sighed. "She's asleep right now. I'll let her know you've arrived when she wakes up in a couple of hours." Neither of them dared to predict her response.

Disappointment, strongly flavoured by relief, slowed Cathy's chaotic thoughts.

Zia Yola tilted her head in the direction Hayley had gone. "You didn't—?"

Cathy pushed her glasses up her nose and checked out the web-free corners of the ceiling. "No, I didn't. My heart forbade me to give her away or destroy her."

"But your heart let you hide her from us? For ten, nearly eleven, years?"

Cathy stared blindly at her purse strap, wrapping and unwrapping it around her hand, reining in her resentment. She lifted her head, chin jutting. "Yes. Mamma was so ashamed, so disgusted with me, so afraid of the scandal. She didn't want me—us—here. So, yes, I left."

Zia Yola gazed at Cathy with sad dark eyes. "You lied to us, sneaking out when we thought you were asleep. Your mother tried to teach you better than that. We both thought you weren't so foolish as to—" Zia Yola gestured vaguely.

Defensive heat crawled up Cathy's cheeks. She had done all kinds of things to escape her mother's haranguing. Especially about sex: dirty, dangerous, forbidden sex. A jolt of near-forgotten desire zinged through her. Sheesh, just being in the same town as her memories of Ryan rattled her nerves.

"So many phone calls from Helen and she said nothing of your child?" Zia Yola's voice pitched high in doubt. "Such a dear old friend of mine. You went to her, you share a house together—and she said nothing?"

Helen had constantly warned no good would come of keeping Hayley's birth a secret or Cathy's relentless stubbornness in staying away.

"I asked Helen not to tell you. To protect my daughter."

Zia Yola sniffed a protest. "Does Helen know who the father is? Do you? Did you tell him?"

Cathy's hands clenched and her mouth tightened. "Yes, I know who her father is. He's on her birth certificate. And if I didn't tell you two, do you really think I'd tell him? If my own family—the only family I've got—didn't want me, refused to help me, why should I expect him to help?" Plus, he'd wrestled with his own family troubles at the time.

But things were different now. Her mother's life-threatening illness demanded at least an attempt at reconciliation before it was too late. Cathy blew a long strained breath to release her defensiveness and laid a coaxing hand on her aunt's shoulder. Only forty-five, Zia Yola looked every minute as old as her sixty-three-year-old sister Lucia. So much premature grey in her aunt's hair, so many burdens she carried. Cathy prayed she didn't add to the heap. "I didn't come to justify my decisions. I got eight weeks compassionate leave to see Mamma, to help you if you'll let me. I brought Hayley in case..."

Her aunt's face held rigid for a long unbearable moment then collapsed in soft folds of grief. She stared up the staircase and Cathy followed her gaze. Pale grey light shone through the landing window, skipped over the once-rich tones of the stair runner. Countless times Cathy had stormed down those stairs and out the door in desperate need of the secret comfort of Ryan's arms.

"What's done is done." Zia Yola raised her hands in

benediction, grasped Cathy by the shoulders, and planted a solemn kiss on either cheek. The warm belated greeting eased Cathy's doubt, yet stirred a new regret. Perhaps she should have come back sooner when the situation wasn't so dire.

Zia Yola crossed herself and tapped her chest over her heart. "*Se Dio vuole*, Lucia will forgive the secret and be happy to see you. And her *nipote*."

Yes, God willing, Mamma would forgive her and greet her granddaughter with an open heart. Cathy huffed a sarcastic breath. As if she actually wanted forgiveness. More like Mamma should beg Cathy's forgiveness for throwing her out in a desperate time. She killed the useless thoughts.

Hayley skipped into the room, arms swinging, curls bobbing. How did she always manage to lose whatever clip Cathy put in her untameable hair?

Hayley stilled as if scenting distress in the air. She gave Cathy a big grin and stuck out her right hand towards her great-aunt. "*Buon giorno, Prozia* Yolanda. My name is Hayley Rossetti and I'm pleased to meet you," she sing-songed her practiced Italian introduction.

Cathy's aunt took the proffered hand with lifted eyebrows and a kind smile at Hayley's irresistible charm. "I am delighted to meet you at long last, *piccola*. You must call me Zia Yola like your Mamma does. Yes?"

"Sure."

With a puzzled frown, Zia Yola scanned Hayley's features closely, took her face gently in her palms and tipped it towards the light streaming in the open door. "You remind me of someone from long ago." She stroked Hayley's wild mop of sandy ringlets.

Hayley's eyes sharpened at the comment. Before her aunt speculated any further, Cathy hustled her daughter out to unload the car.

Whom did Zia Yola see in Hayley? Apart from her curly hair and fair complexion, Hayley looked nothing at all like Ryan. She'd taken only her dark eyes from Cathy's typical Italian face. The origin of her daughter's other features hung hidden on the family grapevine.

Regardless of some phantom resemblance, dangerous recollections must be circumvented until Cathy's second goal was accomplished. She needed to know what sort of man Ryan had become.

As Ryan climbed the stairs of his older brother's sprawling red brick home, an odd noise from across the street snagged his attention. Maybe a branch, broken during the recent storms, rubbed against the Rossetti house. Just as he turned to check it out, Mark opened the door.

"Hey, Ryan. You're late. Tell me you remembered the steaks," Mark said. "Meg will crack my nuts if you didn't."

Ryan handed him the heavy shopping bag. "Sorry. I stopped to get a new watch battery at Streight's Jewellers. Do you remember Luc Tessier from high school?"

Mark stepped aside to let Ryan enter. "Yeah, a big goofy guy, played linebacker. Not too bright. What about him?"

"He's getting married."

Mark whistled his surprise. "He played his cards close to the vest. Who's he marrying?"

"Kate somebody from Sudbury. Anyway, he conned me into helping him pick an engagement ring, a honking big thing that'll make her walk lopsided. I tried to convince him to go smaller, but..."

"Go big or go home."

They chuckled together as Mark mimicked the absurd gait of a woman dragging her left hand as she walked.

Reaching for the screen door's handle, Ryan started to leave again. "I'll be right back. Something sounds funny over at Cath—the Rossetti—house. I want to see if anything's wrong." Old and once-dear habits died hard, like still thinking of the place as Cathy's even though she was long gone.

"Aw, later, Ry. Can't be serious or one of them would've called you. The Jays' game is almost over and it's a real nail-biter." Mark grabbed his arm and dragged him into the family room. Their dad Bucky waved from an oversized armchair. Mark's ten-year-old daughter Lindsey and two young boys hollered a greeting from their scrunched-up positions on the worn couch in front of the wide-screen TV. Mark crossed in front of them to the far end of the couch, eliciting complaints along the way, and plopped down beside his boys.

Lindsey launched herself off the couch towards Ryan. He caught her and tucked his pretty niece sideways onto his lap as he sat down in another big armchair. He tapped the little girl's Blue Jays' cap over her merry grey eyes. "Hey, cutie. How's it going?"

He suppressed a chuckle at the clown fringe of sandy curls—the main reason he never wore a ball cap himself. There was no dealing with the mop inherited from his mother's family.

"Things are tense. Bottom of the ninth, bases loaded, two outs. We're gonna blow it for sure," moaned the mini-announcer.

"I meant, how goes your life?" He breathed in his niece's pinesap and bubblegum scent. She must have been climbing her favourite tree out in the yard.

"It's summer, it's boring." She sighed long and deep and rolled her eyes to underscore her boredom. "Dad's way busy and we're not going anywhere."

"Well, ya know the sad score, kiddo." Mark said, tweaking her foot. "Between my peak-season ranger hours at the park and your school hours all the rest of the year, family vacations are hard to schedule."

Lindsey sagged in pitiful agreement.

"How about we go to the beach next week?" Ryan said to her.

"Cool! Without *them*, right?" She excluded her younger brothers with a haughty pout.

"Sure thing." Chuckling, he bent to whisper in her ear. "We'll get some ice cream."

"Deal!" She squeezed his neck in a vertebra-cracking hug. God, he was crazy about the kid. If he ever had a daughter, he'd want one just like her.

The pitcher wound up and let the ball fly. *Crr-ack!* The ball sailed into the stands and the crowd went wild. Lindsey squealed and bounced on his knees. His dad clapped his hands in satisfaction.

Mark's chubby wife marched into the room and snatched up the grocery bag with an irritated snort. "Steaks aren't gonna get ready for the grill by sitting on the floor," she grumbled and marched back out.

"Sorry, babe. The game was almost over," Mark called after her. Meg slammed the kitchen door for her answer. Mark hunched a shoulder and tried not to look sheepish at Meg's display of temper.

"Mom's probably cranky because of the baby coming." Lindsey nodded, wise in the ways of pregnancy yet oblivious to the stresses an unexpected fourth child put on her parents' limited resources.

Defeated, Mark shrugged and Ryan's mood dipped in sympathy.

"Yeah, you're probably right, kiddo." Mark flicked off the end-of-game show and flopped against the couch. "So how'd the campaign meeting go, Ry?"

Before Ryan answered, his dad twisted in his chair. "Having trouble, son? Let me talk to Bill and see if he can help you out."

"No thanks, Dad. We'll manage without his kind of help."

"Don't be stupid, Ryan. Bill ran every one of my campaigns. He knows a thing or two about getting elected."

"I'd prefer not to smear my opponents with mud from their pasts. It's just plain wrong."

"Right or wrong has nothing to do with anything. That's how politics work. You gotta look good. No matter what it takes."

Ryan cringed at his Dad's most ominous phrase. "I run a clean campaign, or no campaign."

"You're completely unrealistic. I'll make a few calls."

"Dad, no." Ryan forced himself to stay put, to not break up the family get-together. His Dad would never understand clean, honest, open, or any other up-front word. Ryan's current term as the youngest-ever town councillor had really opened his eyes to the damage his father had wrought during his multiple terms as mayor. Damage that Ryan needed to repair to make his town strong, to help it deal with the threat of encroaching malls and an empty downtown.

"I'm with Ry, keep it clean. At least until your competition starts slinging mud." Mark weighed in with his opinion.

"There's no mud to sling at me, so I'll be fine," Ryan said.

"They'll find something. They always do," his dad retorted.

Ryan squirmed. His dad knew plenty about scandals popping up when least expected. "Then they'll have to make something up. I have nothing to hide. Never had, never will."

Except for his youthful relationship with his sweet Cathy. His family knew nothing of their long and increasingly intimate relationship that ended when she left eleven long years ago. Nor how Cathy had gone incommunicado with her aunt revealing only that she was fine. Nor how he forced himself to tend to the house because Cathy asked him to during their final date. Their final date that had meant so much to him and so little to her.

"Everybody has something to hide. Though I haven't a clue what yours might be, you keep your lip buttoned so tight."

Ryan spread his arms wide. "My life is an open book. Transparent—like my slogan says."

"What a stupid way to run a town. People don't want to know all sides to an argument. They only want to know what will line their pockets."

"Closed doors breed misinformation and distrust." As do shady deals with kickbacks for look-the-other-way councillors and their mayors. The shenanigans had gone from bad to worse when his dad left office and stepped into Grandpa's shoes at Chisholm Lakeland Development Corporation.

"Dad, we've been down this road too many times. We'll have to agree to disagree," Ryan said, frustrated with the oft-repeated argument.

His dad jabbed a finger at him. "You'll soon find out people haven't a damn clue what's good for them. Sometimes you just make a decision and don't worry about *full disclosure*." He hung condescending air quotes around the last two words.

"When do you announce your candidacy?" Mark the peacekeeper said.

"Monday, for the *Beacon's* Wednesday print run."

"How's Becca?" His dad cut to his latest favourite nag.

"She's good."

"When are you going to propose?"

Ryan caught a sympathetic glance from Mark. "Geez, Dad. We've been dating for less than two months. She's only twenty-one. I don't want to rush her."

"If you announce your engagement along with your candidacy you'll get her family's support and influence. With the right touch, she'll make an excellent political wife."

"You said so before. And as I said before, I'm—we're not ready to commit." Not by a long shot.

"All you need is an engagement. You can break up after you win."

Ryan shuddered at the crass manipulation. "Oh, yeah, real honest and open."

His dad smirked. "Stop being so naïve. The minute you take office, you'll learn it's the only way to get things done."

Ryan shrugged and changed the topic. Naïve or not, open and honest was Ryan's way to repair his father's damage and make Clarence Bay whole and prosperous.

Later in the evening, Ryan left Mark's place, grateful for the quiet twilight lingering in the early-summer sky. As he opened the door of his truck, the *squeak-eek* noise over at the Rossetti's started up again—a friendly kind of squeak, non-threatening. Ryan smiled at his fanciful idea. Friendly or not, the sound was unusual coming from her house at this hour. He shut the truck door and walked across the road.

The noise stuttered and then the rhythm started up again. Somebody worked the front porch swing. The person who owned the car now sitting in the driveway?

As he stepped silently over the grass by the sidewalk, a quiet chuckle followed by a sigh told his heart it was Cathy. He'd hoped she might come back with her mom so ill. Awful thought—but he couldn't control his thoughts or his heart where Cathy was concerned.

He mounted the steps. His brain needed to actually see her by the extra light of the flickering candles before he believed. The rest of him stood there like a complete idiot.

Cathy? Had merely thinking of her conjured her from thin air?

In the pale evening light, she looked exactly the same—small curvy body and straight dark hair. She sat the same way, one foot tucked beneath her and an ever-present book on her knee. The sexy librarian glasses were new.

She lifted her head. Her big soft-brown eyes still carried a punch strong enough to knock him back in time a whole eleven years.

Her eyes widened in surprise, a trembling hand rose to her mouth. "Oh, hi..." She coughed, skimmed her palm down her throat, visibly collecting herself. "Hi, Ryan."

A surge of happiness pushed up from his gut. He sucked in a deep breath to steady his wobbly knees and swallowed hard against the truth. She was the reason for his years of loneliness and worry. She was not bringing him joy of any kind. "Hi, Cathy. It's...ah...been a while."

She smiled, tentative and sweet. Slowly, she tucked in a bookmark, tapped off the mini-light, and set the book beside her. "Yes, a while. How have you been?" Untwining her legs, the swing moved and her book slapped to the wooden porch floor.

The hollow clunk twanged his taut nerves, scrambled his thoughts. "You've come for your mother?" An obvious comment, but it filled the booming silence.

"Yes. I got eight weeks compassionate leave from work."

"Good. Your aunt will appreciate the help."

"Would you like some wine?"

She leaned towards the small table. Her thin shawl slipped to her elbows, revealing the delicate curves of her bare shoulders. The hem of her sexy tank top flirted with the top edge of her bra. He flashed back to the tongue-tied lust-frozen days of his youth.

"Ryan? Wine?"

A tiny smile tilted the corners of her eyes as she lifted the shawl back over her shoulders. He hauled his eyeballs off her, noticed the two glasses, and lifted a questioning brow.

"Zia Yola intended to join me, but Mamma needed her." She could still read his thoughts. Just like he could still read the hardening of her mouth against her mother's constant interference between Cathy and Zia Yola.

"Where did you go?" His vocal chords tightened against the repressed emotion of eleven long anxious years.

"University. You know that."

He frowned at her flippancy. "I meant, where did you disappear to almost as soon as you got to the city?"

She eased her ruffled skirt out from under her thighs and smoothed it over her knees, avoiding eye contact. "The noise in residence drove me crazy, so I moved out."

"Why didn't you leave a forwarding address? Call, write, visit?"

Finally, she met his eyes with a slight confusion. "We agreed to live our own lives, right?"

Yeah, he remembered the agreement to lead separate lives. "That was before—" He faltered. Unable to forget their last night together, he'd tried to find her. Then his mom died and he'd lost them both.

Her chin dipped. "Did you expect a fairy tale ending?" She stared at the wine bottle.

No, not fairy tales. He had hoped their passion was strong enough to keep them together despite their schools being in separate cities. He wasn't angry with her. She hadn't slunk off in the middle of the night or anything. But he had been disappointed and concerned. "I worried about you, if you were safe."

"Did you ask Zia Yola?"

He nodded. "Of course. She said you were doing fine."

A faint wryness twisted her tender mouth. "Be careful of wanting happy ever afters. They're not always good for you." Deep cynicism, not mockery, lurked behind her quiet words and half smile.

He waited for her tale of relationships gone wrong. Nothing. Her independent spirit remained strong—had likely gotten stronger, more set in concrete.

Sighing deeply, she offered an apologetic smile. "I'm so sorry. I didn't mean to hurt you. But you knew about my Plan."

She poured then handed him a glass. Candlelight transformed the red wine into a luminous elixir. He accepted her peace offering and sipped. The dark rich fullness eased his parched mouth. She moved to one side of the white swing, patted the empty space, inviting him to sit. The wood creaked as he settled beside her. Long-remembered heat swept up his thigh. He slid away and turned sideways in the swing, stretched his arm along the spindled back, and scanned her lovely features. Gone was the slashing black eye makeup of her youth. Mature confidence sat on her as easily as her shawl.

"How did The Plan work out?" He smiled. She'd always used capital letters in relation to her future goals.

She shook her head fondly, releasing her sophisticated spicy-flowery scent to tease his senses. "On the whole, The Plan worked exactly the way I planned." She rolled her eyes at her word choice. "I graduated with a joint Juris Doctor and MBA degree from the University of Toronto and landed a job as a Director of Accounts Management for a large investment firm. I have a good life. The Plan worked out perfectly."

He raised his glass to her. "Impressive accomplishments—law and business degrees. I always knew you'd be a huge success." He dared not ask about her love life. Her earlier cynicism and evasion were answer enough. Funny how she used to raise her hackles like a porcupine did its quills, telegraphing her defensiveness. Now, she hid her spikes behind a subtle facade.

"Thank you." She drank, leaving a dark drop on the sweet plumpness of her lower lip. He curbed an overwhelming impulse to lean forward and lap it up. His glass clicked on his teeth in his clumsy attempt to sip nonchalantly.

Her shawl slipped from her bare shoulder and logic slipped from his mind. Unbidden, his fingertips rested on the warm curve. Her soft hair tickled his skin. Desire scampered up his arm, flew over his chest, and plunged into his groin. His breath jammed in his throat. Smiling faintly, she shifted her back against the swing's armrest and bent her knee under her wide skirt.

Long-ago chatter and laughter, kisses and whispers tinted the air. They'd sat for hours like this in the front seat of his dad's car, parked out at Mill Lake, before Cathy slid back into her house undetected, safe from her mother's wrath.

"What about you?" she asked.

"Umm... Huh?" *Such intelligent conversation.* He shook free of the spell cast by his brief contact. "Uh... I did my Bachelor in Commerce in Sudbury to be close to Mom. After university, I tried to work for my dad—"

She sucked in an audible breath. "Ouch."

Chuckling, he nodded ruefully. "Yep, it was a nightmare. I hated the wheeling and dealing, the hidden agendas and dodgy real estate deals. Didn't last long. So, I bought the hardware store from Mr. Bauer's estate. I got voted to the town council four years ago. I work hard, play not so hard. My life is rather ordinary." In an admittedly peevish move, he skipped the relationships just like she had. He squared his shoulders and sat taller, prouder. "Except, next week, I'll be announcing my bid for the mayor's office."

A huge smile lit her face. "That's amazing! You'll make an excellent mayor."

Her approval flowed through his entire being. Damn, he was blushing.

She touched his wrist and lingered. “I’m so sorry I couldn’t get back when your mom passed away—the exams and essays killed me. Did you get my condolence card?”

“Yeah.” A random wave of grief swamped him. He gripped her hand. Strength and sympathy flowed from her cool fingers, soothing him the way he’d longed for all those years ago. He swallowed back the welling in his eyes. “Dad was devastated and I blew a term at school. I think he still misses her.”

“Caterina,” Zia Yola called from inside the house. “*Vieni e aiutami, per favore.*”

Cathy stood and walked to the screen door. “*Sì, Zia, vengo,*” she replied. She turned back to Ryan. “I have to go. It’s been wonderful chatting with you.”

Impulsively, he took her in his arms and held her close. Hot joy poured through him, warming his body and waking his soul from its long cold sleep.

“Will I see you while you’re here?”

“Soon, I hope. Depends—”

“Caterina!” Zia Yola was panic-stricken.

Without a word, Cathy turned and flew into the house, leaving behind the scent of her sophisticated perfume.

He piled her book and the wine things on the tray and stepped into the hall. Upstairs, the women conversed in rapid Italian. He paused in case they needed help. They didn’t call him, so he left the stuff in the kitchen. Locking the front door on the way out, Cathy’s incomplete statement lingered in his thoughts.

Depends on what?

CHAPTER 2

Seeing Is Believing

"Hey, Ryan!" Bill Hadley, Dad's old crony and campaign manager, flagged Ryan down in the grocery store parking lot. Bill shut Ryan's truck door for him as Ryan settled into the driver's seat. Bill propped a foot on the running board and a hand on the window sill. "How ya doin'?"

"Fine, Bill. How are you?" Ryan put his key in the ignition.

"Good, good. Listen, kid, when are you sending a crew out to fix the boat launch by my place? It's crumbling like no tomorrow."

"I'll ask the town clerk to get it checked, set a priority and place a work order." He fired up the engine to prompt Bill to get off his truck so Ryan could get away.

"Damn it, kid, there's no need to bother Susie with all that paper. You just send someone out next week and get it taken care of. Just like Bucky always did."

"Sure thing, Bill." Not. Yeah, the boat launch was "public," but Bill was the only person who used it, likely even knew of it's existence. There were many such "gifts" still on the Clarence

Bay books from Bucky to his assorted pals. Items that would all be struck off with Ryan's first budget if he was elected mayor.

Bill laughed heartily. "By God, you're a real chip off the old Buckster! By the way, the wife tells me you're giving your girl a hell of a send-off." He gave Ryan a broad wink.

Ryan glanced in puzzlement at the nice bunch of flowers on the seat beside him that he'd purchased for Becca. He'd intended them to serve a double purpose: a small happy-travels gift and to soften the blow of break-up.

A short beep of a horn behind Bill interrupted the conversation. He tipped his head in the direction of a big, shiny truck. "That's the wife waiting for me. She and her gal pals want to watch their show live at eight sharp." He tapped the window sill twice. "Can't wait to see the big day."

A longer beep sounded. Bill tapped the window sill once more and jogged off. Grimacing at Bill's assumption of "service," Ryan continued on his way to Becca's home.

On arrival, he sat in the drive, reluctant to enter the over-the-top monster of a showplace. Beyond the sloping expanse of manicured lawns, assorted vessels and water toys floated beside acres of deck jutting out into the bay.

Weariness pressed down on his shoulders and spirit. Between plans for the mayoral campaign kick-off, staying on top of things at the hardware store, and trying to keep Becca happy he was worn to a frazzle. He rubbed his eyes, squeezed the nape of his neck in the foolish hope of getting rid of his tension.

Now, for extra sauce on top, Cathy was back. Still beautiful, still sexy. Still making him crazy, jumpy, and turned on as hell. Cathy's final word before she dashed inside last night chimed in his ears—depends. Once more, his thoughts spun on the hamster wheel squeaking in his mind.

Did she want to know if he was available? Did he care? Was *she* available and did *she* care? *Geez, get a grip.* Who the hell did he think he was anyway—the King of Clarence Bay? She's home for her mother's sake. God, what an overblown ego he had.

Why was he still dating Becca? Long blonde hair, big blue eyes, and nice curves were good to start with, but at not quite two months into the relationship, the feeble spark had fizzled and died. Even the embers of the fire he'd shared with Cathy all those years ago burned brighter and hotter than anything he shared with Becca.

He unbuckled his seatbelt. Past time to end things with Becca, before he hurt her too badly. Man, he dreaded the drama.

Becca ended his procrastination by flinging herself through the front door and down the driveway. She opened his truck door, dragged him out, and hugged him hard enough to stop his breath. He returned a weak embrace.

"Ryan, why have you been sitting out here for so long? Come on in. I'm so glad you're here, even if you can only stay for a bit. Although there's no point in going to sleep early. I'm so excited about my trip to the Far East, I won't sleep a wink. But Mother's on my case and it's just easier to let her have her way."

Her eyes glowed even more when he handed her the flowers. "Oh, Ryan that's so sweet of you." She flung her arms around his neck for another strangulating hug.

Her flip-flops flapped as she escorted him through the magazine-perfect house, dropping the flowers off in the kitchen for the housekeeper to put in water. She babbled on about her multi-country tour with five of her closest friends as they continued to the family room where a massive television took pride of place. Ryan groaned inwardly when she pushed him down into the blue plaid couch and straddled his lap. She laid a kiss on him and he struggled to find a matching enthusiasm. Damn, the breakup was gonna bite her hard. He wished the deed already done. Dare he swing it so she did the breaking up? Nah, too chicken-hearted for a decent man.

She thrust his shoulders into the couch. "Ryan, what's wrong?"

"Nothing." *Cluck, cluck.*

"Why aren't you kissing me back?"

"Umm...nerves."

"Nerves?"

"Yeah. I've been thinking about...uh...the campaign." He moved her gently to her own seat. She tilted her head in question.

"My dad's been pushing me to use Bill Hadley as my campaign manager."

"Why not? He's good, isn't he?"

"He likes to play dirty and I don't."

She shook her head as if he was a naïve boy. "Dad says all politicians have dirt sticking to their shoes, especially the winners."

"Look, I don't want to talk about this. Let's just agree to disagree. Okay?" He patted her arm and settled back. "Tell me more about your trip?" *While I screw up a bit more courage.*

He grabbed a handful of chips from the bowl on the coffee table. Her words flowed by. He drifted to last night with Cathy. Seemed like her hellion years had passed—her clothes had softened from brass studs and leather to ruffles and shawls. He laid one ankle over the other knee to hide his inopportune woody. God forbid, Becca think it was for her. His foot bounced up and down. *Nervous much?*

"Ryan!" Becca poked his ribs and he damn near jumped out of his skin.

"Damn it, why'd you do that?" He rubbed at the sore spot left by her long fake fingernail.

"You haven't heard a word I've said."

She'd been talking? Guilty heat blistered his cheeks. He uncrossed his arms and legs. "Yeah, that's good. Listen, we need to talk." He cleared his throat, squeezed the back of his neck again. *Like that helped.* "Okay, here's the thing." He cleared his throat again. "We've been going out for a couple of months now and it's been really nice—" He broke off to assess her response. She looked all right, not pissed off or anything. "So, like I said, it's been two months, and it's kinda soon for a person to make up his mind, but—"

"Yes!" Becca grabbed him, squealing and babbling and smooching him wherever skin stuck out of his shirt.

What the—she was *this* happy about ending their relationship? How insulting was that?

"Becca, calm down." He dragged her arms off his neck and pushed her back to her side of the couch.

"Calm down!" She bounced in wild enthusiasm. "How can you possibly expect me to calm down?" Then she drew a deep breath and settled primly beside him, though a big smile still wreathed her face. "I heard you were ring-shopping at Streight's yesterday. Sorry I jumped the gun." She stroked his thigh. "Go ahead and finish, I'll be patient. Just so you know—my answer is yes."

Stark-staring mad, that's what she was. Completely nuts. He

grabbed the beer Becca has set out for him. He needed to buy some time to try and figure out what the hell she meant.

"C'mon Ryan," she wheedled. "I'm sorry I interrupted your proposal."

Shock waves ran up and down his spine, colliding and building to a perfect storm of freak out. The almost-full bottle slid from his suddenly limp grasp and plopped heavily onto his crotch. Yelping in agony, he convulsed forward. The bottle took flight, spewing bubbly streamers through the air.

Once the pain subsided, he unfurled his spine to see Becca with her arms crossed, legs crossed, scowling like no tomorrow. She cut a glance at him. "You okay?"

He grunted for a response. Gingerly rising from the couch, Ryan picked up the bottle to stop the spreading puddle of beer.

"What's going on here? Why is there beer all over my floor?" Mrs. Carleton-Grant stood at the door, glaring down her narrow nose.

Scolded like a bad dog that had done a bad thing on the carpet, Ryan set the bottle on the table.

"Nothing, Mother," Becca said in a shockingly meek voice.

Stunned, he watched as Becca seemed to shrink within herself. He slid a glance at Mrs. Carleton-Grant and winced inwardly at the tension coiling between mother and daughter. Becca had said her mother was even more intimidating in private, now Ryan believed whole-heartedly. The look in her eyes could freeze water at ten paces. Handy around a rink, but terrifying up close and personal. Mrs. Carleton-Grant was one scary lady.

"Sorry about the mess." The unholy God-awful mess that had nothing to do with spilled beer.

"Indeed. You should go home and get out of your wet jeans. Through the patio doors if you don't mind."

Ryan slid open the glass door and took Becca's hand to draw her outside. "See me to my truck?" He had to talk to her, figure out what she meant, before she left for her holiday.

Becca managed a couple of steps before her mother spoke. "Becca, it's time you went to sleep. You'll need to be well-rested. There's a three-hour trip to the airport before you even check in. You can chat with Ryan when you get home." The only acknowledgment Mrs. Carleton-Grant gave Ryan was her nose wrinkling at the brewery odour hanging in the air.

With one eye on her mother, Becca hugged him just long enough to mutter in his ear, "When I get back, you can have a do-over. You get on your knee with my ring and I'll act surprised just like you want me to. Love you."

Back in his truck, Ryan frowned into the glorious sunset. Streight's Jewellers. That was the clue. Gossip had gone wild and transformed his dead watch battery into a fully-charged engagement ring. Had Becca just accepted a proposal he didn't make? Did Becca, Bill, and likely the whole damn town consider him an engaged man?

The next morning, Cathy stroked a gentle fingertip beneath her eyes. "*Dio mio*, I could have used those bags to pack the car two days ago," she murmured to her reflection. With a weary hand, she turned off the water, stepped into the lovely old claw-foot tub, and sank into the hot water. Morning sun glimmered in the rising steam misting the black-and-white tiles.

So much past, so little present, such an unknown future.

On the surface, Ryan still didn't seem to care much for his

father's scheming and conniving. A very good thing if he wanted to get anywhere near his daughter.

"But oh lordy, he's still so gorgeous." Sighing, she eased down the smooth slope of the tub. The hot lavender-scented water cooled her like a dunk in the chilly bay.

Back in the day, she'd been the only girl to call the lean and gangly Ryan a handsome boy. He'd grown magnificently into his long awkward limbs and features too large for his face. She squished the big sea sponge to her chest, hoping to ease the erratic thumping of her heart. Now she bet all the women in town were after him. What would he say to suddenly being the father of a bouncing baby pre-teen?

If he wasn't already.

Painful hot prickles on her skin upped the temperature of the water. Her trembling hand bumped her nose on the way to her mouth. *Imbecille!* Of course, he hadn't frozen in time. Just because he didn't wear a ring didn't mean he hadn't been caught.

Think, dummy. She reached to push up her glasses even though they were across the room on the windowsill. Melody and Emma. Were her old gal pals still in town so she could get the insider info on Ryan?

Now more tense than relaxed, Cathy finished her bath, opened the window to release the steam, and polished every chrome or tile surface. In the rose-papered room shared with her daughter, she redid Hayley's haphazard attempt at bed making, exchanged her bathrobe for a red T-shirt and a denim skirt and went downstairs for breakfast. Only the sight of Hayley shutting the avocado-green fridge stopped Cathy from time warping to her childhood.

"Good morning, Hayley sweetie, Zia Yola." Cathy planted kisses on her daughter's head and her aunt's cheek. Ignoring the apprehension creeping along her nerves, Cathy made herself a *latte macchiato* and toast, and joined Hayley and Zia Yola at the table. "Will Mamma see us today, Zia?"

Zia Yola swept her palm across the table scooping crumbs and dumped them onto her empty plate. "Not today, maybe tomorrow afternoon when her bath is done. Sit and have your breakfast."

Her mother had been duly informed of her arrival and now toyed with Cathy, repeatedly putting her off to another hour, another day. Typical Mamma wielding her matriarchal power. Cathy set aside her guilty relief and joined in her daughter's chatter about nothing and everything. Finished, Cathy rose and rinsed her dishes at the sink.

"Mom?" Hayley turned her head to peek over her own shoulder and Cathy stiffened. Her daughter's tone of voice meant a forthcoming pointed question. All too often these days, Hayley's questions were about her mysterious father.

"Why didn't you tell Zia Yola about me?"

Zia Yola's choked gasp sounded over the hum of the fridge. Cathy flicked a nervous glance at her. How do you tell a child she shouldn't be here?

"Because I wanted you. I loved you and wanted you. You were my baby, a part of me. I *had* to have you."

Hayley beamed her sun-bright smile, jumped up from the table and ran to Cathy for a bear hug. Cathy ignored the twinge of her conscience over her imprecise answer. How on earth to tell her sweet daughter her own grandmother and great-aunt had advised—no, demanded—she be adopted out or, Heaven forbid, aborted?

"Mom?" Her daughter looked up from the circle of her arms.

Cathy froze, fearing another bomb of a question. "Yeah, sweetie?"

"I'm bored out of my brains. Can we do something interesting today? Go shopping or something?"

Cathy sagged in relief and kissed the tip of her daughter's nose. "Well, there's not much in the way of shopping here. Nowhere near like home in Toronto." Hayley's bottom lip protruded. "How about we go to the library instead?"

Hayley considered. "Okay."

"You go get ready and then we'll take off."

Hayley squeezed Cathy one last time then scampered upstairs to the back bedroom.

"*Grazie mille*," Zia Yola rasped. Lips pressed between her teeth until the flesh whitened, she scrubbed hard at the tears on her cheeks. "Thank you for not telling her. I couldn't bear my dear *piccola's* unhappiness."

Cathy's mouth twisted. *Now* her aunt thinks about the child they had wanted dealt with?

"Please don't judge me, *uccellino*."

How long had it been since her aunt called her little bird? Zia Yola had always been so kind. She didn't deserve the harshness, especially when Cathy knew the real instigator of her troubles. Because Mamma was eighteen years older than Zia Yola, Mamma had always treated Zia Yola more as another daughter than a sister. Another delicate answer was needed to dust away the lingering bad feelings between them. Cathy crossed the room to gather her worried aunt in a big hug.

"No matter what was said or done, Mamma believed she acted

for the best. It's in the past, let's leave it there." She kissed Zia Yola's soft cheek and the familiar jasmine scent warmed Cathy. "Except for my gratitude that you sent me to your friend Helen. I don't what I would have done without her. She saved Hayley and me."

Zia Yola cupped Cathy's face and kissed her on both cheeks. "You were always so good to me."

Cathy smiled at Zia Yola's recollections. Zia Yola *had* been so very good to Cathy, providing a safe haven against her mother's harsh old-country parenting.

"So what did Mamma really say when you told her we were here?"

Zia Yola assumed her customary stance—one arm over her waist, the other propped on her hip, protective and assertive at the same time. She stared out the window.

Cathy braced herself.

"She is distressed it took such an illness to bring you home. She claims you've neglected her."

As before, Mamma delivered harsh words through Zia Yola's gentle mouth. Why did Zia Yola allow her sister to use her?

Hayley bounced into the room. "C'mon Mom, let's go."

Grateful for the timely interruption, Cathy swallowed her bitterness and followed her daughter out to the car.

"Look, Mom, a carnival. Can we see?" Hayley danced at the end of Cathy's arm as they navigated around the potholes in the library's parking area.

Books were a lost cause against kiddie rides, fast food, and craft vendors. A stage and podium sprawled by the war memorial in the park fronting the library. A *Carnival for Kids* banner floated on a gentle warming breeze above the stage.

Cathy nodded, happy to engage in some harmless fun. Hayley tore off in the direction of the fair entrance.

"What's the carnival for?" Cathy asked the cute young ticket taker in her teeny cropped T-shirt. Cathy sighed for her long gone belly-baring days.

"The Clarence Bay Volunteers are raising funds for the family shelter. And they're giving out their Helping Hand of the Year award. The purple tickets are for the food and rides, pink tickets for the raffle. The crafts are bought from the individual vendors." She handed Cathy the brochure she'd parroted.

Hayley jigged in place. "Let's go on the Ferris wheel!"

Cathy drew a crisp red bill from her wallet. "I'll take twenty-five dollars in ride tickets and twenty-five dollars in raffle tickets, please."

The teen's eyes popped. "Fifty bucks!"

Cathy grinned at her astonishment. "It's for a good cause, right?"

"Yeah, o'course. Make sure you hang on to your raffle tickets. You've got a fabulous chance to win some great stuff."

An impatient Hayley tugged Cathy into the jostling hoards towards her favourite ride, the long strip of purple tickets streaming behind them. A few minutes later, the scents of stomped grass, corn dogs, and candy floss rose on the heated noisy air as they swayed at the top of the Ferris wheel. Cathy pointed out the features of her hometown—the main drag and bustling harbour, the tree-shaded roads winding up the steep sides of the sheltered bay. The aboriginal island reserve lay near the western horizon. Tucked deep in the woods surrounding Mill Lake, inland to the east, was the parking place where she and Ryan had made out in his dad's car. She didn't tell her daughter the last bit.

Hayley swivelled and pointed. "Look, a beach. Can we go, Mom?"

"As soon as Zia Yola's had some well-deserved time off. It's hard work looking after sick people and she really needs a break."

"O-kay." Hayley drooped. "What's there to do in such a little town? Like, what did you do?"

"The same kind of stuff you do at home. Hang out with friends, go swimming and skating, movies, school, work."

"Where did you work? Was it fun?"

Cathy pointed to the main road forming a big U-shape westwards from the 400 highway, through town, and eastwards back to the 400. "See the red and yellow sign?"

"Uh huh." Hayley leaned against the safety bar, swaying the car.

"That's the hardware store I worked in. Across the street is the restaurant where I waitressed." A reminiscent smile eased the tension in Cathy's face and mind. "And yeah, it was fun. We used to goof around when there weren't any customers."

"Didn't you have enough money—?" Hayley broke off to cheer as the Ferris wheel swept them down and away from the panoramic view.

"When the family moved from Toronto before I was born, the house was paid for by the money we got from the Toronto house. You know, the house three doors down and across the street from our house with Helen. Mamma invested the extra money from the house and my father's insurance money and did very well. But not quite well enough, so Nonna worked in an office and Zia Yola worked in a grocery store and we had enough to get by. Just not enough to pay for university."

"Will I have to work for university?"

"Yes and no. No, because I've got plenty of money for your education. Yes, because it's a good experience and you'll make new friends and have lots of fun."

"Okay," Hayley replied absently as she stared at a car across the wheel where a young girl squealed in fearful delight and tucked her face into her father's shoulder. Cathy steeled herself for an awkward discussion about Hayley's father.

"Your daddy died when you were six, right?" Hayley asked.

Hmm, trying a new tack? Cathy nodded.

"Do you remember him much?"

Relieved at side-stepping dangerous father territory, Cathy slung an arm over Hayley's shoulders and hugged her close. Soft warmth flowed within Cathy. "I remember sitting in Papà's lap while he read me bedtime stories. Just like you and I do. He had bristly whiskers and warm flannel shirts. On Friday nights, he smelled like fish and chips with vinegar on them." She tapped her daughter's freckled nose and ruffled her hair. "Want a hot dog when we get down?"

Hayley puckered her face and scrunched her shoulders. Cathy tensed. As a toddler, Hayley's pucker foretold a scream fest. Now it meant sharp bargaining. "Can we go on more rides first? Use up some tickets?"

Cathy held in her smile at her scheming little cutie. "Sure. Which ride next?"

At the top of the wheel again, Hayley pondered her choices from their sky-high view.

Cathy's heart tweaked with guilt at the successful

distraction. Soon she would answer all of Hayley's questions. Provided Ryan forgave the secrecy and understood her reasons—the determination to live her own life away from her outraged mother; the unwillingness to add to Ryan's burden, especially after his mother's death; and the overwhelming fear of shaming Ryan into a too-young marriage with an unwanted wife and child. University would have been sacrificed, goals compromised, jobs settled for. No. She could never have forced them into such diminished lives.

Six rides and one humorous encounter with a First Nations chief later, Cathy and Hayley chowed down on hot dogs and root beer in the picnic area to one side of the stage. Ketchup dribbled down Hayley's chin and dripped on her white T-shirt.

Cathy wiped her daughter's face and dabbed at the red stain on her chest.

"Mo-om, I'm not a little kid anymore," Hayley protested and pushed Cathy's hand away.

The loudspeakers screeched with feedback and the family at the next table winced and covered their ears. A baby cried out and was comforted.

"Testing. Testing. One, two, three, testing." The deep voice of a good-looking mid-thirtyish man boomed from the podium.

In a group off to the left side of the stage, Cathy spotted Ryan. Her nerves twanged on high alert. The sun caressed the long lean lines of his body. The breeze toyed with his dark-blond curls. Once upon a time, she'd had the right to play with his delicious curls. Regret curdled the food in her stomach.

As if by radar, his head turned to her. Through a sudden split in the kaleidoscope of people, their gazes meshed. The sun beat down on her head, the noise beat in her ears, the blood beat in her veins.

Please stay away.

Please come and meet your daughter.

He nodded, once, briefly. Was he coming over?

He turned to an older woman at his side. Was his grandmother still alive? The press of people hid him from Cathy's sight.

Cathy rolled the cool can of pop over her flaming cheeks. The dampness dried almost instantly in the hot sun.

"Good afternoon, everybody. Are you having fun?" The emcee's bright-blue eyes twinkled to the very edges of the park. A cheer rose from the crowd. Hayley stood on the picnic bench and looped her arm around Cathy's neck. Her familiar sticky touch and ketchup scent settled Cathy's nerves.

"I'm Paul Donner, head of the Clarence Bay Volunteers. Welcome to this year's Carnival for Kids."

Another cheer.

"So far, in the drive for the Clarence Bay District Family Shelter expansion and renovation, we've raised an outstanding—hang onto your hats, folks—" With a showy flourish, he whipped the cover from a fundraising thermostat bursting red from its top. "Seventy-one thousand, two hundred and thirty-eight dollars and fifty-six cents!"

Paul did an impromptu moonwalk around the stage while the fair-goers roared in shared achievement. The man must have supreme confidence to goof around while wearing a suit.

"Has everyone got their raffle tickets handy?"

The audience rustled and rummaged while a couple of teens wheeled a raffle drum onto the stage.

Paul cranked the drum's handle, tumbling the tickets.

"We've got tons of prizes, donated by the merchants of our fair town, to give out to a bunch of lucky people." He waved at the string of corporate logos beneath the large fair banner.

He trolled a hand through the tickets, pulled one out. "And the first number is—389168! Who's our first winner?" A shout from the back of the crowd drew the emcee's attention. Paul shaded his eyes and squinted at the tall whip-thin man with flowing tresses striding towards the stage. "Why it's our own Grady Finn. You've won a haircut and manicure at the Style'n'Scissors. No more excuses to not get buzzed and your daughter will appreciate a little girly time." The crowd laughed as Grady tossed his red hair like a shampoo model.

Paul reached for the next ticket. Cathy and Hayley hooted and cheered as the raffle gave away a pile of prizes.

"And now...for the grand prize. A pair of tickets to the Music Festival's opening gala—including cocktails, dinner, and performance. Donated by Donner Accounting. That would be me." A wickedly charming grin winged its way into every female heart. He withdrew the final purple ticket. "The winning ticket is 393046."

Hayley ran the streamer of tickets through her fingers and squealed when she hit a match. "That's us, Mom! We won!" She jumped up and down, cheering and waving her sunhat.

Paul pointed to Hayley. "Well, little lady, looks like you're our grand prize winner. Come on down to the right side of the stage to collect your prize."

Hayley ran to the stage while Cathy watched over her. She returned with an envelope clutched tightly in her fist and ran straight into Cathy's arms for a swooping hug.

"The Volunteers received many generous donations from

many businesses and individuals, but there is one person who's gone above and beyond. Here to tell you a bit about our Helping Hand of the Year Award is Glory Toussaint."

Paul waved forward a woman with tired eyes and a brave smile. She looked like she'd been through life's war and survived to tell the tale. She rested a hand on a boy's shoulder. He, in turn, held a little girl's hand. All of them sported strawberry-blond curls. This kids were clearly hers. The boy looked about twelve and smiled shyly at the crowd. The toddler pranced and waved like Britney Spears until corralled by her brother and seated on the edge of the stage.

"Hey, everybody." Glory waved.

"Hey, Glory." The crowd, nicely warmed up by the emcee, chuckled and waved back..

"I want to tell you all a story."

Stillness settled over the carnival.

Glory gazed down at her twisting hands. She flattened them on the podium, took a deep breath, and looked into the crowd. For some reason, her gaze connected with Cathy's and she spoke directly to her. "Once upon a time, there was a very young woman who thought she had life by the tail. A home, a couple of kids, a husband with a steady job. Then my husband lost his job and his self-control."

As the story progressed through its downward spiral of blame, rage, and abuse, the girl climbed into her brother's lap. Glory often stumbled to a halt. Each time, she re-connected with Cathy. Each time, Cathy's indignation grew on Glory's behalf.

"After too much abuse, I took the kids and left town. We ended up at the Clarence Bay District Family Shelter." She drew a deep breath and squared her shoulders. "There, we met a man." Shy joy shone from Glory's face.

"He worked at night, putting new doors on the kitchen cupboards. My boy Sebastien wanted to help, to learn about fixing things. But he was afraid." She bent and ruffled her son's curls. "You can imagine his surprise when, instead of cussing and yelling at him to get lost like his dad would have done, this man invited him to help out. He did more than show Sebastien how to saw and hammer. He showed my boy—showed all the kids in the shelter—how a good man deals with kids. And women. No beating, no shouting, no bedtime without supper, no..." Glory stumbled into stricken silence.

Cathy's throat closed and her eyes welled with sympathetic tears.

Glory smiled at her kids, seeming to gain strength from the sight. "This man is full of a big-hearted kindness and gentleness. If I had a do-over, I would pick a man just like him as the father of my children."

The crowd clapped its approval, whisking away the odd tear.

The guy sounded like one in a million, a real peach of a man. Failing Ryan, where did she sign up for one of those as daddy for Hayley? Probably had to get in line.

Paul briefly hugged the young woman to his side, her reddish curls sparkling in the sun against Paul's dark hair. "Thanks Glory, for having the guts to step up and share your story."

He addressed the audience again. "To add to Glory's endorsement, this year's winner has raised the most money among local businesses. Plus he sponsors and coaches the hockey team, and he fixes up the shelter with material donated from his hardware store."

"So, without further ado, ladies and gentlemen..." Paul lifted a plaque from the podium shelf. "The winner of our Helping Hand of the Year award is..." Dramatic pause. "Mr. James Ryan Chisholm."

Cathy's hands paused mid-clap. Ryan? Ryan was the paragon? Hayley cheered, along with everyone else, for her father. She was going to be one happy girl.

Taking his cue, Ryan pushed a hearty grin onto his face as her crossed the stage to wild hoots and whistles. Hopefully the people put his red face down to sunburn, not a girly blush. He shook hands with Paul and received his plaque.

"Hey everyone," he said into the microphone.

"Hey, Ryan."

"I'd like to thank Paul and the Clarence Bay Social Services for today's honour. But the real hero, or rather heroine, of the day is Glory."

Gently he drew her back to centre stage.

"She's a tough survivor who's turned around a bad situation. She studied hard, completed her college degree, and is now manager of The Pits...uh, for you out-of-towners, that's what we call Cherrystone's Bar and Grill on James Street. Glory and the other women in the shelter are stellar examples of what can be done with determination and hope. Please consider joining the volunteer force and being a...Helping Hand."

He raised the Helping Hand plaque to show everyone his small joke. They laughed outrageously and he grinned.

"Now, I'll let you get back to the Carnival for Kids. Have lots of fun and spend lots of money. The kids can use every penny."

Ryan bowed to Glory as the crowd deafened him with hoots, hollers, and whistles. He'd done so little and yet they cheered him like a freakin' caped crusader. Sure, he'd donated time and money. With only himself to look after, he had plenty of both to spare. The admiration shining in Glory's green eyes reflected in her kids' faces. He really wished she'd stop looking at him like some kind of superhero. His cape flowed only in her imagination.

Paul hooked Ryan's arm. "Not so fast, my friend. Time for the big announcement."

"Not now," Ryan hissed back at him.

Paul dragged him back to the podium.

"One more minute of your time please, folks." Paul waited for the crowd's attention. "The formal announcement will appear in next week's *Clarence Bay Beacon,* but I'm so happy, I'm gonna tell you now." Paul slapped a heavy and encouraging hand on Ryan's shoulder. "Our man Ryan here is running for mayor. You already know what a good man he is, an ace town councillor. Just imagine what an excellent mayor he'll make. I'll say right now, for anyone who wants to know, he's got my vote!"

Paul grasped Ryan's hand and raised their joined arms in victory. The roar of approval rustled the leaves on the trees so hard they seemed to join in the cheer.

A backslapping, cheek-kissing group surrounded him at the bottom of the stairs as he came off the stage.

"I thought we weren't going to make the announcement here," Ryan muttered to Paul.

"I couldn't resist a perfect opportunity to get your name out there, reinforce your good deeds, grab some votes," Paul said.

"We're here to raise money for the shelter. The focus belongs there, not on me." He scanned the noisy crowd, waved to a group of friends at the picnic tables. Cathy was out there somewhere. Her presence beat deep in his body.

Paul jammed a soft drink into his hand. "Speaking of focus—where's your head at?"

The cold wet can in Ryan's palm stilled the craziness in his head.

His friend pointed to the far corner of the park where a thickset middle-aged man handed out pamphlets and greeted people. "Adam Baylor over there is stealing your thunder. As your campaign manager, I refuse to let you be out-manoeuvred." Paul gave him a friendly shove towards the milling hoards. "Now get out there and charm the folks who need you to save this town."

CHAPTER 3

Stay or Go

Zia Yola pulled a plate too quickly off the counter and a full serving of hot spaghetti splattered to the kitchen floor. "*Managia!* Look at the mess I make!" She tossed the plate into the sink and it clanged like an odd sort of bell. Cathy exchanged round-eyed glances with her daughter at Zia Yola's unusual display of temper. After several uneasy days of tiptoeing past the closed door of Mamma's room, Mamma had finally agreed to see Cathy and Hayley. Throughout the morning, Zia Yola's face had grown paler and her movements jerkier, ending in the lost and damned food.

Cathy gently pushed her aunt into a chair, scooped up the mess, and threw it in the compost pail. Over Zia Yola's protest, she slid half of her own meal onto a clean plate and set it in front of her aunt. "Please, Zia, take it. I'm not all that hungry."

The meal continued in quivering glances and fractured sentences, Zia's tension snarling Cathy's insides into hideous knots of apprehension.

Even the usually-oblivious Hayley was swept up in the

turbulence. She put down her fork. "Mom, will Nonna be mean to me?" Her voice squeaked and her brows pulled tight over her wide dark eyes.

"No, no, *piccola,* she will be very happy to meet you." Zia Yola tugged one of Hayley's spiral curls and cupped her hand where it lay on the table. The affection and trust between the woman and child shone as clear and strong as the sun lighting the kitchen porch. Hayley leaned into the offered comfort, though she still looked unconvinced. Cathy didn't believe it either.

"Sweetie, it might be difficult. You can leave Nonna's room whenever you want. Okay?"

Hayley lifted a stubborn chin. "We can get through anything together, Mom."

Pride swelled Cathy's heart at her beautiful brave girl. Borrowing from her daughter's confidence, Cathy gripped Hayley's small hand. Cathy reached over the table and took Zia Yola's hand in a reassuring clasp, joining the three of them in a sturdy triangle of hope. "We sure can."

After tidying the kitchen, Cathy and Hayley followed Zia Yola up the stairs and past their bedrooms. Shadows drew closer and the hallway elongated with their every step. The house held its breath. Wariness increased as they approached the large darkened front bedroom. Hayley squeezed hard enough to hurt Cathy's hand, but she didn't scold her daughter or release her.

An old memory of snuggling in the big bed with Mamma and Papà ambushed Cathy on the threshold—Mamma had always turned her back on her and Papà. The wallpaper roses still bloomed and the ornate cherry furniture still gleamed. Today, the frail older woman barely disturbing the smooth lay of her covers contrasted starkly with the round figure of those past, happier days.

Zia Yola leaned over the bed. "Lucia?" she murmured.

The woman in bed sighed, turned her head, and opened dark-brown eyes sunken in a pale, waxy face. "*Lei è qui?*" Is she here? Mamma, born and raised for twenty years in Italy, clung to the language and insisted everyone else do the same. Despite Yola's Canadian birth and schooling, English was very much her second language.

"*Sì.* Let me tidy you up a bit." Zia Yola lifted her sister and tucked another pillow behind her back. She smoothed the sheets and straightened the light toque on Lucia's head. After setting everything to rights, Zia Yola stepped to the other side of the bed to reveal Cathy and Hayley.

"Caterina. You came." Mamma's rusty voice still held its undertone of iron discipline.

"*Sì*, Mamma. We're here." Cathy continued the conversation in Italian. Hayley leaned in and Cathy curved an encouraging arm over her shoulders.

Mamma's sharp gaze fastened on Cathy's face, scanned her up and down, and then moved to her daughter. Hayley surprised Cathy by standing tall under Mamma's assessment. "Good girl," Cathy murmured to her daughter.

Mamma looked beyond Cathy to the empty hallway. "Is your husband with you as well?"

"No, Mamma."

"You're divorced?" The scornful curl of Mamma's lip reduced Cathy to the monosyllabic answers of a sullen teen.

"No."

"He abandoned you?"

Cathy pushed her glasses up her nose, touched her fingers to her mouth. "No."

Many times, she'd imagined this reunion—from joyous forgiveness to outright rejection. This inquisition never happened in any of those imaginings.

"And yet there is a child." Mamma slashed a glance at Zia Yola then aimed her laser-beam stare at Hayley. Her mouth flattened into a hard line. "A bastard. I ordered against this mortal sin."

Shock stilled every muscle in Cathy's body. She prayed the Italian came too quickly for her daughter to capture and translate.

"You know who the father is?"

"Yes."

"*Puttana.*" Whore. She spat the last word.

Zia Yola gasped. "Lucia! Such words for a child to hear!"

Cathy pressed a fist against lips tucked between her teeth. Her glasses fogged with the heat of her anger.

Mamma brushed off Zia Yola's reprimand. "She knows the language?" Mamma spoke as if Hayley wasn't in the room.

"She learns more every day." But, *se Dio vuole*, God willing, not the ultimate slur to throw at a woman.

"Good. She should know the truth of her beginning and her likely end in Hell." Mamma thrust her head forward with a burst of frantic energy. "She should know her mother is disobedient, disloyal. A scandal and a shame to her family."

She should also know her grandmother is a controlling judgmental tyrant. Cathy bit down on the retort, fighting for calm in the face of Mamma's venom.

Hayley's finger teased at Cathy's fist, startling her. The poor girl must be scared stiff by the incomprehensible argument.

When Cathy offered a comforting smile, she found a surprising solidarity in her daughter's gaze. Cathy's fingers relaxed, Hayley's hand slid into its usual place, comforting and strengthening Cathy.

Cathy shrugged lightly, spoke calmly. "There's no shame in being a single mother anymore. I'm proud of my intelligent beautiful daughter."

"There is great shame in giving birth to a child out of wed—" Without warning, Mamma turned dead-pale, and collapsed against Zia Yola who buckled under the sudden burden with a sharp cry.

"Mamma!" Cathy darted forward, gathered the frail body, and settled her mother back onto the pillows.

Zia Yola staggered again with her release from Mamma's weight. Panting, she propped one hand on the bed, the other gripped her back.

Cathy stroked Mamma's cheek. This close, the foul stench of death lingered on her mother's breath.

"Mamma, are you all right? Mamma, say something." Her heart breaking, her eyes watering, Cathy prayed for Mamma.

Mamma stirred, seeming to gather strength before she opened her eyes. The gleaming hatred shoved Cathy upright. "Take that misbegotten child of yours and get out!"

Cathy hustled Hayley out of the room, down the stairs and through the front door before her innocent child understood the exact nature of the Italian words.

"Mom! You're shoving!"

Hayley swerved away from the impetuous momentum. Cathy continued down the stairs to the front walk.

"The old wi—she called me a—how dare she—" Cathy stomped back and forth on the cement, her jaw clenched tight enough to grind gravel from the granite cliffs surrounding the bay. There were limits to what a grown woman should suffer at the hands of her mother. Mamma hadn't changed one bit—still as hard and cold as a damn stone.

I stand by my convictions and my daughter's life.

Mamma might have supported her daughter, might have been happy to meet her granddaughter. But no. She chose to judge, condemn, reject.

The thwack of wood on wood jerked Cathy from her turmoil.

Hayley swung wildly on the porch swing, clipping the railing each time. Had she heard her mother ranting like a lunatic? Jumping up, Hayley stood with her hands on her narrow hips. "Mom, let's go home."

Yep, she'd heard, and responded with a fierce reflection of her mother's wish to escape.

"You're right. Who needs this?" Cathy bounded up the stairs and whipped open the door. "Let's blow this Popsicle stand."

"Yes!" Hayley happy-danced around the porch. "I can't wait to get home!"

Three hours, max, and they'd be safely in Toronto. Where nobody called Cathy a whore or her sweet child a bastard and nobody hated her for sticking to her principles. For doing the right thing. Upstairs, she slammed the bags on the bed. Clothes damn near folded themselves and levitated into place. Cathy marched into the bathroom and snatched up shampoo and other toiletries.

A weak moan came from Mamma's bedroom. *Dio mio!* She refused to be dragged back into the morass. She'd been told to leave and she was damn well going to follow orders.

"Caterina," a small panicky voice called.

Mamma had done well enough all these years without her only daughter. She could continue doing so. Who the hell needed this aggravation?

"Caterina." Zia Yola whimpered.

Cathy froze for a moment, then dropped the toiletries bag onto the counter and hurried into the front bedroom. Mamma slept, a sour expression puckering her face. Zia Yola slumped against the bed as if in prayer.

"Caterina, *aiutami!* Help me!" Tears watered Zia Yola's muffled voice.

Cathy rushed forward and carefully knelt by her aunt. "It's okay, I'm here. What's wrong?"

"My back, I can't get up."

"I'll call 9-1-1."

"Shh, don't wake Lucia."

Cathy bit back her angry "Who cares?" How could Zia Yola possibly be thinking of her sister when she herself was in such pain?

"Don't argue with me, Zia. I'm calling the ambulance."

Cathy started to rise, but Zia Yola gripped her wrist so hard pain shot down her fingers.

"No, it's happened before. Just help me crawl to bed."

"Crawl? No way." Cathy patted her aunt's arm. "I'll be right back."

She raced to the shared bedroom, grabbed the desk chair, and hauled it into Mamma's room. Gently, she guided her poor bent aunt onto the chair, wheeled her into her own yellow-painted bedroom, and eased her onto her bed. Zia Yola wept and moaned. Cathy gently removed Zia Yola's shoes and spread the white-and-gold afghan from the foot of the bed over her suffering aunt.

"*Grazie mille, cara mia. Grazie mille.*" Zia Yola wiped her tears with the tissue Cathy handed her from the maple side table.

"You're welcome, Zia Yola."

"It's such a good thing you are here. It will take me time to get on my feet."

Cathy ached for escape so close she tasted exhaust. Sagging onto the wheeled chair, she surrendered to fate. The chair drifted back and clunked against the old-fashioned dresser.

"How often has your back gone out?"

"Only a few times. Will you please bring me two pain pills from the top shelf in the washroom?"

Cathy retrieved the pills and a glass of water. She helped her aunt to sit up and supported her while she swallowed. Sunlight picked out strands of grey in the wavy brown hair tumbling over Zia Yola's face. Cathy swept the locks into place with a tender gesture, drawing a delicate smile from her aunt.

"*Grazie mille.* I will be well enough tomorrow to look after Lucia. I won't blame you if you want to go." She relaxed into a weary lump.

Resting her hand on her aunt's shoulder, Cathy sat by the bed until Zia Yola's breathing evened out. If Zia Yola couldn't move tomorrow, Cathy would call the doctor. She set the half-empty glass on the bedside table and moved quietly to the door to unpack.

"Caterina."

Her aunt's beaten-down voice turned Cathy back to the bed.

"Sì, cara Zia?"

Zia Yola pointed at the makeshift wheelchair. "Come and sit. I want to talk with you."

Dragging her feet, Cathy sat and then wheeled closer. Her aunt reached out and gingerly, almost fearfully, took her hand. Cathy caressed the careworn skin.

"You may not believe me...I am very glad you did not give the baby away. I never thought you should."

Cathy's grip slackened and her aunt's hand fell to the bed. All these years Zia Yola had supported her choice? "Why didn't you say so at the time?"

"Lucia forbade it. I wanted to go to the city to be with you, to help you."

"Why didn't you?"

"Lucia forbade it. She washed her hands of you and insisted I do the same. She made things—difficult—if I did not do as she wished."

With those resigned words, long-buried memories surfaced of Lucia controlling not only Cathy's life, but Zia Yola's as well. Zia Yola had wanted to attend courses, meetings, go on outings with her friends. Each time, she gave way to the manipulations of her demanding sister.

Cathy had run away to university.

Zia Yola had stayed behind.

How blind Cathy had been in the heated rebellion consuming her teenaged years. While Cathy went to school with makeup, skimpy T-shirts, and tight jeans hidden in her backpack, Zia Yola endured the unrelenting disapproval of an older sister standing in for their deceased mother.

"I am glad you went to my good friend Helen. You take such

good care of each other." She smiled at Cathy's surprise. "Yes, she told me you gave her money in her time of need. And that you would take nothing in return. You have grown into a good woman, Caterina. I am proud of you. I am sorry I was so harsh to you when you arrived."

Walls of resentment in Cathy's heart cracked and crumbled under the weight of guilt for her self-absorption and sympathy for her downtrodden aunt. She kissed her aunt's cheek.

"Oh, Zia, I should have known how much you'd cared. Your support would have meant so much to me. You missed so much of Hayley's growing up."

Sadness and regret swirled with the dust motes in the beam of sunlight.

Yola sighed deeply to gather her resolution. A spasm in her back reminded her of her weakness. She must speak, even though she'd learned the hard way to ask for nothing important. Always, a steep price was to be paid. Gripping Caterina's hand for strength, the words came.

"Caterina, please stay. Please." Yola despised the wobble in her voice.

"A couple more days. Until you're strong."

"For the whole time. Eight weeks."

A mulish stubbornness set Caterina's jaws and fists tight. "Mamma doesn't want to be a grandmother. She never did. I'm surprised she's even a mother. Hayley and I don't need her hard feelings."

Words taunted Yola's conscience. Fist against her mouth, she thrust those words deep, to the darkest corner of her mind before she went *pazza,* demented, crazy.

Instead, Yola reached for words to explain her sister. "No,

cara, no. She hates that you surprised her with your daughter after eleven years of thinking.... She does not like surprises. Give her a chance to get used to being a grandmother."

Lucia was a hard woman to live with, embittered by the disappointments in her life. No sons, a dead husband from an arranged marriage, a young sister desperate for a mother figure, and an unwanted baby girl. Sometimes, Yola wished she'd stayed with Helen's family instead of moving to Clarence Bay with Lucia and Antonio. But family was family. Though Helen was her dearest friend, she was not blood.

"Perhaps she didn't want to be a grandmother before. When she sees what a lovely child Hayley is, she will change her mind. I am sure," Yola continued her persuasion.

"I don't think so."

Yola freed her hand to cup Caterina's smooth young cheek. "Then stay for me. I miss you and I want to know my *cara piccola.*" She would beg if she must. "Please, *cara ucellino,* please."

Caterina pressed her face into Yola's palm, a childhood gesture of acquiescence. "Okay. We'll stay on one condition. Once you're better, you and I will take turns looking after Mamma. I want you to have some time to yourself."

Yola's forehead crimped. "What do I do with time to myself?"

"Read a book, go for a walk. You used to love knitting. The way I remember, the more challenging the project the better you liked it."

Caterina was right. Much satisfaction came from creating a complex garment with a simple pair of needles and colourful yarns. Just two weeks ago, she'd longed for a little girl to wear the charming pattern for a flowered sweater in the knitting magazine.

"Do you think, maybe, Hayley would like me to knit her a sweater?"

Caterina's huge smile encouraged hope. "Oh yes, I still have the pink-and-white snowflake hoodie you made me. Hayley wears it in winter."

Hopeful tears leaked from Yola's eyes. "So, it's decided. You'll stay?"

Caterina dabbed up the tears with a gentle hand, soothed Yola's spirit with a soft kiss.

"Okay, we'll stay for the whole eight weeks."

Hayley got way bored waiting for Mom to come back, so she wandered inside and upstairs. Maybe Mom needed some help packing so they could blow outta here. Hayley desperately wanted to get back with her friends in the city.

At the top of the stairs, Hayley heard Mom and Zia Yola talking in the other bedroom. So, what was happening with the packing? The suitcases were full, but not zipped. Awesome. Mom really moved fast when she wanted to.

With nothing to do, Hayley went back downstairs to get a Coke from the funny green fridge. Everything in this creepy house was way old-fashioned, like that eighties' TV show. Nonna didn't even have Internet. Hayley settled onto the back porch's top step. The long backyard sloped down to a shallow rocky creek making happy bubbly noises. Big old trees threw deep shadows over the grass. Lots of pretty flowers in pink, white, and purple grew along the edges. No swing set though. Just some ratty chairs and an old shed.

The door opened behind Hayley. Mom came and sat beside

her on the step and slung an arm over her shoulders.

She leaned against her mom's side. "We're not going, are we?" Hayley guessed the answer from the vibes.

"No. Zia Yola hurt her back."

"Oh." It was gonna totally suck to keep sharing a bedroom with her neat-nut Mom.

"How would you like your own special place while we're here?"

Sometimes it was like Mom read her mind. Hayley stared up at her. "Really? Where?"

"My old playhouse Papà built for me."

Hayley tried to see what Mom was looking at, but couldn't see a playhouse anywhere. So she went along with her.

"Yeah, sure."

"Wonder if the key is still on the hook?" Mom jumped up and reached inside the door. She cheered and returned with a key looped on a faded purple ribbon. Snatching her hand, Mom hauled Hayley off the steps and down the garden. Amazingly, she stopped in front of the crummy shed. Mom had lost it. Really lost it.

"You kidding me? This is just gross."

"Nope, not kidding. Wait 'til we get it painted and cleaned up. You'll love it as much as I did." Mom opened the padlock and the door creaked open like in a horror movie. She ducked her head under the doorway and went in.

Hayley reluctantly followed. What a reek—old and rank and rotten. Hayley's nose wrinkled hard. Like it tried to climb into her face. "Eww, what a stink!"

Big dingy screened windows on each side let in only a bit of light. All the walls were white-painted wood under layers of dirt. A warped corkboard pinned with some ratty magazine pictures hung on the back wall. An old wooden Muskoka chair, a wall lamp and a side table sat in one corner. A slatted wooden bench occupied a side wall.

Mom went all gooey-eyed as she stood in the middle and looked around at the crappy little dump. "I spent hours in here as a kid with my best friends. We loved getting away from the parents. The secrets we shared...what we did..."

Bending, Mom clicked on the lamp. Hayley jumped when the darn thing actually worked. Too bad everything just looked grosser.

"Eww."

"Only eww for now. We'll clean it up, slap on some paint, get some new cushions for the bench and you'll be all set."

Hayley's imagination stuck on the idea of this place getting even halfway decent.

"C'mon, Hayley, what colours do you like? I think the walls should still be white to make the most of the light from the windows. The rest can be anything you want."

The question got ideas going in Hayley's head.

"Pink like your room at home? Or something different?" Mom asked.

Hayley looked around trying hard to visualize the way her mom did. She saw only ugly dirty grey. She looked out the open door—green grass, blue sky, yellow sun.

"Maybe blue like your new tights and top set?"

Hayley's grinned. "Yeah, like that."

"Okay. A nice clear blue. How about yellow to cheer it up, or maybe light green?"

"Yellow."

Mom smiled and nodded. "Yellow it is. We'll make a list. But first we need to hose this place down because it really is very—eww."

Hayley looked around again. This time she pictured herself sitting in a newly-painted yellow chair with some awesome books and some tasty snacks.

"Yes! Let's do it."

Cathy laughed with relief at her daughter's budding enthusiasm. "Good. Run in the house and get a notepad and pen from the kitchen and we'll do a project list."

Hayley sped away. Drama averted, new goal in place.

Cathy sighed and scanned the battered structure, drifting backwards in time to eleven years ago.

Here in the corner, an old blue trunk had hidden a wardrobe bought on the sly with money from two part-time jobs. The old walls had listened to her rants against Mamma's too-tight control over her not-so-beloved daughter. The wooden chair's wide arms had supported notepad and Coke while Cathy developed The Plan: graduate from the University of Toronto, get a fabulous job, earn fabulous money, live a fabulous life in the big city. And never come back.

Succumb to life in a dead-end town? Not with The Plan....

The Plan had only one day before it kicked off. Tomorrow she would leave for her fabulous life on campus. Tonight, eighteen-year-old Cathy and nineteen-year-old Ryan would share one final joy before they went their separate ways.

"C'mon Ryan, they've been asleep for ages. Even if they're up, they can't see us." Cathy tugged Ryan into the shadows of her hideaway. "I won't even turn on the lamp. A candle doesn't show behind the closed curtains—I already tested it."

Anticipation raced in Cathy's young blood. Anxiety twisted her nerves tight, much tighter than she wished. They'd waited and waited to make love, to be each other's first. With the door shut and latched, she felt for the small table and lit a fat bayberry-scented candle. Sun-dried sheets and clean woolly blankets lay smooth on the cushioned bench.

Ryan's eyes flared in the feeble golden light as she took a wine bottle and glasses from a cardboard box.

"You got wine?" His voice cracked high. He scowled and cleared his throat.

Cathy nodded. "Emma got it." Her old-enough girlfriend did the buy, called it her contribution to the festivities.

She glanced through her lashes at him, hoping he didn't notice the slight tremble in her hand clinking the bottle against the glass. He wasn't the best-looking boy in school, yet he was extremely smart and very good at devising ways of meeting in secret. His excitement was obvious by the bulge in his jeans. "I thought a drink might make it easier. For both of us."

He shoved his hands in his pockets, only to fumble them out again when she handed him a glass of dark-red liquid.

"To us." She tapped their glasses together.

"Forever," he replied.

A small alarm went off inside her. He'd agreed to part ways. A man in her life wasn't scheduled for some years after she'd completed The Plan and achieved The Life. No worries. Another girl would soon chase him, soon make him forget her. A nasty pain needled her young heart.

They'd spent hours talking and laughing, being best friends. Sure, they'd done some kissing and groping. He'd caressed her bare breasts. She'd had her hands inside his pants. They'd made each other crazy heavy breathers.

Tonight they were going All The Way.

He removed a condom from his jeans pocket and laid it on the table. Where he'd gotten it, she didn't care. Now nothing stood in their way.

"Here, Mom." Hayley jolted Cathy back to the present day. Her daughter handed her the requested notepad and pen.

The echoes of long-ago kisses, sighs, and muffled shouts faded in the musty air. Back then was when a condom had failed and a little girl had been conceived on a loving summer night.

Now was when a little girl would meet her father.

CHAPTER 4

New Friends

"Hi. Want some help?"

Hayley, kneeling by her sand castle, peered up from under the wide brim of the sucky sunhat Mom made her wear. A girl about the same age with curly hair and friendly grey eyes, holding a pail and shovel, stood nearby on the beach. Hayley checked her out—cute black-and-white bathing suit, cool black nail polish on fingers and toes, hair as awful as Hayley's own. Sweet—no bragging and hair flicking.

"Okay. You can go on the other side if you want."

The girl knelt and started digging on the opposite side of the moat. Hayley was glad she'd brought her best bathing suit that wasn't all saggy from swim class.

"Nice castle. How long you been working on it?" the girl asked.

"Since I got here."

"Did your mom help?"

Hayley giggled at the idea. "Nah. Her towers always go crooked like they're drunk or something."

The girl choked and giggled. "Then you must be good." She went back to her digging. Water showed in the bottom of her hole and she moved over a bit to dig in a new spot. Looked like she knew how to do it right.

"What happens around here?" Hayley moved to a new spot, closer to the girl. The moat was almost done.

The girl screwed up her face. "Not much. Unless you like water or trees. We have a movie place downtown. The shopping is so lame, we have to go down to Barrie, but it's far away, so we don't go too many times."

No surprise about the lousy shopping. Mom was always right. Except sometimes. Like when she ignored Hayley's questions about her dad. Mom said they were a power team, just the two of them, and didn't need a man messing up their lives.

"Do you have Internet at your house?" Hayley asked.

The other girl's eyes bugged out. "Who doesn't?"

Hayley sat on her heels and rolled her eyes. "My grandmother, and it really sucks."

"Ouch. Even my grandpa has it. And he's old. You can come and use my computer."

"Awesome. What's your name?"

"Lindsey. What's yours?"

"Hayley."

"How old are you?"

"Ten."

"Cool, me too. When's your birthday?"

"May twenty-ninth. When's yours?" Hayley said.

"July sixth."

Hayley instantly became the leader because she was older even if she was shorter.

"Where do you live?"

"In Toronto."

"Are you summer people?" Lindsey made it sound like a dirty word. The opposite of everyone at home, who thought cottaging was the *only* summer thing to do. Like that pest Ricky at school.

"Nope, I'm staying at my grandma's house 'cause she's really sick and my mom is gonna help Zia Yola look after her."

Lindsey's eyes brightened. "Hey, is your grandma's house on Waubeek Street?"

Hayley shrugged. "I guess."

"Mrs. Rosetti and Zia Yola live across the street from us."

"No way!"

"Way!"

"Freakin' awesome." The summer might not totally suck after all.

"Wanna hang out?"

Hayley hesitated just long enough to show she was choosy, but not long enough to be called a snob. "Sure," she said oh-so-casually.

Lindsey grinned like a goofball. Hayley grinned back then jumped up and hauled her into a squealing dance around the sand castle. Friends were so awesome. Treats, they needed treats to celebrate.

"C'mon, let's get my mom to buy us some ice cream." Hayley said.

"All right, ice cream."

They high-fived, grabbed their pails and shovels, and started across the beach.

"Which mom is yours?" Lindsey asked.

Hayley pointed at her, sitting on a beach chair reading a

book.

"Is *that* your mom in the red bathing suit?" Lindsey sounded impressed.

"Yeah. Why?"

"She's so pretty. I wish my hair flipped under like hers."

Hayley looked at her mother again and for the first time saw her the way other people might see her. She was actually really pretty, with her chin-length dark hair in a cool cut, and her nice shape—not too fat or too skinny, just right for snuggling. And she wore some of the best clothes. "Where's your mom?"

Lindsey's face turned red as she pointed to a sorta-fat lady with two little boys running around her. "She's kinda fat 'cause she's gonna have another baby. Those brats are my brothers. They're so annoying. I hate them."

"A baby brother might be cute." Her new friend looked so grossed-out Hayley quickly changed her mind. "Maybe a baby sister would be better. I don't have any brothers or sisters."

"You're so lucky you don't have to share your dad."

"I don't have a dad either." Hayley almost never admitted it, but more than anything, she wanted a dad.

"That's awful. Did he die or something?" Hayley hated the pity in Lindsey's eyes.

"Dunno. I never saw him. Mom says we're fine the way we are." Her heart pinching, Hayley took off and ran the rest of the way.

"Mom! Mom!"

Mom's big happy smile eased the pinch.

"Can we get ice cream cones?" Hayley shouted.

"Who's 'we'?" Mom pushed up her sunglasses. Too bad they hid her pretty brown eyes.

"This is my new friend Lindsey. She helped me build my sand castle. See?" Hayley flung an arm towards the many-turreted creation by the shore.

"Impressive. I guess hungry builders need to be fed, huh?"

Cathy fished change from her bag while the two girls wiggled and giggled. They ran off to the concession stand, shouting out their flavour choices, butterscotch ripple and rocky road.

What a relief Hayley had found a friend. Hopefully, the other girl lived in town rather than out on one of the country roads lacing the vast woods surrounding Clarence Bay.

Cathy's heart jammed into her throat as she spotted Ryan waiting in line for ice cream at the pristine beach pavilion. Lindsey ran up to him and flung herself at him. Ryan scooped her up onto his hip and gave her a big kiss on the cheek. She hugged him tight with her arms and legs in heart-warming joy.

All the sun spangles from all the sand and all the water coalesced in Cathy's vision. All her breath left for parts unknown. *Dio mio!*

Of all the hideous coincidences the fates could have thrown at her. The daughter he knew and the daughter who was a stranger to him were instant best friends. Why hadn't she recognized the mop top? Thank goodness Hayley's sunhat hid her only resemblance to her father.

He spoke to Hayley who offered a handshake. He put Lindsey down and solemnly took Hayley's hand. She chattered away, glowing up at him like an eager puppy. Clearly little girls were as taken with him as big girls.

An unexpected arrow pierced Cathy's heart. Leave her alone! She's *my* little girl.

His eyes followed Hayley's pointing finger and connected

with Cathy's stupefied gaze. She waggled a few limp fingers in answer to his wave. Darn good thing she was sitting or her even limper knees would have laid her flat on her back in the sand.

What a horrendous mess.

Fear rammed up her spine and stiffened all her limp body parts. Frantically, she gathered up the beach gear and called her daughter back. Hayley waved an ice-creamy goodbye to her new best friend and her...dad.

"Hey, Mom, guess what?" Hayley sucked ice cream from the bottom of the cone. "Lindsey lives across the street from us. Can I go over to her place? She's got Internet." Her daughter's dark eyes pleaded as she danced by her side on the way to the car.

Santo cielo! Good heavens! There has to be some excuse somewhere. Whatever it took, the two girls must be separated until Cathy resolved what to do about their obviously-married father.

Three days later, Cathy wanted to scream the house down. Between forcing a stubborn Zia Yola to take some time for herself, distracting Hayley, and waiting on her grouchy mother, Cathy gladly took her turn to escape into town on a beautiful breezy day.

As Cathy and Hayley walked along the downtown streets, Cathy was saddened by the number of empty shops. Cottage country typically weathered out economic storms due to the annual influx of wealthy summer people. Even Clarence Bay wasn't impervious.

The overhead bell at the paint store announced her and Hayley's arrival. Grisham's Paints and Papers still stood in the same location on Gibson Street, marked by a row of classic wide-armed, slat-backed Muskoka chairs on the sidewalk. A scarred wooden counter in one corner of the store held the checkout computer. Hayley wended her way through stacks of cans, racks of brushes, and shelves of the latest how-to books to the rainbows of paint samples lining the back wall. The smell of solvent alone nudged Cathy's creativity.

Cathy's old friend Melody and her father looked up from their work, big grins spreading over both faces.

"Hi, Mr. Grisham. Hi, Melody," Cathy said with a jaunty wave.

Melody cheered and scooted around the counter to grab Cathy in a rocking embrace. "How lovely to see you again. You've been gone way too long." Melody, Emma, and Cathy had been best buds from the first day of kindergarten to high school graduation, ending when Cathy left town.

Her father followed more sedately and wrapped Cathy in a hug. Father and daughter were a matched set with inky-black hair and deep-blue eyes. "Hey, Cathy. I heard you were home to care for your mother. And that you'd brought your cute little girl with you."

"That's right, Mr. Grisham. I see the grapevine still works as well as ever. How's Mrs. Grisham?" The Gossiping Grishams were the clearinghouse for any and all news in Clarence Bay. Nothing escaped their keen observation and clever commentary.

Mr. Grisham nodded heavily. "The missus is good, still has the Style'n'Scissors, still busy in the summers." He nudged his daughter with his elbow. "Our Melody here took a degree in journalism. First university graduate in the family. Now she has a job at the newspaper. Gonna be their star reporter soon."

Melody blushed and elbowed her father back. "Knock it off,

Dad. I only do the Hatch, Match, and Dispatch page and take classifieds. And I still help you out on the weekends."

Mr. Grisham tapped the side of his nose and winked at Cathy. "For now. You just watch my girl."

"Oh, stop." Melody tucked her arm in her father's and leaned into him.

Cathy's conscience stirred at his fatherly pride in his daughter's achievement. Didn't Ryan deserve a chance to be proud of his daughter? Depended on her research results. In her experience, even the best first impressions were not to be trusted.

"What else have you been up to all this time, Cathy?" Melody asked.

Cathy pushed up her glasses. "Well, after busting my chops for seven years, I earned a joint law and business degree then landed a job as a Director for a large investment firm." That sound bite should keep the town happy for a while.

"Nice. No wonder you've been too busy to come home."

Mr. Grisham gestured to Hayley who happily selected paint samples from the racks. "Plus getting married and having a cute little girl. She's what, nine?" His warm smile couldn't quite cover his sharp-eyed search for more intel.

Cathy dipped her head in a gesture that could be either yes or no. "Thanks. I think she's cute, too." She hurried on before the nosy retailer pried further. "We're here to get paint to redo my old playhouse in the backyard."

A sly smile crept over Melody's face and her blue eyes twinkled with mischief. "I remember the playhouse. The scene of many childhood adventures, eh?"

Cathy grinned and chuckled. "Sure, drooling over teen

magazines and gossiping about boys."

"What? Is your memory failing? I recall a bit more than—"

Heat prickled across Cathy's cheeks. She nodded towards Hayley. "Shh. Big ears and all."

Melody copied her dad's nose tap and wink. "We'll chat later. I'll give Emma a call and we'll get together."

"Perfect. Emma's still in town?"

"She's managing the gift shop by the marina for her grandmother."

"Did she ever go on her round-the-world photo trek?"

"No, she came back from art school after the first semester to look after her grandmother when she fell and broke her hip. She's changed, gone quiet, not at all the wild child you probably remember."

Cathy chuckled at her memories of wild Emma. "She was kinda wild. What a shame about her photography; it meant so much to her. At least she has Nico. How many kids have they got now?"

Melody's eyes rounded. "You didn't hear? No, of course, you didn't. You weren't here. Nico, Emma, and a couple of other kids were in a car crash the summer after you left. Only Emma survived."

"How awful for her!" How Cathy wished she'd kept in touch to support her friend through her crisis. Unfortunately, she'd had to sever all but the most perfunctory ties.

"Yeah, she was real wreck for a while, but she's good now."

"Poor Emma." Cathy floundered for something more to say. Hayley chose that moment to summon her with a wave. "I'd better go, before my daughter changes her mind and decides to paint the whole playhouse hot pink. Or worse!" Cathy joined her daughter at the colour display where they rummaged through the samples.

"Mom, what did you do in my playhouse?" Hayley asked.

Sometimes her kid seemed to have the hearing of an owl. "Big ears catch little news."

"Mo-om. Just tell me."

"My friends, Melody and Emma, who you haven't met yet, and I used to hang out and gossip."

"About boys. Eww." Hayley shuddered dramatically.

Cathy grinned and tweaked her daughter's ear. "Yes, about boys. But not until we were much older than you." They'd been all of twelve when a precocious Emma had horrified their little ears with whispered secrets about kissing. *Eww,* they'd responded as well. At least until Ryan kissed Cathy for the first time. Heat danced down her spine.

"Have you—" Her voice came out husky and low. She cleared her throat and continued in more normal tones. "Have you chosen your floor, window, and door colours?" Hayley gave her a puzzled glance, shrugged, and showed her a medium blue, a pale blue, and a sunny yellow. "These ones?"

"Perfect. And we'll get two large cans of white for the walls, inside and out."

While Mr. Grisham rang up their paint and brushes, Hayley's new BFF Lindsey barrelled through the door, almost jangling the shop bell off its hook. Two younger boys galloped behind her, followed by a lumpy woman with messy reddish hair, a baggy T-shirt, and sloppy jeans.

"Look Mom, it's Hayley," Lindsey shrieked and ran down the shop. The two girls hugged and squealed like long-lost sisters, babbling and chattering about Hayley's plans for her hideout. If only they knew they actually were half-sisters.

Cathy stuck out her hand to greet Ryan's harassed wife. "Hi. I'm Cathy Rossetti. Our daughters met on the beach yesterday and became best friends forever over a sand castle and ice cream."

The other woman wiped her palm on her worn jeans and shook hands with Cathy. "Hi, I'm Meg Chisholm. Pleased to meet you. It's nice you came home to look after your mother 'cause it's been real hard on Yola." Accusations of neglect seemed to lie beneath the surface of her pleasant words.

"I agree, Zia Yola does work too hard," Cathy replied.

"Hope you're here for a good *long* time," Meg sneered and questioned at the same time.

Cathy stiffened. Why did this woman feel the need to judge a stranger so harshly?

"Long enough to make a difference, then it's back to work."

"What sort of *work* do you do? I stay home and raise my children."

Ah, clearly Meg didn't approve of working mothers. Well, Cathy could deal with a little disapproval.

"I'm a Director for a large investment firm on Bay Street." Cathy didn't muffle the ring of hard-won pride in her voice. "How long have you been married?"

"Almost eleven years. Did your husband come with you?"

Eleven years? Hot bitterness frothed up from her stomach, scalded the back of her throat. It damn well hadn't taken him long. Ryan's forever vow wasn't worth the breath he used to say it.

"No, I'm—"

Meg suddenly shot down the aisle and grabbed one of her

boys just before he climbed a pyramid of paint cans. She came back with a squalling kid tucked under her arm and a sheepish look on her face.

"Sorry about the chaos, Melody. I'd better get my stuff and get outta here. The nursery won't paint itself for the new baby. The husband always has excuses not to get it done." Meg stood the whining boy on the floor and he wiped his nose on her jeans.

Eww gross, as Hayley said. Cathy muttered feeble congratulations.

Meg charged off to rescue the pyramid from her other son.

Cathy keyed in her PIN for the purchase and dragged a reluctant Hayley away from her new friend.

So, Ryan had been a very busy man in eleven short years—married with three kids and another on the way. Lindsey clearly adored him, though his poor wife was in rough shape. His polished good looks compared to his wife's worn clothes pointed to a selfish nature, but his work at the shelter said something completely different.

Perhaps it would be better he never found out about his other—*santo cielo*—his first child.

"Caterina! *Vieni presto*!" Zia Yola called the moment the kitchen's screen door slapped closed behind them.

Cathy plopped the paint cans on the floor, flew up the stairs two at a time, and dashed into her mother's room. Mamma sat in the middle of the carpet with her flannel nightgown twisted up over her bare knees. Red-faced with exertion, Zia Yola hauled on Mamma's outstretched arms.

Mamma jerked her hands out of Zia Yola's grip. Zia Yola stumbled off balance and grabbed at the window ledge. She moaned and pressed her hand to her troublesome lower back.

"That weakling Yola can't get me off this stupid floor," Mamma raged in Italian. "I've been sitting here forever and I want up." Callously ignoring her sister's pain, Mamma thrust her hands at Cathy. "You get me up."

Zia Yola sank into the chair, buried her face in her palms, and wept. "*Santo cielo*, I can't lift her."

Cathy rubbed her aunt's shoulder. "It's not your fault, *cara Zia*. You can't be expected to lift your own body weight, especially with a strained back," she replied in Italian.

Mamma sneered. "She doesn't want to help me. Good for nothing." She thrust her hands towards Cathy again. "Get me up before I wet the carpet. Though it will serve her right to clean up the mess."

Revulsion swept away all of Cathy's sympathy for Mamma and left a void echoing with years of resentment. Mamma had never been a kind person and now she was a nightmare. *She's sick and scared, so back off.* Cathy reasoned with herself as she scooted the walker into position beside her mother.

"Why didn't you use your walker or wait for Zia Yola?"

"She took too long." Mamma scowled then shoved at the aid, toppling it to the rug with a dull clang. "I don't need that thing. I'm not a cripple."

Mamma can't help her bitterness; she has a right to it. Dredging up patience, Cathy righted the walker beyond her mother's reach. "No, you're not crippled. You're just not well and need some support until you get better." Cathy crouched behind her mother and wrapped her arms around the frail chest. "Okay, Mamma, bend your knees and tuck your feet under yourself."

"Why?" She grumbled, like a crabby child who didn't want to acknowledge she was the author of her own misery. She bent her legs to get her feet closer to her behind.

"Simple physics. It will be much easier to get you on your feet if they're near you instead of stuck out front. Zia Yola, are you able to hold the walker ready?"

Zia Yola wiped her face in her smock and hobbled over.

On the count of three, Cathy straightened, taking the weight of Mamma with her. Zia Yola pushed the walker forward and Cathy placed her mother between the protective rails.

"There you go. Now, let's get you to the washroom."

"I don't need this piece of junk to walk." And yet, she took off with it in a curious knees-together crab-walk. "Find my hat. My head is cold."

Cathy grimaced and rolled her eyes at her aunt. Zia Yola acknowledged Mamma's contradictions with an apologetic smile.

"*Grazie mille*, Caterina. I'm sorry she is so much trouble for you."

Why should Zia Yola apologize for her sister's bad behaviour? Mamma's uncertain temper was aggravated by illness. The very real possibility of death now lashed her resentment to new heights. Compassion laced with a healthy person's guilt flowed through Cathy as she shepherded Zia Yola towards the door.

"It's not your fault, Zia. She's grumpy from the treatments. Why don't you go and rest. I doubt Mamma will need anything for a while. I'll answer if she calls."

"Are you sure?"

Cathy carefully hugged her aunt. "Yes, of course I am. Go.

Don't worry. I'll bring you some pain pills as soon as I'm done here."

Slumping from fatigue, Zia Yola minced from the room, one hand clamped to the small of her back.

Cathy straightened the bedclothes, found the knitted cap and shook it vigorously to remove the stray hairs. Poor Mamma had been so vain about her glorious mane of wavy hair. Mamma shuffled in, set aside the walker, and climbed into bed as if nothing had happened. Once arranged to her satisfaction, Mamma smoothed the blankets over her lap and nodded in a queenly fashion.

"Now, you may stay and look after me."

Cathy tamped down the ridiculous urge to curtsey and say "Yes, ma'am. Thank you, ma'am" like a good little servant.

"You will be more useful to me than Yola."

"Mamma, be nicer to Zia Yola. This has been hard for her, too."

"Hard for *her*?" Her mother jammed her toque over her bald head then pressed a palm to her chest. "*I'm* the one who's got the cancer. *I'm* the one who might die." Tears glistened in her weary brown eyes.

Cathy's vision blurred as she choked on the hard distasteful truth. She gently scooped her mother close. Skinny arms returned her hug. "You're incredibly strong and have great doctors. You're not going to die."

Mamma's breath slowed as she drifted off in Cathy's clasp. She laid Mamma against the pillows and gazed at the sleeping face, so gaunt and pale. Cathy tucked the blankets around Mamma's thin shoulders.

Staring out the window, Cathy drew on her inner strength.

A blue pickup came down the street and pulled in across the way. Ryan slid from behind the wheel. Her skin prickled as sunlight danced off his light-brown curls. Raw lust writhed in her belly. Her palms itched to follow the curving path of light over his back, butt, legs and learn the changes adulthood had wrought. She administered a mental slap upside her head.

Another man, the emcee from the carnival, also got out, and they went up the stairs and into Ryan's home.

Cathy resettled her glasses and turned away. He had a real family of five-going-on-six. The unformed fantasy she'd brought with her to Clarence Bay had never had more than a bluebird's chance in a blizzard.

CHAPTER 5

Truth and Lies

"Thanks, but no thanks, Bill, though I do appreciate the offer of your support. Paul Donner is a capable campaign manager and I have faith in him," Ryan said into his cell phone. In the background at the other end, Bucky issued orders about how to deal with his stubborn son.

If his stubborn dad kept pushing, Ryan would push back instead of merely standing firm. Though there was no *merely* about resisting his father.

Ryan grimaced at his brother Mark seated across the pool table they'd converted to campaign central with the handy addition of two sheets of plywood. The brothers returned joking sympathetic grins.

A grunt blew over the line. "Well, I'll wish you good luck. Call me when the mud starts flying," Bill said.

"I'll keep you in mind. Thanks again. Say hi to Dad for me."

"Roger that, Buckster Junior." Ryan rolled his eyes, said goodbye, and clicked off his cell with Bill's wheezy chuckle in his ear. Why did his dad's friends think the God-awful nickname so amusing? He sagged back in his chair and scrubbed his hands over his face.

His best friend Paul strolled the basement room, peeking into stacked boxes of signs, flyers, and stickers printed with variations of "Vote Ryan Chisholm for Clear Clean Government". For a not-so-tall guy, he seemed to occupy more than his allotted space on the planet. Though Paul was a few years older than Ryan, their mutual interest in the Family Shelter had brought them close.

Everything sat ready and waiting for tomorrow's invasion of envelope stuffers, canvassers and assorted helpers necessary to the burst of effort to elect a mayor for a town of six-and-a-half-thousand people.

Paul clapped Mark on the back. "Thanks for offering your place to us, Mark. No way has Ryan got enough space for a setup like this."

Mark accepted his thanks with a sheepish grin. "Meg insisted we offer our place to help out. Like she says—anything for family."

"Meg's a good one." His inspection complete, Paul propped his chino-clad hip on their makeshift conference table. "Your dad still after you to run a smut-and-smear campaign?"

Ryan dismissed the call with an impatient wave of his hand. "Something like that. Bill Hadley volunteered his services while my dad coached in the background. They're a stubborn pair of old warhorses who *know* only their way is the right way."

"They might have a point though." Meg said as she entered the room and thumped a carafe on the table.

Meg handed out cake and coffee to a round of thanks then sagged into a chair. "Hey, did you hear Cathy Rossetti's back in town?"

Ryan swallowed his shock at Cathy's name. Though why should he be shocked? Clarence Bay's gossip mill eventually turned every event into grist. "That so?"

"Lindsey and I met her down at Grisham's today when we picked up the paint for the baby's room." She shot an aggravated glance at Mark who looked away. Ryan squirmed in his seat on Mark's behalf.

Meg wasn't happy as a stay-at-home mom and had been ready to go back to work for a much-needed second income. Ryan understood Meg's resentment at being trapped at home with the unexpected fourth pregnancy.

She put her mug down on the plywood table with a hollow thunk. "She's some kinda hot-shot investment madame down in Toronto. After she left, Old Man Grisham told me she's a single mom, divorced, and back with her maiden name." She sniffed. "Probably never took her husband's name in the first place—too arrogant, I'll bet."

Ryan had assumed the same about her marital status. Then why did the information depress him and cheer him at the same time? "Being a single mom must be tough."

"And marriage isn't?" Meg snorted. "Guess she doesn't have what it takes to hang in there. Probably couldn't care less about her kid having a dad around. A nine-year-old girl needs her dad." Meg turned and hollered up the stairs, "Linds, you coming?"

Lindsey entered, carefully balancing a tray laden with empty mugs and coffee cake. She slid the tray onto the table and glowed with the success of a safe landing. Ryan winked at his niece and gave her thumbs up.

Oblivious of adult tensions, Lindsey walked around the table to perch on Ryan's knees. She pulled her cake and milk towards her. "Hayley's mom is so pretty. She's got straight hair."

The recollection of Cathy in her look-at-me red bathing suit tugged at the corner of his mouth. Married or not, mother or not, she still carried the power to knock him sideways.

"Hayley says they're painting her mom's old playhouse. I'm gonna help."

Mark nudged Ryan with his shoulder. "You had the major hots for Cathy in high school, didn't you? You gonna try your luck again now she's free?"

Candlelit images of a young Cathy, naked and breathy, danced in Ryan's mind. Oh yeah, major hots. He ducked his head to hide his unrepentant secretive grin.

"No, he isn't," Meg snapped at her husband. "My cousin Becca has other plans for him."

"Oh?" Mark's eyebrows rose. "Something you should tell us, Ryan?"

"Ah...um..." Ryan stalled.

"Becca told me he proposed," Meg answered for him. "Not that we didn't all know."

Paul teetered with surprise on the edge of the table. He flapped his arms to correct his balance then sat there bug-eyed. "I thought you weren't—that you didn't—"

Ryan choked on cake crumbs and coughed until his eyes watered. Lindsey jumped off his lap and patted his shoulder in an oddly effective attempt to soothe him.

"Geez, you okay?" Mark stood; ready to thump Ryan's back.

Wheezing to recovery, Ryan waved his brother into his seat. "Yeah, I'm good. Crumbs went down the wrong way." He sipped his coffee to ease his throat and kissed Lindsey's hand in gratitude.

"So when's the wedding?" Meg prodded.

"Can I be your flower girl?" Lindsey fidgeted at his side, her hands clasped together in little-girl bridal ecstasy. "Please, please?"

Groaning, Ryan scrubbed his face. "It didn't actually happen like she said."

Meg's features tightened with outrage. "You're a fool if you can't see how wonderful Becca is. You'd be lucky to get her."

"I didn't propose...exactly."

"What?" She half-rose from her seat, her palms flat on the table. "She loves you and would make you a terrific wife."

Ryan swallowed hard, glanced at Mark. No help there. "Well, she's nice—"

"Nice?" Meg broke the sound barrier with her offended shriek. "I thought you were smarter than that, you—" She glanced at Lindsey. "You'd rather go after some hot little—etcetera—with all kinds of baggage than a sweet girl like Becca?" She stood all the way up and blistered the men with her angry gaze. "You haven't the sense God gave a goat." She threw up her hands and stomped out.

Speaking glances pin-balled between the men.

Lindsey licked the last crumb off her fingers and wiped them on her shorts. "Can I be your flower girl?" Clearly, she'd tuned out the adult conversation.

Ryan blinked. Mark whistled. Paul smiled. They all chuckled at Lindsey's hopeful determination to have her moment of glory. Lindsey harrumphed and left with her tip-tilted nose elevated in fine imitation of her mother. Her small huffy footsteps echoed in the stairwell.

"Don't do it, Ry." Mark had never been more serious. "Don't marry someone you don't love. Not even if she's pregnant."

Ryan's jaw swung loose in horror. He did a memory scan for Becca's last PMS days. His shoulders sagged in relief. "She's not. We were careful."

"Why didn't you say no right up front?" Mark asked. "Why did you let everyone think you're engaged?"

"It's not like you to be such a coward," Paul added.

Ryan hung his head, embarrassed. "It didn't go down the way you're thinking. Becca's mother dismissed me from her presence before I could talk to Becca, and now Becca's out of the country, and I refuse to break up with her other than in person. Everyone and her family thinks we're engaged, and I haven't a clue what to do." He raised his hands in a futile beg for understanding. "I just don't want to hurt her."

"One way or another you will." Paul's wave encompassed the room and the stacks of boxes. "And all this election prep will become a farce if her family and its octopus of connections decide you're jerking her around."

"God, don't remind me." Ryan groaned and lowered his head into his hands. The mere thought of the might-have-been with Cathy showed him he didn't love Becca and he never would.

Hayley loved brushing paint on the boards of the back wall of her playhouse. And white made everything so clean and nice. Painting was so easy to do. Crouch on a little stool, dip the brush, and smooth the paint. Simple. Not like asking Mom stuff about her dad.

But she needed to know, needed to ask—whether or not Mom

answered. Hayley licked her lips and turned to her mom kneeling by the window.

"M-Mom?" Hayley's bent leg bounced like a maniac rubber ball. She stabbed her thigh with the brush handle to stop the darn jiggling. The brush and her leg bounced together.

"Hmm?" Mom's voice sounded all far away, like she was daydreaming or something. She did a lot of that stuff in the playhouse.

"Will you tell me about my dad?" Hayley tried to talk as if she didn't care. Problem was she cared way too much.

Her mom's hand jerked and blue paint squished all over the glass. "Darn it!" Mom grabbed a rag.

"Mo-om?"

"I heard you, sweetie. Let me wipe this paint off first." Mom wiped off every speck of paint and probably some of the glass before looking at her. "Okay, what did you say?"

A forbidden swear word rolled on Hayley's tongue and she snapped her teeth on it. Mom did that every time—acted like she forgot the question or she changed the subject. Hayley licked her lips and tried again.

"Tell me about my dad." Hayley made herself sound like Mom issuing orders.

Mom stared at her brush as she painted a crooked line on the window frame. Hayley waited. And waited some more. The swearword tried harder to get out and she bit it back. This time, she wanted some answers.

"Was he cute?" A squirmy feeling tickled her heart. If only her own dad was as cute and nice as Lindsey's Uncle Ryan.

Mom sat back on her heels with a funny smile on her face. "I thought so at the time."

Great. Her dad was creepy-looking. Maybe she didn't need a picture of him after all. Mom said people who made babies were supposed to love each other. Ick—not going there.

"Did you like him?" she asked instead.

Another funny smile. "Very much. I loved his great sense of humour and we talked for hours about all sorts of stuff."

Talked? Riiight. Hayley knew babies didn't get made with words. "Where did you meet him?"

Mom's eyes squinted a bit. "Why do you want to know all this now?"

"Because we did a genealogy project at school and I was the only kid with blank spots for my father and his parents." *And because I don't want my teacher looking at me with sad eyes and feeling sorry for me. And because even divorced kids have a dad to fill in. And because I don't need to feel like a freak.*

"Oh, sweetie, I'm sorry." Mom didn't look sorry enough to say what Hayley desperately wanted to hear. Darn it. Hayley tried to forget the hurt from the mean kids' laughing.

Mom tilted her head. "Did I see this project?"

"Nah. I didn't bring it home. It was too ugly." And too empty. And too awful. And too—there wasn't a word sad enough.

"Oh."

"Am I ever going to meet him?" Geez, could she hope any worse for that happening?

"I can't answer that. I'm sorry."

Hayley dug her thumbnail into her index finger to stop the babyish tears. "Didn't he want me?"

Mom slowly painted another bit of the window frame.

Fear shook Hayley's stomach like not-ready-yet Jell-O. She turned to hide the tears in her eyes.

"He doesn't know about you," Mom whispered.

Her surprise chased away the sucky crying. "Why didn't you tell him?"

"Because he—I—" Mom sighed a huge sigh and twirled the paintbrush around. "Well, his mom had just passed away and he was so upset, I didn't think he was ready to be a father."

"Is he ready now?"

Mom sighed. "I don't think he'll ever be ready."

An idea burst into Hayley's mind. An idea as huge as the Grinch's Christmas. An idea so big, she hardly understood it. Mom had seen her dad—like since they'd come to Clarence Bay. Seen him and decided he still wasn't ready to be her dad.

But if he knew about her, he could decide for himself.

Couldn't he?

"Wow, this is like totally awesome!" Lindsey declared from the doorway of the playhouse.

Cathy jumped and peered over her shoulder as if she'd been caught gossiping in school. Lindsey's mother Meg peered in from behind Lindsey.

Hayley placed her brush on the paint can lid and squealed into her new friend's hug. "Totally. Mom let me pick the colours. It sucks you didn't come yesterday."

"I went to Mary's birthday party." Lindsey rolled her eyes. "She's such a dork, but her mom gives out the best goody bags."

Cathy and Meg exchanged knowing glances. Cathy didn't *want* to like Ryan's wife, but the empathetic bonds of mothering pre-teen girls were strong.

"Lindsey, behave yourself," Meg said.

The weak reprimand got an even bigger eye roll and a shrug-off from Lindsey. Why didn't Meg remind her daughter of the good in her friend? Cathy's empathy with Meg dimmed.

"Did you want to help with the painting?" Cathy asked Lindsey. The little girl bore the Chisholm changeable grey eyes, going from silvery to dark as she moved indoors.

"Yeah, cool," Lindsey said.

Cathy waited for the please or thank you. Neither came though Lindsey squirmed with anticipation. Guess with three-point-five kids, manners weren't a high priority. *Meow. Jealous much?*

"Good," Cathy said. "Okay with you, Meg?"

"Completely fine by me. She'll be out of my way."

Cathy winced at the carelessness in her tone.

"Come here, Lindsey. We'll cover your hair to keep the paint off." Cathy slid off her own red bandana and wrapped up Lindsey's curls. If Hayley had looked as much like their father as her half-sister did, this would have been an awkward moment.

Sister. Hayley had a sister. She'd be over the moon if she knew. Cathy's heart twisted with guilt. A father, a sister, brothers—how much could she deny her daughter?

She glanced at the rumpled unhappy-looking Meg. Could she share custody with this woman? Was it better for Hayley if she knew her dad? She'd have to decide before her leave expired in the next six weeks.

A breath gusted from her lungs. She poured some white paint into a smaller bucket and picked up another paintbrush for Lindsey. "Start here in this corner and work your way towards Hayley's corner. Then the walls will be half-done. You two girls can keep going after lunch. Or we can go to the beach."

"The beach. Yay!" Lindsey lifted the brush and slapped white paint on the wall.

"Not so fast, Linds, or it gets all sloppy." Hayley smoothed out her friend's mess. "I like painting and I want to do a good job."

Cathy hid her smile at the comical struggle between good work and good fun.

"Well, if you've done those two walls by lunch, I think you'll deserve a reward—Timmy's for lunch and then hit the beach. Okay?"

The girls squealed their approval and got down to tidy business. Cathy paused long enough to hear Hayley's precise instructions how the paint should be applied: not too thick and not too thin. Then she headed out into the sunshine with Meg.

"Would you care for something to drink? Herbal tea, decaf coffee, pop?" she asked a drooping Meg.

Meg accepted with a tight smile. "Yeah, decaf sounds good."

"C'mon in." Cathy led the way to the kitchen and set to work while lecturing herself to be kind to Meg if only for Ryan's sake.

Meg eased into a chair with a deep sigh. "How's your mother?"

"Better. Thanks for asking. She's still quite weak, but getting stronger every day."

"That's good. Yola's looking good, too. Not so tired."

Cathy sighed with frustration. "It's a real battle to get Yola out of the house and do things for herself. She's worked too hard for too long."

Meg rubbed her protruding belly. "Yeah, I know what you mean. Sometimes I think I'm just a housekeeper and nursemaid. The husband doesn't see me anymore. Except of course, when he wants some action." A bawdy snort accompanied the last statement.

Cathy grimaced at thought of Ryan and Meg in bed. Well, it seemed he was at least faithful. Casting frantically for a safe topic of conversation, Cathy came up empty, so of course out popped, “What’s Ryan up to these days, other than running for mayor?” She hid her painful blush in the bustle of finding biscuits and serving coffee. As if she didn’t already know the answer.

“After he quit working for Bucky, he bought the hardware store and he volunteers for the family shelter and anyone else who asks him. He’s quite the big man about town.” Meg tipped her head from side to side, a dismissive expression on her face. Wow, this woman had a weird notion of her husband’s success. Wonder why? Did he spend too much time away from her?

“What does he hope to achieve in the mayor’s office?”

“He thinks he can make a difference, make the governmental process more transparent for the people.” Meg swallowed a mouthful of coffee and a whole biscuit, and then twisted her mouth to the side. “For some damn reason he thinks people actually care.”

Meg’s deep mockery of her husband’s dreams shocked Cathy, made her feel sorry for him.

The other woman’s eyes narrowed at Cathy. “Didn’t you and Ryan have a thing going on back in the day?”

Cathy flushed at the question, like she’d tell his wife what they’d really done. She pushed up her glasses, touched her lips, and shrugged in what she hoped passed as carefree. “Not really. I’m glad he’s doing well. How’s the baby’s room going?”

“The walls are washed and prepped. I start painting tomorrow.”

"*You're* painting the baby's room?"

"Yep, the husband has to help out the envelope stuffers."

"But you're pregnant!"

Meg rubbed her belly. "Uh, yeah, I noticed. So?"

"You shouldn't be doing work like that. It's not safe."

"Somebody's gotta do it." Meg shrugged. "I'm only five months along."

"Ryan should do the work, not you."

"Ryan?"

"Yeah, you know, the husband?"

"The hus—" Meg halted mid-word and a devious expression blinked across her face. She polished off her mug of coffee. "Aw, Ryan's got more important work than painting our baby's room." She hauled herself to her feet. "Thanks for the coffee. Send Lindsey home for supper, eh? Ryan likes his whole family around the table."

Cathy's world tilted with the Norman Rockwell view of a laughing devoted family around a table laden with food. The fantasy continued with kids tucked in, Meg and Ryan snuggling by the fire. How would things have turned out if she had stayed?

Imbecille. She scoffed at her lunacy.

If she'd stayed behind, she'd have turned into Meg and been stuck with a selfish patronizing despot who spent too much time away from his wife and kids. Who cared only for his own goals and didn't care for his family.

She'd been lucky to get away.

CHAPTER 6

Proposals

The roar of a lawn mower shredded the lazy Sunday afternoon peace. Cathy shot out of her lounger and marched around the side of the house. Why did cretins have to mow lawns on Sunday? There ought to be a law against it.

Rounding the corner, Cathy slammed to a halt. Ryan, bare-chested and bare-legged, was the offending cretin shoving a mower across her mother's lawn.

Frozen in place like an oversized garden gnome, Cathy's gaze followed him as he cut careful lines back and forth, completely focused on his work. Sweat beaded on his brow and trickled down his chest and spine, dampened the ragged cut-offs clinging to his narrow hips.

Her tongue slid between her lips, desperate for a taste of golden salty skin. Her nostrils flared, desperate for the scent of him. Her hands curled, desperate to touch the smooth slick—

Dio mio. She wasn't *that* desperate!

He was married. He had three and a half kids.

He was forbidden.

Cathy's mental slap across her face must have echoed over the grass because Ryan stopped and his gaze nailed her. Embarrassment erupted and Cathy took flight to the safety of the back yard. She flung her overheated self into the lounger on the patio and jammed her book into her lap pretending she had not been watching him with predatory intent.

The lawn mower continued its noisy route over the front lawn. Cathy suffered a few minutes of knife-edged tension. Nothing happened. Her heart rate slowed.

She looked down at her book. *Imbecille.*

She swivelled her head, just the tiniest bit either way, to see if he was coming around the corner.

Safe.

Quickly, she turned her novel right side up and forced herself to read. Well, she tried real hard anyway.

Ryan tooled the lawnmower around the side yard and finally made his way into the backyard. He flashed a sexy grin at Cathy and carried on.

He mowed left. Sleek thigh muscles flexed beneath taut tanned skin. *He's a jerk.*

He mowed right. Slim hips pivoted into a turn, flashing back pockets and zipper. *A married jerk.*

Left. Strong arms and pecs bulged as he guided the machine around a garden bed. *A married jerk with three and a half children.*

Right. Curls tightened in the slick sweat on his chest and neck. *He's the unknowing father of your child.*

Erotic freeze-frame moments of Hayley's conception snapped across her mind. Lava, hot and molten, oozed through her veins. What would his weight feel like now? Cathy's eyeballs got whiplash trying not to follow the glorious nearly-naked man.

Get your eyes off him and onto the page.

Ryan finished the job and put away the mower. Soon he'd go and take all that beautiful, hot, naked, sweaty skin with him. Her eyes widened to take in as much of the view as possible, to store it away for a needy night.

A small ripping sound pulled her gaze down to a page torn by the tension of her white-fingered grip.

"Hey, Cathy."

She lifted her gaze to him and blinked her heavy lids at the interest in his eyes.

Sweat popped on her upper lip and she licked it away. His tongue mimicked the movement over his own upper lip.

Desire steamed up the air between them to equatorial temperatures.

His hand lifted towards her, open, reaching, begging for her touch.

Her hands clenched the book, bending it wide open, cracking the spine.

Clinking, tinkling glass shattered the unbearable tension. The screen door slapped shut as Zia Yola stepped onto the porch. "Caterina, Ryan. I have some drinks for you."

Not yet hot enough, Cathy's entire body blushed. *Guilty, guilty, so guilty.*

Ryan flopped down in the chair beside her. Zia Yola set the tray on the table and handed out iced tea for Cathy and herself, and a cold glass of beer for Ryan.

Zia Yola glanced from Cathy to Ryan, a puzzled frown creasing her brow. "You two look very hot. It's a good thing I brought out something to cool you off."

Little did her aunt know she needed a fire hose connected to a glacier to cool Cathy off. The recent moment with Ryan blazed hotter than anything in the past. Except maybe that night.

Zia Yola patted Ryan's head as she handed him his beer. "You're very good to us. Thank you for doing the lawn."

"You're welcome, Zia Yola." Ryan lifted his glass in a friendly toast, tipped his head, and knocked back half the contents.

Cathy's mouth burned with the need to chomp down on the strong column of his exposed throat. It was true, vampires had more fun.

"Aah." He wiped the froth away with the back of his hand. Touching the dripping glass to his cheek, he sighed in relief. Cathy shivered.

"Caterina, have you caught a summer cold? Maybe you should stay away from Lucia."

Cathy tore her avid gaze from her high-school boyfriend's all-grown-up sexiness. "I'm fine, Zia Yola. Just a bit warm from the sun." She hooted to herself and gulped her iced tea. The coolness spread through her chest in blessed relief.

"Caterina?" The baby monitor on the side table squawked to life. Lucia needed her. Before Cathy shifted to put down her glass, Zia Yola crossed the patio flapping her hand and saying "Stay and talk with your old friend." Footsteps followed by feminine Italian chatter crackled over the listening device, her mother grousing, her aunt clucking. Cathy leaned over and switched off the monitor. The Sunday peace descended and the tension ratcheted up.

"How long have you been doing the yard work around this place?" *Lame, lame conversation.*

"Ever since you asked me, just before you left."

Cathy stared back. "I don't recall...that's...wow... incredible...thank you."

"You asked, Zia Yola is grateful, I do it." He shrugged one shoulder and his gaze drifted.

"So you've been fixing up the playhouse?"

"Yes." Cathy shied from mention of their daughter.

"Show me?"

"Uh...sure." Keeping her glass to fill her hands, she maintained a safe distance from him as they walked down the yard.

"I really miss what we had—the closeness and sharing. I've often wondered what would have happened if we'd managed to keep in touch over all these years, what our lives would have been like."

Cathy frowned at the nostalgia in his voice.

"We could have been really good together. Even better than we were."

Huh? Did he regret hooking up with Meg before the diesel fumes had dissipated behind Cathy's bus? Did he make a habit of knocking up his girlfriends? Had he married Meg out of obligation rather than love?

Arriving at the end of the yard, she waved him into the playhouse but made herself stay outside. In her confused state, she did not need memory and reality colliding.

He stooped to get through the door and remained slightly bent beneath the peak of the roof. He'd been able to stand tall the last time he was there. A dreamy smile spread over his face as his gaze wandered the small space and lingered on the padded bench.

"Do you remember...?" His muted raspy voice resonated with the desire of that long-ago night.

Her mouth hung open. Of course she remembered. But was he in any position to recall the night between them?

"I'll never forget," he continued in a dreamy voice. He joined her outside the playhouse, captured her gaze, let the heat build between them. "I'd like to make some new memories."

Cathy stepped back. *No. No. Please say he didn't just proposition me. Please tell me he hasn't sunk so low.*

Married men were usually sent away with a cold smile and a colder shoulder. It shouldn't matter that *this* married man held a special place in her heart and mind.

Such ugliness beneath his beauty. Her soul wept for her young self and the father her daughter would never know.

Cathy swallowed the last of her iced tea, proud her hand didn't tremble. Then she snatched his half-empty glass from him and threw the cold beer over his hot chest.

She ignored his shocked shout.

"You want memories? Help yourself. But you'll be doing it on your own." She flicked a last drop at him and it trickled down his cheek like a tear. "Or maybe you should ask *the other woman.*"

She stomped into the house, slammed the door, and ignored his pleas to talk it out. There was no way, no way at all, she was having anything to do with such a beast of a man.

"Thank you. I'll be right back with your drinks." The waiter at the Bayside Restaurant tucked the menus under his arm and left Ryan and Nana Jean, his grandmother, to be entertained by the busy marina across the road. The *Island Queen* sightseeing vessel unloaded her crowd of sunburned tourists, float planes whined into the sky, and huge private yachts demanded attention. A lawn tractor traced precise squares over wide swaths of grassy parkland fronting the massive docks.

Ryan nodded with satisfaction to see a paint crew get busy on the long-awaited clean-up of the marina office. Bucky had a long-standing feud with the harbourmaster so maintenance had always been "overlooked."

He rubbed a hand down the front of his clean shirt over his clean torso. What was it with him and getting beer all over himself lately? Some mayor he'd make if he still needed to work on his communication skills.

"Have you heard the latest about Emma and the new doctor?"

At the same moment, a text came in from Becca, full of nonsense and emoticons. Too bad those little hearts weren't from Cathy. Then he'd be singing a different tune. He shook off thoughts of both women. "Okay, Nana Jean, what's the story behind Emma and the doctor?"

She leaned over the table and whispered loudly, "When Lillian was at the hospital's Family Practice Clinic for her check-up; Nurse Daniels said that she saw the new eye doctor kissing Emma in an exam room. Emma's wearing a patch, so obviously, she hurt her eye, but Annie Daniels swears she saw the doctor give Emma a little *extra care.*"

Dr. Stockdale had recently moved to town and Ryan had only met him once. He doubted that such a professional man would allow anything so improbable and improper as a kiss between himself and a patient. But it might be fun to tease his too-serious friend Emma.

Several bites into their delicious fish dinners, Nana Jean

tapped her fork on her white plate. "Okay, Ryan, out with it."

Ryan sipped his wine and carefully placed the glass on the crowded table. "Out with what?"

She scowled lightly. "I'm too old to dilly-dally around. Tell me what's on your mind?"

A cloud drifted by—looked like a puppy he'd once owned. He sighed. "Election things. The polls put me ahead by thirty-three points."

"So why don't you sound excited?"

He put her off by filling his mouth with grilled trout, chewing, and swallowing. "There's possible trouble. Big trouble. Maybe."

She simply waited him out.

"Do you remember Becca Carleton-Grant?" he finally asked.

"Yes, a pretty young blonde, deeply insecure beneath her drama-queen act. She needs to get away from her control freak of a mother."

Ryan choked on his wine, surprised at Nana Jean's accurate character analysis. If only he'd asked Nana Jean before he dated Becca. "That's her. Long story short, she's expecting me to propose." Ryan waited for the automatic congratulations. They didn't come.

She tipped her head. "Somehow I don't think congratulations are in order."

How did she know Becca wasn't The One?

"You know, this reminds me of your father."

Ryan stiffened at the association. "What's Dad got to do with this?" He waited impatiently while she finished her last mouthful of sautéed vegetables.

"Did you know he was once engaged to Becca's mother?"

His knife clattered to his plate, earning him annoyed and startled glances from other patrons.

"Virginia was quite mad for Bucky. Then he met your mother and fell so deeply in love with my sweet Francie, he broke off the engagement. Unfortunately, he didn't tell Francie about the engagement."

His lunch churned in his belly. His old man had started his dishonourable ways early in life.

"Poor Virginia caused a huge fuss and scandal. She never forgave him. The Carletons were always hard on Bucky after the break-up, even though she married someone else. It's why his elections were always so hard-won."

So that explained the bitter feelings lurking between the Chisholms and the Carleton-Grants, especially Virginia's coldness towards himself. "A marriage between us would reconcile the families," he said.

Nana Jean sighed. "It's almost romantic." Her sweet nostalgic expression hardened. "Do *not* marry her."

He grinned at his suddenly hard-core grandma. "Why not?"

"Do *not* marry a woman for convenience."

"She says she loves me, needs me. A lot." He shrugged, caught between a rock, a hard place, and why-me.

Nana Jean captured his hand in a gentle grasp. She peered into his eyes, his heart. "Do you love her?"

He slid his hand away, carefully aligned his used knife and fork to one side of his empty plate, and finished the last drop of wine. The scent of new-mown grass wafted in on the breeze, bringing the image of Cathy's flushed face and delectable mouth. Sweet Cathy lived a life that had nothing to do with him. Beautiful strong independent Cathy didn't need him.

Becca did. And so did Clarence Bay.

Cathy took her after-lunch coffee and headed out back with the sense of a burden shifting, of hope brightening. Her bare feet reveled in the sun-warmed touch of the flagstone patio. She placed her book and coffee on the side table, lifted her face to the sun.

While Hayley and Lindsey had lunched in the playhouse, Mamma had joined Cathy and Yola in the kitchen for the first time since Cathy came home. Her mother's temper was almost back to its normal querulous self. She'd only complained half-heartedly about Zia Yola's cannelloni. Exhausted, her mother retreated to her bedroom for a brief nap while Cathy cleaned up. Cheerful and gossipy from her morning of yarn shopping with her friends, Zia Yola hunted up her needles, took her bag of soft colourful treasure, and settled in the back parlour where the sunlight poured in clear and bright.

Satisfied with a job well done, Cathy lazed in her lounger and savoured the peace of an endless summer afternoon.

Okay, a job almost done.

The only fly in the ointment was her mother's continued refusal to truly acknowledge her granddaughter. Polite enough, she treated Hayley like a stranger's little girl and not a child of her own blood. With five weeks of leave remaining, Cathy had time on her side. Time, determination, and her sweet-natured daughter to bring about a full reconciliation and give Hayley as much family as Cathy could manage.

A breeze tossed strands of hair across her face. She stretched her arms over her head and wiggled her toes. Such a glorious contrast to her high-pressured investment world of meetings morning, noon, and night.

The sound of girls' high-pitched voices lilted up the long green yard. The playhouse looked terrific with fresh white walls, blue window frames, and a yellow door. The two youngsters had stuck to the job set before them and had a lot of fun doing it. Zia Yola had stitched up new blue-and-yellow plaid curtains and cushion covers.

Their voices crescendoed in a fit of giggles.

Cathy drifted into the past when Melody, Emma, and herself whiled away many an afternoon in the playhouse.

"Did Nico kiss you?" fifteen-year-old Melody and Cathy demanded of the sexually-precocious sixteen-year-old Emma.

"Hell no." Two naïve faces fell in disappointment. "*I* kissed *him*!" Two faces goggled in surprise. "Did you like it?"

Emma tapped her cheek and considered her multitude of experiences. "He kisses better than Mark and better than Stephen." She waggled her hand back and forth. "Mark's a seven. Stephen is a nine. Nico..." she sighed dreamily, "he's a ten!" Then they'd all collapsed in a squealing heap.

Cathy smiled to herself and drained her coffee. Multitude, indeed. Nobody giggled so long over so little in quite the same way as innocent young teens.

She yawned, rose from her lounger, and strolled down the yard to ask the girls if they wanted some milk and cookies.

"Uncle Ryan says I have to wait until I'm sixteen to work for him in his store."

"Sixteen! That's ages and ages away."

Cathy stopped in the open doorway as the content of Lindsey's whine penetrated. The words were understood. They just didn't make sense.

"Ryan who?" Her voice squeaked high on the last word.

The girls exchanged puzzled glances and remained silent. Cathy knocked her forehead, hoping to jar something loose.

"Your mother's name is Meg, isn't it?"

Lindsey shot a *is she nuts* look at Hayley. Hayley shrugged back *I dunno, just answer the dumb question.*

"Margaret Louise Chisholm." Lindsey corrected.

"Your father's name is...?"

"Marcus Andrew Chisholm. I'm Lindsey Louise Chisholm and my brothers are..."

Cathy didn't hear the complete recitation as the wheels in her mind ground slowly and still produced no logic. "Mark—Ryan's brother. Ryan is your uncle." Cathy parroted and Lindsey nodded. "You're not Ryan's daughter."

"Nope."

"Nobody is." Hayley piped up, looking very worried at her mother's apparent stupidity.

"Uncle Ryan's not married."

Such precious irony. An incredulous self-mocking shout of laughter burst from Cathy. The girls jumped and nudged closer to each other on the bench. The poor little things must be frightened of the crazy lady.

Cathy sagged onto the comfy wooden chair and stared at the half-sisters. No, not sisters, cousins.

Ryan wasn't married to the deceitful Meg. She struggled to recall—had Meg lied outright, or had Cathy jump to the wrong conclusions? Ugh, a little of both. What was that woman's problem anyway?

He didn't have three-and-a-half kids. He was single, free, available. A huge grin split her face. Hayley could have her daddy-wish.

Cathy's smile softened and the cousins smiled back in relief.

"Nice job with the hair, girls." Butterfly clips in zigzag placements pulled identical curls away from very different faces. Cathy tugged at one of Hayley's curls. Her determined little sweetie had finally got the clip pattern just right.

Hayley glowed at her praise. "I wanted to show Lindsey how to do it because she's gonna be a flower girl." Lindsey squirmed with excitement.

"Oh, aren't you lucky? Who's the bride-to-be?"

"Becca, my mom's cousin. She's got straight long blonde hair."

"Who's the lucky groom?"

"Ryan," Lindsey crowed.

"Lindsey's Uncle Ryan." Hayley confirmed before Cathy repeated the question. "And Lindsey's going to be a flower girl. Isn't that the coolest?"

Cathy gaped at the girls and their faces turned worried all over again.

Santo cielo. The situation finally became clear. Cathy had made assumptions. Meg had lied, confirming those assumptions. Why? Immaterial. One final detail was needed to complete the correct picture.

"When did your uncle Ryan get engaged?"

Lindsey screwed up her face in concentration. "Um, I'm not sure. He asked me to be his flower girl last Friday, when they stuffed envelopes—a whole mountain of them."

That must have been when she saw him out the bedroom window after Mamma's fall. Before he'd come to mow the grass. He'd asked to make new memories with her *after* he'd asked his niece to be his bridesmaid.

Her elation died as suddenly as it had been born. No, he wasn't married with children, he was engaged. She'd got it partly wrong. But one fact remained, Ryan was still a cheater.

Still an ineligible father.

CHAPTER 7

Name Calling

Hayley put her empty milk glass on the tray and swallowed the last bite of Mrs. Grisham's delicious coffee cake. She leaned back in the prickly beige chair in the old-fashioned front parlour and sighed. Old lady conversations were so boring, all about some Emma person kissing a doctor. Gross. Who'd want to kiss a boy? The idea made her want to hurl. Unless Ricky... Eww, no.

"May I please be excused?" Hayley asked Zia Yola. Nonna looked right through her, like she was invisible or something. Creepy or what?

"Of course, *piccola*." Hayley ran to hug Zia Yola.

"Nice to meet you, Mrs. Grisham," she said goodbye to the pear-shaped lady and wandered through the house looking for something, anything, to do. She should have gone grocery shopping with Mom. Had to be less bo-oring.

She wandered onto the front porch and stared across the street at Lindsey's house. She so wanted to be over there, or get Lindsey to come here to the playhouse.

She still didn't get why her mom and Lindsey's mom were so

freaked out at each other. And what did it have to do with Lindsey being a flower girl? It sucked big time.

Dared she sneak out?

Dared she call Lindsey to come over?

She snuck into the kitchen and punched in Lindsey's number. The phone rang and rang and rang. Darn it. Bet their call display showed Nonna's number and Lindsey's mom wouldn't let her pick up. Maybe Hayley could convince Mom to go to the library and she'd chat online with Lindsey. Nah, Lindsey's mom probably blocked the Internet, too.

Darn it. That ticked her off so much.

Hayley went back to the front porch swing and picked up the first in a bunch of old books of Mom's—all about this girl called Trixie Belden who'd just saved her little brother from a rattlesnake bite. Trixie was so brave. Good thing there weren't any rattlers in town, though Mom said there were some in the big woods.

"Psst!"

Scared silly, Hayley yanked her feet up on the swing with the weird idea that snakes talked. A giggle came from the bush beside the porch. She spun around and up to her knees, the swing going crazy. Peeking through the leaves, she saw her new friend.

"Lindsey!"

"Shh." She really did sound like a snake—a really cute one.

"What are you doing here?" Hayley whispered.

"My mom and the brats are napping, so I came over." Both girls stared at Lindsey's house, fearful of Meg stomping over and hauling Lindsey away. All remained quiet.

"Didn't you hear the phone ring?"

"Nah, Mom turned it off." Lindsey flapped her hand. "C'mon let's go to the playhouse."

Hayley wandered down the steps, pretending like she wanted to look at the flowers. She even sniffed a couple. Eww, the white daisies might be pretty, but they sure reeked. Then she and Lindsey ran down the yard, panting with excitement. They flew into the playhouse, slammed the door, and flopped onto the bench laughing their heads off.

Lindsey checked her wristwatch. "We got an hour-and-a-half before Mom gets up to watch the Jersey show she recorded."

"Your mom lets you see the Jersey show?"

"Yeah, I can watch anything as long as I don't interrupt."

"Wow. I wish my mom was as cool as yours."

The girls talked and giggled until the time came for Lindsey to sneak away. Seconds before she left the cover of the front bushes, Hayley blurted. "Do you know what a *puttana* is?"

Lindsey eyes rounded. "Who called you that?"

"Nobody. I heard it at the mall." No way was Hayley going to admit what really happened.

"On the Jersey show, it's a bad lady who sleeps around with a lot of different guys. The other ladies are mean to her 'cause she steals their boyfriends."

"Oh. Thanks."

"Sure. See you tomorrow?"

"Okay." She hugged her friend goodbye and crossed her fingers for Meg not to catch her.

Just as Lindsey went into her own backyard, Mrs. Grisham came out, waved, and took off down the sidewalk. Hayley almost stroked out at the close call. Her heart banging, she climbed the front porch stairs and sat on the swing again. She tried to read her Trixie book and ignore the whole name-calling thing. Didn't work. She got madder and madder. That stupid old Nonna shouldn't be allowed to call Mom nasty names, even if she was her mother. Mom didn't date, except for charity dances with Matt, and Mom said those weren't real dates.

Stomping into the living room, Hayley stopped dead in her tracks at the old lady's squinty-eyed stare. Hayley almost turned around and ran away.

But Mom always stuck up for her, so she had to stick up for Mom.

She clutched her book to her chest and stood up as straight and tall as possible. Hayley Rossetti, princess warrior and snake slayer. She stuck her finger at her grandmother.

"My mom is *not* a *puttana*! And you have to stop calling her that!"

The old lady's eyes bugged out and her mouth hung open. Zia Yola gasped and slapped a hand over her mouth. What felt like hours of dead silence passed then Nonna leaned forward and squinted at her again. "Did your mother teach you that word?" she said in English so Hayley understood.

"No, but I know what it means. My mom does *not steal* other ladies' boyfriends. She only has one boyfriend and he belongs to her."

"How do you know?" the old lady demanded.

Why were Zia Yola's eyes laughing? "Because he said so. I heard him."

The old lady made a gross noise with her nose. "So you've been *ascolatare di nascosto*?"

"What?" Hayley looked to Zia Yola, but the old lady answered.

"It means eavesdropping, listening to things you shouldn't."

Hayley said nothing. She *had* been listening at the top of the stairs once when Matt dropped Mom off at the same time as Hayley crossed the hall to the washroom. They kissed for a second or two and Matt said stuff. After he left, Mom looked sad instead of happy, which made Hayley feel kinda weird. But the old lady didn't need to know all that.

"Doesn't your mother teach you Italian? Teach you your heritage?"

Hayley clenched her fists at the disapproval in Nonna's voice. Sheesh, a mom was supposed to love a daughter, not always criticize her. She scowled and stuttered into Italian. "*N-non solo le—parole difficile.*" So there. Hope she got it right for "Just not big words."

The old lady relaxed back in her chair, crossed her arms, and nodded like she was impressed. For the first time, her grandma wore a regular dress, black and ugly but not pyjamas. She still wore the same little toque, 'cause her hair fell out from treatment Mom said.

"What does your mother teach you about Italy?" Nonna spoke Italian, slowly and clearly, so Hayley understood every word.

"Things in the house, food and how to cook, and songs."

"What songs?"

"For kid's, of course."

"Sing one."

Sheesh, what a bossy old lady. To show she wasn't lying about her mom, Hayley chose her favourite. "*Farfallina, bella e bianca...*" Butterfly, beautiful and white, she began. Nonna joined her in a rusty voice. Zia Yola joined in with a really nice voice. "*E poi poggra sa un fiore.*" And she rests upon a flower, they all finished together.

Nonna's smile made her seem like a lot nicer person. "The butterfly song is my favourite, too. I always wanted to fly from flower to flower. You have a very nice voice."

"Thank you. Not as good as Zia Yola."

"You're right; no one is as good as Yolanda." Nonna said it like she hated Zia Yola. How creepy and weird to hate your own sister. If Hayley had a sister, she'd be her best friend in the whole world.

"Come here, child. What book are you reading?" Nonna reached out to coax Hayley beside her chair.

Hayley glanced down at the forgotten book clutched in her arms. "Trixie Belden. It's about a girl who killed a snake and saved her brother's life." She went to Nonna, not too close because she smelled funny. She stiffened when Nonna drew Hayley to her side.

"My *nipote*." Nonna shot a dirty look at Zia Yola who got up and left, muttering about cooking supper. Hayley followed her great-aunt with her eyes, wanting to go with her instead of being trapped.

Nonna let Zia Yola go and Hayley inched away.

"I'm bored. Read your book to me." Nonna was kinda grouchy now. She must be tired. Hayley was sorry for her sick grandma.

"Mom said I shouldn't bother you."

"Your mother knows nothing. Sit. Read." Nonna waved a skinny hand and pointed at Zia Yola's ratty chair. Nonna's chair was brand new.

Sheesh. Grouchy, tired and way bossy. "Okay, I'll start over again. I love the part when she saves her brother." So Hayley settled in and read about Trixie's adventures.

Across the hall, Cathy lugged the groceries into the kitchen.

"Sorry, I took so long. They didn't have any decent fennel at the big store, so I went to the farmer's market."

"*Bene*," Zia Yola replied from the sink where she peeled potatoes.

Cathy's eyebrows rose at Zia Yola stiff huffiness. "What's wrong?"

"*Nulla*."

"C'mon Zia, it's not nothing if you're upset. Tell me."

Zia Yola hunched a shoulder. "Go to the living room and see."

As Cathy approached, Hayley's voice rose and fell in a story-telling cadence. She halted in front of a scene she'd never thought to see—her mother and her daughter at peace in the same room.

She walked over, stroked her daughter's hair, and kissed Mamma on the cheek. "Mamma, are you sure Hayley's not bothering you?"

"Not at all. We are having a good time." Mamma waved a dismissing hand. "You go and do your business. We're fine here."

Cathy backed away, relieved at any method Hayley used to make Mamma happy. Back in the kitchen, a miserable Zia Yola continued to prepare supper. Cathy sighed. No sooner was one problem solved than another popped up.

"So Emma's having her usual and you're a blue-cheeseburger with fries and a Stella draft," the waitress in The Pits verified Emma's and Cathy's orders. The sunny room full of battered wooden tables and chairs sparkled with cleanliness and friendly feeling—a comfortable place for a casual meal or drinks.

Cathy pushed up her glasses and smiled at the pretty strawberry blonde. "It's Glory Toussaint, isn't it?"

The waitress nodded with a sheepish grin and gathered the plastic-coated menus. "I'd thought we'd met before. Sorry, I can't remember where."

"We sort of connected at the Carnival for Kids. During your Helping Hand award speech."

Glory gazed at the ceiling, thinking. The puzzlement on her face relaxed and she brightened. "Yes, I remember now. You were in the crowd. Your little girl collected the grand prize to the music festival gala."

"Yes, that was Hayley. I'm—"

Melody blew in, black curls flying, and collapsed into a wooden chair between Emma and Cathy. "Sorry, I'm late. Love the hustle and bustle of the summer people, but sometimes the traffic is just awful."

Cathy envied Melody's concept of rush-hour traffic—a real hour compared to four-going-on-five hours in Toronto.

Her friend smiled at the waitress. "Hey, Glory. I'll have my usual."

"Sure thing. I'm just getting acquainted with your friend."

Melody's blue eyes twinkled. "Oh, good, I love making new friends for my friends. Emma you know, of course. And this is our high school pal, Cathy Rossetti."

Cathy held out her hand and Glory returned a warm clasp. "Pleased to meet you. Are you in town for long?"

"A few weeks. Great speech, by the way. You're a real survivor." Cathy said to Glory.

"What speech?" Emma asked.

"You don't remember?" newshound Melody elbowed Emma in the ribs. "Of course not, you were working. At the Family Shelter fundraiser carnival, Glory told her story about taking her kids and getting away from her abusive husband." Melody reached out and tapped Glory's hand. "It took real guts to air all your stuff in public."

Glory blushed at the praise, blurring the freckles on her fair skin. "It was the hardest thing I've ever done. Well, after running away and getting divorced. But I had to do it for the shelter that helped us so much."

"And then she bragged on Ryan being Mr. Wonderful. Got a thing for him, eh?" Melody waggled her eyebrows and winked broadly.

Cathy took a sip of water. Okay, people thought him Mr. Wonderful. How much ugliness did he hide behind the good deeds?

"Nah. Sure, he's a hell of a hunk," Glory said and the other three women fanned their faces and rolled their eyes in feminine appreciation. Cathy couldn't join in. "If I wasn't older and wiser, and didn't have a couple of kids, I'd give the man some attention." She shrugged in resignation, a wistful look in her hazel eyes. "Well, I *am* older and wiser, so I'm steering clear of any more man trouble."

"You're one tough cookie; and for what it's worth, we're proud of you, girlfriend." Emma and Cathy seconded Melody's statement.

"And your kids are real cuties, especially your daughter," Cathy said, remembering the prancing toddler.

Glory grinned. "Chrissy's such a show off. Her confidence

gives me confidence." She tipped her head. "Well, I'd better get back to work. A waitress called in sick, so the manager," she thumbed her chest, "gets to pick up the slack on her own day off."

Leaving with a friendly wave, she strode off to the long bar at the back of the room, greeting other customers on the way.

Melody leaned towards Cathy. "She's done an amazing job filling this place with new customers. Cleaned it up and re-painted. She wants to do more, but the owner is a real cheapskate and won't let her. I keep telling her to buy out the old miser."

The investment banker in Cathy perked up her ears. "You think she'd be interested in an investor?" A select few of her wealthiest clients liked helping out promising small entrepreneurs. The absolute best part of her job was financial matchmaking.

"Why don't you ask her?"

Cathy watched Glory deal, smiling yet firm, with an amorous client. She sure had an effective way with the guys. Had she ever resorted to dumping cold beer on a hotshot? "I'll sniff around a bit more before I approach her."

Melody turned a teasing look at Emma. "Speaking of insider info and your sexy pirate gear, what's this I hear about you kissing the new doctor?"

Emma slumped and rolled her eye. "Not you, too. The whole damn town is asking the same thing. I'll tell you what I told them—I did not kiss Dr. Stockdale. He was checking out my eye so he leaned close. I did not kiss him. He did not kiss me. End. Of. Discussion." She flipped up her patch to reveal her watering bloodshot orb. "See."

Cathy laughed aloud. "Do you flash your..." Her gaze wandered over Emma's shoulder to the man coming through the door. She drew a deep breath and whispered, "Incoming. Wow on legs."

"Oh, isn't he just?" Melody sighed.

"What?" Emma twisted in her chair and spun back fast enough for whiplash, muttering under her breath. "Damn it."

The beautiful man in a fabulous charcoal suit sauntered through the bar towards them, attracting more feminine gazes than sexy shoes at a fetish show. Cathy's eyes opened wider to accommodate all of his tall dark gorgeousness. Wow... Just wow.

"Hello, Emma." His deep voice reverberated around the table.

Emma glanced high to his face then glued her gaze to his middle jacket button. "Hello, Dr. Stockdale," she muttered.

"I'm glad I bumped into you. May I please see the eye?"

Emma flicked an angry hand in a circle. "If you look around, you'll notice this is not an exam room."

What woman in her right mind responded with anger to a caring question?

Dr. Stockdale's rumbling chuckle brought fire to Emma's pale cheeks. He crouched beside her. Chestnut eye locked with dark-brown eyes. Desire sparked between them. Cathy exchanged astonished looks with Melody at seeing their friend so mesmerized.

Dr. Stockdale stared at Emma, equally enthralled. He swallowed so hard, Cathy heard him from across the table.

"I meant to say—you haven't come back, and I need to check on the state of things. Eyes are sensitive, delicate organs and need close monitoring when damaged." His pedantic words sounded oddly out of place in his deep seductive tones. He tucked a curl behind the ear by her eye patch. Emma shivered at his touch and his hand trembled minutely. Then the couple just sat there, staring at each other.

Dio mio. Cathy squirmed in her chair, feeling uncomfortably like a voyeur at a seduction. With perfect timing, Glory returned with their order and popped the fragile bubble around the pair.

"Fine, I'll come see you," a flustered Emma finally said.

Cathy and Melody traded glances brimming with amusement and envy. Dr. Stockdale stood up and stepped back to allow Glory to set down her laden dishes.

"Excellent. No appointment needed. I'll let you get back to your friends." He touched Emma's shoulder and she moved away from his hand. His mouth tightened, flattening the lush Cupid's bow of his upper lip. He nodded at the rest of the women and strode off to the bar. Emma sagged in her chair and stroked her cheek in the exact spot he had touched.

Cathy's hiss of pent-up breath lifted her bangs. "Well, Emma, I take it that was the good doctor?"

Emma nodded.

"No wonder she kissed him, eh?" Melody winked.

Emma shot out of her seat, hands fisted, eye glaring. "I did not kiss him! He fixed my eye!" She jabbed her finger towards her eye and unfortunately poked herself. "Shit it all!" She clamped a hand over her patch. Her good eye watered in sympathy.

Cathy and Melody jumped to her side.

"Leave me alone," she growled and shook them off. Emma rummaged in her purse, tossed a twenty on the table, snatched up her burger in her bare hand, and stomped out of the restaurant.

The two remaining friends goggled at each other. Melody spoke first. "Well, somebody's protesting a tad too much."

"Ya think?" Cathy sat down again, somewhat dumbfounded. Is that what falling in lust looked like? What a hell of a show. Made her skin all hot and twitchy.

"Wanna split her fries and beer?" Melody piped up.

Cathy laughed at Melody's oh-so-innocent expression. "Yeah, sure."

"Just goes to prove you can't have smoke without fire. I knew it all along, as usual." Melody grinned, smug in her ridiculously-accurate guesses for romance.

Cathy sighed to herself. After the pointed demonstration of gossip gone wild and ruining a potentially great relationship, she changed her mind about asking after Ryan. Melody would unerringly add two and two together and come up with Hayley. So, try a less direct approach.

"My daughter Hayley has been hanging around with a little girl called Lindsey. She lives across the street from Mamma's. Do you know anything about her? Is she a good kid?"

Melody tipped her head, her data banks whirring. "Hmm, Meg and Mark Chisholm's kid. As far as I know, she's a good one. Her parents are having a tough time at the moment with another baby on the way and not quite enough money for comfort. Lindsey's nuts about her uncle Ryan."

Melody's gaze sharpened at his name. To delay answering any questions, Cathy chomped a huge piece of her burger then moaned at the burst of flavours in her mouth.

"Good, eh? See what I mean by Glory's hard work."

Melody took her own mouthful of tasty burger and Cathy hoped she'd approached the subject casually enough.

"You know, Ryan carried a torch for you years after you left. None of us could get near him."

"Not anymore, according to Lindsey."

Melody's whole body went on gossip alert. "What do you know that you're not telling?"

Cathy popped some fries into her mouth and chewed. Melody waited her out, a spider to Cathy's fly. Stupid idea to challenge Melody to a standoff. "Well, she said something about being a flower girl."

"I knew it. Becca, right?"

"I think that's the name Lindsey said. Who is she?"

"Becca Carleton-Grant is Lindsey's mother's favourite cousin. You wouldn't know her. She didn't come back to Clarence Bay until you were long gone. She's younger than we are, maybe six years or so, and living with her parents."

"Lindsey said Ryan proposed." The words squeaked out of Cathy's tight dry throat.

"Pfft. Old news. Rumour had it a while ago that he bought a ring. Becca hasn't said anything yet, so I don't believe it. Sure, they've been dating for a couple of months or so. But he just didn't seem that into her. I'd say Lindsey's working from outdated intel." Melody finished off her burger, wiped her mouth. Her blue eyes narrowed to pinpoints and stuck Cathy like a bug to a board. "You want to re-light the flame, don't you? Get a new daddy for Hayley after the divorce?" she whispered.

Cathy's face flamed. She pushed up her glasses and pressed her fingers to her lips. "No, a reunion with Ryan was *not* on my agenda." Not when I got here, anyway. "I came to help Yola and to possibly reconcile with my mother." And to see if Hayley's one and only father would fulfill her daddy-wish.

Melody laughed at Cathy's discomfort and patted her arm. "Don't worry, your secret's safe with me. However, I *will* prod you mercilessly for further details."

"*Santo cielo*, how do I sort it out all?" Cathy pulled aprons out of the kitchen drawer for herself and Hayley. It was days later and Cathy still couldn't discern the truth. What in heaven's name was Ryan's true status: single, engaged, married with children? He'd been each of them over the past weeks. Cathy was beyond frustrated trying to get information and still guard her secret.

"Of course, I could go to the horse's mouth," she muttered under her breath.

"Why would you ask a horse anything?" Hayley demanded.

Cathy stalled for time to cook up an answer while putting on the aprons on herself and Hayley. She sat beside her sharp-eared daughter at the kitchen table. A large cloth covered the battered pine in preparation for manicotti making.

Zia Yola plunked her already-made filling within easy reach of all three of them. She chuckled at Hayley's outrage. "It is a saying, *piccola*. It means you must ask a person directly if there is a misunderstanding."

"Why a horse?"

"In the old days, when someone tried to trick a person into buying an old horse, you got the truth by looking in the horse's mouth to see his teeth. The more worn the teeth, the older the horse. So, if you want the truth, you go to the horse's mouth. *Capisci?*"

Hayley nodded and grinned. “I get it. How do you check other animals?”

While Zia Yola and Hayley speculated and laughed, especially over the ostrich who kept sticking her head in the sand, Cathy mulled over her dilemma. The investment banker in her cried out for reliable data to perform due diligence and rigorous analysis. It seemed even Lindsey might be wrong, or Melody was misinformed or exaggerating.

Cathy had bought herself some time by not correcting Melody’s assumption about her non-existent ex-husband. Hopefully, people assumed an acrimonious divorce and wouldn’t pester her with questions. Hayley was petite and appeared younger than her age, so the math wasn’t clear. So far, so good.

Yola lifted her gaze from her busy fingers. Caterina’s mind had wandered far away and not to a happy place. Yola knew the desolation well. Every once in a while, her faded dreams gathered colour and rose to remind her of what might have been. She’d done her best at the time. No regrets. Happiness was here, now, in front of her, helping her to make manicotti. She smiled and tapped Hayley’s nose, leaving a floury fingerprint behind.

Hayley giggled and swiped at her nose, creating an even bigger streak of flour. It was so good having these two sweet girls at home, filling the vast hole of loneliness in Yola’s heart to overflowing.

“Is something troubling you, Caterina?”

Caterina lifted a wary gaze from her task. “Not really.”

“Are you still wondering if you should ask the horse?” Hayley asked.

“Huh?”

"You know..." Hayley gave her mother a coy twinkling smile. "If you want the truth, ask the horse."

Caterina laughed at her daughter's clever joke. "Right. First I have to decide if I even want to buy a horse."

Jumping out of her chair, Caterina tossed her daughter onto her back and took her on a wild galloping ride around the kitchen. Hayley squealed with joy. Flour drifted across the floor.

Yola grinned with pleasure as her fingers continued stuffing and rolling pasta. Caterina knelt on all fours. Hayley dismounted and opened her mother's mouth. "And then you have to look at the horse's teeth!" Caterina neighed and Hayley crowed in delight.

"And then we have to bring her home and put her to sleep," Hayley said.

Caterina flopped onto her back on the floor and stuck her arms and legs in the air, snoring loudly. Hayley threw herself across her mother and they hugged and laughed and rolled around like kittens.

What a couple of wonderful silly girls. Yola rubbed her stiff cheeks with the backs of her hands. Her poor facial muscles were still getting used to the exercise of laughing and smiling.

"What's going on in here? I'm watching my shows and I can't hear a thing for all the racket." Lucia hobbled into the kitchen, killing the joy and laughter with her angry Italian.

Why was Lucia always and forever a martyr? Yola bore no recollection of any other emotion from her sister. Not when she married Antonio, not when Caterina was born. Never.

The girls scrambled up from the floor. "We're sorry, Mamma." Caterina nudged her daughter's shoulder. "Hayley, say you're sorry for disturbing Nonna." Funny how she didn't sound the least bit sorry.

Lucia thumped her cane. "And so you should be."

A coarse sound of disgust erupted from Yola before she could stop it. Back stiffening in outrage, Lucia turned her wrath on her. Yola hated the familiar quavering in her lungs whenever Lucia ranted.

Lucia pierced her with the devil's own gaze. "Did you say something to me?"

Hayley's eyes rounded in fear and she crept to her mother's side. Something unfamiliar welled up in Zia Yola. Something...fierce, protective...involved.

"Yes, I did." The ferocity gained strength and roared through Yola's blood. "I said, there will be no more apologies in this house for sharing joy and laughter and... and love."

Lucia's face flushed dark red at Yola's back chat. Yola shot a glance at Caterina then aimed her glance at the kitchen door.

Cathy caught her aunt's message, nodded, and tugged her daughter through the back door and out into the yard. Zia Yola's words were muffled by the wood and glass, but the tone rang clear. Mamma was getting a good talking-to. At last.

"Mom?" Hayley warbled as tears trembled in her eyes. "Is Zia Yola gonna be okay?"

Cathy kissed her daughter's forehead. Amazing, as young as she was, Hayley knew Zia Yola to be the weaker of the two sisters. "I think so. Why don't we go down to the playhouse? I'll check on Zia Yola in a while." She gave her daughter a rib-cracking squeeze and Hayley flew off down the garden.

Through the window of the door, Cathy saw Mamma, incandescent with rage, spit a few more words, and hobble from the room. Zia Yola sank into a chair, buried her face in her apron. Her shoulders shook with her tears. Cathy stifled a cry with both hands over her mouth, her spirit savaged in equal parts with love for her aunt and hatred for her mother. Tears fogged her glasses and trickled over her fingers. She put her hand on the knob to go and comfort Zia Yola.

Suddenly, Zia Yola snapped upright in the chair, grim determination on her face. Her mouth moved in a staccato burst of muffled Italian. Her hand slammed on the table, raising a puff of flour. She jumped to her feet, spun to the doorway, and tossed a vicious Sicilian salute towards Lucia. Dusting off her hands, she wiped her face with her apron, and calmly set about saucing the manicotti.

Cathy blinked, transfixed by Zia Yola's show of defiance. Never mind that Mamma hadn't seen it.

Withdrawing her hand from the doorknob, she followed Hayley to the playhouse, worried by her daughter's tears. No need to worry; Hayley was sound asleep on the bench.

Cathy sagged into the Muskoka chair and leaned back. Whatever was the world coming to? Didn't matter. If Zia Yola was finding her backbone, good for her.

Cathy wished she could find her own backbone and deal with her secrets.

CHAPTER 8

Sorting Things Out

A tickle ran along Cathy's left index finger. Without opening her eyes, she shook off the ant and rubbed her thumb over its trail to soothe the skin. The tickle restarted on the inside of her left wrist and crawled up her forearm. She raised her right hand to slap the damn ant dead.

"Please don't hit me," a small high-pitched voice begged.

The wooden chair rattled as she bolted upright to be greeted by Ryan's grey eyes twinkling with mischief. Her heart swelled, her breath stalled, her laugh jumped from her throat. She wanted to hug him to bits. Just like the old days when he'd played sneaky little tricks.

Instead, she stayed seated and opened her mind to the possibility that everything she thought she knew could be wrong. *Shame on me.* Bearer of a law degree, she'd judged him with lies, hearsay, and circumstantial evidence. Head dropping and shoulders hunching, she gestured for him to sit and stay awhile. Staring at the floor, she searched for words in the spiral braid of the new rug.

He nodded at Hayley sound asleep in a tight ball on the bench. "She's cute. Especially with the apron and the flour face paint." Sunbeams highlighted blonde strands in her wild curls, creating a soft glow in the dimness. "She looks chilly." He pulled the afghan from the foot of the bench up and over Hayley. A deep yearning flickered in his face. Cathy's chest squeezed with a sharp new guilt as Hayley relaxed and unfurled.

She must tell him the child he covered so tenderly belonged to him.

But first, she had to sort out a host of misinformation. Go directly to the horse's mouth. She smiled and gestured for Ryan to step outside. He ducked under the door, but didn't go far as if he understood Cathy's need to be near Hayley.

He turned to face her in the bright sunshine. He raised a hand to touch her cheek, but stopped just short of contact. "You've been crying."

Cathy lifted the apron's neckband over her head and scrunched the apron to scrub at the dried tear tracks. "Mamma and Zia Yola had a fight."

"One of these days, Zia Yola will get her back up and then we'd all better run for cover."

"I think the day has arrived." She recounted her observations.

He shook off his astonishment and nodded with satisfaction. "Well, more power to her."

"Umm...are you here to mow the lawn?"

"No, I'm here to answer some questions you probably have."

"How did you...? Melody called you. I will never tell that woman anything in confidence ever again."

"I wouldn't be here if it weren't for Melody's busybody

caring. I don't want any secrets or confusion between us."

"Why?"

"Because I let you get away once and I won't let it happen again." He sidled up to her, the intent to kiss her lighting his eyes. She held up a shaky hand and backed away from the kiss she wanted to get as much as he wanted to give.

"Not until we clear the air."

He frowned, his disappointment clear. "Okay, fair enough. Tell me what you've heard." He mimicked her crossed arms.

Cathy debated how much to tell him about his sister-in-law. She didn't want to cause trouble in his family but, it was past time for honesty. He deserved as much of the truth as she could handle.

"Did you know you're married to Meg and the two of you are expecting your fourth child? And you're a lazy bastard who's making a pregnant woman paint the baby's room?"

If ever a man looked shocked beyond belief, that man was Ryan.

"And you're also engaged to Becca Carleton-Grant and your daughter Lindsey is going to be your flower girl."

If ever a man looked guilty, that man was Ryan.

"And last but not least, Glory Toussaint does *not* want to get in your pants."

If ever a man looked relieved, that man was Ryan.

"Wanna sit?" She sank to the grass, wrapped her arms around her knees.

"Yes, please before I fall down." He sagged down beside her, crossed his long legs. The poor man, she'd put him through the emotional wringer. No more than he deserved if any of the crap was true.

"So, what's truth and what's fiction, please?"

He heaved a deep sigh. "Well, you've certainly got a shitload of misinformation—only one item of which is correct. I'm not interested in Glory. Sure, she's good-looking and her kids are great—" He shook his head. "She's not for me. Paul maybe. But that's anybody's guess."

She nodded. "Glory was the easy one. Why did Meg lie?"

"Likely because Becca's her spoiled and pampered cousin and Meg wants me to marry her?" He shrugged. "Who knows why people lie. Though if I ever do get married, Lindsey will be a flower girl." His gaze widened and whipped away to the leaves bobbing in the breeze.

She shook out her apron and folded it into a tidy square.

Ryan cleared his throat, rubbed the back of his stiff neck. "Anyway, about Becca." He paused. "She might think we're engaged. We're not. It's a misunderstanding based on an assumption."

Her eyebrow curved upward in doubt.

Hell, he barely believed the snafu himself. The words pressed forward and piled up like lemmings at the edge of a cliff. "I hesitated when I was trying to tell Becca that I wanted to break up with her and she thought I hesitated because I was proposing because she'd heard gossip about me buying a ring at Streight's. But I was just helping a buddy buy a ring for *his* girl. And then I dropped a bottle of beer on my crotch and her mother booted me out before I could correct her and there wasn't time to fix I before she left for the Far East and she still thinks it's a go even thought I haven't actually asked." His neck tightened in memory at his lame responses to her effusive emails. He shrugged his shoulders hard to ease the tension. More words backed up and flung him over the edge with a final humiliating confession. "And I'm a coward and I don't want to hurt her. But she's back, and I'm telling her tomorrow because I can't live with myself any more." He dragged in a breath. "Even if it costs me the election. There, I'm done." He closed his eyes and clenched his whole body, bracing for the impact of Cathy's justifiable ridicule.

"Oh. Um. Okay."

He opened his eyes, more than a little self-conscious. Blank-faced, she appeared stupefied with the information overload.

"That's it?" he asked.

"I'm trying to decide which bit to consider first."

"Any questions?"

"Bottom line. Are you or are you not engaged to Becca?"

"Yes and no, like I said."

"Huh?"

Feeling a complete fool, he reiterated, in excruciating detail, the entire disastrous evening. She had the absolute balls to start laughing.

"I'm sorry, the visual is hysterical." She teetered back onto the grass.

"I'm so glad you find my humiliation amusing." A wry smile tugged at his mouth despite his best efforts to frown.

She stopped laughing though her mouth twitched a couple more times. "After today, I needed a good belly laugh. Oh, don't sulk. I sympathize with your pain. *Dio mio*, that must have hurt. And then to be chastised like a bad dog." A wheeze escaped her and was quickly corralled. She turned onto her side and rested her head on a bent arm. "Poor you. What a mess."

He rolled his eyes and rubbed the back of his neck again. "An understatement. I'm a complete idiot."

"And what's this about losing the election?"

"Paul's convinced that if I hurt Becca, her family will blackball me. I don't know if you remember, the Carleton-Grants are a huge and influential family who love to throw their weight around."

Her eyes bugged at the ultimatum. "That's outrageous! And illegal! Don't they realize how much good you'd do for the town?"

Her confidence in him warmed his heart. "I doubt they care one way or the other. Especially her mother who has a grudge against my dad for dumping her back in the day."

"Really? Nice family."

"So Nana Jean said. Anyway, no matter what the Carleton-Grants want, I refuse to be blackmailed into marrying anyone. If and when I marry, it will be for love, and only love." At hearing his own words, his cheeks burned. He stared at the small creek that marked the back boundary of Lucia's property and debated ways and means to get the hell outta there without further embarrassment.

Juicy tearing sounds came as Cathy plucked blades of grass and tossed them into the breeze. She'd almost hit dirt before she cleared her throat and asked, "So are you...um... in love with anyone?"

After an agonizing moment, he faced her. "No. Are you?"

She peeped up at him from the corner of her eye. "No."

The world stood still—not a bee buzzed, not a flower bent to a wayward breeze. He met her soft brown eyes. A tiny encouraging smile tugged at her kissable mouth. Turning to kneel before her, he slid his hand into her silky hair. She cupped his wrist, but didn't push it away.

She lifted a chagrined face, her smile a tad crooked. "I have to start all over again with you."

"Let's start here," he murmured.

He drew closer, giving her time to back away, until her beautiful eyes filled his vision. Amber flecks flared and swallowed the dark brown. He leaned in and touched his mouth to hers. The tentative touch heated his blood. They both sighed, exchanging breaths. He slid his tongue along her lower lip. She whimpered, soft and low, and opened for him. The rush of familiar tastes and scents wheeled him into the past like a gull on the wing. Bound him again to the only girl, the only woman, he'd ever loved.

Breaking the kiss, Cathy twisted to face him more fully. She cupped his face, his stubble scratchy on her palms.

"Can you forgive me for misjudging you so badly? I should have known better," she said.

"How could you know? You haven't been home in ages, barely kept contact..." His voice trailed away on a question. *Why?*

The confession sat just above her heart, hovered at the back of her tongue, pressed for release. No, not now, not with her daughter so close. Ryan had to be told first, so Hayley would receive a prepared welcome from her father, not an outraged rejection.

Disappointment at her non-response drifted through his eyes. "Your mom treated you so badly, was so strict and judgmental, it's no wonder you stayed away." He stroked her hair. "But you're here now."

She shook her head. "I'm here for now, Ryan, not forever."

"Good enough for me." He slid a hand up her arm, into her

hair and drew her close for another soul-searing kiss.

Hayley stirred, threw off the blanket, took a sec to figure out she was in her playhouse. Hot and thirsty, she got up and wandered to the open door. She gasped and covered her mouth with her hand. Mom and Ryan were kissing. It was a way different kind of kiss from the one she gave Matt. She let Ryan get a whole lot closer for a whole lot longer.

Holy cripes, just wait until she told Lindsey.

"Did you bring the ring?" Hope and doubt in her voice, Becca opened Ryan's truck door for him and he slid out into the misting rain. She was back home from her trip and, apparently, lying in wait as the door to her parent's house stood open.

"Yeah, about that..." He cupped her shoulders, held her at arm's length, and stopped her intended hug.

Her welcoming smile wilted. God, he hated what he was about to do. He sighed. But it had to be done for both their sakes.

"Let's go inside before we get soaked." When she didn't budge, he took her elbow and led her into the grand foyer.

"Good morning, Ryan." Becca's impeccably-dressed mother strolled from the library, appointment book clasped in hand, expectation in her hard blue eyes. "So are we ready to set the date? The second Saturday in June next year is good for us."

"Good afternoon, Mrs. Carleton-Grant. I'll get back to you on that." He nodded and ushered an un-responsive Becca into the family room, away from her mother.

Not even the tiniest whiff of beer lingered from the night of the proposal fiasco. He guided Becca into a seat on the couch and took the chair for himself.

"You've changed your mind." Becca toyed with the hem of

her dress.

"No—"

"Yes!" She met his eyes, face radiant. He groaned and dragged his foot from his mouth.

"No, I haven't changed my mind. We're not getting married."

Her forehead crimped drawing her brows together. "I don't understand. You proposed on the Friday night before my trip, right here in this room."

"No, I'm sorry, but I did *not* propose." He scrubbed the back of his neck, forced himself to maintain eye contact. "It was a misunderstanding on your part."

"You said it had only been two months, but you'd already made up your mind and you bought a ring..." Her voice trailed away while she worried over the puzzle. She slumped and hung her head. "Oh. You meant you'd made up your mind to break up."

"I am so sorry. I didn't want to hurt you. I hesitated when I should have gone forward. I know I should have clarified immediately. But your mother threw me out for widdling on the carpet." He tried for a laugh in hopes of lightening the atmosphere.

Bad idea, doofus.

Tears gathered in her eyes. "You weren't proposing. You were dumping me."

He squared his shoulders. "Yes. I'm sorry."

"You were supposed to be my hero and get me out of this prison." She waved around the over-styled family room.

He cringed at the h-word. "I'm nobody's hero. And you're strong enough and smart enough to get yourself out."

"Why are you dumping me?" She completely ignored his

words of encouragement. "I worked so hard to make you happy. I told all my friends. I even bought a dress in Japan."

He swallowed hard against the noose around his neck, gripping his fingers together so tightly they went numb. "The...um...spark is gone. The...um...romance has faded." Man, those emotions were damn hard to pinpoint, never mind say.

"You don't love me anymore." Becca sighed in deep and painful resignation. The tears spilled down her cheeks, leaving dark tracks of mascara.

"I like you. A lot. You're smart, strong, gorgeous. But no, I don't love you. I'm sorry."

"I'm gorgeous enough to like, but not to love?"

"Yes—I mean no—" He pinched the bridge of his nose, gathered his words. "Isn't that what dating is all about? Like test driving a car?" *Damn it, remove foot and shin from mouth.* "I mean, like trying on a dress before you buy." Her eyes darkened and her lips pinched. *Not much better.* "Men really are useless at this, aren't we? What I really mean is—I'm not the one who's destined to love you."

"You love someone else?"

Cathy danced into his head, eyes shining with suppressed laughter at his silly ant joke. He bit his inner cheek and called his face to order. *Not the best time to be smiling about Cathy.*

"You bought the ring for that Rossetti bitch, didn't you?"

His mouth flattened into a hard line to lock down the words of vindication. Becca lashed out in all directions with her pain. She needed his compassion.

"She's a divorced mother with a load of emotional baggage you'll have to lug around. She'll soon blow this hick town and head back to Toronto. I'm single, I'm here."

"Becca, don't—" He paused.

"What?" She slapped the leather couch, the sound like flesh on flesh. "Don't what?"

How to say this? Honesty is the best policy. "Bargain. Settle. You're better than that."

She bristled and thrust her finger at the doorway. "Get out."

He stood. "Becca, I'm so sorry."

Grabbing a cushion, she wound up. "Take your ridiculous sorry and get out of my sight."

He turned in the doorway, calmed himself. "Becca, I really am so sorry. You deserve better than—"

She fired the cushion at his head. He ducked and it smacked into the wall behind him, knocking a painting askew. A few feathers floated to the carpet.

"You're damn right I deserve better than you. Now, get out!" She flopped into the couch, crossed her arms and legs tight against herself.

"I'm sorry," he said once more in useless regret.

She gave him one final scathing glance then turned her nose up and away.

Mrs. Carleton-Grant intercepted him in the foyer: queen and judge in one stiff chilly package. "You've rejected her, haven't you? Well, no real loss. I've always felt Becca needed a bigger, stronger man to guide her, make decisions for her."

"Sorry," he mumbled and stepped towards the door and freedom.

She sniffed delicately, like he was a bad smell she was trying to ignore. "It wasn't unexpected, you know."

"Pardon?"

"You're just like that cretin of a father of yours."

Ryan's steps faltered with her perfectly-aimed poisoned dart. "Thank you. I'll let him know. He will be pleased." Sarcasm and bitter truth coated his words.

"You're rather naïvely running on a platform of squeaky clean honesty, aren't you?"

Wary now, Ryan nodded.

"What will the voting public say when they get the dirt on you?"

He crossed his arms over his chest. "Oh, yes? What dirt would that be?"

"You've dumped a perfectly beautiful single girl for a trashy divorcée. And her child? Who knows who the father is? Could be anyone." She leaned in as if to impart state secrets. "Well, what do you expect from such a family? They're not from here. We've always wondered whether Yolanda was Lucia's sister...," her voice fell to a venomous whisper, "or her bastard daughter."

Blood boiling, tongue unleashed, he strode across the hall and stopped within centimetres of the too-smooth face. According to Nana Jean, this woman had once been engaged to his father, might have been his mother. Creepy.

"They'll label it the revenge of a bitter woman brooding over a dead romance from so long ago most of the town can't recall." He paused and leaned in real close. "Yet," he whispered.

When his threat penetrated and understanding widened her eyes, he stuffed his hands in his pockets, sauntered through the foyer, and closed the front door quietly behind him.

It wasn't until he sat safely at home in front of the TV that truth smacked him between the eyes, giving him an instant headache. The old witch was right.

He slung mud and pond scum almost as well as his old man.

"Hoo whee. Don't you look spiffy in your suit?" Paul, his campaign manager, flicked an imaginary bit of lint from the lapel of Ryan's dark-blue suit. Around them bubbled the cocktail hour of the Saturday-night opening gala in honour of the sponsors of the Clarence Bay Music Festival. Dark suits and colourful gowns swirled, glasses clinked, voices ebbed and flowed, occasionally punctuated by laughter.

"Go away," Ryan grumbled, scanning the shifting crowd for Cathy.

A sumptuous dinner would precede a night full of music ranging from a string quartet to a country-rock band. The angular theatre of stone and wood with its companion hockey museum was the pride of the Waterfront Committee.

Paul snagged a glass of red wine from a passing waiter and pushed it into Ryan's hand. "Here, misery guts, you need this more than I do." Ryan sucked back half the contents in one gulp.

"Geez, Ry, what's gotten into you? Your poll numbers are way up." Paul gave him a congratulatory slap on the back. "How in hell did you dodge the bullet of breaking up with Becca? I thought for sure her family would nail you six ways to Sunday."

"I'd hardly call Mrs. Carleton-Grant saying 'He'll do' a wild endorsement."

"Yeah, but combined with her husband's resounding approval, they've made a hell of an impact. You're up fifteen points to sixty-three percent. You're a shoo-in."

"Don't get too excited. The Carleton-Grants could pull their support in a nanosecond." Speaking of whom, Becca swanned by in a big poofy dress; her blonde hair piled a mile high. Her glance skimmed right over him. Who knew invisibility was the price of manning up to a difficult deed.

He hated that his honesty had hurt Becca. He'd done what he had to do. But why had he uttered that stupid threat to her mother as if anybody cared? His dad was right—when the going got tough, the tough slung mud. His dad would be so proud of his younger son. Too bad said son wasn't so proud of himself. "Clean and clear" he proclaimed at every speech and promised with every sign. It ground his gears that the damn threat appeared to have worked where honesty had failed. For now.

"Nah, you're golden. They always stand by their man. And you are The Man, buddy. Way to go." Paul leaned in close, grinning. "Your dad must be sick with jealousy."

"Huh?"

"He never got a Carleton-Grant endorsement. Every election was a squeaker for him. Such is not your fate." Paul lifted his glass to Ryan and gloated.

Ryan dared not gloat along. He expected at any second to hear boos and hisses condemning him for being a hypocritical asshole. It was bad enough he condemned himself.

Paul scanned the noisy crowd. "Where's Cathy?"

"The ladies' room."

Cathy appeared, smiling and waving from across the crowded room.

He'd done it for her—to protect her and her family against slander. This was personal, not politics. Mrs. Carleton-Grant must have absorbed too many chemicals through her scalp along with the gossip at Dahlia Grisham's hair salon.

What kind of people gossiped with malice?

Apparently, his kind of people, his town, the people he asked to vote for him.

Paul nudged Ryan with his elbow and gave him a sly wink.

"Seems like another lady is endorsing your success in a very *personal* way. You risked the wrath of the Carleton-Grants for her, didn't you? Do I hear wedding bells in your future?"

Embarrassed heat crept over Ryan's cheeks, burning away his guilt, revealing his affection. "It's still way too early... Fingers crossed, man, fingers crossed."

"The Force be with you, my friend." After laying another slap on Ryan's shoulder, Paul moseyed across the room to chat up a slinky raven-haired beauty dressed in killer red.

Cathy slid her hand into the crook of Ryan's elbow and took the white wine he captured for her from another passing tray. "Thank you."

"You're gorgeous," he repeated for the third or fourth time since he'd picked her up a short while ago.

Dark silvery fabric clung in folds to her lush breasts and fell smoothly over her waist and hips. From the front, the dress appeared fairly demure with shoulder straps and a hint of cleavage. In the back, demure took a long slow slide down a deep plunge. Pearly discs on a web of silver chains spread over her bared skin and tempted his fingers to caress the shadowed hollow at her waist.

He tried to puzzle out if she wore anything beneath the silver column. He hoped to find out later tonight. His groin twitched and swelled in anticipation. Dinner jackets had their uses for hiding things. Cathy was easily the classiest woman at this classiest of town events, attracting admiration from men and women alike.

"I'm so glad you accepted my invitation for the other ticket I won at the carnival. It wouldn't have been the same without you," she said.

He smiled down at her, lost to the world in gentle brown eyes glowing with a happiness that warmed his heart and soul. "I'm happy to oblige. It's always a good show." He'd passed his already-purchased ticket along to a reluctant Glory. She'd come for the music if nothing else.

"To new beginnings," she toasted.

"I'll second that," he said gazing his fill of her from her stylish hair cut to her red-painted toes. Was her instep still sensitive to the lightest touch? Unable to stop himself, he bent and kissed her cheek. Her spicy sophisticated scent blurred his senses.

Over her shoulder, Ryan observed a slick dude, blond hair shellacked in place, cut across the room and head precisely for Cathy. His custom suit made Ryan feel like a slob in his expensive off-the-rack gear.

"Sorry to interrupt, I've been looking everywhere for this little lady." He tapped Cathy's shoulder and she spun around wafting her scent between the two men.

"Matt! What are you doing way up here?" Cathy placed her hands in his and turned her cheek for a social kiss. Right on top of Ryan's own kiss.

Ryan wanted to wipe the oily smile right off the snake's face.

"We're corporate sponsors for the gala, so a bunch of us made a long weekend of it. I was hoping to see you while we're here." He eyeballed her. "Cathy, you're stunning as always."

"Yes, of course, I'd forgotten." She beamed up him.

He beamed down at her.

Too much beaming going on.

Ryan's chest swelled on a thick dark wave of primitive possessiveness. He slugged back the rest of his red wine along with his rage. "Hello Matt." He interrupted the gaze fest.

The guy released Cathy. He spoke to Ryan but couldn't quite peel his eyes off her. "I'm sorry?"

"Oh, excuse me." Cathy gushed. "Matt Bartholomew, meet Ryan Chisholm. Ryan, Matt is my VP at the investment firm. Ryan is a dear friend from the old days."

A friend from the old days? Shit on a stick. He was more than a lousy friend. Wasn't he?

"Correction, Cathy." Matt touched her shoulder. "I'm not your boss anymore. I've been promoted to senior vice-president of the new division."

If the asshole didn't stop touching her, his fingers would soon be broken.

"That's wonderful, congratulations! You deserve it." Cathy stood on her tiptoes and laid a kiss on the guy's cheek. Grinning smugly, he took out a handkerchief and pressed it to his cheek. He kissed the dark-pink lipstick mark on the pristine white cloth, winked at her, and tucked the handkerchief away.

Ryan rolled his eyes so hard they hurt.

"Can I steal you away for a moment? I've news to share," Matt said.

They both looked at Ryan and he not-so-graciously gave his permission for the newly-appointed big-wig to take her off to the balcony.

The couple stood outside, silhouetted black against the lurid evening sky. Cathy shivered in the cool evening breeze. Matt took off his jacket, wrapped it around her shoulders and she snuggled into it. He spoke for a few minutes. Cathy shouted in joy and threw her arms around his neck, tossing his jacket to the deck. Matt spun her around once and put her back on her feet.

He scooped up his jacket and replaced it on her shoulders. They spoke rapidly together for some minutes. With way too much touching.

Unable to bear the scene any longer, Ryan turned and headed for the bar. "Hey, Grady. A double Canadian Club, hold the ice," he ordered from Emma's brother who manned the bar in one of his many jobs.

"My sympathies."

No point in asking what Grady blabbed on about. The whole damn room had seen the next best thing to Ryan being jilted. The tweeting and twittering deafened him.

"The same for me," Paul said from beside him.

"Good man, keep your friend company." Grady tossed down a napkin and poured another double rye with a flourish.

"Put down the whiskey, boys. Grady, I need champagne to celebrate." Cathy squeezed between Ryan and Paul, her energy swirling around her like a happy tornado. "A bottle of your finest," Cathy ordered over the bar.

"He's a lucky man, Cathy," Grady said.

"Who?"

"Your new fiancé."

Puzzled, Cathy looked first at Ryan then followed Grady's gaze across the room to Matt joining a large jovial group. She laughed and blushed at Ryan. "He's not my fiancé. He is—was my boss. And a friend. He had some excellent news for me."

Relief perforated the gloom hovering over Ryan.

"He's just been booted up the ladder and over to a new division, and offered me his previous job as vice president," she practically squealed with delight. "You two come join us, drink to my outrageous success."

Air hissed from beneath a released champagne cork and Grady poured three flutes. "Congrats are still in order. I'll send the rest over, Cathy."

"Thank you." Cathy's wide toothy grin and excited eyes lit up the dark corners of the room.

Grady winked at Ryan as he handed over the napkin-wrapped bottle. "Still in with a chance then, Ryan."

"You go ahead, I've got other plans." Paul gave Ryan a subtle wink and sauntered off to join a piratical Emma Finn looking devil hot in her angel-white dress.

Cathy hooked Ryan's arm and dragged him off to be introduced to a congratulatory crowd of Cathy's co-workers and their significant others. Matt was the only one on his own. The expression in his eyes as he watched Cathy said he didn't plan to stay that way for long.

"Over my dead body. Or better yet, Matt's dead body," Ryan muttered.

"Sorry?" Cathy asked

Before he could come up with a reply, the lights flickered to call people to dinner.

Ryan plastered a smile on his face and followed Cathy into the banquet hall. Instead of the hoped-for romantic tête-á-tête, they were absorbed by her coterie of sophisticated city friends. Beside him at the white-draped table, Cathy chattered to one and all, clearly happy to be among them. On his other side, Ryan enjoyed sporadic and stilted conversation with Matt.

"So, Ryan, how do you contribute to the bustling burg of Clarence Bay?"

Ryan ignored Matt's mockery. "I own the hardware store."

"The big franchise on the way into town? Impressive." Matt

raised his glass in a faint salute.

"No, the small place in the center of town."

"Ah, a Mom-and-Pop shop. How...quaint."

Ryan itched with a defensive urge to pop him a good one in his smooth sneering face. Instead, he matched his wide insincere smile. "Don't underestimate the value of family proprietorships. Dozens of small shops make this town what it is—give it a strong sense of community, shared goals and values. You can't buy those things with any amount of money."

Matt sat back, his invisible cloak of power and money swirling around him. "If I ran this backwater, I'd go for the big employment numbers. It takes a hell of a lot of the little people to match, never mind exceed, the tax levy on a single big-box store."

Cathy turned at their brisk exchange of words. "Well, you don't run this town. And Ryan is about to." She gave him a look of pride, more than making up for her interruption. "He's running for mayor and is currently sitting in the polls at..." She turned to Ryan for the information.

"Sixty-three percent." Ryan put his arm around Cathy and grinned obnoxiously.

Matt's eyebrows rose and finally he shut up. A few minutes later, he forcibly switched places with one of the other men. Ryan shrugged off the snub. He couldn't care less about the smog-sucking tower-hugger.

Cathy stroked his thigh, drawing his attention back to his silver nymph. "I'm sorry. He's a big-city snob. I suspect it needed a direct order from the CEO to get him to the gala. For some reason, he can't bear small towns. Hence the entourage." She included the rest of the table with a sweeping glance.

"As long as *you* don't feel the same way."

"Not when I come from a small town."

Which she'd left as soon as possible, then taken more than a decade to return.

Cathy got distracted by an intense conversation with the sleek woman next to her. The woman wore a red dress so tight it was a wonder she breathed at all. Her fingernails were painted a livid matching red; her painted smile revealed small pointed teeth.

During dessert, he left the rowdy big-city crew and headed to the bar where Grady poured a single shot. "Your lady sure can party hearty with her city-slicker friends. Who are they?"

"The CEO has a thing for the music festival, so they're sponsors for tonight's shindig."

"Whew, serious money."

"Not a big deal for a bunch of investment bankers." Ryan sipped and a lovely burn slid down his throat.

"She's one of them, ain't she?"

"She was born here, though it's been ten years since she came home."

"So she went over to the smoggy side."

"Yep."

With a promotion shattering the glass ceiling, she'd be gone. And her small-town fling would be left eating her dust. Again.

CHAPTER 9

Wishes and Words

Cathy pondered last night while she waited for a lull in the intense political discussion between Ryan and Paul. She'd fully expected to return to Ryan's place for some all-night loving, had even slipped some day clothes into a satchel. Instead, he'd delivered her to Mamma's doorstep, kissed her unenthusiastically for a few minutes, and left. Took the shine off a girl's triumph, it did.

Today, she'd brought a surprise picnic lunch to Ryan's house in the hope of some time alone. Instead, she'd found Paul already there. Finally, the guys stopped at a point of agreement. "Ryan, I get the feeling there's more than climbing up the political ladder in your drive to be the mayor."

The two men exchanged glances. Ryan flushed and looked down at the table. Paul laid a hand on his shoulder. "You tell her. He's your dad."

Cathy expected Paul to leave, but he settled in his chair in the rust-and-cream kitchen of Ryan's sprawling fifties brick bungalow on the high forested cliff at the south end of town.

"When I worked for my dad—I told you that, right?"

She nodded. "The night we met again for the first time."

A soft answering smile flitted across his face. "Anyway, I hated all the shady not-quite-illegal stuff I saw going down. When I was voted to the town council four years ago, I saw even more. Dad used his power to grant favours to old friends—"

"Like boat launches in select locations," Paul inserted.

"Road-paving contracts to guys that would pave his friends' driveways—"

"And leave municipal parking lots riddled with pot holes—"

"Expedite requests for maintenance when his cronies asked—"

"And ignore his enemies altogether, even though they had fair requests."

Ryan grimaced. "I could go on, but you get the picture. He ruled the place like a despot. I want to balance the inequities, free the town from his corruption."

"But why *you,* Ryan?" Cathy said.

"Tell her the whole story," Paul encouraged Ryan.

Ryan flushed again, looked at her steadily, then glanced away. "Dad duped me into casting the swing vote that ended with a family homeless and penniless, without resources."

"What? How could you?"

"He didn't," Paul said. "His father took advantage of Ryan's inexperience to have a home repossessed for unpaid taxes. The town, meaning Bucky, sold the house to a developer who tore it down and put up a parking lot."

"What happened to the family?"

"They went to Barrie, where the wife had family. Last I heard, they'd divorced and the son was arrested for stealing cars."

"It's all my fault." Ryan pounded the table, making the cutlery jump. "I should have known. I should have investigated. I knew what he was like."

"It's not your fault, my friend. You believed your father one last time. Those folks did have some say in how they managed their finances."

"But it shouldn't have come to that."

This sounded like a well-worn topic between the two men, so Cathy didn't mind interrupting again. "Ryan, do you feel responsible for the well-being of Clarence Bay?"

"For the welfare of my town, its people, its places? Yes. Absolutely. We have to shake off the filth and take out the garbage."

Paul grinned hugely and clapped his hands. "Bravo, Ryan. Speeches like that will get you elected. Cathy, swoon at his feet."

Ryan's cheeks turned ruddy and he laughed along with Cathy and Paul. "Knock it off, will ya?"

Cathy spun her empty water glass. "Larissa told me something last night at the gala." She'd argued with herself until dawn about whether or not to tell Ryan and Paul. She'd weighed the slight risk of exposure against the huge benefit of helping Ryan to win the election. His conviction had tipped the scales in his favour.

"Which one was Larissa?" Paul popped the last potato chip into his mouth.

"The barracuda in babe's clothing. All in red. Sat at Cathy's right," Ryan answered for her.

"Ah, Larissa." Paul nodded with a sly gleam in his eye and finished off his beer. "What did the lovely Larissa have to say?"

"She told me that the Big Deal Corporation is planning a major expansion across Canada. One of the locations they're considering is Clarence Bay. She says it's only a matter of time before they start an aggressive assault on the town council to put in a massive big-box store. And you know what happens once they move into a small town."

The three of them contemplated the grim statistics of hollowed-out downtown cores, councils with their hands tied, unfulfilled promises of stable employment.

"How does she know what BDC is doing?"

"It's her job to know what has the potential to hit investors in their bottom line," Cathy replied.

"So it's only hearsay BDC is planning to build a megastore in Clarence Bay?" Ryan asked. He munched his last bite of dill pickle.

"No. Hearsay prompted Larissa's investigation. Her analysis is bankable."

"It's interesting. Possibly useful." Paul said.

"It's unethical." Ryan reared back as if a rattler hissed among the remains of lunch. "I can't use your information in my campaign."

His response was exactly what Cathy had expected him to say.

Ryan got up and started to clear the table. Cathy stood to help and he pressed her down into her wooden chair. He stroked her cheek with his fingertips, smiled tightly and went back to tidying his sleek maple kitchen. She followed his movements and a tiny sigh of longing escaped. Handsome and domestic—perfect husband material. Her eyes widened at the sneaky thought. *Not happening. I'll be gone before the summer is over.*

Paul tilted his chair on its back legs, caught her eye, and tipped his head in Ryan's direction. He raised a brow over twinkling hazel eyes as if he'd seen her girlish imaginings on YouTube.

She pushed up her glasses in a pitiful attempt to hide the telltale stinging in her cheeks. *Imbecille,* dreaming of domestic bliss with Ryan.

Paul handed the last of the used tableware to Ryan. "I get your hesitation and agree you can't broadcast the information, or use it for personal financial gain. How about if you add another plank to your platform showing your determination to protect Clarence Bay?"

Ryan closed the dishwasher and started the coffeemaker. He walked over to stand gazing out the sliding doors—arms crossed, feet wide, sunk in on himself.

Birdsong and the heady scent of pine floated through the screen. Sunlight sparkled off the bay far below. Didn't look like he noticed any of it. Long minutes ticked by. She shuffled her feet and Paul raised his hand in a leave-him-be gesture. Restless, she went to pour coffee into the mugs Ryan had set out.

"Double-double for me please," Paul murmured.

"Okay," Ryan said into the quiet, startling her and Paul. "I like the new plank idea—give more scope to the platform." Ryan squared his shoulders, turned away from the view. "We use the information in a general, rather than specific, way. I can get onside with that. Besides, we can't do anything concrete until the application comes before the new council."

"Then you, my friend, can persuade council to deny the request." Paul said.

"Or we pre-empt the application with a visible protest—" Ryan withdrew a box of Timbits from a cupboard and plopped them in the center of the table. Cathy took a chocolate doughnut hole.

Paul sat up straight, buzzing with enthusiasm. "Like the voters making it clear they won't stand for monster corporations gutting the town core with their monopolistic strategies. We can learn from the other big-box franchise the previous council let in." Paul finished Ryan's thought in triumph. The two men huzzahed and bumped fists.

She rejoiced to see the renewed energy and hope bursting from Ryan. Something had been pulling at him, draining his spirit.

"One more thing, Cathy. Did Larissa mention a timeline on the application?" Ryan asked.

"Spring next year, possibly late winter, if their people green-light the project."

"Excellent, we should be able to get an amendment to the town plan by then. Plus we can work up a strategy for rejuvenating the center of town."

"When, or if, the BDC applies to build, it will seem like a prescient move on your part," she said. A brilliant plan, subtle, not connected to Larissa's information, yet true to Ryan and his commitment to Clarence Bay.

"So we expand the message—keep it clean, keep it clear, keep it small."

Cathy's pride threatened to swell and bust the buttons off her blouse. Ryan and Paul had driven themselves hard for two days, re-crafting today's speech to expand the core message without any hint of what prompted the revision.

"In conclusion, ladies and gentlemen," Ryan's strong voice boomed around the jam-packed school auditorium. "A vote for me is a vote for clear, clean government and a vote for preserving small-town Canada."

"Go Ryan, go Ryan!" Hayley and her crowd of instant girlfriends bounced their cute little butts and circled their arms along with the rest of the cheering sweltering crowd. The entire town had turned out for the candidate's debate and free barbeque.

"Now that my able opponent Adam Baylor and I have discussed everything from beach maintenance to bus routes, let's all party!"

More cheers erupted for both candidates and then everybody piled out to the schoolyard for food and music. The hot offshore breeze blew the smoke from the barbecue grills out over the water. Heavy weather threatened, but for now, people milled about, gossiping and visiting.

Cathy and the girls ate at a picnic bench near the candidates' table. She listened in as Ryan and Adam continued to debate the issues with the small crowd gathered around them. The people of Clarence Bay would be very lucky to have him at the helm of their beloved town.

He was a good man—honourable, caring, upstanding—and sexy. Her blood surged with affection and desire, warming her soul. She wanted to give him a great smacking kiss to show everybody how proud she was that he belonged to her. She sucked in a startled breath. Belonged to her—as in he's mine and keep your hands off? Nah. Only time-warping back to high-school days.

Shaking off her fantastical thoughts, she snagged Hayley just before she ran off with her gaggle of friends.

"Mo-om," Hayley protested the hug. "Lemme go."

"Where are you off to in such a rush?"

"Ryan ordered an ice-cream truck."

"Well, all righty then. Away you go." She released her daughter. Hayley squealed and tore off through the crowd with her posse in tow, a leader just like her daddy.

"Soon, sweetie. Soon, your daddy-wish will come true," she said under her breath.

The capricious breeze blew snippets of conversation her way.

"Ryan's a hometown boy," from a group of seniors

"Adam's got the big picture," said a supporter.

"Baylor's in the pocket of big business. Big business brings big jobs."

"Did you know Baylor had an affair in his last job? He married her, but still. Ryan would never do that, he's too honourable. Don't want a home-wrecker for Mrs. Mayor," from a group of women watching over kids in the inflatable castle.

"Don't trust Adam."

"Ryan did all the work and didn't tell anyone."

"What would we do without Ryan?"

A wry smile curved Cathy's lips. Some things never changed. Clarence Bay loved a good scandal, especially with romance involved. Yet they expected their leaders to be perfect in every way. Ryan would win by a landslide.

Unless....

Unless the town discovered he'd fathered a child and abandoned her and her mother.

Cathy floated into another realm where ordinary things

happened on the other side of a pane of heavily-smoked glass. *Santo cielo*, what a complete idiot she was. Had her analytical ability gone up in a puff of smoke from a few hot kisses? *Imbecille!* No, it wasn't the kisses, good as they were, scrambling her brain. Giving him privileged information had been a pathetic attempt to give him something in return for ten lost years with Hayley. *Stupid, stupid, stupid woman.*

"Mom, Mom!" Hayley grabbed her arm, shattering her eerie outward calm. "Can I go on the pony ride?"

Cathy nodded absently. Hayley ran off, followed by her faithful posse. Lindsey was among them, even though she shouldn't be. They were destined to know each other as friends only, never as cousins.

Of course, Ryan hadn't abandoned his pregnant girlfriend or his child. How can a person leave something he doesn't know exists? But the town wouldn't understand. And if they did, they'd ignore it. Ryan would be laughed out of the mayoral race. Even if she waited until after the election to tell him, his constituents would lose all respect for him and, with it, their support. Support he would need to achieve any of the gains he planned for his town.

What aboriginal dream pipe had she been smoking? Tears blurred her vision as her heart broke for the joy her innocent daughter would never share with her unknowing father. So much for Hayley's daddy-wish and any other wishes her mom might be cherishing.

At least Cathy's Mamma-wish was coming true as her mother's health improved in fits and starts and grumbles.

"Is the biscotti ready yet?" Mamma stood in the kitchen

doorway, thumping her cane on the floor. Wispy white down now covered her scalp and her step was firmer, seldom needing the cane to walk. She used it to express her frustration if Zia Yola wasn't quick enough serving her. "I hope you didn't put any nuts in my biscotti. I don't like nuts." As always, Mamma spoke Italian.

Zia Yola tossed a belligerent look over her shoulder. "*Santo cielo,* it will be ready when it's ready," she muttered in English under her breath.

Helping her to prepare an afternoon coffee tray, Cathy touched her aunt's arm and they exchanged subversive grins. Since the astonishing Sicilian salute, her aunt's defiance had grown stronger and more vocal. Cathy was thrilled and terrified for her aunt at the storm brewing between the older women. Cathy hoped she'd be around to support Zia Yola when the storm broke.

Cathy patted Zia Yola's shoulder. "Time you left."

"Left? Where are you going when it's time for my coffee?" Mamma rapped her cane against the door frame. Zia Yola jerked. Her mouth pulled tight and her hands flew at her work.

Cathy grabbed those flying hands and gazed firmly into her aunt's eyes. "Zia Yola has a knitting circle meeting."

"A knitting circle? You can knit perfectly well at home. Why go out?"

"To put on a pretty dress and meet her friends."

"*Sta zitta.* Who needs friends? They're so nice to your face then spit on you when your back is turned."

Dio mio, where did Mamma get this new paranoia? Had the cancer made her excessively anxious?

"I'm sure Zia Yola hasn't seen them for months. Since you

got sick."

"I'm still not better. I still need her here to look after me."

Zia Yola hesitated, staring with desperate longing through the screen door.

No, Cathy refused to allow Mamma to browbeat Zia Yola into staying home. She untied her aunt's apron strings and lifted the neck strap over her head. Zia Yola grabbed at the apron and Cathy tossed it out of reach.

"I'm here, Zia Yola. You go." She infused extra firmness into her voice to strengthen her aunt's resolve.

Still Zia Yola hesitated. Cathy snatched her aunt's purse, car keys, and knitting bag off the table and thrust them into her unresisting arms. She turned her aunt around and gently pushed her out the door. "We'll see you when you get back." Zia Yola halted, blew a grateful kiss, and disappeared with a quick hunted pace.

Mamma's whine interrupted Cathy's internal celebration. "Why did you let her go? I need her to serve my *caffe.*"

Cathy dredged up a smile. "I'll take care of your coffee, Mamma. You go and sit in the parlour."

Mamma harrumphed and scowled. Cathy cut her off before she spoke. "Hayley's there. Why don't you ask her to read some more of her book? You know how much she likes reading to you."

"Yes, yes, she does." A satisfied smile broke out on Mamma's face and she left with a smug set to her shoulders. For some incredible reason the two older women had gone from wanting no part of Hayley's life to competing for her affection. Cathy gave up trying to solve the riddle.

She groaned under her breath and turned to the preparation

of afternoon coffee. When she got a good look at the biscotti, she laughed aloud and shook her head. Her mischievous aunt had made a huge pile of her own favourite hazelnut biscotti and a few of the plain vanilla ones preferred by her sister.

"What are you doing?" Mamma shrieked from the parlour on the other side of the house.

Cathy slammed the tray on the table and shot across the hall. Hayley cowered by the black dial telephone, her hand on the receiver, her terrified eyes glued to Mamma's raised hand.

"Mamma! No!" Cathy lunged forward and slapped her mother's hand down. Mamma dropped her cane from her other hand, clutched her heart and fell backwards into her flower-cushioned chair.

"How dare you abuse me?" Mamma ranted.

Hayley flew into Cathy's waiting arms. "I-I didn't d-do anything, Mom. Honest." The frightened words tore at Cathy's heart.

"Are you okay? Did she hurt you?"

"No."

"Don't worry, sweetie. Don't worry. We'll get it sorted out." Cathy soothed her daughter with gentle tones and stroking hands. Over her daughter's head, Cathy scowled at her mother. "You may have hit me, but don't you even dare so much as threaten my child. What was she doing that you felt you had to strike her?"

"She was using the telephone." Her mother picked up her cane and jammed the shaft into the crease between the chair's arm and the seat cushion.

Cathy goggled at Mamma. "Using the phone?"

"*Sì.*"

"So?"

Mamma curled her upper lip. "She—," thrusting her finger at Hayley, "was whispering, having a secret conversation, making arrangements—with a boy!"

"What!" Cathy released her daughter, lifted her chin, and gazed with reassurance into her daughter's brown eyes. "Hayley, is this true?"

Hayley swallowed hard and returned a direct gaze. "I wasn't talking with a boy. Eww." She wrinkled her nose in distaste.

Cathy bit back a smile. "Then who were you talking to?"

The little girl's gaze roamed into every nook and cranny of the old-fashioned room.

"Hayley." Cathy put a note of warning into her voice.

"Okay. I phoned Lindsey." Cathy waited. Hayley rolled her eyes. "Like, I *know* you told me I'm not supposed to talk to her. I don't know *why*. I'm bored and she's my only friend here."

"What about all those girls you were running around with yesterday?"

Hayley popped her fists on her slender hips. "Oh, yeah, let me call my PA for their numbers."

Cathy tucked her lips between her teeth trying not to laugh at Hayley's mimicry of herself. She chuckled and Hayley started to giggle. A sudden painful jab in the thigh from Mamma's cane recalled Cathy to her senses. "Ouch!"

"Go to your room, you nasty child!" Mamma ordered Hayley. So much for the affection competition.

A shattered Hayley catapulted into Cathy's arms. Cathy lurched back at the impact and hugged her daughter close.

"Leave her be," Cathy ordered her mother.

"She's in my house. She will do as I say."

"No." Cathy glared at her mother, determined to protect Hayley at all costs. Cathy drew a deep calming breath and caressed Hayley's curls. "Why don't you grab some biscotti and milk and go out to the playhouse. You can use my cell phone to call Lindsey. I'll join you later." Hayley burrowed deeper against her chest. Cathy cupped the soft little-girl cheeks, smiled encouragingly, and kissed her daughter's nose. "Go on. I'll fix it."

Hayley threw a sullen glance at her grandmother, but she didn't stick out her tongue like Cathy knew she desperately wanted to. Cathy waited to hear the clap of the screen door before she turned to her mother.

"Mamma, if you're going to treat Hayley like a delinquent, we'll leave. I remember how much you hurt me and I will not tolerate—"

"Discipline is necessary for obedience."

If her mother's mouth puckered up any harder, it would freeze that way. "*Dio mio,* she's a little girl. Not an animal. Nor was I."

Mamma stood up, groping for her cane. Cathy dug deep for the courage not to cringe before her mother. No more fleeing before her mother's rage. She squared off, ready to give as good as she got.

Mamma's eyes widened then narrowed. She harrumphed. "I know you're not an animal. Though you protect your daughter like a lioness. I like to see that."

Cathy puffed up with pride at her mother's first ever nod of approval.

Then she cried out as Mamma crumpled to the floor.

Hayley grabbed a couple biscotti and a glass of milk on her way through the kitchen. The screen door slapped shut behind her and she sighed in relief at her narrow escape.

"Psst!"

Hayley jumped and almost dropped her glass of milk. "Darn it, Lindsey. Quit scaring me!"

Lindsey giggled so hard she fell out of the lilac bush beside the stairs. "You shoulda seen your face. You looked ready to poop your pants."

Hayley scowled at her best friend. "I did not. I was thinking."

"About what?"

"I'll tell you later. Want a snack?"

"Zia Yola's biscotti?" Lindsey closed her eyes in ecstasy. "They're *so* good."

Hayley led the way to the playhouse and they settled on the bench. She dunked her biscotti in her milk and slurped up the softened cookie.

"I can't wait to go home. My horrible old *nonna* won't let me use her phone to call you. Told me I was sneaking. The old grouch." Now that all the excitement was over, she was getting mad.

"You were sneaking to use the phone?"

Hayley squished her soaking cookie so hard; the wet piece broke off and fell to the bottom of the glass. Eww.

"Yeah. Can you believe it? Nonna was gonna hit me, but my mom stopped her."

"Are you okay," Lindsey asked, wide-eyed.

"I guess so. I've never been hit before. Did you ever get hit?"

"Nope." Lindsey nibbled a dry biscotti. Hayley held out the goopy milk and Lindsey dunked.

"Oh, and suddenly she's okay with you and me hanging out. I still don't know why I couldn't. But she was gonna let me use her cell phone to call you. So I guess now we can hang out." Hayley shrugged and rolled her eyes at Lindsey. "Moms."

Lindsey rolled her eyes, too. Then she went all silly and flopped on the floor like she'd been shot. Good thing she wasn't holding the milk.

"It totally sucks, 'cause now my Nonna is probably yelling at my mom like she's a little kid."

"Yeah, totally. My Nana Jean is always nice and she never yells at my dad. She talks to me like I'm a grownup. I don't always get what she says but I like it."

"You're so lucky. I wish Zia Yola was my grandma. She's so nice and she sings so good she should be on *Canadian Idol*."

"You know, it's too bad you don't have a dad. Then he could take you home. That's what my dad does when Mom wants to yak forever with her cousin Becca at her house."

Hayley sat like a stone dummy, staring out at the grass, her mind spinning with a scary possibility. She grabbed Lindsey's arm making her jump a mile. "Mom and Ryan were kissing the other day."

"Eww, kissing." Lindsey made a sour face.

"Yeah, totally gross. She let him kiss her like she never let Matt kiss her."

Lindsey's eyes bugged. "Your mom has a boyfriend?"

"Nah." Hayley waved Matt away. "He takes her out to charity dances and stuff for work but she's just not that in to him."

"I don't get what you're talking about."

Hayley rolled her eyes. Sometimes her best friend was just a little dim. "Mom's single and available. She invited Ryan to a dance. They kissed each other like all smooshy and stuff. Get it?" Actually it was kinda nice the way Mom and Ryan kissed and laughed at the same time. Gave Hayley the warm fuzzies.

Lindsey sat quietly, chin on her fist, thinking. Finally she looked up with a blank face. "Nope."

"If my mom and your Uncle Ryan got married, I'd get a cool dad, and I'd move here and we could be friends forever."

"Yeah, friends forever!" Lindsey thrust her hand into the air. "We'd go to school together and ballet class and everything."

Hayley squealed with delight and grabbed Lindsey for a happy dance around the playhouse. Dancing done, Hayley plopped onto the Muskoka chair. "All we need now is A Plan."

CHAPTER 10

Photograph and Memory

Yola hurried down the hall and into her bedroom, shut the door behind her, and snatched up the ringing phone. "Hello?" she said quietly. Lucia slept peacefully after her minor fall and the subsequent doctor's visit.

"Yola? It's Helen. Are you crying? What's Lucia done now?"

Yola warmed at her friend's classy British accent. "I'm not crying. I ran from Lucia's room to my room to get the phone. Yesterday, she overtaxed herself and fainted. The doctor checked her out and she's fine. She needs to rest and be more careful."

"I see. Well..." Helen's voice faded.

"My turn. We spoke two days ago. Why have you called off-schedule? What's wrong?"

"Nothing's wrong with me. But, I have to tell you something." Helen paused long enough for Yola to develop palpitations. "I've heard from Leo."

Yola's heart skittered to a ragged stop. Tremors raced over her skin. With a great thump against her ribs, her heart started again. Reaching behind her to ensure her chair hadn't moved away on its own legs, she slowly sank into its seat. Her hand crept to her mouth.

"What did you say?" she croaked like a bullfrog in the creek at the end of the backyard.

"This will be a huge shock for you, I'm sure. Leo is looking for you."

Clearing her throat, Yola took a steadying breath. "He is? Why me? Why now?"

"He's visiting Canada and he wants to see you."

Yola heard a certain knowing in her friend's voice. Helen knew his reason, but wasn't saying it aloud. As Yola had recently learned, Helen was an expert at keeping secrets.

"Why?" she wailed.

"You must ask him when you see him."

"Ask him? See him?" Bewildered, Yola could only think of Hayley telling her to ask the horse.

"That's what I said. Shall I let him know where you are? Give him your number perhaps?"

"No!" The word rushed forth without thought.

"I think you must see him."

"No!"

"Don't you want to see him? He's still as lovely as ever, better in fact."

Images of her only love chased through Yola's mind; laughing brown eyes, dark curls, tall, young, and full of promise. So incredibly young. At fifteen, they'd sworn to love each other forever. Then he'd gone forever.

"I'm so old now, Helen. Old and tired and worn out. Stuck in this town, in this house, with her."

"He will think you're beautiful." Helen had such a diplomatic way with words. "I expect you're looking younger already just thinking of him."

Yola moved to stare at the reflection of a stranger in her dresser mirror. A rosy bloom coloured her cheeks, her eyes sparkled, and her hair seemed darker. *Santo cielo,* a freaking miracle as Hayley said. That Hayley was a clever little girl, just like her sweet mother.

"Okay, you may give him my number." The words tumbled over each other. Yola giggled, on the edge of hysteria.

"Well done you." Yola pictured Helen's firm head bob. "He'll likely call you quite soon."

Yola nodded still transfixed at the turn of events.

"Well, I'll let you get back to Lucia. By-ye," Helen sang in her funny British way.

Yola waved goodbye to herself in the mirror, put down the phone, and wandered down a very short memory lane. They'd had only a year before his executive father had been transferred to England. A year that had filled a lifetime.

Se Dio vuole, dare she dream? Dare she wish for more?

The loud electronic beeping of a phone off the hook ripped through Cathy's peaceful reading in the parlour. Mamma. She raced up the stairs and stalled at Zia Yola's room. Puzzled, she crossed to the dresser, lifted the handset off the jewellery box, and put it in its proper place.

Zia Yola sat in her chair, staring at nothing, an odd distant expression on her face.

"Zia, are you okay?" Cathy laid her hand on her aunt's forehead. Her forehead was cool, but her cheeks burned. "You look feverish. Do you want to lie down?"

Withdrawing Cathy's hand from her temple, Zia Yola kissed the back and rested it against her hot cheek.

Cathy bent and peered into her aunt's unfocused eyes. "What's wrong? Tell me."

"I'm sorry to worry you. It's nothing."

"It's not nothing that upsets you like this." Cathy sat on the bed, needing its solidity beneath her. "Please, *cara Zia*, tell me if there's something wrong. Don't hide anything from me. I couldn't bear it if you were ill like Mamma." Her voice tightened over the last words.

Zia Yola blinked and she was back inside herself. "No, no, *ucellino.* Forgive me. It is not bad news at all. It's...it's good news, I think. Definitely not bad." She smiled and ducked her head. "An old, very old, boyfriend of mine telephoned Helen. He wants to meet with me."

Cathy flopped spread-eagled on the bed, nearly dead with relief. After getting her heart rate and breathing in order, Cathy lifted her head from the yellow quilt and peered at her aunt. "Did you say an old boyfriend?"

Zia Yola pressed her hands to her face. "*Si.* My Leo called. That's his name, Leo Giacometti."

Aw, how cute and flustered her aunt was at the mention of her youthful romance. "Zia, what's Helen got to do with an old boyfriend of yours?"

"I knew him when our family lived in Toronto and Helen lived beside us. A long time ago."

"Was he your first love?"

"Sad to say, he was my only love."

"Your only... Didn't you have boyfriends here? You were

what—seventeen, eighteen—when we moved here?"

Zia Yola took her rosary from the bedpost and ran it repeatedly through her fingers. "I was too busy helping Lucia to have boyfriends."

A fragment of memory floated to the surface of Cathy's mind. Mamma had scolded Cathy for some misdemeanour and slapped her face. Cathy had run with streaming tears into the warm safe embrace of Zia Yola's arms. Zia Yola shouted back, protected her. Mamma had handed out punishment to the pair of them, as if they were sisters.

Cathy gasped. Could the idiotic rumour be true? Impossible. "Zia? This is a stupid question..."

Wariness flickered in Zia Yola's eyes before going back to the anxious twisting of her rosary.

"There's an awful rumour going around... Haven't a clue where it came from..."

"*Sì,* Caterina?" Zia Yola whispered, an odd edge of fear in her voice.

"Lucia's behaviour, the age difference..."

The bright colour faded from Zia Yola's face.

"Are we sisters?" she blurted before she talked herself out of it.

Zia Yola's gaze flew up, her mouth gaped. After a moment, she began to laugh. The merry sound came more frequently the longer Cathy stayed. How Cathy had missed it while she was gone.

Wiping the tears from her cheeks, Zia Yola said, "That old rumour? The gossips have speculated since we moved here. At one time, they thought I was her illegitimate child by another man and your father took pity on her. Can you imagine Lucia running around getting pregnant before marriage? Never."

Cathy tried hard to picture her uptight mother coy and flirting. Nope, the image wouldn't gel. "Well, settling in Clarence Bay instead of Toronto, where the *paesani* are..." Cathy defended her logic, "Lucia's obsession with our chastity..."

"Let me tell you about my sister." Zia Yola folded her hands in her lap. "Lucia is eighteen years older than I and she looks older than her age. I was born after our parents moved to Toronto from Italy—a late-life gift to them. They were so happy to have such a gift, I'm afraid they made a favourite of me. When I look back, they treated Lucia almost like a poor relation. After our parents passed when I was eight and Lucia twenty-six, she raised me like a mother. She tried very hard, but without husband or parents to guide her she became a very strict demanding mother. She married Antonio when she was thirty. She loved him in her own way. He opened his heart to me—we were good friends and I think Lucia resented me for that, too. As much as I care for her—well, she is a difficult woman to love."

"True, she's not overly affectionate. Not like you and Papà." Cathy hesitated. "You know, I always fantasized you were my real mother. You were so much more understanding and loving. But I don't even look like you or Mamma. I must look like Papà—too bad we don't have any pictures."

Zia Yola's rosary snapped, flew across the room, and clicked wildly against the windowpane. Stunned, Zia stared first at Cathy, then at her empty hands, then at the fractured chain on the windowsill. She giggled hysterically and fisted both of her hands over her mouth as if to stop the madness.

"Zia, are you okay?"

"*Sì, cara.* I guess I'm more worried about meeting Leo than I thought."

Hayley tugged her end of the afghan up over her chilly knees and tummy. Mom was so right about the coziness of reading in the playhouse while rain tapped on the roof. She read a couple more pages of *The Mystery in Arizona*, volume six of the Trixie Belden mystery books. These kids had the coolest adventures, but not cool enough to stop Hayley's buzzing thoughts.

Hayley peered at Lindsey under her half of the afghan at her end of the bench. "I've been thinking about my dad," she said, a little nervous.

Lindsey eagerly put her book face down on the narrow bench. She didn't read much, but she talked a lot. "Yeah, what about him?"

"Well, I still don't know who he is."

"I thought you wanted Uncle Ryan for a dad."

"Yeah, I do. But I want to know my real dad. He might be better than Ryan."

Lindsey blew a raspberry and flapped her hand. "Better'n Uncle Ryan? Fuggettaboutit." She loved the Jersey show and copied the slang all the time.

Hayley stuck a marker in her book and dropped it to the floor. "I *wish* he was my dad. That would be the best thing ever! But I can't stop thinking about my real dad."

"So?"

Rolling her eyes, Hayley tucked up her knees and hugged them. Didn't Lindsey know friends were supposed to care about what their friends cared about?

"So-o, I thought we'd solve the mystery. Y'know, like Trixie and Honey and Jim."

"You mean they do more'n find the money in Jim's uncle's haunted house? Way cool."

"Yep, they find the money in the first book. In the others, they solve all kinds of mysteries. I thought if *they* can do all that, *we* can find my real dad."

Lindsey pushed her book and cushion onto the floor, and flopped onto her back. "Uh...how?" She shoved off the afghan and stuck her feet in the air.

"I already tried eavesdropping. They all spoke in Italian about other stuff," Hayley said.

"So, ya got nuttin. What else you gonna do?"

Her friend started doing ballet exercises with her feet—point, flex, first, second, fifth. Hayley's feet followed along then she stood up and added arms. Lindsey got off the bench and copied her.

"Well, a little while ago, my mom said she'd seen him here in town. *Pliés.*" Lindsey followed her through the standard warm-up, turning as needed, keeping perfect time. Cool.

"And she didn't tell you who he is? Why not?"

"Mom said—" She screwed up her face to help her remember. "She thought he was cute but other people didn't, and she loved him, and he was funny, and his mom is dead—that's so sad—and he didn't know about me. Once she almost told me I had hair like him. *Battements tendus.*" Hayley couldn't wait until she was old enough for her first pair of shiny pink satin toe shoes—awesome.

"Whaddya mean almost told?"

"She was brushing my hair once a long time ago and said her fingers got stuck in my curls just like they did in his. Except she didn't say my dad, she said something else I can't remember. But I knew she meant my dad. *Rond de jamb en l'air.*"

"You mean your dad has curly hair like you and me?"

Hayley's arms and legs fell out of their graceful poses like a rag doll. The Grinch's Christmas feeling grew in her chest again. "Holy cow! We might be related!"

Lindsey screamed and waved her hands over her head. Totally Kermit.

"We just have to prove it."

Lindsey drooped like a balloon with the air let out. "How?"

Hayley sank to the floor cross-legged. "Let me think." She twiddled her hair, followed an ant across the floorboards, squished it dead. "Having the same hair isn't enough proof. We need pictures."

"We've got tons of them at my house."

"Is your mom home? Can we go over?"

"Nah, she has a doctor's appointment and then she's going to Becca's. She took the brats with her, so the coast is clear."

Hayley stuck out her hand to Lindsey who grabbed hold and yanked her up.

Lindsey shoved aside the curtains. "Good, it stopped raining. Let's go."

Hayley yanked her back just before she shot out the playhouse door. "Shh. We have to sneak so they won't guess what we're doing."

"Why?"

"Du-uh. Because that's how Trixie Belden does it. You don't tell the parents until you solve the mystery."

"Oh."

"So c'mon, what are you standing there for?" Hayley

crouched and flew down the drippy yard. She leapt the small creek and ran into the forest bordering the lot. Lindsey followed quickly. She cursed loudly when her jump didn't quite clear the creek and she got a soaker.

"Shh!" Hayley hissed at her friend. She grabbed her hand and hauled her through the trees behind the neighbour's thick hedge and the next neighbour's board fence at the end of the street. They ran along the fence, turned its corner, and kept going until they hit the sidewalk. Hayley halted to check for cars and then they ran as fast as they could across the street, scooted along two open backyards and onto Lindsey's kitchen porch. Hayley wriggled impatiently while Lindsey got out the house key she wore on a string around her neck.

Finally, they made it inside. Hayley ran into the living room and peeked out, her heart in her throat, sure they'd get caught. Nope, nobody shouting or anything. Safe.

As she'd never been in Lindsey's house before, she looked around while she caught her breath. It was like Nonna's house only backwards with the kitchen and parlour on different sides. And it smelled different.

"Where are the pictures?" she whispered to Lindsey.

"Over here in the bookcase," Lindsey whispered back.

They ducked below the level of the windowsill and crept across the room. Lindsey got a fit of the giggles and fell down. "It's just like we're on TV."

"C'mon, let's do this before your mom comes back." Disgusted, Hayley hauled a limp Lindsey to the bookcase. Yeah, the smart one and the goofy one—just like on TV.

"Crap, how we gonna look at all these?" Hayley sagged at the sight of, like, a million photo albums, all decorated with swirls and stars and sparkles. They'd be really pretty if there weren't so darn many of them.

Lindsey shrugged. "My mom scrapbooks."

"Yeah, she sure does. Where do you think we should start?"

"Mom looks at this one the most." Lindsey took out a white book. "It's their wedding. It's got my whole family in it. 'Cept my Grandy 'cause she was in the hospital."

The girls sat down and flipped through book after book after book.

"How many pictures did your mom take of you?"

"Too many. And she goos over every darn one of them."

"Let's go back to when your mom was little." So they went through those, laughing like loons at the silly clothes and stupid hair. Still no luck. They were down to the last book, stashed on another shelf and plain brown,

"That's the Chisholm family album. All the families have copies of all the pictures. Mom never looks in it."

Lindsey's mom's car came up the driveway. Squealing, they grabbed the book, flew up the stairs to Lindsey's room, and stuffed it under the bed.

"Hi, Mom, I'm up here." Lindsey called down the stairs.

"Get down here and help put the groceries away." The boys were whining on about cookies and Coke.

Lindsey groaned and slouched downstairs.

Hayley dug the book out from under the unmade bed. On the very first page, it was like looking in a mirror with the time dial set to old-fashioned. The little girl looked so much like herself it weirded her right out. The only difference was the girl in the photo had grey eyes like Lindsey while Hayley's eyes were dark brown like Mom's. Freaky.

When Lindsey finally came back, she whistled in surprise at the photo.

"Who is this?" Hayley asked.

"My Grandma Francie when she was ten like us. She died before I was born, while I was inside my mom, so I never met her."

"Whose mom is she?"

"My dad's."

"So that must mean... I'm this little girl's daughter when she grew up and got married? No way, I'm my mom's daughter."

"Jeez, this is complicated. Let's ask my mom," Lindsey said.

"No! You don't tell the parents. Gimme some paper and a pencil." After a huge search through Lindsey's messy room, they found an old notebook and a green pencil crayon. Hayley carefully drew a family tree like she learned in school and wrote in the names and relationships and showed it to Lindsey. "So here's your Grandma Francie, then your dad, then you, and I'm the same as you 'cept I have a different mom, so that makes me...," she screwed up her face and drew the last line, "your half-sister." Hayley dropped the paper and pencil in shock. Her eyes were gonna bug right out of her head.

Lindsey sat statue-still and stared right back at her. "You're my sister!"

"You're my sister!"

They squealed and shouted and danced loud enough to make Lindsey's mom holler at them to pipe down.

"Can I borrow the picture?" Hayley pulled open the binder rings and lifted the page out.

Lindsey grabbed for the page and Hayley snatched it out of her reach. "No! If you wreck it, Mom will kill us!"

"Not if you don't tell her. You said she never looks in this book."

Hayley took the notebook she'd been charting in and slid the picture between some clean pages then stuffed everything under her T-shirt.

"C'mon, we need to hide it until I figure out what to do." Hayley thrust the photo album into her friend's arms. "And we gotta put this back to cover our tracks."

Hayley lead the way down the stairs and into the living room. Just as Lindsey slid the album into its place on the shelf, her mom came in.

"What are doing in here?" she demanded, scaring the life out of Hayley and making Lindsey squeak.

"N-nothing, Mom," Lindsey said.

Cripes! This lady was her stepmother—better be nice to her. "Lindsey was just showing me your scrapbooks. They're very pretty. Especially your wedding album."

Her stepmother stared at her with narrowed eyes and her hands on her hips. Hayley exchanged a wary waiting glance with Lindsey. Then Mrs. Chisholm *humphed* and dropped her hands. "Thanks. What have you got under your shirt?"

Hayley pulled out the notebook. "Just a book to write in. We're playing detective like in the Trixie Belden books. I put in under my shirt so I wouldn't drop it."

Meg snorted. "Detectives...cute. Now, you two get outside and play."

Hayley didn't wait around for her to ask to see the notebook. She grabbed Lindsey's hand and they ran as fast as they could straight across the street and back to the playhouse. Out of breath and panting, she lifted the bench cushion and carefully slid the notebook underneath it. She lowered the cushion and stroked over the hiding place.

"There, it's safe now."

"Whaddya gonna do with it now you got it?" Lindsey went to sit on the spot and Hayley yanked her away.

"Don't sit on it!"

Lindsey gave her a bug-eyed look. "Whatever." She sat at the other end of the bench. "So, whaddya gonna do with it?"

Hayley settled in the chair, stared at the hiding place. "Not sure. But when I have A New Plan, I'll have the picture ready for it."

Seated on a bench in the park by the marina, Yola drew water-scented air deep into her lungs and raised her face to the sun's blessing. Hayley ran back and forth on the grass with Lindsey. A shy joy swelled Yola's heart. How she adored Caterina's little girl. *Grazie a Dio,* Caterina had defied Lucia and kept the child. Yola did not allow herself to think of the many missed years of Hayley's life. The enchanting child was here now. Learn to live in the moment, leave the past behind.

Astonishing that her Leo had come back after thirty years. Yola smirked. *Her Leo, she says. Silly woman.* Her heart fluttered with fearful anticipation in spite of herself. She raised a trembling hand to her wind-ruffled hair. Should she dye her grey hair? Her hands fell to her newly trim waist thanks to the stress of Lucia's care and the fun of Caterina's exercise tapes. If only her mental state firmed up like her muscles.

"Hello, Zia Yola."

Yola looked up at the halo of chestnut hair belonging to one of very few people who might address her so familiarly. Both

Emma and Melody claimed her as an honorary aunt—Yola's reward for countless biscotti and glasses of milk served in the playhouse. Emma looked very pretty in her grey skirt and mint-green tank top. Yola brushed a hand down her ugly black dress. When had she turned into an Italian crone—at only forty-five? All she needed was a headscarf, a frumpy sweater, and granny shoes.

"Hello, Emma. Come, sit. How's your eye?" Yola marvelled at the transformation from boy-crazy teenager to responsible woman. Emma had stopped running around with all sorts of inappropriate young men, took good care of her grandmother Myra, and managed Myra's shop.

Emma blushed and touched the patch covering her eye. "It's getting better."

"What happened?"

Emma pointed a thumb in the vague direction of Finn's Fine China and Gift Shoppe across the street. "A clumsy customer dropped a pottery bowl and a big chunk hit me in the eye. She paid for the bowl and sent flowers to apologize, but I still have to wear this dumb patch."

Wincing at the imagined pain, Yola touched Emma's arm in sympathy. "*Santo cielo,* how awful for you."

Emma patted Yola's hand in gratitude. "Yes, it really hurt and being a one-eyed monster is very tiring. The doctor says I can take the patch off soon."

Yola smiled teasingly. "Ah, yes, it seems you've found some special medicine with the new doctor."

Emma groaned. "Not you, too. Why can't this town mind its own business?"

Yola chuckled at Emma's discomfort. "Because everybody

else's business is more interesting than our own. Most of the time." She muttered the last under her breath.

A sudden sly expression crept over Emma's face. "Why Zia Yola, I think you've got some of your own interesting business going on. At long last."

Yola gasped, a hand flew to her mouth. "How did you know? Did Caterina tell you?"

Emma pealed with laughter. "I guessed from the secret smile on your face when I saw you sitting here."

Yola huffed and joined in the laughter. "I gave myself away. Silly me."

Emma nudged her with a shoulder. "So, out with it. Why the little smile? A man in your life at long last? Where did you find him?"

Yola waved the suggestion away and pointed at her knitting bag on the picnic table. "I've been going to knitting circle with my old friends. I can't remember the last time I laughed so much. Busy hands make busy tongues. Isn't it wonderful to have Caterina home again? And her little girl." A blush stung Yola's cheeks. She babbled far too much.

As expected, Emma smirked lightly. Of course, she'd seen through her flood of words. "Okay. We won't talk about your romance. How's Mrs. Rossetti doing?"

All temptation to laugh and tease died at the mention of Lucia. "My sister is too impatient and has setbacks when she pushes herself. As she gets stronger, it happens less. Caterina will go home soon." The black weight of depression bowed Yola's shoulders. "I don't want her and Hayley to go."

Emma touched a shy hand to Yola's arm. "I'm sure she'll be back at Christmas. Now that she's come back once, she'll come again."

"Zia Yola, Zia Yola, can we have some ice cream?" Hayley charged over to the bench and placed sticky hands on Yola's arm. "Please?"

Yola caressed Hayley's springy hair. Her baby finger caught in a curl and she carefully freed herself.

"That happens with Mom all the time. I hate my hair."

"Many women would pay—" Yola started.

Hayley joined in. "Good money—"

Emma joined as well. "To have hair like yours."

Yola hugged the laughing little girl.

"Zia Yola, ice cream?"

"Shame on me. I forgot all about it. *Sì*, you may have your ice cream. First you must meet someone special. Hayley, this is your mother's childhood friend Emma. Emma this is my—niece." She tapped her heart. "What a joy to say the word."

"Hi, Emma."

"Hi, Hayley. Hey, Lindsey," Emma greeted Ryan's niece as she ran up to join them.

"Hey." She prodded Hayley. "Did she say yes?"

"Yep." Hayley glanced expectantly at Yola, too polite to remind her again. Yola got the money from her wallet and the girls raced off to the concession stand.

Emma stood and stretched her back. "Well, work awaits. See you soon. Enjoy your knitting classes."

The young woman's naughty wink drew another chuckling blush from Yola. Turning her gaze back to the harbour, Yola rejoiced at the happy bustle Caterina and her friends had brought to the cold and lonely life she shared with Lucia. When Caterina and Hayley were gone, the joy would dim. Even more than when Cathy left the first time. Her mind rested again on her long-ago lover. Questions and doubts dipped and swayed like a cloud of dragonflies.

The two little girls raced back, ice cream melting down their hands, chattering like the sparrows in the big pine tree in front of the house. Lindsey spotted her father who'd come to pick her up. "Ask her about our dad," she whispered not so quietly in Hayley's ear and raced away with hurried thanks for the treat.

Our dad? Had Yola heard correctly?

"Zia Yola..." Hayley began then stopped and licked her ice cream cone. "Zia Yola..."

"Yes, *piccola*?" So jumpy, the little one.

"Do you know who my father is?"

The question vibrated a chord of regret deeply hidden within Yola's soul. Looking into the past with sharpened hindsight, she still discerned no other choice for her to make.

"Zia Yola?"

What had the dear child asked? Oh, yes, she dug for information about her father. Yola looked into the earnest little face. A recollection teased her, but ran away before she captured it. "No, I'm sorry; I don't know who your father is. You must ask your mother."

Hayley's face fell. She didn't notice the drips of ice cream running down her hand and plopping on her sandaled foot. Yola pulled out a wet wipe and cleaned Hayley's hand and toes while she diligently licked down to the cone.

"Thanks. D-do you know Lindsey's dad?"

A silly question. Who in Clarence Bay didn't know their neighbors almost too well? "*Sì,* they live across the street from us."

"Well, the other day, Lindsey and I were looking at her family pictures and—" She bit off the bottom of the cone and sucked out the ice cream.

Dio mio, would she ask her question already?

"We found an old-fashioned picture." She munched down the rest of the cone and wiped her hands on her shorts. "You're never gonna believe it." She dug through her knapsack and pulled out a notebook. From between the pages, she withdrew a photograph in an album sleeve and handed it to Yola.

Yola took it gingerly and stared at a child who looked just like Hayley but with grey eyes. Her memory started to twitch—she knew this little girl somehow.

"She's Lindsey's dad's mother. So, I was wondering—is Lindsey's dad my dad? Are me and Lindsey half-sisters?"

Yola's mind whizzed through a portfolio of memories, sifting, analyzing. She gasped. No. Why hadn't she thought of that? Francine, Mark and Ryan's mother. Francie was older than Yola—Yola forgot how many years. They'd met in Clarence Bay; Francie always came to Yola's cash-register aisle at the grocery store. An unlikely friendship had grown through further contact at the knitting circle. Yola would never have known what a ten-year-old Francie had looked like. Any mental images of a grown-up Francie had faded in Yola's mind. Plus, Yola had been so busy with Lucia lately, she simply hadn't noticed.

All the pieces clicked into place in Yola's mind. When Cathy had come to beg for help all those years ago, she had refused to name the father. Yola and Lucia had assumed Cathy had gotten pregnant at university. Cathy had reluctantly admitted that Hayley's birthday was May twenty-ninth.

Other old memories welled up of Cathy creeping into the

house while Mark… The memories cleared as she concentrated. No, not Lindsey's father Mark. His younger brother Ryan. It was Ryan who watched from his father's car while Cathy crept into the house. The silly young things thought no one noticed. It was just that no one remembered. *Imbecille.* It was so obvious. Ryan was Hayley's father. Now, this child thought her father was Ryan's brother Mark?

Dio mio, what a mess.

"Zia Yola? Is he?"

Yola pressed a hand to her mouth. "I don't know, *piccola.* Your mother never told us." As sure as she was about the identity of this child's father, Yola was equally sure it was not her place to tell either Hayley or Ryan.

Those very big jobs belonged only to Caterina. And she must tell them soon before someone else, namely Lucia, saw the resemblance and also recalled Francie.

CHAPTER 11

Secrets and Bargains

"Your secret's out, my friend."

Cathy's grip slackened at Melody's casual remark. Her fork clattered to the plate of pasta, onto the wooden table, and down to the linoleum kitchen floor. Which secret? Ryan and Hayley? Yola and Leo? Emma and Asher? No, Melody already knew about the last two. Was there an unknown secret?

Melody stopped chewing. She swallowed and tipped her dark head like an inquisitive chickadee. "Oooh. What an interesting over-reaction. Tell all to Miss Mellie. You *know* I'll figure it out."

"Umm." Cathy stalled by retrieving the wayward fork, hoping Melody would clue her in as to which secret she meant.

"About you and Ryan?"

Cathy dropped the fork again. *Dio mio,* what a loud mouth on Melody. "Shh, Mamma might hear." Cathy tiptoed to the door and peered down the hallway. Nobody. Cathy picked up her dirty utensil, got another, and returned to the table of inquisition.

"C'mon, she can't hear us with the TV so loud."

Mamma didn't want to sit with the flighty Melody yet still needed to make her presence felt.

"She detests secrets and has no problem eavesdropping to find out about them."

"Don't you *want* to tell me?" Melody put the back of her hand to her forehead with a mock cry. "Your best friend, true to you through thick and thin."

Cathy chuckled. "Cut the melodrama, 'cause I ain't buying it."

"Too much?" Melody drooped in her chair and made pitiful-puppy eyes.

Snickering, Cathy shook her head. "Nope. Not buying that either."

"Dang." Melody straightened to her usual perfect posture, but let a pout pull down her pretty mouth.

Cathy's continued resistance brought a comic twist to Melody's lips and a twinkle to her dark-blue eyes. "Oh, just tell me, will you?"

"Tell you what?" Cathy asked in feigned innocence.

Melody's face went blank. Cathy rocked back and laughed until her ribs ached.

"Keep the noise down!" Mamma hollered in Italian from the parlour.

Cathy rolled her eyes. "Okay," she hollered back in English and ignored the rest of Mamma's crabbing.

"Grr. You were always too dang good at misdirection." Melody curled a lip.

"Only because you're such a show-boater from too much community theatre."

"*Moi?* Acting?" Melody spread a hand over her heart with a wounded look.

"Don't play innocent with me, young miss." Cathy wagged a scolding finger. "I've heard all about your recent performance of the sparkling Raina in *Arms and the Man.* Dozens of men fell at your feet."

"You flatter me—there were only a few and all of them yucky." Melody slumped. "Dang it."

Another successful dodge.

"I want my *caffe!"* Mamma shouted from the back parlour.

Cathy got up to start the machine.

"Why are you letting her still boss you around? At your age?" Melody demanded.

"I'm choosing my battles. This morning she didn't want Zia Yola and Hayley to go out. I won. So this afternoon, she can demand lunch service."

Visibly impressed, Melody nodded. "Ah, a delicate balancing act. When did you start fighting back?"

Cathy shook her head and laughed ruefully. "Hayley started it. Zia Yola told me Hayley screamed at Mamma that I was not a whore."

"What?" Melody's eyes popped and her mouth hung open. Such a satisfying thing to flummox Miss Mellie of the Gossiping Grishams.

"Yep. My spunky little girl stuck up for her single mom." Cathy brushed away a crocodile tear. "And—" Cathy lowered her voice and leaned toward her friend, "Zia Yola tossed Mamma a Sicilian salute." Melody gasped. "Too bad Mamma didn't see, but still a promising start to standing up for herself. Since then, Zia has been acting out like a teenager."

"Well, good for her. It's about time you two stopped getting pushed around by that—" She clapped a hand over her mouth. "Sorry," came out muffled.

"Don't worry. I'm beginning to see her for the bully she is. As obvious as it sounds, age and distance does give perspective."

"Caffe!" The order came accompanied by a thump of Mamma's cane.

"But it still gets ree-eal annoying," Cathy whined and Melody laughed in sympathy.

Cathy made the espresso, added a few vanilla biscotti to the tray, and took it in to Mamma. She cringed as the soap opera diva on TV spewed her venom at top volume all over some poor sucker. Great example. Mamma pretended to ignore Cathy as she removed the lunch dishes and placed the dessert on the TV table.

Good, I can ignore her foul mood right back.

How ridiculously childish.

Refusing to stoop to her mother's level, Cathy bent and gave Mamma a kiss on her forehead. Mamma's struggle not to respond was visible and comical. Finally, Mamma surrendered and allowed a smile to crack the concrete of her set face. Her sour mood lightened, though she still didn't deign to look at Cathy in spite of the suspicious glimmer in her eyes.

Huh, fight fire with kisses. Who knew?

Cathy smiled all the way back to the kitchen where she found Zia Yola and Hayley spilling all their goods about her relationship with Ryan. Looks like Melody's tactics worked with those two. Fortunately, neither of them had much info beyond the invitation to the gala.

Melody stayed for an espresso and Zia Yola's hazelnut

biscotti. After she left, Hayley disappeared into the playhouse with her latest volume of Trixie Belden. Except for the loudly continuing sagas in the back parlour, the neighbourhood snoozed in the afternoon quiet.

Yola cupped her hand around Caterina's forearm. "Come outside. I must speak with you." Yola quivered at the discussion to come—for Hayley's sake, this must be done.

"What's up, Zia," Caterina asked as Yola led the younger woman to the front porch. Yola said nothing until they settled in the swing and gently pushed off.

Yola flicked a glance through the front parlour windows. *Nulla.* Nothing. "When Hayley and I were out, she asked me a very funny question."

"Yes?" Caterina scratched her arm.

Yola leaned closer and murmured, "She asked me if Mark Chisholm was her father."

"Mark? Mark!" The swing rocked wildly with Caterina's surprise. Her gaze jerked across the street to where Mark and his family lived. "How? Where? Why did she ever come to such a bizarre conclusion?"

Yola dug Francie's photo from her knitting bag and handed it to Caterina.

Instead of clutching her heart in panic, Caterina smiled. "Oh, how nice." She ran her finger over the scalloped edge. "You went to the photo studio for a novelty shot." Her eyes narrowed. "You put coloured contacts in Hayley's eyes?" Her voice sharpened as she looked up.

"No, I wouldn't do such a thing. This is not Hayley, though the resemblance is remarkable. *Sì?*"

Caterina paled. "Who is it?"

"Mark and Ryan's mother, when she was ten. The same age as Hayley is now."

Understanding dawned in Caterina's face, quickly followed by dismay. "*Santo cielo,*" she whispered.

"You must tell Ryan and Hayley what they are to each other—father and daughter."

"No! Not yet. Don't tell Ryan yet."

"They have the right to know."

"I completely agree, though I can't tell them yet. Not with the election coming so soon. Ryan will be ruined. All his hopes and dreams gone down the drain. The town needs him."

"True. But a little girl needs her father more—and he needs her." As Yola had ensured Caterina had a father to hold her on his knee.

"Don't you think I haven't tried to tell him? Just two days ago, I tried after the fund raiser. And failed miserably. I can't get him alone long enough. It kills me that I can't speak up." Caterina groaned. "He'll hate me. She'll hate me. The town will hate him." Yola felt Caterina's trembling where their thighs touched on the swing. "Do *you* hate me, *cara Zia*?"

Yola's heart welled with empathy. Long-held secrets were extremely difficult to uproot and expose to the light of day. She hugged Caterina tight and soaked up the comfort for a brief moment, almost as if she'd revealed her own secrets.

"No, no, *ucellino,* I don't hate you. How could I not love someone so precious to me?" Yola held Caterina at arm's length and gazed sternly into her watery brown eyes. "Caterina, how much do you love Hayley?"

Caterina gasped indignantly. Yola gave her a gentle shake of admonishment. "Answer me."

Caterina looked directly into Yola's eyes. "She changed my life. I gave up so much for her but I did it willingly. She's the most important thing in my life."

Yes, a child's happiness and well-being are more important than anything. Yola stiffened her spine and her resolve to make Caterina do what must be done. "Do you still love your Ryan?"

Caterina looked like someone had hit her with a *pizelle* iron. "I-I don't know, Zia. When we—" A blush hot enough to fry those *pizelle* coloured Caterina's cheeks. She stared down at her fiddling fingers. "When we were young, we were so much in love. It might have lasted forever, but we went our separate ways. I don't know if I love him. I'm terrified he'll hate me."

Yola shook her head. "He doesn't hate you, *cara.* He loves you."

"Really?"

What a child this grown woman seemed, so unsure of herself. Her little pink T-shirt and cut-off jeans didn't alter the perception.

"Yes, really. His eyes don't lie. You *must* tell Ryan and Hayley. They *deserve* to know." She gave Caterina a firmer shake by her shoulders.

"Can't I wait until after he wins the election?" she pleaded with fear in her eyes.

"The town will still be angry with him. They will feel tricked. Cheated. You must tell him before the vote."

"But if I wait, he'll do such a good job, the town will forgive him. Won't they? They love him. Don't they? Please don't say anything to either of them?" Caterina placed her hands on Yola's knees and leaned into her embrace. "Please?"

Yola knew the delay would make it more difficult. As always,

Yola capitulated to a plea from her beloved Caterina. She took both younger hands into one of her work-worn ones and caressed the soft young cheek. "I have no say in this. It is *your* secret to tell." Besides, who was Yola to be giving advice she herself should take?

"Secret? What secret?" Lucia demanded from the window to the front parlour. Yola jumped so badly she hit Caterina's cheek.

"Ouch!" Caterina fell back against the swing.

"Lucia, stop sneaking up on people!"

"What secret are you talking about? You have no right to keep secrets. You must tell them to me." Lucia was half-hidden in the shadow cast by the screen. Her hair formed a bizarre fuzzy halo around her sepulchral face.

Startled and trembling, Yola took shelter in the comfort of lies. "*Dio mio,* Lucia. Now you've spoiled the surprise with your sharp ears. We were planning a small party to celebrate your return to good health."

Ryan couldn't stop smiling. The wind tugged at his hair despite his rarely-worn ball cap.

"You'll get bugs in your teeth," Cathy teased.

Ryan's smile only grew wider. Sun spangles bounced off the water as he steered his boat between the tricky submerged rocks and numerous islands of Georgian Bay. Hayley scampered fore and aft to absorb all possible views. She waved at the occupants of every single boat they met. True to boating tradition, everyone waved back, thrilling Hayley.

Cathy stood near him at the center console. Each time they bounced over the wake of another boat, their arms brushed and a glowing awareness streamed over Ryan's skin like a permanent sunburn. Though sunglasses hid Cathy's eyes, he knew the amber flecks reflected the same glow. Yes, it was a bad thing to wish your life away, but he couldn't wait for tonight when they were alone at his place.

Arriving at Franklin Island beach, Ryan dropped the anchor on gentle swells in about three meters of water. He loaded the picnic gear into a wake tube and stowed his life jacket. He stripped off his T-shirt and plunged into the cool green water, surfacing with a shout of relief at the rapid dissipation of pent-up body heat. Cathy splashed in beside him, also surfacing with a shout from the contrast of hot air and chilly water. They corralled the tube and looped arms over the inflated rim.

Hayley hesitated on the deck. Her small hands clamped, white-knuckled, on the gunwale.

"C'mon sweetie. Jump in, the water's lovely," her mother coaxed.

"It's too deep," Hayley, quavered.

"Don't be afraid, we're right here. We'll catch you." Treading water, Cathy lifted her arms.

"Can I leave my life jacket on?"

"Of course you can."

"I don't wanna jump. Can't we stay on the boat?"

"C'mon, sweetie, you're an expert swimmer. This is no different than jumping in the deep end from the low diving board. You've done that hundreds of times."

Ryan floated patiently while mother and daughter worked through the girl's reluctance.

"There aren't any fish in the swimming pool." Her big brown eyes rounded with fear, her narrow shoulders clenched beneath her life jacket.

Ryan bit the inside of his mouth to stop the grin. He laid a hesitant hand on Cathy's arm. "May I give it a try?"

She tipped her head, consideration joining the frustration in her beautiful expressive face. A confident smiled bloomed to replace the doubts. "Sure. Go for it."

"Why don't you take the gear to shore?"

Taking the tube's rope from him, she hesitated to leave her daughter.

He shooed her towards the shore. "Don't worry, I won't let any harm come to her."

Cathy chuckled ruefully. "I know you won't. I'm just not used to anyone looking after her except me."

"What? You never left her with a sitter?"

"Only with family and, until recently, only for business events."

He scowled as the face of the arrogant Matt Bartholomew popped into his head.

"*Very* recently. Like within the last few weeks." She lifted her sunglasses and winked saucily. Matt's ugly mug swirled down an imaginary drain with a satisfying glug.

"Nice to know. Go ahead. I'll get Hayley to shore."

Cathy mischievously flashed her red-clad butt at him and swam away, taking the tube with her.

Grinning, Ryan turned to the frightened child. "Hold on, Hayley, I'm coming onboard."

Once beside the little girl, he peeled her death-grip off the gunwale and looked her in the eye. "Yes, Hayley, there are fish in Georgian Bay. But fish are really shy and your mom and I already scared them away."

"I can't see the bottom."

"You can once you get a few meters closer to shore."

Her brown eyes stared after her mother. "Can't we park the boat by the sand?"

Ryan chuckled. "No. It's not a city street. We'll smash the transom and propeller on the rocks before we hit sand."

"I'm scared." Her small body trembled beneath his hands.

"It's okay to be scared." Just because he and Cathy had jumped fearlessly into deep water all their lives didn't mean Hayley couldn't be frightened of the unfamiliar. He tapped the brim of her sunhat. "Tell you what—I'll put the ladder over the side and you can climb down into the water."

"Ladder?" A thin hope threaded her high voice.

He climbed between the seats and dug the ladder out from under the foredeck. "Yep, see, here it is."

Even with the ladder hooked over the side of the boat, Hayley still hesitated. Her little hand nuzzled into his and she gazed up at him with huge trusting eyes so much like Cathy's it hurt.

"Will you catch me?"

He cupped her skinny little shoulder in reassurance. "Of course I will." He stepped up and over the side of the boat into the clear green water. Upon surfacing, he swam over to the ladder and held onto the side rails. "Okay, honey, turn around and go backwards down the ladder. I'll be waiting at the bottom for you."

Hayley cautiously lowered herself to the first step. She twisted to make sure Ryan still floated at the bottom and he winked up at her. She smiled broadly and came down another step to where the water lapped at her feet. This time when she twisted to check his location, Ryan pushed back into the water and raised his arms.

"Jump now."

Fixing her gaze on his, she leapt. She bobbed to the surface, squealing at the cool touch of the water. She lunged for his neck and drove him under. He surfaced, spouting like a whale, making her laugh. They started to swim—his slow breast stroke keeping pace with Hayley's rhythmic front crawl. She really was a good swimmer. His feet touched bottom and he slung her into piggyback position. She clung like a barnacle, her life jacket chafing his bare back, until they reached the blanket Cathy had spread on the soft golden sand.

"I did it, Mom. I jumped in."

Ryan knelt on the warm sand and Hayley climbed off his back.

Cathy tapped her daughter's nose. "Good for you. I knew you could, my brave girl." She unbuckled her daughter's life jacket, dried her off, and exchanged the wet T-shirt over her bathing suit for a dry one.

Once free of Cathy's fussing, Hayley surprised Ryan by hurling herself at him and laying a smacking kiss on his cheek. "Thanks for helping me, Ryan."

Hugging her back, Ryan was surprised again by the depth of yearning this little girl stirred in him. Before he'd had enough of her sunscreen scent, she released him and ran to the water's edge with her pail and shovel.

Cathy's cool hand on his arm startled him. "Thanks, Ryan."

He switched his gaze to her sitting on the blanket and sketched a bow. "We had fun. She's a great kid. Wish I had one like her." And a bunch more where she came from. The thought pounced out of nowhere and he welcomed it with open arms.

Behind him, Cathy wrapped her arms around her shins and

dropped her forehead to her knees. She groaned quietly into the hollow of her body.

Alarm skittered over his skin, raising all the hairs on his arms. He sat close beside her. "Cathy, you okay?"

"No. Yes. Mostly."

"You look a little green around the gills." He sat beside her.

"I'm fine." She waved away his concern. "Hungry, I guess. How about you?"

The corner of his mouth kicked up. "Hungry, you ask?" Bumping shoulders, he skimmed her body with his gaze. "In that red bathing suit, you tempt me almost beyond endurance." Fever-hot blood throbbed in his veins.

A throaty chuckle curled from her throat and she flirted her eyes over his chest and up to his face. "You always were a hungry fellow, weren't you?" She quirked her brows at him, yanking a sharp exhale from his lungs.

"Come here you temptress." He stroked the curve of her thigh. The fine tremor in her muscles vibrated through his hand to his groin. She pivoted towards him and tilted her chin up. Her mouth touched his, honey sweet, unbelievably wonderful.

The past scorched a path to the present—the glow of candlelight, the taste of wine, his weight pressing her into the sun-dried sheets. Then as now, her tongue swept across his bottom lip, seeking entry. He parted his lips and met her tongue with his in a hot wet dance of seduction.

He should never have let her go. He should have pursued her, found her, kept her and her daughter for himself. Not let some stranger marry her and make a child with her.

Hayley's laughter from the shore penetrated the red haze of sunlight and passion as she and a bunch of girls raced past them and into the water. They dove and splashed, screaming and squealing. Guess her fear was only of fish and not water.

Cathy broke away with a guilty expression. "*Dio mio,* you're a temptation to sin," she groaned.

He desperately wanted her to climb on top of him, take him inside her, and ride him until the sun went down.

Instead, she stood and headed for the water. "Must. Cool. Off." She walked straight into the bay and plunged in.

Flopping to his back, Ryan lifted a knee to hide his painful erection from the people on the beach. He dropped a bent elbow over his eyes. Oh, God. That kiss. That woman. He loved her, always had. Always would. A heavy fatalism settled over him like a shadow, killing his ardour.

A real shadow moved over, giggled, and dumped a pail full of cold water on his naked skin. He shot upright with a roar and tore off after a wildly screaming Hayley. "You little imp," he scolded when he finally caught the squealer. "I think you deserve a dunking." He scooped the flailing Hayley up into his arms and marched into the water. When the water hit his waist, he tossed her. She came up spluttering and laughing and threw her arms around his neck.

"Do it again," she demanded. He obliged over and over until his arms ached and his back muscles screamed for mercy. She swam over to him.

"Float me."

"What do you mean, honey?"

"You hold onto my hands and walk me around while I float on my back. 'Kay?" She arranged them to suit herself and soon they were cruising. They chatted about Lindsey and her family, swimming versus diving, dresses versus jeans. The last topic was an "Uh-huh, okay" conversation on his side.

"Ryan, can I ask you something serious." She barely waited for his consent. "Why did Becca think you were getting married to her?"

His heel caught in the sandy bottom, he stumbled backwards and went under with a mighty splash. Surfacing, he dragged the water from his face, she latched on again, and they resumed their tour.

"So, why?" Hayley continued her inquisition like nothing had happened.

"Who told you about that?"

"Lindsey told me her mom is really mad at you because you made Becca cry."

How to explain the mess to a kid? "Well...adults sometimes... No, let me start over. Do you know what a misunderstanding is?"

"Umm, yeah, sure."

"Not really, eh? Do you know what gossip is?"

She nodded vigorously, sending ripples through the water. "That's when people tell stories about other people and some of them are mean."

"Good answer. Well, I helped a friend pick out an engagement ring for his girlfriend and somebody must have seen me—"

"Oh, oh!" She pushed out of his grip to stand in water up to her neck. "And they told Becca and she thought the ring was for her. Right?"

"Wow, you are gonna be a great detective when you grow up."

"Yeah, just like Trixie Belden."

"Trixie who?"

Her teeth chattered and she shivered hard. He grabbed the opportunity to leave Becca and her misunderstanding behind.

"C'mon, let's get outta here. You're all blue and pruney."

In the warm ankle-deep water near shore, she tugged him to a stop, made him look right at her. "If you're not gonna marry Becca, will you marry me and my mom?"

Wow. Good thing they were out of the deep water or he would surely have drowned. In her big brown eyes, anxiety mixed with bravado warned him not to laugh. Looking at her serious little face, he acknowledged the brilliance of the idea.

It could work. They could team up and....

No. As much as he wanted to fall in with her plans, he couldn't. A little girl, smart as she was, didn't know what she asked. Damn it all, he hated to snuff her bright hope. Bending on one knee, he took her hands.

"Listen, honey. Sometimes, a person wishes so hard for something, they don't see how it affects other people."

Her bottom lip trembled and tears blurred her brown eyes. His gut twisted at her disappointment.

"Don't you love us?" she whispered.

He simply wasn't cruel enough to stomp on her precocious little heart. Besides, then he'd be lying to her. He gave her a brief hug. "I do love you and your mom and I'd be delighted to marry you both. But it's not for a little girl to ask. It's for a man to ask the woman he loves."

She heaved a huge sad sigh and hung her head to watch her toes burrow into the sand.

He gave her a few minutes then lifted her chin to connect with her sad eyes. "We okay on this?" he asked gently.

She nodded. The bright twinkle flared again as something occurred to her. "Wickedly awesome. Do I get to be your flower girl?"

He chuckled at her easy joy, took her small hand in his, and led her up the beach for lunch. "You sure do. Just give me some time."

Ryan guided his boat home over water gilded by late afternoon sun. Hayley snoozed in the prow, exhausted by her endless fun in the sun. Cathy relaxed against him with her arm around his waist. She stood on her toes and kissed his cheek, purred a sexy promise for later.

As they passed Bateau Island, several people on shore jumped up and down, hollering and waving both arms overhead, signalling for help. Ryan drew alongside the dock where they were greeted by a family of three.

"Damn, I'm glad you stopped. We haven't seen anyone for hours," a stout grey-haired man said.

"Ages and ages," accused a stout teenaged boy with a nasty sunburn that was going to be agony tonight. "We're frying out here." Like it was Ryan's fault for not showing up sooner.

"What's the problem?"

"Engine won't start. Because *somebody* didn't think to gas up." A scrawny leather-skinned woman jabbed the man in the ribs with a sharp elbow. He flinched and gave her a dirty look. She gave him a haughty nose in the air, vaguely reminding Ryan of someone.

"Did you happen to have a spare tankful?"

"Sorry, I've only the one tank left. Enough to get ourselves safely back to Clarence Bay." All three faces fell. "But I can give you a lift to a marina and they should be able to help you out."

All three faces lifted. "That would be wonderfully kind of you," cooed the woman. Ryan's skin crawled beneath her lascivious gaze.

"First let me check if you really are out of gas. It might be something else easy to take care of right here." Ryan passed a rope to the older man who looped it around a cleat. Mother and son stood uselessly by, watching and whining.

Ryan boarded the other boat and performed several preliminary tests. When he was done, he reached for the soap in his vessel's dash and washed off the oily grit from his inspection. "Well, you're not out of gas."

"I told ya," the man grumbled at the woman.

Ryan held back his chuckle. "You've got a clogged fuel line, so the engine won't start. Likely a clogged filter as well."

"Can you fix it?" the man asked.

"I can, just not here. Is this a rental? We should head there."

"No, we're visiting friends and it's their boat, their problem."

"Who are you staying with?"

"The Carleton-Grants. My wife is younger sister to Virginia." He seemed to suddenly recall his manners and stuck out his hand. "I'm Jerry Dyson. This is my wife Alicia and my son Todd."

Sister to Becca's mother, no wonder the wife's sour face looked familiar. Ryan sighed and accepted the inevitable demands of rescue.

"I know exactly where their house is. Your boat is bigger than mine so I can't tow it safely. But I'll take you back to their place. You and Evan can make arrangements to pick up his boat."

Jerry dumped all their stuff in Ryan's boat and climbed aboard. When Ryan introduced Cathy, he restrained himself from punching the lecherous look off Jerry's face. He organized the women in the rear seat and invited Jerry to stand with him at the console. While the arrangement kept Jerry's eyes off Cathy, it didn't work so well keeping Alicia's eyes off his own ass. Good thing his bathing suit was dry and loose, not all wet and sticking to his skin.

The two children sat on the foredeck. Suddenly Hayley yelped and leapt away from Todd with her hand clamped to her thigh.

"You pinched me," she accused him.

Todd rolled around, laughing at her indignation. Jerry laughed along with his damn brat. Alicia ignored the whole incident and dug into her beach bag.

Hayley looked to Ryan, silently asking permission to retaliate. Ryan grinned and shrugged, expecting she'd holler a few choice phrases.

"It's not funny," Hayley yelled, wound up, and punched the mini-cretin on his sunburned arm. He cried out and clutched at the sore spot. "Leave me alone!" she shouted, stuck her tongue way out, and moved as far away as the seat allowed.

Ryan hooted. "Atta girl, Hayley." He was so damn proud of her, like he was her real dad.

Frowning, Cathy stood, clearly intent on scolding her daughter for violence.

"Wait," he murmured as she started to squeeze by the console.

She stopped, brows raised.

"Don't know if you saw, but he pinched her first. She

retaliated against a bully."

Her mouth opened and he braced to receive the sharp edge of her tongue for interfering. Cathy gave him an inscrutable look. "No, I didn't see." Turning to the bow, she fired a long hard look at Todd who cringed then grumbled an apology to Hayley. Her daughter looked to her for next steps. At her nod, Hayley reluctantly accepted Todd's apology.

Cathy laid her hand on Ryan's forearm. "Thanks for telling me, Ryan. And thanks for looking out for her. It's good to have another pair of eyes." She surreptitiously stroked his thigh and returned to the rear seat.

Hot damn, he felt like a real part of their little family. He resettled his ball cap and focused on driving to the Carleton-Grants' place and getting rid of the three Dysons.

Not soon enough, they drew alongside the vast property. Dozens of people dotted the green sloping lawns. Mark, Meg, and their kids were there, as well as a few political bigwigs from nearby towns and the province. Mr. and Mrs. Carleton-Grant broke away from the crowd and hurried down to the dock when they saw her sister's family.

Evan Carleton-Grant tied up Ryan's boat and helped his in-laws out. Jerry gave him a run-down on the rescue, sidestepping the pinching incident. Mrs. Carleton-Grant and her sister and brother-in-law wandered off. Todd headed for the food. Ryan stayed in the boat, reluctant to allow Becca anywhere near Cathy.

Lindsey squealed to announce her arrival at the dock. Hayley squealed back, scrambled ashore, and vanished into the party with her friend.

Evan slapped Ryan heartily on the shoulder. "Well, Ryan, no

way you're leaving now. Come join the party. I'll give you some gas to get you home."

A tight noise of distress from Cathy's direction glued Ryan's feet to the floor of his boat.

A puzzled crease appeared between Evan's brows as he glanced from Cathy to Ryan. "Ah, got it." His face cleared. "This is the lady you chose instead of Becca. Let's say we bury the ludicrous hatchet between our families and forget all the nonsense. It's gone on long enough. Your choice is your own." He held out a hand to Cathy. "Now, I've got some influential people I'd like Ryan to meet. You're not going to make a fuss, are you?"

Cathy turned questioning eyes on Ryan, peeked inside his head, read all the pros and cons, and graciously made the decision easy for him. "These influential people will have to overlook our beachwear," she said.

Ryan gave her a quick hug of gratitude, hopped onto the dock and took Cathy's hand to help her up. Together, they joined the party.

Santo cielo, Cathy really wished Becca would stop cold-shouldering Ryan so pointedly and Virginia would keep her disdain under wraps. Every last one of Cathy's nerves was screwed tight, leaving a hollow in her belly. Countless times, she had dredged up her hard-learned control and checked the words she longed to let rip.

An hour before sunset, Ryan excused them, saying they needed to get to the harbour before dark. While he and Hayley readied the boat, Virginia sidled up to Cathy with a mean look in her eye.

"Have you told him yet?" Virginia appeared to be watching Ryan though her real focus was firmly on Cathy, a curl of disgust on her lip.

All the little hairs on Cathy's arms stood on end, her head pounded with an instant headache. "Excuse me?" The blank expression wasn't hard to come by.

"Have you told Ryan that Hayley is his daughter?" Virginia rolled her eyes and swept an impatient glance over Cathy. "Oh, stop pretending you haven't got a clue what I'm talking about. Look at your hands, they're shaking. Your face couldn't be redder if you painted it. I was guessing until you confirmed it just now. Thank you for that."

Who knew such softly-spoken words had the power to tilt a world into mayhem?

As if sensing her distress, Ryan stopped his work, glanced between the two women, and silently asked Cathy if she wanted help. Cathy's hand rose of its own accord and waved that she was okay.

"Not to worry, however, your secret is safe with me." Virginia spared her a brief pitying glance. "But what would the news do to *him*? How much would he care about you then? It doesn't bear thinking about." She gave a mocking little shudder. "And what would it do to his mayoral aspirations? We must do everything we can to keep him and his precious ideals safe. Mustn't we?"

Cathy managed a nod that nearly broke her stiff neck.

Virginia smiled graciously. "How much longer did you plan to stay?"

Forever.

Jolting a little with surprise, yet completely unsurprised, Cathy discovered she never wanted to leave. She wanted Ryan's forgiveness, wanted his love, wanted to stay forever. She still loved Ryan with an endless soul-deep passion.

With her next breath, Cathy also knew what Virginia demanded of her. The temporary silence Cathy had already demanded of herself was to be extended. Until when? How long would be long enough to satisfy this awful woman? Forever?

Once again, Cathy visualized Ryan, humiliated and humbled, crushed by the weight of the town's rejection. His own father would mock him, his brother and grandmother would turn away.

The sweet leaping joy, born moments ago, died on the blade of blackmail.

"I've got three weeks left of my compassionate leave. My mother still needs me." Cathy's reply shredded vocal chords rigid with fury.

Virginia tapped a thoughtful finger against her chin. "I suppose I can wait for your dear mother to get strong enough to do without you. But you must *stay away* from Ryan. Or the town might discover that he knew everything all along. You know how important optics are in politics." She stroked Cathy's arm in a consoling way.

Cathy stared at the beautiful blonde bitch. A crystalline glitter lit her blue eyes and her mouth mocked a caring smile.

Under everyone's watchful gaze, Cathy glared at the cool delicate hand. She lifted her gaze to Virginia's and refrained from bitch-slapping the phony smile right off her face. The older woman dropped her hand and stepped back.

Just a single tiny step, but enough to grant Cathy a grim satisfaction. "What makes you think that just because I go home to Toronto he'll marry Becca? How deluded are you?"

"He's meant for Becca, not you. He just doesn't know it yet."

Reeling with shock, Cathy turned towards the dock. Because she loved Ryan, though it broke her heart and crushed her daughter's dreams, she would stay away from him until her leave expired.

Virginia put her hand at Cathy's back and gave her a light shove. Not enough to knock Cathy over, just enough to make her slip on the dewy lawn.

"Oh, do be careful," Virginia purred in gracious hostess mode. "The grass can hide all sorts of irregularities. It was such a pleasure to meet you and your little girl."

CHAPTER 12

Revelations

"She's hiding, Yola, and I just figured out where." Ryan turned away from the front door, stalked across the Rossettis' front porch, down the rain-wet stairs and around to the backyard. A whippoorwill called out in the humid night. He slapped a mosquito on his bare forearm, stinging his own skin in his anger. Lamplight glowed behind the blue-and-yellow curtains. As expected, he found Cathy holed up in the playhouse, just like when she was a kid hiding from her mother.

He snatched the door open and stood on the threshold, glaring at her.

Cathy startled and dropped her book. *Trixie Belden and the Happy Valley Mystery*, he read on the cover—straight out of childhood—fucking priceless.

"Damn, you're a hard woman to find. I've been hunting for three days now." He released the doorframe and ducked into the playhouse. The spring-loaded door slammed shut behind him.

"I've been here all along." Yep, sweet as pie in battered denim shorts and a baggy blue sweater, looking all of sixteen.

"Why have you been avoiding me?"

She pushed her glasses up her nose. Her gaze slid down the buttons of his plaid shirt along his jeans to his sandals.

Her rejection frosted his anger with resentment. "Hmm. What happened to your 'make hay while the sun shines' philosophy?"

She nonchalantly lowered her hand from his view and he knew she was crossing her fingers against telling lies. Old habits died hard. "The sun went away. It's raining cats and dogs."

He clasped his hands behind his neck and pushed back against them. "God, this is so stupid." Abruptly, he stepped forward and plopped down on the bench.

Gossamer memories floated in his mind: Cathy risking her mother's wrath by sneaking out of the house to vent her teenaged angst, Cathy revelling in passionate kisses, Cathy laughing over some silly joke. Their abiding friendship and young love had smoothed the ragged edges of their lives.

He wanted that again, all of it and more.

Squeezing his head between his bent arms, he purged the useless anger and resentment. Catch more bees with honey and all that jazz. Lowering his hands, he looked around. "Nice reno in here. Lindsey really bent my ear about it. Now she's nagging her dad for a playhouse of her own."

"Thank you."

"You're welcome." He leaned against the wall and crossed his arms, waiting for her to say whatever he knew was on her mind.

Nothing came. She cleared her throat a couple of times, resettled her glasses.

He sighed, resigned to a fishing expedition. Appropriately, the rain started again, tapping on the roof, fogging the windows.

"I saw you talking to Virginia last week after we rescued the Dysons. The whole trip home, I expected you to fill me in. I didn't expect you to ditch me."

"I had to get Hayley home."

He tipped his head, forced himself to stay silent. She shuffled her feet and tucked one foot under the opposite knee.

"Virginia said something that's turned you against me. She'll say just about anything to get her way. Even lie." He swallowed. "Did she tell you that Becca and I are engaged?"

Cathy flinched. "Are you?"

"No. Like I said before—never was, never will be."

"Okay."

"She didn't care for Hayley's handling of her precious bully?"

"She didn't mention it. Though I'm incredibly proud of Hayley and grateful you caught my mistake."

"You're welcome. You've done a great job raising her. Someday I want kids just like yours."

Cathy gasped, her hands fisted at her mouth. She sighed, blinked, placed—almost forced—her hands one over the other in her lap.

Good, she was thinking along the same lines—a future together for three or more. The thought of laying Cathy down and making more kids with her heated his blood. He shifted, settling his errant thoughts.

"This is ridiculous," he snapped. "Tell me what she said to drive this damn wedge between us."

"Fine, I'll tell you." She crossed her arms over her breasts, crossed her legs, leaned back as if she had all the time in the world.

Well, good! Finally, he would get to the root of the problem and get his sweet Cathy back in his arms. Where she hadn't been in too damn long.

"Virginia didn't say anything I didn't already know. This relationship between us can't work. We have different goals for our lives, different agendas to pursue. You have a life here in Clarence Bay. There's a damn good chance you'll soon be the mayor of a small town with an identity crisis. I've been promoted to a major vice-presidency in an industry that still derides women—a huge achievement I've worked incredibly hard for, for a very long time. I need to be in Toronto, the financial capital of Canada. And you, Mr. Future Mayor, need to be in Clarence Bay. How can you expect to have a relationship when we live two-hundred-and-twenty kilometres apart?"

"It's called driving. Besides, I may not win."

"Don't say that. Of course you'll win."

"If I don't, I'd move to Toronto in a heartbeat if you wanted me to." *It'd kill me, but I'd do I for her.*

She shut her mouth so fast, her teeth clacked. Then she melted before his eyes. He shot off the bench to kneel before her in the chair.

"Whatever happens, we'll figure it out. I'll move there, you'll move here, or we'll get a place in-between and commute. *You* are more important to me than any town."

She raised a hand to his face. "You're still a sentimental fool, Ryan Chisholm." She shook her head, a tender smile playing over her features.

"And you're still my one and only, Cathy Rossetti."

"No," said her mouth. *Yes* said her eyes.

Words of love sprang from his heart to his tongue. Her fingers slid over his parted lips, locking his marriage proposal behind his teeth.

"Only for now. Not forever."

"Now will do." Though he wouldn't push for more at the moment, he was planning on forever.

Pressing his tongue to the fingertips resting against his mouth, he drew a gasp from her. He took her hand, turned the palm up, and kissed the delicate skin from her wrist to the inside of her elbow. She shivered and her mouth opened on a quick inhale. He drew her, unresisting, towards him. Leaning forward, he met her mouth with his.

Soft, oh God, still so soft.

He sighed. She took his breath, gave him her own. He threaded his fingers into her silky dark hair. She spread her other hand on his chest as if to stop him. He leaned into her palm, testing her resolve.

She stared into his eyes. Her fingertips moved, delicately caressing his face. His skin quivered under her touch. Sliding her palm over his pounding heart, she pulled his shirt from his jeans and thrust her hands beneath the fabric, over his heaving ribs to his back. She pulled him closer, buried her face in the curve where his neck met his shoulder, licked and bit down.

A deep shudder rattled down his spine, thrust into his cock. Groaning, he cupped her butt. She hitched forward on the chair, her legs opening wide to nudge him against her center. She yanked off his shirt, not bothering with buttons. Her slow hot hands and quick wet tongue caressed the bare skin of his torso.

Memory-drenched mind-bending kisses lashed his passion. Only Cathy had ever whipped him into a froth of desire that blurred the edges of sanity.

Pressing her breasts against his chest, she invited his touch.

He cupped her luscious flesh, moaned in delight when her nipples greeted his palms with braless joy. He lifted her sweater, bunching it under her arms.

Allowing a single sweet caress, she pushed his hands away. He damn near died of sexual frustration, but not for long. She pulled the sweater up and over her head and he damn near died of lust at the sight of her naked breasts. Lush, full, cherry-tipped, and begging for his kiss, his touch.

If only his knees weren't begging for mercy on the hard floorboards. Joints snapping and cracking, he shoved off the arms of the chair to stand, and smacked his head on the playhouse roof. Clutching his head, he moaned in pain and sagged onto the bench.

Her breasts jiggled with her laughter and his pain receded almost instantly.

"Geez, we were better at this eleven years ago." He moaned, hoping for some sympathy.

"Aw, you poor thing." She knelt between his knees and toyed with his belt buckle. "Tell me where you hurt and I'll kiss it better."

She chuckled, deep and low in her throat. Capturing his gaze with her aroused amber eyes, she undid his belt, his button, his zipper. And just stared at the shadowed opening of his jeans.

She barked a laugh. "Superman? You've got red-and-blue Superman underwear?"

He groaned in embarrassment. "A gag gift for Christmas. Lindsey thought they were cute."

"Stand up. I wanna see." She waggled her eyebrows. "I'll take them off after you show me."

Embarrassed and clothed, or naked and not embarrassed,

which did he prefer? He stood and his jeans slid down his legs as if they couldn't wait for the big reveal.

She twisted his hips to check out the unmistakable logo on his butt. Did she have to laugh so hard? It got a man down. Really it did.

To end the agony, he toed off his sandals, kicked his clothes aside, and got totally naked. Her sudden lack of words and wide gold-glazed eyes cured his embarrassment and spurred his recovery.

"Your turn, dear heart."

A fiery blush swept up her breasts, over her cheekbones and blew into her hair.

"Oh? Do you have special underpants on, too?"

"Umm..."

"C'mon. Off with the shorts."

"Umm..."

He reached across the cramped space and hooked her by the waistband. She struggled unconvincingly to get away. He drew her closer and popped the button on her ancient cut-offs. The zipper obediently slid down by itself and her shorts bit the dust. Now that's what a man liked—self-stripping clothes.

Candy-pink panties with... He pivoted her hips. "Disney princesses on your butt? Don't tell me, Hayley thought they were cute." He leaned down and kissed the side of her neck. "Get rid of them," he breathed in her ear.

She shivered and yanked them off.

They stood, each comfortably dressed in nothing but the pale ghosts of their bathing suits, measuring the changes wrought by the years. Gazes cruised over rounder curves and broader muscles.

"You're gorgeous," they said in unison and smiled. One step each and chest touched breast, thigh touched thigh, past met present. Future didn't matter.

"One final thing has to go." He grasped each side of her glasses and lifted them away to reveal bright desire.

Cathy blinked as her vision blurred then cleared. She smiled and pressed her palms to his abdomen, savoured his smooth warm skin, the sight of his jutting erection, the familiar scent of him. She slid her hands over his tight butt, around to his taut belly, down to his coarse curls. She reveled in the jerking of his hips and the catch in his breath when she clasped his erection and cupped his balls. Her mouth curved in lusty satisfaction—he'd grown in more than height in the past eleven years.

Her insides clenched with anticipation. She tipped her face, inviting his warm wet kiss. Instead of taking her mouth, he pressed delicate kisses to her eyelids, rubbed her nose with his, flicked his tongue over her lower lip.

Ah, she remembered how he liked to drive her crazy with longing.

Shuffling him backwards, she stopped and eyed his height against the length of the bench. "There's no way you're going to fit laying down, so..."

He chuckled when she pushed him to sit on the padded bench and made to climb atop him. His hands on her hips, he stopped her, and chuckled again at her frustrated pout. "Condom, left front pocket, please."

After a quick rummage in his jeans and a quicker rip of a foil packet, she knelt before him, lust in her gilded eyes, and spread his knees. She tiptoed her fingers up his thighs and stomach, scattering goose bumps in all directions. She thumbed his nipples, zipping tingles into his crotch. Leaning forward, she sucked his cock into her mouth. He grunted with surprise, hips flexing upward of their own volition.

No freaking wonder women loved the three-point treatment—two nipples and a....

He closed his eyes and thumped his head against the wooden wall in the struggle to control his driving need. With an audible pop, she released him from his ragged stupor and rolled on the condom with endearing ineptitude. She prowled up his body, straddled his lap, and slid him deep inside her. She wrapped her arms over his shoulders, fisted her hands in his hair, and using her sweet tongue and soft lips, kissed him senseless.

"You always did know what you wanted."

"Always. And right now I want your hands right here." With glittering eyes, she grabbed his wrists and planted his palms on her lovely breasts. Dropping her hands, she clasped his throbbing cock and rubbed her slick folds along the length. "Do like you did once before. Make me cry for happy."

"Whatever you want." Cupping the lush heaviness of her breasts, he rubbed his thumbs lightly over her taut nipples, back and forth, up and down.

"More."

"Yes, dear heart." He tweaked her nipples, hard and quick. Not enough he knew. She growled her encouragement. Laughter bubbled in his chest.

"More. Harder," she commanded in the rough whisper he still adored and obeyed.

"As you wish."

Capturing both begging nipples between his thumbs and forefingers, he tweaked and tugged in an escalating rhythm that was matched by her hips. Her internal grip on his cock tightened to pleasure-pain as she drove against him. Panting, she strained for her climax. When frustration creased her forehead, he leaned forward and pressed a nipple to the edge of his teeth with his tongue. She spread her knees wider, seating him deeper. Crying out, her entire body went rigid with her orgasm except for her juicy pulsing core.

Triumphant tears welled in his eyes at her intense strangled shouts of pleasure. Her breasts were still so sensitive. He grabbed her clenched little ass so she wouldn't topple to the floor. His nose, buried in her quivering chest, filled with her musky female scent of sexual gratification.

After giving herself time to recover and savour him, Cathy opened her eyes to stare at his lust-flushed cheeks and molten-silver eyes. She smiled crookedly and her vision blurred with unshed tears of the promised joy. "I lied earlier. We're much better than before." She smiled wickedly. "But, we're not done yet, are we?"

He rolled his head from side to side, his sandy curls clinging to the boards like an abbreviated halo. Wiggling in his lap, she settled him deeper inside her until he touched the very center of her being. He clamped his hands to her butt and swivelled her hips in rhythm with his thrusts.

She wrapped herself around him as she had done before, loving him now as always. She had but a moment to feel the truth before passion swept them into a bright hot delirium of sighs, moans, and a soul-wrenching climax.

Collapsing against him, she reveled in his sweaty exhausted state. He tucked her head into his shoulder and planted a tender kiss on her hair. She nuzzled the side of his neck, her tears making his skin damper still.

"Ah, Cathy. What have you done to me?"

"Dunno, but you made me cry for happy."

"My job here is done." He squeezed her tight and broke his word. "I love you too much to let you go. Marry me, Cathy."

Tears of joy turned bitter with guilt leaked from her tight-shut eyes. Cathy gulped down the toxic brew of emotion. "I can't, my sweet sentimental fool. Forgive me, but I can't."

Marry me.

In the morning, the words still ricocheted inside Cathy's skull like a demented ping-pong ball.

Don't go. I'll go with you.

He'd ignored all her arguments of space and time, goals and agendas. She grimaced into her empty coffee cup. Last night, after their world-shattering sex, she'd called Ryan a sentimental fool and then left him in the playhouse. How could she be so utterly cruel?

A plan began to grow in her mind. Still tell Ryan before the election. Take full blame for his apparent dishonesty. Marry Ryan, give Hayley a daddy. Poke the damn Virginia in the eye. She bobbed her head from side to side, weighing ways and means. Not an easy job. But she'd faced down difficulties before.

"Caterina, what are you doing?" Mamma asked in Italian.

Cathy focused on her task of putting the coffee pot—in the fridge. The carton of cream sat on the coffee maker. The hissing stench of burning wax fired off the smoke alarm. *Imbecille.* She snatched up the melting carton and tossed it in the sink then grabbed a tea towel and flapped at the alarm. The sudden silence rang with beautiful words tempting her to damn her fears and take what she wanted.

I love you. Marry me.

"Caterina? What is going on in your head to make you so absent-minded?"

"Nothing."

Mamma harrumphed. "*Bugiardo.*" Liar.

Weary from hidden tears and lost sleep, Cathy begged. "Please, I'd rather not talk about it, Mamma."

"Is Hayley worrying you? She looks like a trouble-maker."

Cathy rolled her eyes. "No, I'm not worried about Hayley." Her father, on the other hand....

How Cathy longed to blurt out her problems, to discuss them rationally. Unfortunately, after a bitter battle between the sisters, a determined Zia Yola had left for Toronto yesterday. Hopefully, Zia's long-lost love brought her fewer problems than Cathy brought to Ryan. Zia Yola deserved some easy times.

Still on the rampage from her lost argument with Zia Yola, Mamma thumped her cane on the floor. "You listen to me. She'll give you trouble a whole lot sooner than you'll be ready to deal with it."

Cathy rubbed at the pain blooming in her temples. "Whatever."

Mamma snorted and jabbed a finger in Cathy's direction. "You were exactly the same. All cute affection until you turned thirteen."

Cathy groaned. Not again. She didn't want or need a scolding about her bad behaviour as a teen. What difference did it make now?

"I know what you're thinking. Regrets. For having the child."

"Regrets? Yes, but not for Hayley, never for Hayley. For...other things."

"Your life is not what it should have been, Caterina. You should have found a rich man to take care of you. Not be burdened with a child you didn't want."

Cathy's head ached from banging it against the wall of her mother's disapproval. "Mamma, stop making assumptions. I wanted my baby from the moment I knew of her existence. I loved her from her first breath. You didn't want another mouth to feed, another body to clothe. You suggested, ever so kindly, that I get rid of her."

"You deserved better than the struggle, the shame, of an unwed mother."

"I've said it before and I'll say it again—"

"*Sì*, Caterina. You say there is no shame anymore in birthing a bastard. All is sweetness and light. Tra-la. But what of your child? She has no father. No family. No name."

Mamma's vicious mockery squeezed the air from Cathy's lungs and tested her love for her mother. Cathy gazed at the woman who'd given her life and a sudden truth hit her like a slap in the face.

"You're not talking about Hayley, are you? I've always wondered if you loved me. Now I know."

Moving in sticky slow motion, Cathy cleaned the kitchen. She half-expected a dramatic fainting spell. Instead, Mamma—*Dio mio,* how the word hurt—watched with an almost scientific detachment.

Done with her work, Cathy faced Mamma. "And you wondered why I was such a bad girl." She shrugged off her defeat, made a decision. "Hayley and I will leave when Zia Yola gets back. You're doing so well, she'll be able to manage on her own."

She'd tell Ryan before she left and set up a visitation schedule. He'd retract his love and his proposal. She'd leave town with an empty life and an empty heart. At least Hayley would have her daddy-wish granted.

Giving her mother a wide berth, Cathy headed out of the kitchen. Her mother stopped her motion with the only words having any power.

"*Mi dispiace.*" I'm sorry.

The words caught Cathy like a fist between the shoulder blades. Grabbing the doorframe, she turned and leaned against the solid dark wood. Her mother's back bowed to rest her forehead on hands clasped over the cane planted between her black-shrouded knees. Her thickening white curls captured the thin gray light of another rainy day. Had Mamma said she was sorry? Doubting her hearing, Cathy remained in the doorway, twisting her fingers in the fraying edges of her cut-offs.

"I found the thought of you leaving so distressing I pushed you away. *Stupido, sì?*" An astonishing humility flattened her mother's voice.

"*Non so.* Not stupid. But incredibly careless to throw away the gift of love." Like she was careless with Ryan's love? Something to think about later.

"*Sì.* Careless." Mamma unfurled to her usual stiff-necked posture. "I have been harsh with you. I did it for the best, to keep you safe." She shrugged, tilted her head in the classic Italian for gesture *go figure.* "You were so determined not to be safe. You wanted your friends and your fun. And so you had them."

Cathy nodded. "Lots of fun. Rebellion gave my life the spice that was missing at home—a lesson I plan to use with Hayley."

Mamma's face softened. "Your daughter is precious beyond price."

"Yes she is."

"She will still bring you tears."

"I expect so."

"She is Ryan Chisholm's child."

After her mother's apology, nothing surprised Cathy. "How did you guess?"

"I overheard you and Yola on the porch that day. Francie was a little older than Yola, but they were so close. It was terribly sad to see such a lovely woman waste away. She was always so *vivace*. Hayley is very like her other *nonna*—she has no fear."

"No, she doesn't." Unless you considered fish in the lake. But then her daddy helped her overcome that fear.

"I am glad you didn't give her up. You have done an excellent job raising her."

Nope, Cathy was wrong. A complete reversal of opinion, plus compliments, from her mother topped an apology for shock value.

"Thank you. Though I don't know how I managed without Helen. She's always known everything."

Mamma's mouth twisted. "Yes, Helen knows a great deal."

Cathy puzzled over what Helen's extensive knowledge had to do with anything.

"You've already told Yola. She was more of a mother to you than I. You haven't told Ryan yet."

Cathy stopped being surprised now—numb would have to do.

"He would be claiming her if he knew," Mamma continued.

"I think he wants to claim her anyway, as your child. Ryan and Hayley are like you and your father, so close." She bowed her head again, her fingers working an imaginary rosary. "Antonio treasured you beyond anyone or anything. Even me." She scoffed at herself. "Do not laugh, a grown woman jealous of her own child. Pitiful."

"Mamma, no—"

Her mother ended the discussion with a slash of her hand. "May I ask a promise of you?"

"Depends."

"Tell Ryan because you must. Tell Hayley. But please, do not tell the town."

"Why shouldn't we tell the town?" Revelation was a package deal, tell all or tell none.

Mamma sighed. "When our parents passed, may they rest in peace, I was twenty-six and Yola was eight. Already my sister, she became my child. Antonio and I married and you came along. When we moved to Clarence Bay, people gossiped that Yola was my illegitimate daughter from a man before my husband. Antonio was devastated. The scandal died, but he never forgot the insult."

Cathy dare not tell her mother the rumour still lived.

"Typical Sicilian, that Antonio—hot-headed, hot-blooded." She eyed Cathy. "You were so like him. Explosive! Where has your passion gone?" She shrugged and answered herself. "Your child took it from you, of course. When you told us you were pregnant, I didn't want more scandal for our family. That is why I pushed for an adoption. You surprised me again. It seems you have taken care of the problem. The town thinks Hayley is the daughter of some man in Toronto. Let them believe the story. I can't bear the scandal. For all of us, but especially for your proud father's memory, don't tell the town."

"Paul, where have all the women gone?" Ryan hung up the phone in frustration, pushed away from the oak desk in his home office and leaned back in the leather chair. He hadn't seen them while out campaigning today. They weren't answering their phones. The town wasn't that damn big. Where were they?

Paul looked over from the large wall calendar dotted with Ryan's public appearances. "Where are you looking, because I see plenty of women? Or, more to the point, which *one* are you looking for? As if I didn't know."

"I can't find Cathy or Becca or Yola or even Hayley."

Paul twirled the marker in his fingers. "Okay, I can figure three of those. What do you want with an ex-girlfriend who once presumed to be your fiancée?"

"Her mother said something to put Cathy's nose way out of joint and I want to know what it was."

"Dangerous territory, my friend, getting between the current and the ex and her mother. Avoid it at all costs. Or you will live to regret it."

"Some expert advice from an older man?" Rolling his sleeves to his elbow, Ryan lifted a brow at Paul.

"Only six years, Grasshopper."

"Whatever. Where are the women I want to find?"

Paul gazed over Ryan's shoulder to the view of his driveway. "Hold that thought 'cause you've got a visitor."

"Cathy." Ryan couldn't stop the joy ringing in his voice.

Paul winced and threw Ryan a puzzled glance. "What would Virginia Carleton-Grant want with you? You finished with

Becca before you started with Cathy. Right?"

"Damn straight I did." Ryan twisted around to watch Mrs. Carleton-Grant climb gracefully from her car and smooth her suit. "Brace yourself, Paul, looks like we're about to get screwed." Grimly determined to get to the bottom of Mrs. Carleton-Grant's problems with Cathy, Ryan wrenched the front door open before she rang the bell. "Mrs. Carleton-Grant, hello."

Her brows rose at his sudden aggressive appearance. "I've come for a chat."

He leaned against the doorframe. "How nice. Did you want to make a campaign contribution?"

"A contribution?" She tipped her head to one side, smiling like a satisfied spider. "Yes, I like that. A very special contribution." She stepped forward. "Do you mind if I come in?"

Trepidation pricked along his spine, his armpits got a little damp. Witness, he needed a witness to whatever was coming. He shook off the odd thought.

They engaged in a brief stare-down. Ryan ceded and stepped back because she still had info he wanted.

"By the way, have you seen Cathy lately?" she asked.

A powerful urge to protect Cathy rose from deep within his core. Protect? From Virginia Carleton-Grant? "Last night. Why?"

Her posture stiffened to impossible heights while her gaze briefly turned internal like she debated with herself. She sniffed delicately and cleared her face of all expression. "I think she lost an earring the other evening and I thought you could give it to her." She slid a hand into her jacket pocket then dropped an unfamiliar diamond ear stud into his open palm. "Is this hers?"

"I don't think so. Why don't you hold onto it? I'll tell her about it and if it's hers, she can get it from you."

"Thank you," she took the earring and sashayed down his hall, through his kitchen and into his office as if sizing the place up for a remodel. He swallowed and tugged at the collar and tie getup he'd put on for a breakfast meeting at the Masonic Lodge.

"Paul, not that it isn't a delightful surprise to find you here, but I was hoping to speak to Ryan privately." Her words hustled Ryan into his office. His campaign manager had risen from his chair.

"Paul, sit," Ryan ordered. Paul blinked and sat back down in the plaid armchair.

"Mrs. Carleton-Grant, a seat?" Ryan indicated the couch then sat behind his desk, desperately needing to at least pretend to be in control.

Virginia smoothed the back of her skirt, eased onto the brown leather couch. She crossed her legs at the ankles and swung them to the side then arranged her skirt and purse.

Ryan guessed at her real reason for showing up. "Please don't tell me your contribution is Becca. That you want us back together again. That you'll withdraw your support, and your husband's, if I don't propose again. Even if it will simply hurt Becca in the long run."

"I admit that was my initial intention. It's a mother's job to give her daughter everything she wants. However, I've changed my mind and have a different sort of contribution to make. Though I'm not sure you want Paul to hear what I have to say."

Paul cut a teasing glance at Ryan and grinned at Virginia. "Telling tales out of turn, are we?"

Virginia focused a sardonic smile on Paul. "Hmm, depends

on how well you know your candidate." She adjusted her watch to the precise center of her wrist. "I heard a story lately that I thought might amuse you." She spoke to Paul though Ryan felt her slanting gaze as if he was a squeaking mouse under her cat's paw. Sweat popped on his palms.

Paul smiled, broad and full of confidence. "I stand behind my candidate completely."

"Oh? No matter what he's done?"

Paul eyeballed Ryan, nodded, and turned back to the sleek blonde. "No matter what. He's a good man."

"So fortunate he has such a steadfast friend. He'll need you."

"For fuck's sake, will you cut the crap and get to your point?" Ryan erupted.

Virginia shook her head, a mockingly-sad look on her face. "Such language your friend uses."

Paul leaned forward. "Virginia, what's on your mind?"

She dropped all pretence to coyness. "Well, Paul, what would say if your *good man* had fathered a child and abandoned the mother?"

Paul goggled at her for a long moment then started to laugh, tossing his head back and slapping his thigh. Even Ryan chuckled heartily.

Virginia was not pleased. Her eyes narrowed and her mouth prissed up at their mockery. "How typical. The men have joined forces." Her voice hardened. She rose and tucked her purse under her arm, strolled towards the door. "Well, Ryan, I suggest you begin looking through your old family photographs. Your mother or your grandmother, perhaps? You might find a photo of interest to—" She pivoted, paused, and tossed her grenade lightly. "Cathy Rossetti." She grinned smugly and strolled out.

"Cathy Rossetti?" Paul repeated, staring at Ryan in confusion. "Huh?"

The grenade exploded with gleeful abandon in Ryan's mind. Fragments of dialog, curtailed glances, fractured images shifted and re-settled. His blood roared through his body, banged in his ears, battered his heart against his ribcage.

Hayley.

Hayley was his.

His daughter.

"Ryan!" Paul's shout paused the intense mental gymnastics.

Ryan blinked, breathed. "Yeah?"

"Yeah?" Paul ranted. "All you can say is yeah?"

"Yes?"

Paul growled at him, rose from his chair, and strode to the window to watch Virginia leave.

"Yes. Cathy Rossetti and I had a child, Hayley. Damn it. I assumed, like the whole town did, that Cathy was divorced, that Hayley was her ex-husband's kid. You knew when I knew. Though I should have figured it out sooner." Ryan leaned forward, head in hands, tugging at his hair, trying to think better, swifter, smarter. "God, I am such a dumbass."

"I'll say." Paul agreed sarcastically.

A horn tooted gaily as Virginia drove away.

Ryan's world had gone sideways in the time it took an angry woman to make her exit.

"Shit!" Paul shouted. "What's she gonna do with that precious tidbit? She could screw you forever! I'm going after her—do some damage control." He shot out of the house, slammed into his car, and followed Virginia at the speed of light.

Calm as the lake under a dead wind, Ryan shrugged his

shoulders. "Tell you what Paul," he said to the space recently occupied by his best friend. "You find out what she wants in exchange for her silence and I'll get out the family album."

"Ryan?" Hours later, at the edge of night, Cathy's voice called from his front hall. "Are you here? The door's unlocked."

He debated whether or not to reply.

"Ryan?" Footsteps moved through the house, pausing briefly in the kitchen.

Goaded, he called, "I'm in here." *I think. I was earlier today. Now? I'm not so sure.* "In the living room."

"Ryan? Why didn't you answer?" She spoke from the shadowed doorway. "Why are you sitting in this dim light? Did you get my message?" She crossed the room to turn on a lamp.

He closed the photo album on his mother's smiling little-girl face, set the book on the side table beside his chair, and folded his hands in his lap. His eyes tracked Cathy's curvy shape in a printed dress to a second lamp, a third lamp, blinking against each flood of light. Finally, she stood before him with a playful scowl on her pretty face and her arms akimbo. He should be repelled, not drawn, to slide his tongue over her pouty bottom lip.

"Don't tell me. You worked out my surprise," she said.

"Shame on me."

"I hope you don't mind, I cancelled our reservation at the Inn. I thought you'd prefer a home-cooked meal for your birthday."

He flinched with the surprise of the ordinary. "I forgot."

"Racking up too many birthdays to bother celebrating?" She ran teasing fingertips over the rasp of his whiskers.

"No, not enough birthdays." He let her puzzlement deepen.

"I've missed ten of them."

The colour leached from her face, apparently taking her strength with it, as she collapsed gracelessly onto the couch. Odd how comical she looked. He lifted the crystal glass from the table at his elbow and sipped, barely noticing the fine peaty whiskey.

Her jaw worked several times before her words sounded. "Who?"

"I heard an interesting story lately." He would have winced if he'd been able to climb out of the deep dark well trapping his emotions.

Her colour surged back, eyes narrowing, fists clenching. "Virginia."

"Clever guess. How many others knew before I did?"

Her mouth clamped shut.

"It's not important. I'm merely curious."

"Zia Yola, Mamma, Helen."

"So Hayley's still in the dark, too. Nice to know we have something in common. Other than our curly hair, of course." He tugged on the curl by his ear which had fascinated her two nights ago—a night of false loving and rejection. A blow from a mighty invisible hammer slugged him in the gut. He held his breath until he absorbed the pain.

"Why didn't you tell me back then? I would have married you, worked through school."

"We were so young. We'd agreed to separate lives. Remember? You had your own schooling, your own goals. And I had—"

"The Plan which had no place for me."

"I know you would have married me."

"Damn straight I would have."

"I didn't want you to worry about me when your mother was so ill."

Another blow fractured the hard casing around his emotions.

"Did it not occur to you Mom would have fought harder if she'd known? I might still have her." He shot from the chair and flung his glass into the fireplace. Shards twinkled amid the ashes, like stars fallen to earth. He grabbed Cathy by her shoulders, hauled her from her seat, and got in her face. "Mom adored you. She would have adored Hayley. I adored you. I would have loved any child you gave me."

"May I explain?" she whispered, eyes huge, lips quivering.

"Can you?" he demanded. She trembled in his grip.

"Yes," she cried.

"Go ahead. Explain to me why *you* have been a mother to *my child* for ten years and *I*—" He swallowed hard against the weight of emotion in his throat. "I have been *nobody* to her—to you." His voice broke on the last word. He released her and she plopped back to the couch.

He turned his back on her, his face buried in shaking hands. Tears dripped through his cupped fingers to splat on his shoes.

Behind him, she wept quietly.

Around them, night closed in, the lamps cast pools of silent light in the gathering gloom. Her hand crept into the crook of his elbow.

"Don't." He jerked away, across the room to sit on the back of the chair, facing away from her. He gazed out the window at the dark waves heaving under the moon far below. Jamming his heels into the carpet, he forbade himself to follow the glimmering path to nowhere.

Reflected in the dark glass, Cathy rocked back and forth, flattened hands stuffed between her clamped thighs, staring at the floor. "Yes, I had my Plan. And you had yours. Can you imagine what our life would have been like? You'd have skipped university and gone to work for your dad. And hated every second. You wouldn't have risked buying a run-down hardware store and transforming it. You would have been trapped. I'd have been miserable with regret. Sure, we would have started out loving each other, but how soon do you think the grinding pressure of that life that would have turned our love to hate? Just ask Glory. And how do imagine Hayley would have responded to that atmosphere?"

He stilled deep inside, listening to her reasons, acknowledging them, yet resisting just the same.

She lifted her pale face. "Mamma wanted me to adopt the baby out, even suggested an abortion. She wanted me to get rid of my baby. So I never came back, never told them, never told you. They only guessed. All of them guessed, but only recently."

Each drop of information dripped into the stone well of his doubt and despair, rippling the surface with reason. An unwilling sympathy stirred in him for a pregnant young girl, alone and abandoned, terrified.

He turned slightly to speak over his shoulder. "Where did you go?"

"I went to Helen Lomax, a childhood friend of Yola's from when my family lived in Toronto. We share a house now, Helen, Hayley and me. She's been an incredibly good friend. She insisted I put your name on Hayley's birth certificate."

So Cathy had been cared for, had a mother figure to stand beside her. Better than the ex-husband the town had assumed.

Someday he'd have to thank the unknown Helen. Reluctant understanding growing, he turned towards her.

"What's Hayley's middle name?"

"Francine."

"After my mom?" He didn't know what to make of the gooey sensation clogging his heart.

Cathy nodded.

Headlights streaked across the fireplace. Presumably, Paul had returned.

"Why didn't you say something when you came back to town? Lindsey introduced me as her uncle. Hayley shook hands with me like a stranger."

"I thought you were married to Meg with three-point-five children. Remember? And then I thought you were engaged to Becca. Remember?"

"And then why not?"

"The election. The news about the BDC development deal. How important it is to the town for you to win. How important it is to you." She raised her head and met his gaze. "So the scandal wouldn't kill your chance to be the best damn mayor this town ever had!"

"You didn't tell me about my dau—" His vocal chords tightened. He lifted his chin, rolled his shoulders to loosen up, and tried again. "You kept my daughter from me for the good of Clarence Bay?"

She stood and walked towards him. "I know it sounds so horrible, but please listen to me. You said you'd follow me to Toronto. But you'd die down there. You love this place. You wouldn't be happy anywhere else but Clarence Bay." She waved her hand north towards town. "You can't look at yourself in the mirror every morning if you don't do the best you can for your town. So yes, I kept my secret for your own good, for your redemption in the eyes of your town, for your dream. For you."

"All excellent reasons," Paul said as he strolled into the room.

Ryan put up his hand to stop Paul. "Not a good time, my friend. Cathy and I have more important stuff to sort through. Come back tomorrow."

"Don't you want to know what happened with Virginia?"

Ryan sighed raggedly and let his hand flop to his side. "Fine, tell me. And then go."

"After a knock-down drag-out fight, she surrendered. She won't say anything. Word of honour. You owe me for some incredibly fast talking."

"Do you believe her?"

"Yes."

"Then I do owe you one. And yes, Hayley is mine. Cathy and I will tell the town our way. As soon as we figure it out."

"What? No!" Paul said. "You can't jeopardize your position. Baylor is narrowing your lead in recent polls."

"We have to. It's the right thing to do. The people need to know who they're voting for. Remember my campaign promise? Clean and clear. Honest and open. It's more than my philosophy for government. It's how I run my life. It's exactly what Dad would not have done." He shot a narrow-eyed stare at Cathy. "Wish more people were honest like that."

Cathy's face reddened and she dropped her gaze.

"Ryan, wait. Give yourself time to absorb the news. Think what it will do to your campaign."

"That's stalling. Do you seriously think I can absorb the new me—I'm a father for fuck's sake—in a few of lousy weeks?"

"Were you not prepared to be a father if we got married?" Cathy piped up.

"Married?" Paul, all over the idea, rubbed his hands with glee. "This town loves a wedding. Two old flames with their little secret. I can feel the warm and cozy already."

"No!" Ryan's shout rattled the windows. He stood and leaned on his hands over his desk. "We are not getting married to make the town happy or to get votes. That's just sick!" He glared at Cathy. "The last ten years of my life are a lie. Who the hell am I?"

"You're the mayor who will help this town redefine itself and guide it into the future," Paul said.

"I'm running on the principle of honesty. Not secrets revealed only to con and manipulate. I am *not* my father. Don't you get it?" Ryan's throat tightened with every word.

Cathy shuffled her feet and exchanged glances with Paul who felt less like a good friend to Ryan and more like a despised spin-doctor.

"And don't you get that sometimes a whole town is worth more than one man's sense of honour?" Paul argued.

"May I make the argument personal? Umm, more personal." Apology lay beneath Cathy's request.

"What?" Ryan turned on her, snarling with frustration.

She cringed at the whiplash of the word. Paul moved toward her as if to protect her and Ryan choked on the irony.

"Well, spit it out."

Ryan expected her to get huffy and leave. Good, save him the trouble of kicking them both out.

Courageously, she squared her shoulders and pushed her glasses up her nose. "You've heard the rumour about Yola being

Mamma's illegitimate child?"

"So? It's ancient news."

"Mamma's afraid the nightmare will start all over again. She wants to protect Papà's memory and I don't think her condition will be improved by the scandal—"

"You think I want to do anything for a woman who wanted to throw away my child?" he shouted.

"No. I want you to keep the secret for Zia Yola. For the love you have for her. She's just starting to gain some strength around Mamma, just starting to get out again, to reconnect with her friends. Can you imagine how people would greet her? The scandal would destroy an innocent woman. Can you live with the collateral damage?"

CHAPTER 13

Reunion

At about the same time, in Toronto's west end, in a three-storey home overlooking High Park, an unfamiliar woman stared back at Yola from the mirror in Helen's spare bedroom. Gone was her long stringy hair and hideous housedress. A short neat bob and a stylish teal pantsuit replaced the ugliness dictated by Lucia. Even mirror-Yola's face seemed younger. She drew back her shoulders to show off her generous breasts, tucked in her slender tummy.

I am never wearing black again.

"Forty-five sits well on you," Helen said in her crisp British accent as she rested an affectionate hand on Yola's shoulder. "Now stop fussing and get going."

"Does Caterina have your number?"

Helen gave an exaggerated huff of impatience.

Yola groaned and flapped her hand. "Of course she does. I don't know what's come over me."

"Umm..." Helen rolled her eyes, waggled her head from side to side, doubting Yola's sanity. "Could it, or rather he, go by the name of Leo?"

Yola rejoiced in the warm womanly conversation of her oldest and dearest friend. Especially when compared to the harsh judgmental fear-mongering of the fight with Lucia.

"She's got Ryan's number if she needs help." Worry creased Yola's forehead. "Something's happened. I can feel it."

"They're in love again and everything's grand. Isn't it?"

"So it seemed. Now something's gone wrong. Caterina didn't say anything when I called, but she didn't sound happy. For once, Lucia is behaving herself, so it's probably Ryan." Yola's hand fluttered to her rose-painted mouth. "*Dio mio,* Ryan must have found out."

"Secrets are always difficult to deal with when they come out." Helen gave her a pointed look. "The longer they've been buried, the greater the impact."

The doorbell rang and startled them both.

"Saved by the bell," Helen said with teasing smile. "Leo is right on time."

Tension knotting her stomach and legs, Yola stumbled in her hurry to get down the stairs. She rescued herself and rushed to open the door.

And there he stood, Leonardo Giacometti, her one and only love. Her hand fluttered to her wildly beating heart. *Santo cielo.* He looked exactly the same to eyes that had ached for the sight of him. His dark gaze still glowed with vigour and his dark curls were still plentiful. His youthful promise was fully realized in this tall expensively-clad Italian man.

"Yolanda deBartolo, is it really you? Looking as beautiful as the day we parted so very long ago?" His accented voice was deeper now. Moments passed while Yola stared at her once-upon-a-time lover.

"Why don't you come in, Leo?" Helen's pragmatic suggestion prodded Yola.

"*Dio mio*, of course, come in, come in. I'll only be a moment." Yola flew up the stairs to retrieve her purse, almost tumbling back down them in her unaccustomed heels. *Zitta, what a clumsy oaf.*

Kissing her cheek, Helen whispered, "I won't wait up and I'll cover for you if Lucia calls—just like in the old days." Louder she said, "Have a good time."

Yola halted on the stoop, listening as Helen's footsteps went into the front room and a lamp burst into light. She and Leo had talked briefly on the phone to arrange this meeting. Yola wanted to save all the rest until she sat face to face with him. Suddenly, she had nothing to say. *Imbecille.*

"Come, my dear, we'll be late for our reservation." He held out his elbow with old-world courtesy and Yola settled her hand in the warm crook. He gazed down at her as he patted her hand. Heat moved through her, stirring her body. He cupped her cheek with his warm palm, setting up fine tremors in every nerve ending. For one tender terrifying moment, she thought he meant to kiss her.

"Come, *cara*, we have the evening before us." He ushered her down the wide stone steps to a shiny black limousine. A chauffeur opened the rear door and they settled in the roomy back seat.

"*Pronto, signore?*" the chauffeur asked permission to set off.

"*Si, avanti.*"

They drove away from the curb in a dignified surge of power and headed downtown.

Yola nervously stroked the soft black leather. "You shouldn't have hired a fancy limousine for us."

Leo took her chilly hand firmly in his large warm one. "The car is mine. Carlo is my employee. His wife is my chef."

"You didn't say—"

"That I'm very rich? No, it is not something I brag about."

"Was your family successful in England?"

"My unfortunate father did not do very well. I did better." No disparagement of his father sounded in this bald statement. Only simple facts. And a lot of pride in the last three words. "I did well when I expanded my hotel chain into the Mediterranean. We have lived in Italy for many years now." His accent was a charming blend of British and Italian.

She stared out the window. "I have not done much—an ordinary grocery store clerk in an ordinary small town. I quit recently to care for my sister when she was diagnosed with cancer."

"I'm so sorry."

"She's much better now."

"I'm sure your excellent care helped her." He caressed the back of her hand with his thumb, bringing her gaze to his face. Tingles ran up her arm and danced in her heart. "An ordinary life does not make you an ordinary person, *cara*."

She ignored the tingles and the warmth of his endearment. "Helen said your wife passed on. May I offer my condolences? She'll be missed, I know."

He shrugged eloquently. "We had a good marriage. But since her passing, I thought about you. Wondered how you were, what your life had become."

"I thought of you for many years, but—"

"Yes. Let us blame the circumstances of our youth."

Yola smiled and turned to watch the city flow by as they picked up speed along Lakeshore Boulevard. When he tugged her hand, she looked into his handsome face. A small scar paled the skin beneath his left eye. His mouth was still a lush invitation.

"Why the little smile, Yola?"

She couldn't stop a second twitch of her lips. "You didn't used to be so formal in your speech. Shall I call you Leonardo?"

He sighed deeply and shook his head. "I don't often speak English now, so it has become a little stiff. Especially when I am nervous."

"You're nervous? *Dio mio*, so am I. I'm terrified of you."

"Why?"

She assessed his carefully groomed hair, custom-tailored suit, wafer-thin gold watch, gleaming shoes, and his private limousine. "Look at all this luxury. You've done so incredibly well."

He tapped his chest. "Inside, I'm still the boy who used to buy you veal sandwiches and Brio at the bakery on St Clair. Do you remember?"

She smiled fondly. "How could I have forgotten? Those sandwiches were so messy and so good."

"You know, I've never found their equal anywhere in Europe. Though the goodness was more to do with you than with the secret tomato sauce, I think."

Yola chuckled and the tension drained away, leaving two old friends to reminisce about young love.

At the end of the evening, Leo escorted her to Helen's front stoop. The exterior lamp had been discreetly left off. Light from the hallway streamed through the fanlight and the narrow windows beside the glossy black door.

"Thank you for a wonderful evening, Leo. I can't remember the last time I had such a good time. The play was so funny."

"You're very welcome, *cara mia.*"

"W-would you like to come in for a drink?"

"Yes, please." Leo insisted on taking Yola's key and opening the door for her. She led him into the front parlour where the thoughtful Helen had laid out a selection of drinks. Yola poured brandy and Frangelico into two glasses. They sat on the couch, a single lamp casting its warm glow.

Leo sipped his drink. "May I see you again?"

Joy skipped through Yola like a giddy young girl. "Tell me why you are really here, thirty years later."

"Why did I not come sooner?" He nodded. "It's a fair question." He reached inside his jacket for his billfold and held it, unopened, in his lap. "When my family and I moved to England, I thought of you constantly, daydreamed of returning to you. I missed you with the ardent ferocity of youth. Then my father was dismissed from his lucrative position, went into a depression, and committed suicide. I was left as the head of a shamed family."

The bald recital of facts didn't mask the anguish, pain, and worry she heard in his voice. Her gentle heart suffered with him.

"I don't regret marrying the daughter of my wealthy boss. We loved each other and were good together. My reward is four handsome sons. Barbara, my wife, passed three years ago, God rest her soul." He gazed into his brandy, sipped, and set it on the coffee table. Opening his billfold, he withdrew a small photo. He ran his thumb tenderly over its surface.

Yola resolved to be suitably responsive to a photo of his wife. She was struck speechless to see, not a blonde English girl, but her own self at fifteen. Worn and faded and well-fingered, the photo had been laminated at the last moment to prevent disintegration.

"I carried you next to my heart during the early years. Foolishly sentimental, but there you go. A few months ago, I found your photo again in an old box I was going through." He tucked the photo away. "I was never unfaithful to Barbara, but I believe a small bit of me always belonged to you."

Yola doubted, yet savoured, the devotion in his eyes. "I don't know what to say. It seems so improbable. I'm so forgettable."

"Not to me. This summer when I came to Toronto on business, I couldn't stop myself and went for a walk in the neighbourhood. I knocked on your door, hoping you were still there. The young people sent me to the next house. Helen answered and remembered me at first sight. We shared some laughs about old times."

Yola smiled. "Yes, Helen told me you were looking for me. I wanted to see you so very much... I feared and hoped...and here we are."

His gaze slipped from her eyes to her lips.

All moisture evaporated from her mouth on a single indrawn breath.

"May I kiss you?" he asked.

"Oh, yes, please. I've waited all night to see—"

"If the magic still lives?"

She nodded, shy and girlish once more. He set her drink on the table. Tugging her to stand with him before the unlit fire, he drew her slowly into his embrace. She dipped her head in sudden embarrassment at her first kiss in thirty years that didn't land on her cheek. He lifted her face and her lips parted in anticipation. His eyes gleamed dark and deep, his lips curved in a gentle smile.

"I did not know how much I missed you," he murmured. Then his lips met hers in sweet short kisses. She purred her encouragement and he returned for deeper kisses, drugging kisses. Kisses that swept her away to a place of passion.

Yes, the magic still lived.

Until her secret killed it.

Yola gasped at the chased golden bracelet in the velvet box. "Leo, you're spoiling me. You have to stop." She closed the box with a painful reluctance and held it out to him.

He raised his hands, palms out, refusing to take the gift back. "It is to celebrate our anniversary."

"Our anniversary? It's only been two weeks!" She'd spent the days constantly in his company, wandering over the city like avid tourists. The nights, oh, the last few nights in his bed, were intimate and sweet.

She thrust the box at him again. He walked over to the large windows overlooking Lake Ontario and its islands.

Determined not to take advantage of him, she pursued him across the hotel suite. He slipped out onto the penthouse balcony and around the furniture grouping. When she followed, he tucked her to his side and drew her to the railing. She slipped the box into his jacket pocket.

He shook his head and said nothing more about the gift. "I know how foolish I appear. A widower with four nearly-grown sons, making eyes at his old girlfriend." He pressed a finger to her mouth, stopping her protest. "I don't care if I am foolish. I hope with all my heart to spend more time with you."

"Leo, don't say such things. I'm leaving tomorrow. Lucia needs me."

"My darling, I must speak while we are together. I do not wish to lose you again."

She gazed out to the sailboats flying across the water, wishing she could sail far away from the moment to come. "Why?"

"I love you, *mio tesoro.*"

My treasure. The words melted her heart. "How can you? Foolish or not, it's still only been fourteen days."

"Days measured in moments are much longer than ordinary days, so your argument is useless."

Dio mio, her heart fluttered at his romantic words. His old trait of brushing aside opposition had strengthened over the years. However, Yola had forged her own brand of stubbornness.

"What will your sons say? They'll call me a gold digger." In addition, much more once they knew how wicked she truly was.

"They'll congratulate me for finding my old love and making her my new love. They'll be very happy because I am very happy."

"Oh, Leo. I don't have your faith in them. I'm a nobody from nowhere. I own nothing more than my clothes and some money in the bank. What could you possibly want of me?"

"Yolanda, I am getting a little angry with you," he scolded gently. "You're a loving giving woman with gentle hands and a warm heart."

He sank to his knee, took her cold limp hands in his warm

strong grip. "What I want of you, my beautiful darling, is to allow me to adore you with all my heart for the rest of my life. Please, say you love me and that you'll marry me."

Tears welled in her eyes and spilled down her cheeks. She was the happiest, and the most miserable, woman in the world.

He loved her. Such joy swelled in her heart.

Soon, he would hate her. Such fear shook her to the core.

"Yola, what's wrong?"

Both hands fisted over her mouth, she stepped back and turned away.

"Why do you cry?" he pleaded.

Her loneliness echoed in the cry of gulls on the wing. Her soul ached with the pain she would give him.

"I see. You don't love me back. It's just the pathetic illusion of a lonely man." He sat back on his bent knee, his head sunk in his hands.

Her throat seized on her secret, tears ran down her knuckles.

Slow as a tired old man, he stood and turned to the balcony door. "Carlo will take you home."

In agony, she listened to his sad footsteps move down the balcony.

"No! Leo, no! Come back!" She chased after him. Tears blurring her vision, she stumbled into a wicker table and fell to the cold hard stone.

"*Cara*!" Leo thrust the hapless table across the space, scooped her up into his strong arms. Placing her gently on the balcony's couch, he held her close while she wept all the tears dammed inside her soul for thirty years. She snuffled to a stop and he offered her his linen handkerchief.

"*Cara mia,* why you cry so hard?"

"I have to tell you something that will make you hate me."

He grasped her hands. "First, please, tell me the love in your eyes is also in your heart."

"*Sì, ti amo.* I love you with all my heart."

He dropped his head back on a huge sigh of relief. "Thanks be to God. How can I hate you when you make me so happy?"

"Because I've done something so horrible—" She hesitated, tried to shift herself away from him. His grip tightened. "No my dear, I can't let you go."

"You will."

"Tell me what it is and I will judge whether or not I hate you."

Words and phrases, English and Italian, swirled in Yola's mind. If only she could find the words to calm his expected anger. Such words did not exist.

"You have a daughter and a granddaughter."

He looked faintly puzzled at this earth-shattering news. "No, I only have sons and I have no grandchildren as yet."

Cupping his face, she gazed directly into his beautiful brown eyes, measuring every nuance of his passionate Italian soul. "You don't understand. *I* gave birth to your daughter and *she* has a daughter."

The wheels of his mind turned behind his blank expression. "You mean to tell me I got you pregnant?" Horror-struck, he gaped at her. "*Madonna mia,* you were only...*sixteen* when you gave birth?"

"*Sì.*"

"And I had vanished when my family left the country." A blush of shame coloured his dear face. "What happened? Where is she—they?"

"I was too young to keep our daughter myself. Lucia and her

husband pretended the baby was theirs. We moved to another town where no one knew us. It was the only way to keep my child with me."

"*Madonna mia,* the generosity and the cruelty are staggering. To deny a mother her child. To mask as the rightful parents. And yet to save you both." He hugged her tight. "Yola, I *cannot* hate you for your sacrifice. I hate *myself* for the burden I gave you."

"Caterina was never a burden. She has only ever been a delight to me. Even when she did not do as Lucia wished." She huffed a laugh. "Caterina did not take kindly to Lucia's ideals of behaviour. I think that is when I loved her the most."

Hesitant joy shone from his eyes and grew to a powerful beam. "Her name is Caterina? And my granddaughter? How old is she?"

"Caterina is twenty-nine and Hayley is ten."

"What of Caterina's husband?"

"Ryan is Hayley's father. Though he is not Caterina's husband—yet."

He frowned at the situation. Priceless, when she considered it. "I don't understand."

"Caterina followed in my shameful footsteps. She also had her child out of wedlock and did not tell the father. Like mother, like daughter." Hopefully, Hayley wouldn't do the same. Yola crossed herself.

"And now she has told him and they're getting married?"

"I don't know if she said anything to him yet. I know they love each other and I hope they can solve their problems."

"I completely understand the situation," he said wryly, toying with her fingers. "When can I meet my girls? Where do they live?"

"There is a problem. Caterina still believes Lucia to be her mother."

"What! We must tell her immediately." He tried to stand, but she held firm and wouldn't let him rush off to find his daughter.

"I swore to Lucia, on our mother's grave, to never tell."

"Yola, your mother would not deny you the joy of loving your daughter and granddaughter."

"Lucia has been very ill. It would kill her if I told the truth. Caterina will never forgive me."

"I don't like secrets. If only my father had revealed his troubles, we could have done something to help him before— Tell Lucia we go to Caterina whether or not she approves."

"She won't agree. She did what she thought was best. Imagine, for one moment, where I would have been without her."

He stared blindly at the lake, his gaze turned inward. Finally, he nodded. "You're right. To my everlasting shame, I wasn't there and she was. It is my punishment to live in the shadows of my daughter and granddaughter's lives."

She pressed an insistent hand to his mouth. "No, Leo. No more talk of punishment. You were half a world away, you didn't know."

"But I—" he said against her fingers.

Pouting playfully to ease his sombre mood, she tapped his lips. "Now I will get angry if you insist on beating yourself with circumstances beyond your control."

He smiled wryly and kissed her fingers. "In that case, *cara mia,* can you think of something else to do with this mouth of mine?" He twisted his head so her hand fell to her lap. Then he kissed her until she made helpless little noises. "While we're on the subject, you still haven't answered my question."

Yola blushed fiercely. "Ask me again, Leo. Please?"

With a happy shout, he set her on her feet and she grinned happily, as he knelt before her and took her hands.

"Mi sposi, cara Yola?"

"Sì, caro Leo, ti sposo."

After helping Zia Yola to lug bag after bag of shopping from the car to her bedroom, Cathy followed her aunt into the kitchen and smiled at her daughter's eager tugging of Zia's hand.

"Come and sit, Zia Yola. We missed you so much," Hayley said. "We made biscotti and you have to tell us if they're good enough. I said they were. But Mom said we need your stamp of approval first." Hayley set cups before them, while Cathy and Zia Yola exchanged tolerant glances at Hayley's excited babbling. "Here's some espresso, just the way you like it. Mom taught me how to use the machine."

Zia Yola thanked Hayley with a hug and kiss. Hayley pulled a chair close to her adored great-aunt and joined them at the table.

"*Ciao,* Zia Yola. How was your trip?" Melody had sat back down, even though she'd been about to leave before Zia Yola's prodigal return.

"*Ciao,* Melody. My trip couldn't have been better." Zia Yola glowed with an unfamiliar soul-deep happiness.

Cathy was crazy glad to have her aunt home. The place hadn't felt the same: as if Zia Yola had packed up all the joy and took it with her, leaving Cathy in uncomfortable intimacy with her mother. Cathy disregarded the other reason for her sour mood—the distance between herself and Ryan. The last time she'd called him, he gave the feeble excuse of "thinking things through" to end the conversation. He'd always been a strategist, which was good for politics, but not so good for personal relationships.

"I love your new look. Very up-to-the-minute," Melody said, interrupting Cathy's brooding.

Her aunt blushed, ran a hand over her shorter hair, and over her khaki twill pants. "*Mille grazie,* Melody. Helen and I went mad shopping. I spent a fortune and had a fabulous time."

"Well you deserve a new you."

Zia Yola turned to Cathy. "How has Lucia been?"

"She's napping at the moment. We had the final appointment with the oncologist on Tuesday. Mamma got the all-clear until her next check-up in three months. Her appetite's fully recovered—I'm worn out with cooking. The doctor's pressing her to start an exercise program and get out more. She says Mamma's been sitting around too long."

"*Bene,* good." Zia Yola beamed. "I will take her to the knitting circle. Helen's circle call themselves Stitch and Bitch." Yola winked at the naughty pun.

"Mom, she said bi—"

"Shocking!" Melody covered her mouth with a playful hand.

Cathy rolled her eyes and laughed. "Yeah, Hayley, she said bitch. I'll tell you later when it's appropriate." She shot a mock scowl at Zia Yola. "Thanks for that."

Zia Yola grinned, stunning Cathy with her mischievousness.

"One last thing about Mamma—the doctor had a lot of complimentary things to say about the care you've given her. Says you were instrumental in her recovery."

"You deserve some credit as well, Caterina."

"Me, too. I read to her," Hayley added.

Lucia had been unexpectedly kind to Hayley, showing patience with the little girl. Too bad Cathy had such a hard time returning the favour. But then Hayley didn't have quite as many buttons for Mamma to push.

Zia Yola tapped Hayley's nose. "You read very well, with lots of expression. How far did you get? Are Trixie and Honey and the gang back from Arizona yet?"

"Yep. Now we're reading *The Mysterious Code.*"

"You're reading Trixie Belden? I adored her when I was a kid." Melody said to Hayley. "Don't you wish you had a real mystery to solve?"

"Be careful what you wish for, Melody," Cathy teased.

Melody smirked. "Like that will ever happen in this little half-horse town." Melody's dismissive smirk changed to real affection as she poked Zia Yola gently in the shoulder. "Speaking of which, did you meet your old flame while you were in Toronto?"

Zia Yola turned a shocked expression on Cathy. "You told her?"

"No, she didn't." Melody answered. "Cathy was very coy, but Hayley was a much easier nut to crack. It's so romantic. Do tell." Melody propped her elbows on the table.

"Was it supposed to be a secret, Zia Yola?" Hayley cast a worried look at her great-aunt.

"No it wasn't Hayley. We just like to tease Melody, make her work for her newspaper column," Cathy reassured her daughter.

Zia Yola hugged Hayley. "No worries, *piccola.* It's not a

secret."

"So, Zia, is he still handsome?" Cathy was just as eager to hear about Zia Yola's old boyfriend and just as eager to turn Melody's insatiable and highly accurate curiosity away from herself.

Zia Yola blushed to the roots of her cute new hairstyle. Repressed joy twinkled deep within her eyes. Goosebumps of anticipation swept over Cathy's skin. Hayley bounced on her toes, jiggling Zia Yola's arm on her shoulder.

"Yes, he is still handsome—" Zia Yola said. The girls oohed.

"Still very charming—" The girls aahed.

"Still sexy—" The girls giggled.

"Incredibly rich—" The girls clapped.

"He still loves me and asked me to marry him," Zia Yola finished with a crowing laugh. She drew her left hand out from under the table and flourished a magnificent diamond. A sumptuous gold bracelet circled her wrist.

The girls squealed and hugged Zia Yola to bits and she basked in the approval. She was going to need every ounce of confidence when Lucia found out.

"Can I be your flower girl, please? Pretty please?" Hayley begged.

"The bride decides, the little girl does not ask." Cathy chided her daughter.

Hayley jigged and whined. "I'm desperate to be a flower girl before Lindsey."

"Hayley, stop it," Cathy barked then felt instant remorse for her quick temper. She wasn't herself these days. Zia Yola frowned at her. Even Melody gave her a beady-eyed questioning glare.

"I'm sorry I snapped at you, sweetie."

"S'okay, Mom. I know I have to follow the bride rules."

Hayley slouched away and Cathy shrank to the size of a crumb on the table.

"Hayley," Zia Yola called and Hayley turned back, a stubborn hopeful pout on her little face. "Will you be my flower girl?"

Hayley squealed and rushed back to hug her great-aunt some more.

"I have to tell Lindsey! Please can I tell her? Can I?"

Cathy looked to her aunt. "Are you ready to tell the world?"

Zia Yola winked at Melody. "Too late, I think."

"Hey, I resemble that remark!" Melody said, hands on hips in mock outrage.

Cathy laughed. "So, that's a yes, Zia?"

Yola nodded and Hayley slammed out the kitchen door to brag to her friend. Cathy secretly shared her one-upmanship. Score one for the Rossetti team.

"Caterina, will you be my maid of honour?"

"Yes!" It was more a jubilant shout than a proper acceptance. So much for the rules.

Melody smiled gaily. Cathy knew she was taking mental notes to hang on the grapevine.

"What's all this racket going on?" Mamma stumped into the kitchen. "No sooner do you get home than you turn the house on its ear. Where's my supper?"

The celebration screeched to a stunned silence. Cathy exchanged terrified glances with Zia Yola.

"Thanks for coffee. Deets tomorrow, Cathy." Melody's black curls streamed behind her in the breeze of her hasty retreat.

"I don't like that Melody." Mamma grumbled. "One of these

days, her gossiping will get her into trouble."

Mamma turned her sharp disapproving glare on Zia Yola. "Why did you cut your hair? And look at those frivolous clothes. Go and change immediately."

Cathy put a restraining hand on Zia Yola. But it was unnecessary. Zia Yola drained her cup and placed it in the saucer with only the faintest clinking of china to betray her tension. "I cut my hair because I wanted to, and I will not change my clothes."

"What's wrong with your housedresses? They're perfectly serviceable."

"They are perfectly ugly. I want pretty clothes." There wasn't the least bit of cowed self-defence in her aunt's voice. For the first time, Cathy heard implacable decision.

"She's so pretty. Eh, Mamma?" Cathy piped up, hoping to intervene.

Mamma gave Zia Yola a scathing up-and-down look and harrumphed. "Why were you gone so long?"

"You know I went to visit Helen."

"That one?" Mamma's eyes narrowed. "She's been lying to us all these years, keeping our *nipote* from us." Cathy choked on Mamma's blind disregard for any fact not suiting her version of the truth.

"She's been a good friend to me, and I will not have you say anything against her." Cathy interjected with little hope of deflecting the conversation.

Mamma's sharp glance cut Cathy's heart. "Your precious Helen is a good liar."

Cathy borrowed a little courage from Zia Yola. "Even though she didn't agree with my choice, she supported me. Unlike some other people I can think of—Mamma."

Mamma ignored Cathy's bold accusation and pinned Zia Yola with a harsh narrowing of the eyes. "And what do you think of Helen's secret-keeping, *sorella*?" Sister? Mamma never called Zia Yola sister. Cathy's gaze flicked between the two women. She sensed a hidden undertow in the question she couldn't puzzle out.

Zia Yola straightened, returned Mamma's look with a hard one of her own. "Helen knows the secret is not hers to tell." They were still talking in coded messages. What secret did they share with Helen? *Dio mio,* was it true? Yola was Lucia's child and not her sister? Had Yola lied? Cathy staggered with the thought.

"So then why did you visit Helen after all these years? When you were content to stay here with me?" A film of guilt crossed Cathy's mind. They hadn't considered for even a nanosecond what to do about Mamma.

A sly triumph radiated from Zia Yola. "A little while ago, Helen contacted me. An old friend of ours is in town and wanted to see me."

"And who is this old friend who makes you so impertinent?"

"Leonardo Giacometti, you remember him?"

Lucia went rigid at the name. "Another one who's more trouble than he's worth."

"You always said so, I always disagreed. Anyway, Leo and I met. He still loves me. He asked me to marry him and I accepted."

"Even though he left you with a broken heart and a—?" Mamma cut her eyes in Cathy's direction.

"He was sixteen. He had no control over his situation."

"Why has he waited so long to come back and declare his

undying love for you?" She made undying love sound like something you should flush away.

Zia Yola hesitated.

Mamma pounced. "So he hasn't pined for you all these years? He got on with his life, probably married. Now he's a widower, wants an easy replacement to cook and clean and look after his children. And—oh, let me guess—he remembered his first love and came from God knows where to find his soul-mate." Mamma laced her words with poisonous mockery.

Zia Yola flinched and tears shone in her eyes. Cathy couldn't take it anymore. She wrapped her arm around Zia Yola's shoulder.

"Enough, Mamma. Why must you destroy Zia Yola's precious happiness? She loves Leo and he loves her. After being trapped with us all these years, it's time she had a life of her own."

"Happiness? What rubbish. Do you think there's happiness for the likes of you two? Go, do what you want for love." Mamma waved her hands in a travesty of celebration. She all but spat on the floor. "I wash my hands of the pair of you." Forgetting her avowed need of her cane, she grabbed it in her fist, stomped up the stairs without using it, and slammed her bedroom door.

CHAPTER 14

A Funeral

"Is Mamma talking to us yet?" Cathy asked after breakfast two days later. Zia Yola prepared to go out, dressed in one of her fashionable new pantsuits, her knitting bag and purse ready to go. Cathy was over-the-moon happy for her beloved aunt. At long last, after years of sacrifice, Zia Yola deserved all the good things coming her way.

Zia lifted her hands in prayer and rolled her eyes to the sky. "*Dio mio,* she accuses us of betraying her, abandoning her, being selfish, ungrateful, and stupid. If you call that talking, there's plenty of it."

Cathy grinned at her aunt's wry assessment of Mamma's cantankerous mood this morning.

Zia Yola's diamond ring flashed in the sunlight filling the big room. She held her hand high, spraying tiny rainbows. Her wide elated smile flashed even brighter. "She thought my ring too large and vulgar. Any smaller, she'd say it was as insignificant as Leo's love." Zia shrugged. "There will be no pleasing her today."

"Do you think she'd like a special meal this evening? Is her favourite still cannelloni with red and white sauce?" Cathy asked.

"An excellent idea. I'll buy the ingredients while I'm in town." Zia Yola smiled brightly.

Cathy loved to see her aunt taking such joy in the prospect of a day out.

Zia Yola glanced around as if for spies. "Good, Hayley's gone off to her playhouse. I wanted to see what you think of this." Zia Yola pulled a gorgeous child's sweater from her knitting bag. A cardigan in Hayley's favourite sky-blue colour sprouted a multi-coloured garden of spring flowers around the hem.

Cathy gasped with delight, took the bundle of knitting, and held the softness to her cheek. "This is the most beautiful thing I've ever seen. The colours are perfect together. You've done an amazing job. The stitches are so even and *Dio mio*, you've lined it with matching satin."

"Will Hayley like it?"

"She'll adore it. In fact, she'll wear it to rags." Cathy laid her hand over her heart. "I'm sick with envy."

Zia Yola beamed her pleasure. "Emma told me about some flower-shaped buttons at the sewing center—so much prettier than the plain ones I bought. I'll give the sweater to Hayley at dinner tonight."

"I can't wait to see her face." Zia Yola tucked the sweater away just as Hayley's footsteps echoed across the back porch and she bounced into the room. Her curls, tightened into corkscrews by the summer humidity, bounced on after she stopped by Cathy.

"Mom? Is Nonna mad at me too?"

"No, sweetie." *You haven't betrayed her in any way, shape or form.* Cathy tugged and released one of the wild corkscrews. She'd done the same to Ryan's hair once when he let it grow past his collar just to please her.

"Should I read to her?"

Cathy and Zia Yola exchanged a silent question. Would Mamma want any of them anywhere near her?

"Sure, why not?" Cathy tapped her daughter's nose. "I'll see you later, Zia?"

"*Sì,* once I find my car keys. We'll cook for Lucia this afternoon."

"Perfect, I can get a load of laundry done. Hayley, want to go shopping after lunch?" Then Zia could finish the sweater in secret.

"Well, duh," she replied with a mischievous grin. Cathy and Zia Yola laughed.

Cathy hooked an arm over Hayley's shoulder. "Okay, let's go read to Nonna." Arriving at Mamma's bedroom, they found it unoccupied. Mamma's cane hung on the closet doorknob. Finally, Mamma had given up the useless thing.

"Nonna?" Hayley called.

"In here," Mamma answered from the washroom down the hall. "Don't rush me."

Hayley settled on the chair and found her place in her book, ready to start the moment Mamma nodded her permission.

"*Buon giorno*, Hayley," Mamma greeted her granddaughter with a loving smile. She looked straight through her daughter. Typical. Mamma walked firmly over to the bed, adjusted the pillows behind her back. "What are those two girls in our book up to today?"

"They've just arrived at—what's wrong, Nonna?"

Cathy gaped. One side of her mother's features seemed to be sliding down her skull. *Santo cielo.* Mamma's mouth worked. Only fragments of words came out. Her confused gaze met Cathy's.

What was that darn acronym? F-A-S-T: face, arm, speech, time.

"Quick, Hayley! Go get Zia Yola!"

Hayley ran out, hollering for Zia Yola before she hit the stairs.

Cathy forced a surreal calm into her voice. "Mamma, can you lift your arms?"

She lifted both arms. The right stayed aloft, the left slowly drifted down to the bed. Mamma's eyes rounded with abject fear.

"Caterina, I'm here." Yola spoke from the doorway while keeping Hayley behind her.

"Mamma's having a stroke. Stay with her while I call 9-1-1 from your room."

A wild grunting and rustling drew Cathy's attention to the bed. With her good arm, Lucia beckoned for Zia Yola.

"Go to her, keep her calm. When the ambulance comes, I'll go with her. You take Hayley to Lindsey's place then meet me at the hospital."

While Caterina hustled Hayley down the hall, Yola approached the bed with a deep foreboding. Lucia thrust out her good hand. Yola gasped at the desperate strength of her sister's grip. Lucia struggled with words, not making any sense.

Yola patted Lucia's hand, praying she reassured her. "Don't speak. Save your energy."

As usual, Lucia didn't listen. After much trying, she garbled out, "*Sulla tomba di nostra madre—non dirlo.*" On our mother's grave, say nothing.

Lucia once again demanded Yola's secrecy for the rest of her life, Caterina's life, Hayley's life. And all the lives beyond.

"*Prometti mi,*" she commanded. Promise me.

Yola hesitated and hesitated. Leo's words came back to her—the cruelty of denying a mother her child. And the child her mother.

A siren sounded, growing louder by the second. Red lights flashed across the ceiling.

Frantic, words failing, Lucia used the strength of her grasp and the plea in her eyes to exact her promise.

Loud sounds of entry shattered her insistent grunts. Paramedics stormed the house and took charge, issuing orders back and forth. They transferred Lucia to a stretcher and carried her down the stairs. To the last moment, with wide eyes and flagging lips, Lucia persisted in her demand for a binding promise.

Seeking a desperately needed respite, Yola returned to tidy Lucia's room before leaving for the hospital. She lifted the pillow from the mattress and found her car keys.

Lucia had hidden her keys so Yola couldn't go out, couldn't have a life of her own.

Rage, refined by thirty years of grinding submission, consumed every guilt, every obligation in Yola's heart. Three times she raised the pillow over her head and slammed it down on the spot Lucia had occupied in the rumpled bed. "*Ti. Prometto. Niente.*" Feathers flew like confetti on the final word. *I promise you nothing.*

Emotionally purged and eerily calm, Yola joined Caterina in the emergency waiting room. They huddled together while time stretched and bent. Other lives were discussed in whispers by other people as they waited. News items on the television mounted in the corner repeated and repeated. Coffee and tea were offered by sympathetic hospital volunteers and denied.

A doctor came to them, his face sad, his voice sombre. "Lucia has a standing Do Not Resuscitate order in her file. She gave a good fight. There's nothing more we can do. She's unconscious and near the end. Come and say your farewells."

Yola and Caterina followed him to a curtained bed in a bare white room. No machines whirred or beeped or blinked.

Lucia's chest heaved and collapsed, labouring for breath. Her white curls lay mashed to her head, her dark eyes closed, her rough Italian tongue still.

The priest greeted them softly and continued his Last Rites.

Weeping, Caterina took Lucia's still hand, kissed her still cheek. *"Ciao, Mamma. Ti amo."*

Dry-eyed, Yola kissed her sister's cold forehead, patted her cold hand. *"Ciao, Lucia, grazie mille."*

The priest murmured through the odd rattle in Lucia's throat, the final breath, the doctor's quiet declaration. Caterina and Yola crossed themselves when the prayers ended.

The iron discipline had failed.

Maria Lucia deBartolo Rossetti went to her just reward at 15:33 on August the seventh. *Riposa in pace.*

"Caterina." Zia Yola stood at the threshold of the rarely-used dining room where Cathy had set up office to deal with the astonishing amount of paperwork associated with executing

Lucia's will. Cathy took off her glasses feeling like she removed her eyes, and placed the black frames carefully on the stack of papers to her left.

"Yes, Zia Yola?"

"Sorry to interrupt when you're so busy." Her aunt, dressed in warm peach tones, moved briskly into the room bearing a lunch tray.

Cathy sighed and wondered at her aunt's calm acceptance of losing her sister the day after Lucia had been granted a clean bill of health and the prospect of many more years of life. Cathy wasn't blind to the fateful timing of her mother's death just as her aunt embarked on a new life that had caused major strife between the sisters. *Santo cielo,* what a guilt-inducing thought.

"You're not interrupting, Zia. I needed a break, anyway." Cathy smiled as Zia Yola slid the tray onto the one bare spot in the table right in front of her.

"Sitting over those papers for two days can't be good for your peace of mind. She never trusted me with her finances, but I'm sure Lucia left everything in perfect order." Zia Yola sat at the head of the table and gestured for Cathy to *eat, eat.*

"If only half my clients were half as well-organized, my life would be a lot easier." Cathy's stomach growled a greeting to the food at the heart-warming aroma of tomatoes and garlic.

Cathy took a bite of Zia Yola's delicious lasagne, closed her eyes to savour the taste. "Mmm, this is so good." Despite the pressure of paperwork, Cathy cheered up at the satisfaction on her aunt's face.

"You'll be returning to Toronto and your new job?"

"Yes, my compassionate leave of absence has ended. I'm expected back at work in six days."

"You will leave Ryan behind?" Distress watered her aunt's voice.

"Under Canadian law, silence cannot be construed as consent. But it sure as hell can be construed as rejection!"

"*Scusa*?"

"Sorry, that's lawyer speak for it's been over a week and he hasn't come to visit Hayley and I think he must ha-hate me." She sipped the red wine to clear the tears from her throat. "I get that. But to reject his daughter? When he's just found her?" Cathy's whole body squeezed tight to contain the urge to weep uncontrollably. She stuffed in another mouthful seasoned with the salt of her tears.

"You haven't told Hayley yet?"

"Don't you think she's suffered enough this week without being rejected by her father? When he's ready to step up, I'll tell her. Not before then."

She touched the pile of paper—much better to talk of cold hard cash. "Zia, Mamma left this house and all her assets to you. She left no debt to speak of, so it will be a tidy estate."

Zia Yola crossed her hands over her chest, refusing the gift from her sister. "No, she never spoke to me of her investments." She rose and walked to the window. "Caterina, I do not want what is rightfully yours."

Cathy raised her hand. "Stop right now. I left. You stayed. I know one doesn't speak ill of the dead, but let's admit you deserve every penny of Mamma's estate." Cathy halted Zia Yola again with a raised hand. "Consider it a nest egg, *una dota*, so you won't go empty-handed to Leo."

Zia Yola blushed at the name of her fiancé and gazed at her sparkling diamond with love glowing in her eyes. "At least let me give you a part. Or give Hayley a part."

"Absolutely not. My portfolio is perfectly healthy without taking the food from my aunt's mouth. Not that Leo will see you starve exactly." Cathy wiped her lips with a napkin. "Though I'm delighted to take food prepared by your talented hands. Thank you so much. I needed to eat more than I thought."

Cathy went to her aunt and laid an arm over her shoulder. "Zia, I've asked Helen and she agrees. Will you come home with Hayley and me?"

Zia Yola's mouth trembled and she turned to give Cathy a rib-cracking hug. "*Grazie mille*. I do not want to stay here anymore."

"Excellent, after the funeral service, we'll close up this house and get a caretaker until you decide if you want to sell."

"You're such a good girl." After a gentle pat on Cathy's cheek, Zia Yola re-stacked the tray and lifted it, hesitated, put it down, lifted it. She walked towards the archway and turned around.

"Is something else on your mind?" Cathy tried, really tried, to keep the impatience out of her voice. Though the estate was straightforward to Cathy's expert eye, it included several properties about town and a surprisingly diverse portfolio. The list of contacts on the pad at Cathy's elbow grew with a steady pace.

"Caterina? Do you think I caused Lucia's stroke?" Zia Yola finally blurted.

"Why on earth would you think that?"

"Because I was leaving her, and me... I broke a promise to her. I didn't tell her, but she knew."

Cathy slowly shook her head. "No, Zia, I don't think anything you said or did would have given Mamma a stroke."

"She was so angry."

"When wasn't she angry? Was the promise important to Mamma?"

"*Sì.*" She opened her mouth, closed it.

Cathy waited, hoping Zia Yola would reveal the promise. Nothing. "Does it matter now?"

"Do you think she will know?" Zia Yola glanced skyward.

"I have no idea. Before you keep or break the promise, consider the consequences. Will anyone be hurt by the disclosure?" How weird to be giving secret-keeping advice to her aunt. Especially given her own dismal record of accomplishment and the pain she'd inflicted on Ryan. Would he in turn hurt Hayley?

Zia Yola stared blindly at the tray in her hands and Cathy drew breath to prod her aunt to reveal her difficulty. Her cell phone rang and she checked the display. Damn, one of the contacts she'd been trying to reach all day had chosen this ill-timed moment to return her call. Cathy grimaced apologetically. "We'll talk about it later, okay Zia?"

Her aunt nodded and left the room. Cathy got on with her executor's duties.

"Mom?" Hayley asked.

Mom looked up from the huge stack of papers on the table, a not-all-there expression on her face.

"Can I bring the Trixie Belden books home?" Now that she'd solved her own mystery, she wanted to read all of Trixie's adventures. Maybe there were some mysteries at home to solve.

"What, all thirty-something of them?"

"Yes, please."

Mom shrugged *no biggie* and scribbled on the notepad. "I'll get another box."

"Okay." Hayley's tummy cramped and her throat tightened. "Mom, who will I read them to now?" She pulled her bottom lip between her teeth but the stupid crying started anyway.

"Come here, sweetie." Mom opened her arms and Hayley ran around the table into her Mom's great big hug. She cried until her chest hurt and her eyes puffed out sore. Hayley hated that just as she'd got more family, Nonna had died. Mom cuddled her until all the tears were gone and then they cuddled some more because it felt so darn good. Mom gave good cuddles.

"If you want, you can read to me," Mom said quietly in Hayley's ear. "I know it won't be the same as reading to Nonna. But we can share her memory when we read together. Okay?"

Hayley smiled soggily. "Do you think she'll hear us in heaven?"

"Absolutely. No doubt about it."

Hayley fiddled with Mom's cell phone on the table. A doctor was the last-dialled number. Hayley got real scared, real quick.

"Mom? You're not sick are you?"

"What?" Mom took the phone, saw the number and smiled. "No, sweetie. I'm in perfect health. Zia Yola had some questions about Nonna, and I asked the doctor to speak to her. No need to worry."

Hayley sagged with relief. "Mom?"

Mom's eyes were on the papers. She sighed, a bit pissed.

"Are we going home after the funeral?" Hayley asked. Mom looked up from the papers, the checked-out expression back on her face.

"Yes, our work here is done." Funny, Mom shook her head no at the same time she said yes.

"Aren't we gonna stay and marry Ryan?"

Mom's eyes got all big and watery behind her glasses. "I don't think so, sweetie," she said in a croaky voice.

Hayley bowed her head to hide the hurt. "Doesn't he like us anymore? He hasn't phoned or come over or anything. Did you have a big fight?"

Mom's face got all red and she shook her head. "No, we didn't fight."

"Then why isn't he here with us?"

Mom took off her glasses and rubbed her eyes. "Sometimes things just don't work out the way we want them to. And there's nothing we can do but learn to live with it."

Hayley knew it was too good to be true. Good thing she still had her real dad. "Can I come back and stay with Lindsey?"

Mom got a way funny look on her face, weirding Hayley right out. Didn't Mom want Hayley to see her dad because he was married to somebody else? That totally and completely sucked!

Mom's cell phone rang and she took the call.

Well, if Mom wasn't gonna let her see her sister Lindsey or their dad, Hayley would have to do something. She had to tell Mark Chisholm that she was his daughter before it was too late.

Cathy wanted to pull her hair out, or pop a sleeping pill, or knock back a stiff drink. Something—anything—to help her cope with all the horrendous crap in her life.

The stiff drink appeared as if by magic.

"You really look like you could use this." Emma and Melody closed ranks around Cathy, keeping the mourners at bay for a brief respite. Cathy gratefully sipped at the brandy, letting it ease the tension from her neck and shoulders.

"Respectable crowd. Your mom would have been pleased." Emma slipped behind Cathy and added a discreet massage to the brandy's soothing effect. Cathy quietly groaned her thanks.

"I've been to a lot of funerals for the newspaper and this has been a very classy service. I can't believe the number of people here to support you and Zia Yola." Melody said polishing off the last bite of a triangle-cut tuna sandwich.

"I had no idea how much was involved in putting on a funeral, even with the pre-arrangements Mamma made. The times I choked up..." Cathy sipped again, hoping for the brandy to loosen the vice of shock, grief, and tears clogging her throat. The silent guilt of keeping Ryan and Hayley apart screwed the vise tighter. The timing for everything couldn't be more wrong.

"Speaking of class, Zia Yola looks amazing, like a very merry widow. Especially with that gorgeous rock on her finger. And where did she get her incredible dress?" Melody asked.

Cathy smiled at the only beam of joy in the gloom clouding her mind. "She's trying real hard to appear suitably sad, but every night at eight o'clock when Leo calls, she beams so bright."

"Aw, that's so sweet. She deserves every ounce of happiness coming her way. Does she talk long with her fiancé?" Emma asked, finishing her massage and stealing a sandwich from Melody's plate.

"An hour or so. It must be costing Leo a fortune to call from Italy. He had to go back for urgent business reasons."

"Speaking of Zia Yola, why is she hanging on Asher's every word?" Emma nodded across the room where Zia Yola was clearly relieved, listening to Dr. Stockdale.

"She's feeling guilty she caused Mamma's stroke. I already told her she didn't, of course, but she needs to hear it from a professional, even if he is an ophthalmologist. The more times she hears, the less guilty she feels." Cathy must remember to thank the gorgeous doctor later.

"And when did the good doctor become *Asher* to you, Miss Emma?" Melody arrowed the question at Emma who blushed profusely beneath her eye patch.

"I've seen him so often about my eye he insisted I use his given name. Said he felt like his grandfather to be called Dr. Stockdale."

"He certainly isn't old, is he?"

"No, definitely not." Emma returned Melody's sharp glance with a frown. "Get your mind out of the gutter, Miss Mellie."

Melody pouted charmingly. "You have so much fun in the gutter, I'd think you'd want more."

"Not for a while and not with Asher," Emma replied.

Cathy exchanged a glance with Melody as they waited for Emma to state her reasons. When she maintained a steadfast silence, Cathy shrugged.

"In that case, mind if I have a go at him myself?" Melody chuckled at Emma's disgruntled look.

"What play are you acting in next?" Emma changed the topic.

Cathy's attention was dragged across the room. Virginia and Becca Carleton-Grant had their heads close together, speaking with a great deal of discreet finger pointing at Ryan, Cathy and Hayley. Virginia was telling Becca the truth of Hayley's parentage. Someone beside them avidly joined their conversation. Was Virginia vindictive enough to spill the secret here, at Mamma's funeral?

Melody's monologue on her starring role in the next community theatre production melded into blah-blah-blah in Cathy's ears. Cathy shoved a fist against her mouth. Her vision blackened at the edges and she tottered on her heels.

Standing by the door with Nana Jean and his father, Ryan saw Cathy wilt. His feet started walking before his brain engaged. He stopped as Emma and Melody sprang into action. Shielding her from view with their bodies, they sat her down, and got her to sip at her drink some more. Melody scanned the crowd and headed to Zia Yola.

How was it possible to still love Cathy so much he ached to scoop her up in his arms and take care of her? And at the same time, he was so angry and so disappointed. All he could do was avoid her like a mossy bog, unwilling to sink up to his neck in conflicting emotion. He longed to kiss his daughter and cheer her up, help her deal with the loss of her grandmother. Neither of them deserved the resentment he couldn't quite control. So, he stood gawking at them both like a lovesick fool.

"Looks like your little lady's in trouble," his dad, Bucky, spoke up from beside Ryan.

"Cathy's not my little lady." Her daughter on the other hand....

When did Cathy plan to tell Hayley? Could he tell her instead? Walk up to her and say, "Listen, Hayley, remember when you asked me to marry you and your mom? Not necessary, because you're already my daughter. We don't need your mom." He groaned under his breath. Yeah, that would go down real well.

Would Hayley still like him after the big reveal? Were kids so easy to deal with? He'd never raised a kid, but he and Lindsey got on really well. He rolled his shoulders in his black suit and wished he were way out on the water, far away from all these aggravating unanswerable questions.

"...too damn bad," his dad's voice interrupted Ryan's troubled musing.

"Huh?"

His dad nudged him with an elbow. "Wake up, son. I'm talking about Cathy. She woulda been a notable asset to the company. Brains and financial smarts like hers are very useful."

Cathy in his dad's clutches? Revulsion churned in Ryan's gut. Maybe it wasn't such a bad thing she was leaving town.

Hayley and Lindsey walked, oh-so-solemnly, to the buffet table. They were clearly on their best behaviour—his daughter was such a cutie. Now he knew the girls were cousins, the similarities were ridiculously obvious. Why didn't other people see the likeness?

Zia Yola and Melody made a beeline back to Cathy, right past Hayley and Lindsey. Emma started taking Cathy down the hall, presumably to a private room.

Bucky's eyes suddenly narrowed. "Cathy's little girl looks awfully familiar. I can't precisely place her. What about you, Nana?"

Nana Jean studied the two girls, her chin tipped to one side. Alarm bells clanged and banged in Ryan's head.

"Doubt it, Dad. You know how everyone has a double. You've probably seen a little girl somewhere just like her." He could have bitten his tongue out. Talk about giving the game away.

Did he want someone to guess? Maybe get the info out sort of accidentally on purpose? How ironic if Bucky, the great manipulator, ended up being the one to clear the air accidentally.

"Francie?" Nana Jean's eyes widened and snapped to Ryan's face.

"Mom says we're going home and never coming back," Hayley complained. Lindsey whined along then took a huge bite of her sandwich.

"Such manners," Nonna's voice lectured in her head. Hayley grinned to herself. Nonna sure had a point sometimes. Hayley sneakily wiped away a tear and took a neat bite of her own triangle. Egg salad with little green oniony bits—yum. "I'll never see you again."

"How fair is that?" Lindsey said after she swallowed hard.

"No-ot," they said under their breaths. Hayley was really gonna miss Lindsey and the way they always thought the same thing at the same time.

"And I'll never get to call our dad Dad. We gotta do something."

Mark handed Meg a plate full of food and she made a sick face and pushed the plate away. Poor Dad tried so hard to make his wife happy. Her half-sister blamed it on her mom's pregnancy. Maybe she'd wait until after Meg had the baby before she visited her dad and half-siblings.

"I can't believe Dad hasn't figured it out yet. Why don't we go over and tell him?" Lindsey interrupted her thoughts. "WWTD?" She added their secret code for "What Would Trixie Do?"

"Trixie would trick him into figuring it out by himself." Hayley tried hard to think of a scheme worthy of the heroine of her favourite books.

"What about Uncle Ryan being your other dad? It'd be easy to get him to marry your mom. He's way sweet on her."

"I asked him to marry us, remember?"

"That's for grown-ups to decide." They groaned together. It was awful when adults said such boring stuff.

"Why's Dad ignoring me?" Hayley whined.

"Who's ignoring you, honey?" Mom's friend Melody stopped and bent down. Zia Yola kept on moving past them.

"My dad," Hayley said.

"Your dad? Your mom didn't say he was coming to the funeral. Decent of him be here for her." Melody stood and looked around. "I don't see him. What's he look like?"

Lindsey giggled. "He looks a lot like my dad."

"Looks like Mark? You mean Ryan? They don't look that much alike. What are you talking about?"

"No, silly, I mean *my* dad. Marcus Andrew Chisholm." Hayley said, and rolled her eyes at Lindsey.

Melody clicked her head back and forth like the clockwork doll in the toy museum. Hayley giggled. What a goof!

"You mean Mark is your father?"

Hayley giggled harder at Melody's squeaky voice.

"Course he is. We saw a picture and everything." Geez, adults had a real hard time figuring out such a simple thing. "But nobody's supposed to know, so you have to keep it a secret. All right?"

Melody blinked faster and faster. "Dang! I need my eyes examined. I should've seen something so obvious."

"What's obvious, Melody?" Dr. Stockdale asked from way overhead.

"Mark Chisholm is Hayley's father." Melody said right out loud in a shocked voice. Right away she slapped her hand over her mouth.

A big space suddenly opened up in front of Hayley. Everyone stopped talking. Weird.

"*What* did you say?" Meg yelled. She stared at their dad, really really mad.

Their dad panicked. "No, I'm not! I swear, Meggie, I never had anything to do with Cathy." He grabbed her hand. "You're the only woman I ever loved. That little girl is *not* mine!"

Everybody looked back at Hayley, waiting for her to say something, like that time she forgot her lines in the school play. Hayley's stomach hurt—she was gonna hurl. Her dad didn't want her. Hayley's heart hurt like somebody stuck a stick in it. Lindsey said something and tried to hold her hand. No way. Lindsey got her dad and she didn't. Not fair. Not fair!

Ryan stepped into the empty space. "No, Hayley. Mark isn't your father. I am," he said in his speech-making voice. He crossed the room, bent down a little to look straight into Hayley's eyes. "I'm your father, Hayley. Not Mark. Me," he almost whispered.

Hayley stared at the crowd of adults staring at her. Some of them started talking, pointing, smirking. Others looked at Ryan like they suddenly hated him. Lots were shaking their heads like she was a stupid little kid.

Frantic, she looked for Mom, but couldn't find her.

Mark called Lindsey to his side. "Sorry," she whispered and went to her parents.

Ryan knelt down and held out his arms.

Why should she go to him when he didn't want her either?

Hayley shook all over, tears poured from her eyes as she pressed her fist to her mouth. Only one person looked at her with a kind face, and that's where she ran. Straight into Zia Yola's open arms.

CHAPTER 15

Choices

"Yes, you heard correctly. Cathy Rossetti's little girl is my biological daughter. Not Mark's. Mine." Ryan sagged in his desk chair, fielding questions from yet another potential voter.

"No, I have no further comment. However, I'd be delighted to talk about my rejuvenation plan for the downtown core." He listened to some slight excuse. "Nice chatting with you, too. Goodbye."

Ryan clicked off the phone, shoved it into the charger stand, and met Paul's gaze. "I should rent one of those scrolling neon signs and stick it to my forehead. Then I wouldn't have to repeat myself over, and over, and over."

Paul nodded wryly. "Who knew gossip was more important to voters than something that actually impacts their lives."

"I just want them out of my personal life."

"Personal, political—same difference. Welcome to Clarence Bay."

"No, it isn't. Or it shouldn't be."

"Maybe not, but it is." Paul raised his hand to stop more

words. "When you ran for mayor, your private life became public property. The muddying of your squeaky clean image by your own daughter is just too tempting a morsel to ignore."

Ryan clunked his forehead on the desk and conceded the futility of the circular argument they'd been having all morning. The frequent interruptions from the nosy town made it even more difficult.

"Whatever you're feeling, this will affect your campaign."

Ryan lifted his head and stared at his best friend. "You think I still have a chance?"

"Yeah, sure. Got any brilliant ideas for damage control?"

Ryan cringed at the implication he'd done something wrong like manipulating council votes or massaging the numbers. He'd only done the honourable thing and claimed his daughter. Not to mention saving his brother's ass.

"My poor kid. What an awful scene for her." His heart still cramped at the stricken look on her face before she'd run to Zia Yola. How he had longed to cuddle and comfort Hayley, tell her he loved her. Even if she had left him kneeling like a publicly-rejected suitor.

His pain was not Hayley's fault. Instead of planning the best way to tell people, he should have just shown up the day after he found out and he and Cathy could have told her together. All this agony might have been spared. That would teach him to ignore his heart.

"I heard Bucky was damn amazing how he hustled everybody outta the funeral parlour."

Nana Jean had left with Hayley and Cathy while Zia Yola returned to the funeral and did her duty by her sister.

"Yeah, he surprised the life out of me." Ryan rose from his

seat, rubbed a hard hand across the back of his neck. "Anyway, I have some explaining to do to my family and then I'll go see Cathy."

"While you're with your dad, you might ask about damage control."

"No fucking way! Good as he was yesterday, doesn't mean he can help me today."

Paul surrendered with a shrug, but wouldn't meet his eye. Ryan thrust a finger at his campaign manager. "Do *not* do an end run on me. If anyone asks my dad for help, it'll be me. And there is no way in hell that's gonna happen."

An hour later, Ryan had explained all to Mark, Meg, and a long-faced Lindsey. Crazily, the situation seemed to have cleared the air between Mark and Meg, because they were sitting close and friendly, holding hands no less. Meg rubbed her tummy and eased back. Mark patted the bulge that moved visibly below her maternity top.

Their togetherness filled Ryan with sadness. He'd missed the pregnancy with Hayley, getting acquainted before she was born. And everything after for ten whole years. Resentment joined the sadness, leaving him conflicted and antsy. Again.

"Well, if you ask me, you should marry her," Bucky said from the big chair in Mark's family room.

His dad's words penetrated his gloom. "What did you say?"

"I said marry Cathy. You'll get the best optics. Show you for an honourable man."

"You think I'm not honourable?"

"Calm down. Of course you are. Have to admit, it's reassuring to see you're as fallible as the rest of us ordinary human beings."

Ryan was more than a little creeped out. Regardless of the lousy advice, his dad was there for him. It was unnatural. If Ryan had known bad behaviour was the way to win his dad's approval... Nah, too weird to think about.

"So Becca didn't stand a chance," Meg said. "You should have said something. It would've saved her a broken heart."

"Damn it, Becca's heart is not broken. And I didn't know about Hayley until Becca's mother, of all people, told me."

"Virginia knew before you did?" Meg asked. A roomful of people sat with slack jaws and popping eyes.

"The whole damn world knew before I did. You think that doesn't grind my gears?" Ryan got up to leave.

"Marry her, Ry. Dad's right." Mark said.

"Marry her," Meg repeated.

"Hayley says you're crushing on her mom," Lindsey said.

"Crushing on a person is not enough to marry them." He turned to Bucky. "I will not marry her for the optics of the thing."

"Well, then, how 'bout you marry her for the same damn reason I married your mother?"

"To beat your rival?"

"Well that, too. But I married Francie because I loved her with everything I had in me. Marry Cathy because you love her. And if it happens to be good for your numbers, why complain?"

Ryan huffed a startled laugh. "Dad, sometimes, you are just so damn right." Ryan loved Cathy and Hayley, needed them in his town, in his life, in his heart. If the town didn't like it, they didn't need to vote for him. With determination in every step, Ryan left his brother's house and crossed the road to Lucia's—no, Zia Yola's—place.

"If you had told me, I wouldn't have made such a stupid mistake!" Hayley shouted loud enough to rattle the cutlery on the kitchen table. "I followed all the clues just like Trixie. But you...withheld evidence!"

Cathy cringed at her mini legal eagle. "He needs to stay here for his town, they need him—" Cathy started again, though her patience was wearing thin.

"I don't care! You lied to me my whole life! I hate you!" Her daughter ran from the room. Moments later, the bedroom door slammed. Cathy threw her glasses onto the table and they skittered off the other side. She ground her knuckles into her gritty eye sockets. Sometimes, life really truly sucked.

Zia Yola wrapped an arm around Cathy's shoulder. "Don't worry Caterina, she doesn't mean it."

Cathy leaned against her beloved aunt. "I know, Zia. I don't blame her. She's still mortally embarrassed by the scene yesterday. And I wasn't there for her. Hayley just needs some space. She'll come around soon. I hope." She gazed out the kitchen window. "I hate to think what Ryan's going through."

"Much worse, I expect."

"Mmm. I'd help him if I could. But my instinct is telling me I'd just make it uglier." Cathy also resolved to stay out of Clarence Bay politics. Forever and ever, amen. "Let's get on with the packing. I'll go get some cardboard boxes from the grocery store." She picked up her purse and kissed her aunt's silken cheek. Clearing out nearly three decades worth of stuff was not an easy chore, but it would give closure to her mother's life.

As Cathy opened the front door, Ryan stood with his fist raised to knock. They stared at each other through the screen, frozen in position like a pair of shop-window mannequins.

"Hi," they said at the same moment then exchanged sheepish smiles.

"C'mon in. I guess we have a few things to talk about." She stood back and he followed her to the dining room. The piles of paper shrank every day as Cathy worked her way through Mamma's estate.

Ryan stared awkwardly at her. Feathery lines etched tiredness on her lovely face. Her eyes were red and shiny, as if she'd just stopped crying. He looked away from her gut-wrenching sadness and tamped down the need to give comfort, seek comfort.

"Yeah, a few things," he said. "We—"

"How's your morning been?" she interrupted.

"Crazy with phone calls, all asking for verification of Hayley's paternity. I didn't get as many calls when I announced my candidacy. We—"

"What do you tell them?"

"I confirm it, of course. Then I ask them if they'd like to talk about the election and suddenly they have plans."

"I'm so sorry I've jeopardized your chances."

He brushed aside her concerns. "Listen, I—"

Cathy tossed her purse on the table and paced away from him, dodging chairs and stuffed file boxes. "Zia Yola's coming home with us until her wedding next spring. She's so focused on her new life with Leo, I doubt the mess made a dent in her happiness. I get the feeling she was never very happy here." She raised her hands and let them flop in a gesture of futility. "So all the secrecy was a pointless waste of energy."

He cornered her by the window, grabbed her shoulders.

"Cathy, you need to marry me."

Her mouth trembled then firmed. After a deep breath, she locked gazes with him. "Why," she croaked. "Why are you asking?"

Not the response he was hoping for. He released her shoulder to smooth the silky hair away from her beautiful face. "Because I love you, I love our little girl. I want us to be together."

He pulled her gently into his arms, lowered his head for a kiss. She placed her hands on his chest, halting his movement.

"Do you forgive me for keeping her a secret from you? Do you understand why?"

"I understand, sort of." What did she want from him? Was he supposed to be grateful for years of deception?

She pushed against him, increasing their distance. "You're proposing for damage control, aren't you? Did Paul suggest marriage again?"

"No, my dad did."

"Your father?" Her voice, her entire body, stiffened. She gave him a good push, enough to get away and put the table between them again. "You're taking advice from your father of all people?"

He pursued her, needing her back in his arms. "No. Yes. No. I asked you to marry me before, in the playhouse when we made love. I get why you said you couldn't. The secret's out, the problem's gone. I've asked you again, and you haven't answered."

"When you didn't return my calls, I assumed you'd withdrawn the question after Virginia's revelation."

"Point taken. But you have to understand that I needed time to process the facts. I've done that and I've figured out that I want you and Hayley in my life. I love you. You love me. We both love Hayley."

Propping a hand on one hip and wrapping the other over her waist, she gave him a narrow-eyed scowl. "You're being noble."

"I sincerely hope so."

"No." Flat voice, flat mouth, flat hand sliced through the air. A negative to his statement of her love. And a flat-out lie.

"No, what?"

"No, I won't marry you. I won't have you sacrifice us all for the sake of your pledge to the town. You got your wish, they know about Hayley. It's up to you how you manage their knowledge."

"Damn it, you're not getting it. I want to marry you," he shouted.

She walked to the doorway, trying to out-manoeuvre the issue of their future. "Not really. You want to do the right thing. You can see Hayley though. Do you want it made legal?"

"Yes. I want you and her to marry me, live with me, make a family." When did this get so damn complicated? Did she have no faith in him, in them?

She gave him a tolerant smile and crossed her arms. "Nice of you to insist. It's almost heroic, romantic. It won't work."

Ryan growled in total frustration at her stonewall stubbornness.

"I'll call my lawyer when I get back to Toronto." Her smile faded to real sadness.

Hands clenched, he held her gaze, demanding her surrender. She clenched her own hands, clamped her mouth shut, and stared him down. They'd have stayed that way for hours, but Cathy broke the standoff with an insincere smile. "So, if you don't mind, I've got a house to clear out."

Ryan wilted at the fractured tension, no longer wondering at her success in a man's world. She was one damn tough cookie. "Okay, I'll leave it." For now. Cathy didn't own stubborn. "I want to see Hayley while I'm here."

She paused a long time. "If Zia Yola is with you."

He scowled. Why did his acknowledged fatherhood make him less trustworthy? "I'm not going to run off with her."

She gave him a smart-assed smirk. "I know. It's not you. Hayley's a little weirded-out, in her words, so I think she'd be more comfortable if Zia Yola were with her."

Slightly mollified, he shrugged. "Okay, not a problem."

"Zia Yola's in the kitchen, Hayley's upstairs." Cathy stood so still, staring over his shoulder out the window, Ryan heard the gears of her mind grinding. She met his gaze, drew breath as if to say something. He waited, hope rising. Instead of speaking, she turned, snatched up her purse, and marched out the front door.

He let out a long slow sigh, venting his crazy hope. She didn't want to marry him, but she trusted him. He mulled over a multitude of flawed options. All he found was the stubborn determination to try again. In the kitchen, Zia Yola worked through the cupboards, sorting stuff into labelled boxes. Packing wouldn't take long given the speed she was going. Or was the current speed a cover for eavesdropping? Didn't matter, Zia Yola knew it all anyway. The huge rock on her left hand flashed and practically blinded him. Maybe he should've stopped at the jewellery store on the way through town. Put his money where his mouth was.

"Zia Yola," he said.

Her fake surprise gave the game away. “Ryan, I thought you’d gone.”

He acknowledged their conspiracy with a slanted smile. “No, you didn’t.”

“Caterina is being a lot stubborn and a little stupid.”

He shrugged his agreement.

ZiaYola crossed the room and patted his arm, looked up at him with eyes so like Cathy’s, the pain of giving her up knifed through him, destroyed him. With a strangled sound, he allowed Yola to hold him tight and surrendered his grief to her motherly murmurings. Embarrassed at his unmanly struggle with emotion, he released her as soon as possible. He went for a glass of water to push down the unshed tears.

“Don’t worry, she’ll come around soon,” Zia Yola said from behind him.

“Not soon enough to suit me. Anyway, I stayed to talk to Hayley. My daughter.” A consolation prize beyond compare.

Yola patted his back encouragingly. “I’m glad the secret is out now. Secrecy is a poisonous thing.”

A note in her voice caught his attention. Too much vehemence? Nah, what secrets did Zia Yola have?

“Cathy’s gone for boxes. She said Hayley would likely want to have you with her when I talk to her.”

“Why would she say such a thing?” Zia Yola dismissed her own question with a wave of her hand. “Hayley’s in the bedroom at the back of the house. She’s very angry with Caterina right now. I’m sure she’ll open the door for her father.” Yola flashed him a smile full of reassurance and encouragement.

Ryan soaked up the energy of her good wishes and tried to balance his trepidation. “I’ll try anyway.”

Slowly climbing the stairs, he tried not to let his footsteps sound like doom coming for his little girl. The front bedroom had an empty feeling though it was stuffed full of heavy old-fashioned cherry furniture. The women weren't wasting a minute packing up. Likely, they couldn't wait to lay rubber down the 400.

A puzzling number of feathers clotted a corner of the room—a split pillow maybe? He spotted a book partially hidden under the stripped bed. He picked up a kid's mystery novel and tucked in the loose bookmark. Carrying the book down the hall, he passed Zia Yola's cheerful yellow bedroom and the huge old bathroom with a claw-foot tub. A picture of Cathy up to her chin in bubbles flirted with his imagination. Not gonna happen any time soon. He sighed with ragged regret.

The shut door had the air of having been slammed real hard, as if the vibrations hadn't settled yet. He screwed up his courage and knocked on his daughter's—his daughter's—bedroom door.

"Go away," came the sulky dismissal.

"Hayley, it's—Ryan." He dared not call himself *dad* without her say so.

"Is my mom with you?"

"No. I'm alone."

Nothing. Geez, the kid had aced her mother's lessons about the art of speaking silences.

"I found something that might be yours," he tempted feebly.

A long pause. He was turning away when Hayley said. "Just a sec." Some rustling and scurrying went on behind the door. Then it cracked open a couple of centimetres. Hayley bobbed her head, trying to peek around him.

He stepped aside, controlling his smile. "See, all alone."

She disappeared, leaving it up to him to open the door all the way and enter the room. Twin beds with pink-checked blankets flanked a large window overlooking the back garden. Hayley sat cross-legged in the center of the rumpled bed. He sat on the tidy bed opposite her and squirmed like a kid in uncharted territory. He handed her the book. "I found this down the hall in the big bedroom."

She laid the book on the bed as if she was afraid of it. "I was reading to Nonna wh-when her face went crooked and she had a stroke." Her struggle showed in her quivering chin and white-knuckled grip of one hand on the other.

Going on pure father instinct, Ryan opened his arms.

She sat unmoving; tears trickled down her cheeks retracing the dried tracks of previous tears. She gazed at him, hopefully reading his love for her written on his soul.

He leaned forward, beckoning with his hands. "Come here, honey. It's okay to cry."

His daughter unwound her legs and flew across the room. He tucked her into his lap and murmured nonsensical comfort while huge sobs wracked her slender body. His throat choked in empathy with his little girl's misery. As deep in misery as she was, Ryan rejoiced in the feel of his daughter, his little girl, his child. Her curly hair snagged on his day-old stubble; her skinny arms wrapped tight around him. Her messy soggy face pressed into the side of his neck. He'd loved her before as Cathy's daughter. Now, he loved her as his own.

Hayley wouldn't be here if not for Cathy's determination to protect her regardless of the cost to herself and others. His heart swelled with gratitude and his arms tightened around his weeping little girl. Tears of pure joy slid down his cheek into his daughter's hair. What a weepy dude he was today.

After a few minutes, the storm of her sorrow subsided into the occasional shudder. He grabbed some tissues for her, which she insisted on using herself. Sadly, he'd lost the opportunity to wipe her nose for her as a baby. He wrestled with a twinge of resentment and tossed it over the ropes.

What was done was done.

Hesitantly, she moved back to the other bed and clasped her hands between her knees. "Are you really my dad?" she asked, her gaze stuck on the floor as if fearing his answer.

"Yes, I am. Your mother says my name is on your birth certificate." Should he add he loved her? Or would that pressure her to state an affection she didn't feel? Even if she'd asked him to marry them that day at Franklin Island?

"Why didn't you tell me?" She flicked him a sour glance. "I feel really stupid asking my own dad to marry me and my mom, and then telling everybody my uncle was my dad." She rolled her eyes fiercely. "People were laughing at me and everything."

"Nobody was laughing at you, honey. They were just shocked. But, don't worry, people will forget the whole thing as soon as something else catches their attention," he replied, conscious of her vulnerability. "And I loved your proposal. I smile every time I think about it."

"Do you know why my mom kept me a secret?"

Ryan hesitated. Despite all the harm Lucia had done with her judgmental, overbearing ways, he couldn't desecrate his daughter's memory of her grandmother or upset her relationship with her mother. "Do you remember that day when we went to Franklin Island and we talked about misunderstandings and marriage?"

"Yeah, you said marriage was for grownups."

"That's right. Well, some reasons are for adults, too."

"Will you tell me when I'm a grownup."

"If you still want to know, I'll tell you."

"Okay." She played with his shirt button. "Do you still want me to be your daughter?"

He smiled the biggest smile he had ever smiled. "More than ever. Do you still want me to be your dad?"

"Uh huh." She giggled then twinkled at him from beneath her lowered lids.

"Are you and Mom getting married?"

This time, only the truth would work. He shook his head, hating to crush her hope, watching her closely. "We're not. Your mom said no when I asked her a few weeks ago. She said no again about an hour ago."

Downstairs, the door opened. "Zia, I come bearing boxes," Cathy called.

Hayley was about to stomp off and ask her mom what he guessed were some very uncomfortable questions. He lifted his arm to stop her. "No, don't make her change her mind. I know you can, just don't. I don't want to force her to marry me."

Hayley crossed her arms, stubborn as a little mule. She got her determination from her mother as well. Suddenly, she relaxed. "Okay, let's go see if Mom bought ice cream."

That was easy, too easy. Warily, Ryan allowed his daughter to lead him downstairs. A cautious-looking Yola joined Cathy in the front hall as Ryan went down the staircase hand in hand with Hayley.

"Mom, my friend Ricky says his dad has visitation rights."

A frantic, blameless guilt burned in his cheeks as Ryan

rapidly shook his head.

"What about Ricky's father's rights?"

"Does Ryan—my dad—have those?"

His little girl had called him *my dad.* His knees turned to mush.

Cathy's gaze pierced Ryan like she tried to peer through his blood and bone, straight into his heart. A fine sweat broke out along his spine. He swallowed and opened up, let her see the truth about his love for Hayley and herself. He stroked Hayley's shoulders where she leaned against his hip.

Cathy stared at him some more, then transferred her gaze back to her waiting daughter. "Yes, he can visit you."

"Good, because I want to stay with him when you and Zia Yola go home."

Cathy and Zia Yola's gasps sucked all the air out of the room. Leaving Ryan only enough air to squawk.

Hayley turned huge puppy-dog eyes up at him. "Please, can I stay with you, Daddy? Please?"

Saturday, five days later, Cathy returned to her Toronto home by herself. Zia Yola would arrive in a couple of hours, in her own car. Cathy closed the kitchen door from the garage and leaned heavily on the solid panels. Her chest heaved with the anger and resentment stalking her since Hayley's bold demand to stay with her father. The little wretch had used every form of guilt known to children. And she'd won.

The big three-storey house greeted her with bleak emptiness. Tremors of rage began deep in her belly and worked outwards. Her hands shook so wildly, the car keys clattered to the tile floor. Unable to restrain herself any longer, rage scorched over her vocal chords and into the air. She ranted and raved, stomped and stalked, screeched every cuss-word purged from her vocabulary until she embarrassed herself with her own foul mouth.

Lungs heaving, she wilted into the kitchen rocker. "Damn, what a relief."

"Whew, I broke a sweat just listening." Helen entered from the mudroom, wiping her brow.

Cathy started and hot colour steamed her cheeks. "Where were you? You weren't supposed to hear me."

Helen's teasing smile welcomed Cathy home. "Out in the garden, of course. It's ever so nice to know you're as normal as the rest of us." Ruffling her short feathery dark hair, Helen stripped off her gloves and tossed her hat on the rack by the door. "By the way, those came for you today." She pointed at two envelopes on the table: one an invitation, the other an express delivery.

Cathy opened the embossed invitation to the museum gala for this coming Saturday.

"*Santo cielo,* I'd forgotten about this darn thing. Guess I'll be buying a new dress."

"What about the lovely grey one you just bought? The one your co-worker with the long red nails—"

"Larissa," Cathy said.

"That's the one. The grey dress she took up to Clarence Bay for you. Something wrong with it?"

"I don't want to wear it anymore." Not with Ryan's indelible handprints all over it.

"Why? It's so lovely and fits you so—" Helen broke off with a sympathetic smile when tears welled in Cathy's eyes. "O-kay.

Let's talk about something else equally emotional. Are you sure you're okay leaving Hayley with Ryan?"

Cathy grimaced at her friend and more tears welled. "You were right. I shouldn't have kept the secret all these years. Now, it's tearing me apart. Hayley wants to know her dad and she has the right. *Dio mio,* she asked Ryan to marry us! She'd already picked him for her father when she'd thought her 'real' father was already married."

"I always said Hayley was one determined little girl. Just like her mother." Helen hesitated. "Do you trust Ryan to give her back in time for school?"

"Completely." Cathy's firm voice tried to contradict her quivery chin—and failed. "I'm not so sure about Hayley. I th-think my little girl h-hates me."

"You poor dear," Helen said.

Cathy trembled with the longing to run into Helen's sympathetic embrace and cry away all her grief and anger. But she was terrified once she started to cry, she would never stop. Surrendering on a hard little sob, she ran to Helen's comforting embrace anyway. Great sobbing gulps of pain for her mother's death, her daughter's defection, and her lost love tore at her soul. She was left hollowed out, achingly alone and desperately lonely for Hayley and Ryan. Thank God for dear Helen and her murmured denials and support. Pulling another tissue from the box on the table, Cathy mopped up and summoned a watery smile.

Helen gave her one last hug and set about making a pot of tea. "How did the clear-out of the house go?"

Cathy drew a shuddering breath and tossed out the mess of tissues. "Not bad considering the three decade's worth of stuff in the house. Yola choked when we came across some of my baby clothes. Especially my knitted lace christening gown—incredibly delicate work. The moths had eaten holes everywhere. She cried at the damage and regretted Hayley hadn't worn it."

Helen slid the cardboard envelope over the table to Cathy. "Don't forget this."

Inside, Cathy found the official job offer for her vice-presidency with its lovely fat salary and delicious bonus. Only her signature was needed. Cathy stuffed the pages in her handbag and climbed to the third floor where she and Hayley had their rooms. She dropped the contract on her bedroom dresser while she unpacked.

For a few shining hopeful moments, she toyed with the notion of returning to Clarence Bay. Could one man realistically be persuaded to propose for a third time? Not damn likely. Hope wilted and died on the bleak plains of her despair.

Monday morning, dressed for success in her navy-skirted suit and moderate pumps, she walked into her new corner office suite and stared out at her south-facing view. Crowds speckled the Toronto islands, cramming the last days of the summer full to the brim with family activities.

Tears welled and blurred her vision. She allowed herself one quiver of her jaw and blinked back her tears.

Drawing a determined breath, she squared her shoulders, sat at her big teak desk, and signed the damn contract. Her first assignment was a complex restructuring of her dysfunctional and unwieldy department into lean product-oriented units. Through the resulting dozens of meetings, teleconferences, and delicate negotiations that consumed her mind, Cathy's heart longed for her daughter. And her daughter's father.

"Caterina, there's something we must discuss," ZiaYola presented a worried face in Cathy's home office.

Harassed, Cathy glanced up from her phone that had been ringing, dinging, and chiming all day and well into the evening. The price of success was measured by the noises issued by a little black box. Cathy scrolled through an email. "Yes, Zia Yola, what can I do for you?"

"Caterina, are you paying attention?"

Cathy sighed in aggravation, set her phone on her desk, and looked at her aunt standing in the doorway. "Okay, I'm paying attention."

Zia Yola sat down on the blue floral couch. "Will you come shopping with me for my wedding dress and your maid-of-honour dress?"

Cathy picked up her phone to look for a date and the damn thing beeped another incoming message. Cathy sighed. The CEO wanted to ensure the latest item had been added to the agenda for tomorrow's meeting. Cathy ignored it and flipped to her calendar, thumbing her way down to look for an empty day. "Looks like I can do three weeks from next Tuesday."

ZiaYola slapped her hands on her thighs. "I guess it will have to do. Were you able to give any thought to the colour you prefer?"

Cathy dropped her chin abruptly to her chest, weighed down by guilt. "No, I'm sorry. You're so happy, I've ignored you, and I shouldn't have. Let's decide now. What colour did you have in mind? What day is your wedding again?"

ZiaYola pressed her lips together in a hard thin line. "And

this is what you call paying attention? What if I had something really important to discuss?"

Her phone chimed with her assistant's reminder note to see her boss in the morning. Moments later, Hayley's personal ringtone sounded—a tinny Justin Bieber song.

Her smile barely cracked the tension in Cathy's face.

"It's Hayley."

Yola nodded. "She comes first. I can wait." Cathy took the time span of a ring to loosen her shoulders and throat so Hayley wouldn't hear, and worry about, the tension in her voice.

"Hi, sweetie, how's it going?"

"Finally you're answering your phone I've been trying all day and I've been getting nothing but voice mail."

"I'm sorry, sweetie, I'm just so wrapped up with my new job." Cathy settled in her chair, ready for a nice long chat. "How's it going?"

"Can you remember if my bike is too small? Daddy wants to buy me a new one."

Cathy winced as Hayley rushed past the niceties. "If your daddy wants to buy you a new bike, tell him to go ahead. He doesn't need my approval." Cathy rubbed her forehead with her fingers to soothe the sudden headache. She reached into her purse for painkillers. *Santo cielo.* She'd bought the bottle only last week and now it was empty?

"Do we have any more painkillers?" Cathy asked her aunt.

"I will get them for you," said Zia Yola as she sprang up and hurried from the room.

"So how was your day today, sweetie?"

"Okay, I guess. Lindsey and I were in the playhouse. It's not the same because you aren't here," Hayley complained.

"Don't you remember we discussed this before I left? You know I had to come back to work. My leave is over. I've got a big job taking a lot more time."

"Yeah, I remember. Even Daddy said that about your job."

Ryan talked to Hayley about her job? Was this a good thing? "Don't you like spending the days at Lindsey's house?"

"Yeah, it's okay. Except sometimes her mom sleeps so much and the little boys are a real pain in the butt."

"You know you could have come back to Toronto with me." Cathy hated herself for playing tug-of-war with her daughter in the middle. But she couldn't help it. She was jealous of Ryan for their daughter's time. Zia Yola quietly handed Cathy the painkillers and a glass of water. Cathy mouthed her thanks and gratefully knocked back the pills.

Cathy listened with half an ear to Hayley's chatter while scanning for an earlier day for Zia Yola's shopping expedition. Her thumb hovered over a calendar entry. The day scheduled for picking Hayley up from Clarence Bay was the same day the CEO expected her to attend a corporate opera function with Matt. The round trip up north took six hours at a bare minimum and she'd wanted to spend the weekend. There was still so much to be done to get the Clarence Bay house ready to put on the market.

Santo cielo. Her heart dropped into her shoes. She'd have to beg Ryan to bring Hayley down to Toronto. "Is your dad home?" she asked Hayley reluctantly. She'd only had stilted conversations with Ryan—confined to the topic of their daughter—since the final discussion of Hayley's visit to him.

"Yeah, but Paul came with Grandpa. They went into Dad's office and shut the door."

Cathy went limp with relief at not having to talk to Ryan then stiffened at the meaning in the message. Ryan was in trouble with his campaign. Dead serious trouble if he was behind closed doors with Bucky of all people. What had she done to them all?

"Don't interrupt them. I'll call back later."

Fortunately, ZiaYola read her expression and jumped to her rescue. She would get Hayley. Cathy hung her head in shame. She didn't even have the time to drive a measly 220 kilometres and back to get her daughter. The happy job had to be delegated to her aunt.

And this was supposed to be a better life?

A timid knock sounded on Ryan's home-office door. He glanced at his father and Paul sitting across from him. "Hayley wants me. Do you mind if we break for a while? Clear our heads?"

"Not at all," Bucky agreed to the interruption. "Every minute I spend with my new granddaughter is fine with me."

Paul shrugged his agreement and Ryan called to his daughter. She barrelled into the room, around his desk, and straight into his lap. Her Flower-Power sweater from Zia Yola glowed in the grey evening light of yet another miserable day in an endless week of chilly late-August rain.

"Hi, Daddy." She added a smack on his cheek to her greeting. They grinned at each other, still stoked about their newfound relationship. "I called Mom like you said. She's okay with the new bike."

"What's wrong, Sweetpea?" She wrinkled her nose at the nickname. "No good, eh?" They were having fun choosing nicknames for her—the more outrageous, the harder she giggled. So far, only honey and my girl made the grade. Sweetie was out because that's what her mother called her.

"Mom's really busy and she sounds really tired and kinda sad. She wanted to talk to you but I said you were busy and she said she'll call back."

"Did she have anything specific to talk about?" Ryan grimaced at the pathetic longing in his voice.

"She didn't say."

"Come and give your granddad a hug, kiddo," Bucky said. Hayley went for another hug and leaned against Bucky's leg. After the initial shock, they'd taken to each other like bread and butter. Paul tossed her a cheery wink from the plaid chair. The men laughed at her facial contortions in a comical attempt to wink back.

Damn, his little girl was a doll and a half. She brought a whole new dimension to his life—and lots of redecorating and shopping and other girly stuff.

"Mom said she has to go to a dance, but she didn't sound like it would be much fun. Why wouldn't she want to get all dressed up and go to a dance?"

The music festival's opening gala swamped Ryan's memory. Cathy in her silver dress with the pearly discs had driven him nuts with desire. He brushed his palms over the studs of his jeans to ease the itch.

"Did she say if she was going with anyone? Larissa maybe?" Paul asked with a naughty gleam in his eyes. Apparently he, too, had reminiscences from the same party.

"Matt's gonna take her. She didn't talk about Larissa's going."

"Who's Larissa?" Bucky asked.

"Just you average corporate barracuda," Ryan joked.

Matt Bartholomew's contemptuous city-slicker face and tower-hugging attitude oiled its way into Ryan's mind. Jealousy twisted in his gut. "Is the dance for something special?"

"Mom's company made a big donation to the opera so they're invited to a fancy party." She rolled her eyes. "I think companies donate a lot of money just to show off and get free tickets."

Ryan exchanged stunned looks with Paul at the world-weary sophisticate masquerading as his daughter. Bucky laughed and gave his granddaughter a playful bump on her chin with his big fist. "That's my girl, calling them as she sees them—a regular chip off the old block."

"So are you finished? Can you drive me to Lindsey's?"

"Sorry, honey. We're still not done. Probably won't be for a while. Why don't you read some more or watch one of the movies I got for you?"

A huge pout formed on her delicate features and she crossed her arms. He opened his mouth to start a losing bargaining session with his sharp-dealing kid. An abrupt motion from his dad caught his eye. His dad gave him a minute shake of the head. *Don't bargain.* Who knew he'd be getting parenting advice from his father? And even more astonishing, taking said advice and that it was working.

"No, Hayley. I know you're mad, but this is a business thing just like your mom's—I have to do it. I'll take you to Lindsey's tomorrow while I give my speech so you don't have to listen to me bore the town. Okay?"

She sulked for a bit then finally, reluctantly, gave up.

"Will you read more Trixie to me tonight?"

He grinned at her relentless bargaining. "Why would I pass on the best part of my day?"

She threw herself at him for a hug then bounced her way out of the room and shut the door behind her with a little slam. He sighed and rubbed the back of his neck. As challenging as he found the new enterprise of fatherhood, a huge hole would be ripped in his gut when his little girl went back to her mother at the end of the Labour Day weekend. At least he'd see her every second weekend after that.

"Being a dad ain't easy, is it, son?"

"Nope. Would raising her be any easier if I'd had more practice, started when she was a baby?"

"Good question. No clue about the answer. However, I now have the answer to your crappy poll returns."

"Excellent. What have you got for us?" Paul slapped Bucky on the shoulder. As good as Bucky's advice might be about parenting, Ryan still hated asking his father for political advice.

Ryan drew a breath to protest then used it scoffed at his worn-out declarations of transparency. More like spin-doctoring. Managing voter perception, Paul called it. Spinning, managing, whatever label you stuck on the action, Ryan knew it was subterfuge. He hated the deception and was beginning to hate himself for succumbing to the need to staunch the bleed-out of his poll numbers.

"As you refuse to use Baylor's affair against him—"

"I've slung enough mud already."

His dad perked up at the muttered confession. "You have? When? Who?"

"Virginia Carleton-Grant wanted revenge because I didn't want to marry Becca. She threatened me with malicious gossip and—thanks to your history with her—I did the same back."

A huge grin spread across his dad's face. "So that's why she endorsed you. Well done, my boy."

For a foolish second, Ryan grinned at the unfamiliar approval. A scowl grabbed his whole body, more at his own weakness than his dad's morals. "I figured you'd liked that. It's not something I ever want to repeat. Regardless of the consequences."

"Just because it turned out to be politically advantageous to you, doesn't mean you did the wrong thing. How would you have handled it differently?" Bucky sat back, clearly waiting for an answer.

Ryan scowled. "I wouldn't have. But I refuse to go down that muddy road again."

Before the discussion could go any further, Paul cut in. "Let's call it a draw and get back to the current problem."

Ryan and his dad exchanged spiked glances, agreeing once again to disagree.

"To fix the current problem, you need to use a variation on the love-my-family spin," Bucky said.

Drawn back to his dad's words, Ryan laughed derisively. "How can we spin my family when I don't have one?"

His dad jabbed a thumb over his shoulder. "You forgot your little girl already? She's your family."

He stared, aghast at the suggestion. "Typical. See a person, use a person. It's tantamount to abuse when it's a little kid."

Bucky rolled his eyes. "Showing off your family in public is not abuse. Paul, talk to the boy. Tell him what abuse really is."

Paul withdrew deep inside himself for a long moment. Ryan had seen the closed expression before, knew his good friend relived some hideous event of his childhood.

Ryan's mouth twisted in disgust at his dad's careless

reference. "He does not need to talk to me. I volunteer at the family shelter, remember? There are many ways to take advantage of a person."

Paul shook himself like a wet dog and returned from his shadows in full campaign-manager mode. "Your dad's right, you're not abusing her. You're exercising your political astuteness. Your support faded with the exposure of your past."

"But I didn't know—" Ryan thumped his fist on the desk.

"True. Some people understand the fickleness of human nature. Others, not so much."

"But I didn't—"

"Stop right now, shut up, and listen," Paul ordered.

Bucky grinned and tilted his head in Paul's direction, seconding his command. These two were ganging up on him? Ryan's teeth clacked as he snapped his mouth shut, crossed his arms, and leaned back in his chair.

Paul got up and paced, thinking out loud. "Some people have made up their minds that since you lied about Hayley, you're lying about your political convictions. The way you've been sending Hayley off to Lindsey's every day makes it seem like you're still trying to hide her."

His dad ended Ryan's protest with a stabbing forefinger.

Paul continued. "It's been construed as dishonest. I'm thinking if you take her around with you, people will see you care about her. If they see you connecting with her, being with her, you might reverse the tide of disapproval."

Bucky nodded vigorously.

"Don't you think parading her around is like waving a red flag at a bull?" Ryan asked.

"No, it's a delicate balance. Everyone is dying of curiosity about you and Hayley. Hiding her turns the curiosity into malicious gossip. You take her with you, the gossip goes for you instead of against you."

His dad leaned in. "I'll tell you something I've learned over the years as mayor of Clarence Bay. This town is nuts about happy ever afters. Give them one and the mayor's office is yours."

Paul was impressed. "Huh. I never thought about why they love to gossip about romance."

"You mean, why they love to gossip about you and your long string of conquests and when are you finally going to pick one and settle down?" Bucky teased Paul. The sudden bleak look on Paul's face killed Ryan's laughter in his throat.

"All kidding aside," Bucky continued, "Clarence Bay is an optimistic place. Always looking on the good side first and standing behind you when you try to fix a mistake. Provided you acknowledge the error of your ways."

Ryan agonized over the arguments of the two more experienced men. Every morning, he tussled with Hayley about dropping her off. This would make them both happy and give them some quality time together. Hope rose in him, lifting his spirit, for the first time in a long, long while.

"Okay. Maybe you're right. It does look like I've been hiding her. But I won't bore her with campaign stuff. We'll go to public places—have dinner at The Pits, see a movie. It might be fun to take her to buy back-to-school supplies. Maybe Mark and Lindsey might go with us because Meg isn't up to shopping these days."

"Now you're talking, son. Now that's family!"

CHAPTER 16

Election Results

"Dang, I can feel it in my bones, Ryan. You're going to win this thing," Melody squeezed his arm.

Ryan gave her a tight doubtful smile on the evening of the third Monday in October—Municipal Election Day for all the municipalities in the province. Crammed into the school auditorium, they watched the returns along with a few hundred friends and supporters. Adam Baylor's crowd had gathered on the other side of town in the basement of the largest church.

The distinctive scent of fallen leaves breezed through the open doors, ruffling the red and white streamers and balloons. In a corner, a wide-screen TV reported the province-wide results.

"It's too close to call, even with half the returns counted," Ryan said. He glanced at the white board showing the Clarence Bay vote count. He currently stood behind Adam Baylor by ninety-two votes. Ten minutes ago, he'd been ahead by eighty-nine votes.

"Have you heard from Cathy lately?" Melody asked with a

boldly avid look on her face. "Will I have an item for my Hatch, Match, and Dispatch column?"

Ryan flinched at the direct question from the only person in town who owned the brass pair to dare. During the last intense weeks on the campaign trail, everyone had tiptoed around the topic of him and Cathy oh-so-delicately. He'd played deaf to the subtle hints and questions, and focused on the issues and let Hayley field the questions about her mom. His brain hurt thinking of his increased skill in avoidance and deflection. What hurt even more was the slow learning that maybe his dad was right. Sometimes you had no choice but to fight fire with fire.

He knew Cathy's exact location tonight—the opera ball. He pictured her in that clinging silver dress, sashaying through the swanky crowd with the creep Bartholomew fawning at her side. Every second Friday night and following Sunday afternoon when he either picked up or dropped off Hayley, he expected to see the creep in the place that belonged to Ryan. Ha! He hadn't seen Cathy, never mind anyone else but Helen. Cathy always managed to be elsewhere.

A red balloon bobbed before his eyes and snapped him from his jealous and futile musings. Hayley, with him on this important night, tugged on his hand. "Are we gonna win, Dad?"

"Of course we are. I can feel it in here." Melody tapped her chest.

He sproinged one of his daughter's curls. "We'll have to wait and see."

"Grandpa says the exit polls are favourable." Ryan chuckled at his pint-sized expert. Puzzlement creased her forehead. "What are exit polls?"

"Reporters stand around outside the polling station and ask

people who they voted for."

"Really? Sounds kinda silly when they have the real vote in the box."

"Yep, it is kinda silly. Though it can be a prediction of how things are going."

"It doesn't count. Does it?"

"Nope."

"Way stupid." Hayley voiced her frustration with bizarre election rituals.

"Yep. Did you get some ice cream?"

"Yep. I had three."

"Oh. Guess that's enough for one day." Ryan looked up from his daughter's big brown eyes to the plaid-covered belly of his father. "Hey, Dad."

"The exit polls are good," Bucky said.

Ryan slid Hayley a knowing glance. Laughing, he tapped her nose and she ran off to join Lindsey and the little-girl posse. Meg and Mark were home with their new baby boy.

"What was the joke?" Dad asked suspiciously.

"We were talking about the uselessness of exit polls and too much ice cream."

"The kid is going to be Prime Minister some day." His dad puffed with pride. Ryan could only agree. He'd been doing that a lot lately. If felt weird. Good, but weird.

The whistle blew to announce an update from the central counting desk. He was ahead by fifty-four votes. The smallness of the number depressed him. Even for a town of 6,500 people with just over 3,000 on the electoral list, fifty-four votes in the lead was a pitiful thing.

"I've never seen such a tight race." His dad shook his head, gave Ryan a hangdog look.

A tight race—talk about useless information. The hovering failure dragged at Ryan's shoulders. He should be used to the weight by now.

"Whatever the outcome, I'm still proud of the way you handled the last couple of weeks. I couldn't have done better myself." His dad's arm slid around Ryan's shoulders in an awkward half-hug.

Surprised, Ryan lit with the glow of his father's approval even in the face of a total flop.

The whistle shrilled again. Now he lagged six votes behind. A groan vibrated in every throat in the room.

Nana Jean approached and tucked her hand beneath his arm. He bent his elbow, cradling her slender wrist against his side.

"All the seniors voted for you, Ryan."

He patted her hand, knowing Nana Jean and Hayley had worked the dining room at the residence. "I'm grateful for your support. If I actually win this thing, I'll throw a thank-you party for the residents."

She beamed up at him, looking exactly like an older version of Hayley. It still amazed him how blind he'd been to their similarity. If his mom were here, they'd look like a science fair project—a perfect progression of look-alike generations.

"Ooo, party! And there's no if about it. You're going to win." She wagged a delicate finger at him. "Isn't he, Bucky?"

"You betcha, Jean."

Another whistle blast sounded. One-hundred-and-six votes ahead, three polling stations left to report. The crowd muttered satisfaction. Nobody cheered, saving their energy.

A flurry of activity burst across the control table. The last three polls reported in rapid succession. Hayley appeared out of nowhere, tucked herself into his other side, and wrapped one skinny arm around his waist. Standing between generational bookends, he missed the women in between. He hoped his mom watched with pride from the beyond. Cathy's absence was an ache in his soul he couldn't figure out how to soothe.

The room drew its collective breath. Held it, waiting, watching.

The official approached the white board, raised her marker.

He was two-hundred-and-twenty-seven votes ahead.

Three-hundred-and-two votes ahead.

The more optimistic among the crowd began to cheer.

Three whistle blasts warned of final results.

Four-hundred-and-seventy-nine votes ahead.

A full-throated roar erupted from the crowd. Hayley squealed and jumped up and down, jostling his arm. Nana Jean rose on her tiptoes and kissed his cheek. His dad hugged all three of them. Ryan's heart burst with relief.

How he wished Cathy was part of the family hug.

Two months after his December first installation as mayor, Ryan sagged back in the big leather chair behind his heavily-carved desk. The novelty of being His Lordship, the Mayor of Clarence Bay had worn off like cheap paint after a single phone call three weeks ago.

An environmental assessment had reversed the town council's approval of an important land deal for an up-market residential and marina project. All the hard work to ensure the deal met the new requirements was done in by a snake. Not the typical snake in human clothing. A real snake—the endangered massasauga rattler to be precise. Millions of dollars of potential long-term revenue were gone in the shake of a rattler's tail. He groaned at the horrendous pun. The town council now scrambled for ways to meet the huge fees resulting from the cancelled project.

The thick folder of failed suggestions taunted him, the computer chimed a new message, the desk phone blinked with more messages.

Today, the expected mega-mall offer by the Big Deal Corporation landed on his desk along with a demand by council to fill the coffers immediately and ignore future costs.

Now he understood what his father proclaimed all these years. High-flown principles filled the ballot box, but money greased the wheels of local politics. Ryan refused to renege on his campaign promise to preserve Clarence Bay's small-town atmosphere.

Small town versus mall town.

He'd have to think of some other way to compensate for the lost tax revenue, find some other land for development. At least the council backed his downtown rejuvenation plan—so far.

He wished he could talk to Cathy, get her savvy big-picture input on his dilemma. But, she continued to be invisible on his trips to Toronto. The only light in the dark days of winter was Hayley. Christmas had born a double-edged quality as having Hayley in Clarence Bay took her away from Cathy.

Wearily, he shoved upright to stroll down the hall to discuss the money problem with Adam Baylor. He still congratulated himself on the strategic appointment of his opponent as deputy mayor. The town had gossiped for days over the announcement. Fortunately, general consensus landed on the favourable side.

The cell phone at his hip vibrated. Cathy leapt first into his thoughts. He shut down the useless hope. She was gone and not coming back. Twice he'd proposed. Twice she'd rejected him. He'd read between the lines of her politely enthusiastic email of congratulations. She didn't want his love. She only wanted him to be a father to their child.

He stopped in Adam's doorway with the idea of Hayley calling from Toronto firmly in his mind. She loved to call at odd moments of the day on the purple cell phone he'd given her.

"Let me get this." He always made time for his daughter, so he unclipped the phone with a ready smile, checked number. Hmm, not Hayley.

"Hello?"

"Ryan Chisholm?"

"Yes."

"It's Nurse Daniels from Emergency at the Clarence Bay District Health Center. Your father's here. He's suffering from arrhythmia and he's asking for you."

"He's having a heart attack?" He about-faced and headed for the front exit. Adam followed from his office.

"You need to get here as soon as possible."

"I'm already on my way." Ryan snapped his phone shut while running down the hall. He tossed out a few words to a startled Adam and blew past his assistant on the way to his truck. Coatless, he white-knuckled the brief trip to the hospital, parked haphazardly among the snow banks and ran into the emergency wing.

Nurse Daniels waited for him. "He's in the OR now, being prepped for surgery."

"How did he get here?"

"Called 9-1-1 himself from home. He instructed us to call you. He said you have Power of Attorney for Personal Care? Is that correct?"

"Yes."

"Will you sign this permission for a bypass, please?" She thrust a clipboard at him.

"Dad can't sign for himself?"

"Not at the moment."

Struggling with a sudden terror, Ryan signed his permission and handed it back to the worried nurse.

"Thanks. The waiting room is on the third floor. You can call people from the pay phone, no cell phones allowed in hospital." She rested a sympathetic hand on his arm. "Don't worry, he's in the best of hands with Dr. Clemmons."

Ryan hustled to the waiting room where he called Mark. He gave his white-faced brother a man-hug when he arrived. Together they waited as the clock ticked its way through six hours. To bolster their hopes, they reminisced about their dad, recalled their mom, laughed at incidents both proud and profane.

Finally, Dr. Clemmons arrived, a tall balding man wearing clean scrubs, his face was drawn with the strain of cardiac surgery.

"Mr. Chisholm is in Critical Care, doing as well as can be expected. He suffered a major heart attack and we performed a double bypass. His condition is touch and go at the moment. You can both visit him, talk to him. Though he's unconscious, he might hear you. Give him a few words of encouragement."

His brother glanced back at Ryan as they crept into the room where Bucky lay still and pale beneath the sheets. Machines hummed and beeped in comforting rhythm. Mark scrubbed eyes red-rimmed with exhaustion, likely as gritty as Ryan's own. They moved in unison to either side of the bed and each took one of their father's hands, bracketing the unconscious man with their strength. Dr. Clemmons hovered at the glass door.

"Dad?" Mark's voice had a gravelly edge. "We're here, me and Ryan."

"The doctor said you might be able to hear us. So we're here to tell you we—umm—we love you. We're waiting for you to come home," Ryan said.

"Yeah, Dad. Meg and the kids send their love."

"And Hayley said it's not time for your exit poll yet." Ryan attributed the words to Hayley just to cheer up his dad. If he heard them.

A faint movement tugged at a corner of his father's mouth. Damp-eyed, Ryan looked across the bed at Mark. "Did he just smile?" Ryan hissed.

"Yes," Mark hissed back.

Mark planted a kiss on Bucky's forehead. "We'll be back tomorrow, Dad."

"Yeah, don't go anywhere without us." Ryan gripped his father's hand.

Bucky responded with a faint curl of the fingers of both hands for both sons. He sighed deeply and relaxed. Ryan and Mark questioned each other, then glanced at Dr. Clemmons who smiled reassuringly.

"He's asleep. It's the best thing for him right now." The steady beeping backed up the doctor's opinion. Bucky lived and breathed.

The brothers straightened. Mark gestured with his head and

Ryan followed his older brother from the room. Self-conscious from the display of emotions, they avoided each other's gaze as they waited for the doctor.

"Thanks, Dr. Clemmons."

"We did everything in our power. The rest is up to your father." He grasped a shoulder of each brother and turned them towards the elevators, gave them gentle reassuring slaps. "You did good work in there, guys. He's resting easy. Now go home and get some sleep. We'll call you if there are any changes during the night."

As Ryan flopped into his empty bed in the wee hours, he longed for someone to talk over the tumultuous day. Not just anyone—Cathy. He wanted Cathy by his side. He reached for the phone, but stopped dialling after six digits. It was the freaking middle of the night. She didn't need his burden added to her own. She didn't need him at all.

Ryan sauntered into the semi-private room where his father had been moved after a tense week in Critical Care.

"Hey, Doctor. How's my dad?"

Dr. Clemmons looked up from his note-making. "Much better than expected. We'll send him home in five days, if all goes well."

"Five days too late." Bucky grumbled. "I've got a corporation to run. Get me out of here now."

The doctor raised his grizzled eyebrows at Bucky's demanding tone. "No, you don't."

"What do you mean?" Bucky growled at the doctor.

Ryan cringed for the man facing his father. Even with a temper reduced by a tour of the cardiac wing, his father still made grown men nervous.

"I mean you will not be running any corporation in five days, five weeks, or five months. There is significant tissue damage needing considerably longer to heal. You'll have a strict regimen of aftercare. Any stress of any kind will jeopardize the healing process. So consider yourself retired."

Bucky jabbed an intimidating finger at the younger man. "Now listen sonny boy, I'm not ready—"

The doctor raised his own long skinny finger to interrupt his patient, deliberately placed the medical chart in the box at the end of Bucky's bed. Dr. Clemmons gave Ryan a slight heads-up with a dark glance, crossed his arms, and turned to Bucky.

"I can see you're a straight forward sort of man, Mr. Chisholm, so I'll be very blunt. You have two choices regarding what happens next. Retire and live. Or work and die."

Bucky's eyes rounded with the force of the ultimatum. Ryan reeled in the shock wave rolling off his father. Then reeled some more, when his father's eyes narrowed in his direction.

He instinctively raised his hands in self-defence. "No, Dad."

His dad gave Ryan an innocent look. "What?"

"I will not run your company for you."

"But—"

"I've barely been mayor for three months."

"A job you got with my help."

"I'm grateful for your help, just not grateful enough to quit."

"Ryan, may I have a word?" Dr. Clemmons' quiet tones cut through the increasing decibel levels.

Alarmed, Ryan took stock of his father's flushed cheeks and ragged breathing. He turned abruptly and left the room. The doctor followed, shutting the door behind them and moved down the hall to a tiny seating area.

Ryan turned on the doctor. "Do not tell me to resign as mayor and take over my father's company."

Dr. Clemmons raised his hands. "I wouldn't dare suggest it. My concern is your father's health, which is too fragile at the moment for contentious issues. Do whatever you must to calm him down and keep him that way. It's up to you how you do it."

CHAPTER 17

Mother and Daughter

Caterina was an hour-and-forty-five minutes late, leaving very little time before the engagement party began. Yola glanced at her watch and smiled uneasily at Leo. "She promised she'd come home early. She probably got caught up in work. She's very busy with her new job. Vice president you know." She tipped her head, listening hard, certain the tiny noise came from Caterina's key in the door.

"Yes, I know *cara mia*. You have said many times." Yola's handsome *fidanzato* tried to soothe her fear with a calm voice and gentle caress.

It worked for a moment then the tension screwed her shoulders tighter than ever. "I'm sorry. I'm just so nervous. I want you to love Caterina and her daughter." She spread her apology to each of Leo's four handsome sons as well. They'd travelled all the way from Italy to meet Caterina, and she wasn't here to be met. *Santo cielo*, could anything be more frustrating?

"No worries, Mamma Yola, we are ready to love our sister and niece as much as we love you." Giancarlo, Leo's eldest son, spoke for the brothers who ranged in age from seventeen to twenty-two. Of course, they had been shocked at first then gradually delighted to discover an older sister and an adorable niece. Today, they welcomed their stepmother-to-be with open arms. The romance of their father's first love was an irresistible story to these fine Italian boys.

"We are looking forward to more women in the family." His fourth son, seventeen-year-old Ilario, waggled his eyebrows at her. Trey, his third son, snickered and nudged him in the ribs. Teenagers were the same the world over.

She rewarded him with a tight smile. Tonight, friends old and new were invited to the engagement party. Ryan had declined due to his father's poor health and the pressures of the mayor's office. Too bad, because Yola missed him.

She paced around the front parlour, checking everything again—drinks, snacks, dips—all in order and ready.

For seeming ages Yola had intended to reveal the truth of her motherhood, introduce Caterina to her father and the half-siblings to each other. These momentous events were supposed to take place several weeks ago, before Hayley returned home. Unfortunately, Caterina had been harder to pin down than a definitive recipe for tomato sauce. Every single time Yola approached Caterina; there had been excuses, delays, and brush-offs. Leo had been nothing but sympathetic and supportive. If Yola had been a true mother, she would not have tolerated such neglect. As a very cowardly aunt, there had always been another time to divulge the news. Her hand fluttered to her mouth.

Now Caterina and Hayley would find out everything, meet everyone, all at once.

And *santo cielo,* of course, Caterina was late. And Hayley waited impatiently upstairs with a long-suffering Helen. And Yola's nerves were like un-cooked spaghettini—stretched thin and brittle, ready to snap at the slightest touch.

Caterina's key scraped in the lock for real this time. Yola bustled into the hallway, pulling the pocket doors together behind her.

"I'm so sorry I'm late. My boss needed to analyze and debate every tiny little thing." Caterina tossed her briefcase on the closet floor and hung up her coat. "I'll run upstairs to tidy up and be right back down. Your guests will be coming in about half an hour, won't they? I'm so sorry I wasn't here to help you." After dropping a quick apologetic kiss on Yola's cheek and giving only a brief glance at the closed doors, she ran up the stairs.

Hayley flew down, meeting her mother halfway. "Finally, you're home. Helen's been keeping me upstairs while they're having a party down here."

"Really?" Caterina turned to Yola with a puzzled stare that went coy. "Why, Zia Yola, have you got a secret? Other than finally meeting Leo?"

Yola twisted her hands and swallowed hard. Her engagement ring dug deeply into the palm of her right hand. She barely felt the pain.

Hayley giggled. "I'll bet she does. She's been whispering with Helen for ages about this party. Why else would I be stuck up here until you got home?"

Caterina tapped her daughter's nose and tossed a naughty wink down the stairs. "Let me get washed up and then we'll discover Zia Yola's big secret together. Okay?"

"Do I have to wait? I'm so tired of waiting," Hayley begged.

Yola put her foot down. "*Sì,* you must wait for your mother." Like tearing off a bandage, she wanted to do the revelation only once.

After an eternity, Caterina and Hayley came downstairs. Behind them, Helen gave Yola an encouraging smile, which didn't help to still the tremors making it difficult to slide back the pocket doors. All five men jumped to their feet, lined up from youngest to oldest. Yola's heart slammed against her ribs. Caterina was going to hate her.

Cathy drew a quick breath at so many beautiful Italian men in one room all at the same time. They smiled at her in an oddly expectant way. She hoped she lived up to the reputation Zia Yola had clearly built for the step-relations-to-be. She and Hayley walked toward the oldest man, Zia Yola's fiancé Leo, she guessed. As she passed his sons, a sense of déjà vu crept over her. Had she met these men before?

Zia Yola moved to Leo's side. Helen stood just behind her. As if for support?

"Caterina, this is Leo Giacometti and his sons, Giancarlo, Emilio, Trey, and Ilario. Leo, this is my Caterina and her Hayley."

"Welcome to Toronto, Leo." She received a kiss on each cheek, as did Hayley. The sense of knowing strengthened. "Excuse me, have we met before?"

Leo's smile broadened. He tucked Zia Yola under her arm. Why did she look so terrified?

"Are you my grandfather?" Hayley asked.

Leo and all his sons laughed as if Hayley said something extremely clever.

Cathy squeezed her daughter's hand. "No, sweetie, he's not. But soon he'll be your great-uncle, your *prozia,* when Zia Yola and Leo get married."

Hayley rolled her eyes. "I know, Mom. Leo and the other guys look just like you—if you were a man. You know, how I kinda look like Dad but mostly like his mom?"

"You have to stop the face-matching. Remember how much trouble that got you into?" Cathy looked at Leo. "I'm sorry. Hayley likes to play detective."

Leo shrugged as only an Italian man can shrug—acknowledging much, saying little. "I'd say she's an excellent detective. She has deduced correctly with very little evidence."

Cathy blinked at him, cut a glance at the tense and worried Zia Yola and the stalwart Helen at her elbow. "What?"

"Hayley is my granddaughter—"

"Way cool! Now I have two grandpas." She released Cathy's hand and turned to the four younger men. "So are you guys my uncles? Wicked!"

The young men laughed hugely and greeted Hayley with cheek kisses and hugs. Cathy watched her daughter cavort with them as if from another dimension—somewhere far away yet intimately close.

Cathy's gaze skimmed over Leo's hopeful face and locked onto Zia Yola's desperate brown eyes. Zia Yola held out a trembling hand. Cathy took it without thinking, startled by its coldness. "Zia, did Mamma have an affair?"

"No," she said in a strangled voice.

"So how...he...?" She flicked a glance at Leo.

Zia Yola tucked her hand into her fiancé's, linking Leo and Cathy. "Leo is your father. I am your mother. *Dio mi perdoni.*"

Words formed in Cathy's mind, struggled to gel into coherent thought, slid away as more words took their place. Nothing made sense, all was gobbledy-gook.

Helen brought sanity, meeting Cathy's gaze with deep honesty in her own. She nodded, affirming the wild story. Cathy's knees wobbled, her hand clenched around—her mother's? The sound of her own heartbeat boomed in Cathy's head.

Hayley skipped over to Zia—her grandmother? "So now you're somebody's *nonna*. Mine!"

The older woman grabbed Hayley's face and kissed her soundly on both cheeks. "*Sì.* I am also somebody's mamma." The word filled the space between them, swelled to occupy the room, the house, the whole upside-down world.

Mamma?

Zia Yola was her biological mother.

Hayley squealed with joy. "When school ended, I only had my mom and Helen in my family. Now I have a great-grandmother, two grandfathers, a new grandmother, five uncles, one aunt, four cousins and, best of all, a dad!" She flung her arms wide. "My family is huge! Awe-some!" Hayley spun until she staggered with dizziness. "I can't wait to tell the other kids."

Hours later, Cathy lay in bed staring at the ceiling. Her mood swung wildly between fierce denial and joyous acceptance. Hayley's blithe welcome of her newly expanded family was a stunner. Guess she'd grown accustomed to new family members springing out of nowhere.

All evening, Cathy had tried to call Zia Yola by the name of "Mamma". The word jammed at the back of her tongue. Maybe she'd call her Mamma Yola like her half-brothers.

Dio mio, she had four brothers. Each had welcomed her to the family. Each had rejoiced in their father's happiness at finding the three women. They teased her about being a wicked elder stepsister. Ilario even joked she could boss him around if she wanted to have a bit of fun.

All these years, she'd known herself as Caterina Lucia Rossetti. Turned out she was Caterina Lucia deBartolo. Or should she have been Caterina Lucia Giacometti?

Hayley, too, had been going under an assumed name. Cathy scoffed at the new meaning of *assumed name* spun from the tatters of her life. How ironic she'd almost changed her name to deBartolo when she'd left Clarence Bay so long ago.

All these years, she'd believed her mother hadn't loved her. Her real mother had loved enough to sacrifice her own identity for the safety and security of her daughter.

Yola had clung to her family. In the same circumstances, Cathy had run away from hers.

A small memory eased its way forward. She was very young, lying in bed, a closed kid's book on the bedside table. Papà stroked her hair, kissed her forehead, and tucked the blankets around her small body. "You'll always be my *bella figlia.* I'll always be your Papà. No matter what," he said, seemingly out of the blue. The puzzling determination in his voice suddenly made sense.

She was Antonio's little girl and Leo's grown daughter. Both men were Papà.

Had Ryan experienced this bizarre out-of-body alienation? He'd assumed he was a single man without kids. Then, bam, he's a father. The news and subsequent secrecy had ground him up and spit him out. No wonder he'd flinched away from her on the night of Mrs. Carleton-Grant's revelation. No wonder he'd never since met her eyes without hurt and confusion in his own.

She had committed a grave wrong against the father of her child. She should have told Ryan. Regardless of her fears, she should have told him.

She pressed a fist to her trembling mouth.

Silent tears trickled into her hairline. She'd always be grateful for her trip home this summer. She'd made peace with her—with Lucia—and done the right thing in giving Ryan and Hayley to each other.

But what had she done to him? How could this be called love? Was there any way on earth to make it up to him?

No, there was not.

She rolled to her side and jammed her head under her pillow in a foolish attempt to hide from her guilt and remorse. And to muffle the sound of the sobs that wracked her, body and soul.

A soft rap sounded on her bedroom door.

Cathy lifted her pillow from her sodden face.

"Caterina?" Zia Yola—her mother—eased the door opened and peeked in. "May I come in?" she asked, her voice thin with fear and doubt. Her aunt's—mother's—silky yellow robe glimmered in the dim light from the hallway.

Cathy snapped on the bedside lamp. Zia—Mamma—Yola timidly approached the bed and Cathy shifted to make room for her. A hopeful smile gleamed and faded and her head bowed almost to her knees.

"I couldn't sleep. I heard you crying so I came." She reached to the bedside table and handed Cathy a few tissues to mop up the remnants of her crying jag. "I am *pazza* with worry,

Caterina. I want to apologize again for the secret and the manner of its revelation. I'm a terrible coward. I was afraid you would hate me."

The whispered words, vibrating with fear, wrenched a painful empathy from Cathy. She had known the same fear of losing a daughter's love too well and too recently not to sympathize.

Hand to mouth, Zia Yola—Mamma struggled with tears. "Do you remember the day, the moment, you discovered you were *incinta,* pregnant?"

Cathy wiped away a fresh fall of tears and nodded.

"Do you remember how happy you were? And how very very afraid?"

"I came to you for help. Mam—Lucia didn't want to help. Instead, she wanted me to give up my child." The angry shouting and the brutal ultimatum resounded in the pounding of Cathy's heart.

"You were nineteen. I was fifteen when I got pregnant, barely sixteen when I gave birth to you. In the eyes of the law, I was too young to raise a child. It was either give you away to a stranger and never see you again, or give you to Lucia and Antonio and see you every day. Which would you choose?"

Cathy took Zia Yola's clenched fist, stroked the fingers open, and held on tight. "Why the lie?"

Zia Yo—Mamma stilled, moved back in time. "To protect us all from the scandal of an underage unwed mother. To keep you with me."

"Did Lucia want me?" Cathy swallowed hard. "Please don't lie."

"She was unable to have children. Antonio wanted a child so

much. He couldn't bear the thought of his dear little niece in the hands of a stranger, so he convinced us to deceive the world for all our sakes. But mostly for you, *ucellino*."

"I don't know what to call you," Cathy said.

"When you were born, Lucia gave her name to you, to mark you as hers. I named you after Caterina Sforza, a medieval *contessa* of great strength. I felt you would need a great deal of strength." Zia—Mamma pressed a hand to her heart, tears quivered in her eyes, her jaw worked convulsively. "Every time you called her 'Mamma', I wept. Every time she treated you so un-motherly, I wept. Every time you turned to me, hugged me, kissed me, I wept."

Zi—Mamma swallowed hard. The noise clawed at Cathy's throat.

"I don't want to weep anymore. I want to be your Mamma. I want to be Hayley's Nonna." She held out her hands in supplication to Cathy. "Please let me?"

Tears blurring and streaming, Cathy gazed at the dear face always so full of love for her, no matter the name. She scooped her Mamma into her arms and they cried for each other and they cried for joy.

Ryan rubbed his aching eyes as he closed yet another file. Gusts of wind-driven snow clattered against the night-blackened window reflecting himself and his tired brother. Towers of cardboard boxes crowded the spacious corporate offices of Chisholm Lakeland Development Corporation.

"Dad always hoped one of us would take over." Mark said as he lifted the last box to his side of the conference table. "He really meant you. I was totally useless during my time here."

Ryan grunted. "Yeah, that's a year of my life I'll never get back. He shot down every single proposal I put forward. If he didn't do it in person, he got some flunky to do it for him."

They'd already spent days going through the confused mass of their dad's files in preparation for the arrival of a public trustee to manage the company while Ryan stayed in office. Want ads for the trustee had been posted ten days ago. No one had yet shown any interest.

"Being a park ranger is the perfect job for you, Mark. The camper's kids are nuts about you," Ryan said.

Mark's mouth curled crookedly, acknowledging the truth.

"Plus you'll need all the benefits you can get if you keep having kids at the current rate."

Empty pizza boxes leaned against the overflowing recycling bin. Bags of shredded paper slumped in the hallway outside the door. Why had his dad kept all those defunct documents?

Ryan rolled his tight shoulders and opened another file, read another document. The blood drained from his head at the speed of sound, leaving a ringing hollow in his ears. He read the document again, and a third time. The pages crackled under his clenching fingers.

"What did you find?" Mark's concerned question slowed the anger rushing through Ryan.

"Dad's been negotiating with the Big Deal Corporation for months now."

"Huh? Lemme see."

Ryan handed over the offer. "Apparently, Dad's company—now our company—owns the parcel of land BDC wants for their mega-store. He's been holding out for an incredible amount of money. Way more than what the property is worth." He pointed to a figured buried in the depths of the counter-offer.

Mark whistled long and low. "Go, Dad."

Ryan saw his brother spending the money for his growing family. For a split second, he considered giving his brother the huge gift. "Sorry Mark, but I can't participate in this. The simple fact I know the offer exists puts me in conflict of interest."

"So, I'll sign the offer then."

"Can't. When you agreed to share the profits as silent partner, with no responsibility for the corporation, you didn't get signing authority. Damn! No wonder Dad was so secretive when he signed the company over to me. He knew this mess was waiting to blow up in my face."

"What's the problem with conflict of interest?"

Ryan tried not to groan over Mark's lack of knowledge. "A mayor has quite a bit of influence over his town council. If the mayor is also a land developer, he can influence council decisions for his own purposes, good or bad. Who benefits the most, the mayor or the town? That conflict of interest is illegal."

Mark nodded his understanding.

"BDC's application for approval hit the mayor's desk the day Dad had his heart attack. So, now I can influence a decision in the corporation's favour, or not. I'm in conflict of interest. The situation is rotten with an opportunism that makes Dad's previous tricks look like child's play."

He slammed his hands on the table, thrust out of his chair, and paced the room. "And I'm damned if I'll turn into a man worse than Dad."

Anger seethed under his skin as he cursed long and loud. "Damn it, I don't want to resign. Cathy was right; I can't look at myself in the mirror every morning if I don't give my best to our town."

"So? Who cares what some people will think?"

"I could go to jail for this. Plus, it's a matter of moral integrity. The town trusts me. If I turn my back on my publicly-stated beliefs to make a mega-profit, my reputation, my word, my self-respect won't be worth shit. Anything I did after would become suspect."

Mark's deep sigh told Ryan he'd said good-bye to all the things he'd get for Meg and the kids. "So, what are you gonna do?"

Three stressful days later, Ryan's knuckles cracked under the strain of his death grip on the podium in the Town Hall auditorium. The heaving sea of faces blurred before his tense vision. Ryan blinked, breathed, and tried hard to relax. He cleared his throat and sipped some water.

"Good morning, everyone, and thank you for coming." As he waited for quiet, he looked out over the shuffling crowd. The council members, seated front row center, nodded their support. Damn, he wished Cathy's friendly face was out there cheering him on. Paul tossed him a thumbs-up from the wings.

I can do this. I have to do this.

Ryan smiled, rolled his shoulders and crossed his hands over his notes. He looked out over the townspeople.

"During my campaign for mayor, I spoke with many of you about my deeply-held beliefs on effective transparent government. Many of you share those beliefs. The majority of you voted for me because of them. Thank you. Your vote of confidence in my commitment to my new-found family moved me deeply." A wave of wry chuckles and nods crossed the room at his veiled reference to Hayley's spectacular announcement at a spectacularly inappropriate moment.

"When I took office, my mandate stated 'Keep it clear, keep it clean, keep it small'. My mandate has now been threatened."

"Got another kid you didn't know about, Ryan?" some wag called out from way in the back.

The gossip lovers in the audience—the whole town—sat forward in anticipation. Ryan popped his eyes in overdone surprise, shook his head, and laughed along with the crowd.

He turned over the page for the introduction.

"Our beautiful town has many valuable assets. Foremost of these, is our civic-minded citizens. Each of you contributes to the reputation Clarence Bay has for caring, compassion and respect—the main ingredients in our small-town lifestyle. Another of our valuable assets is the land held by our town and her citizens. Each owner is guided by the principles of good stewardship. We try to balance land use with land protection. As proof of our good stewardship, a large marina project was recently cancelled in order to preserve the habitat for the endangered massasauga rattlesnake."

A chorus of *eww, yuck* rustled through the room.

Ryan spread his hands and grinned. "C'mon folks, even a snake deserves a safe neighbourhood."

The chuckles subsided and Ryan continued. "Good stewardship often has costs in the world of man. In this case, our town is liable for rather large fees related to the cancellation of the marina contract with the Althorp Group. Fees the town can't cover."

Gasps and murmurs greeted this grim statement.

He flipped over the page for the first point. He glanced at Mark in the second row and got a reassuring nod.

"As friends of the Chisholm family, you all know about Dad's heart attack." He raised his hands and smiled to forestall speculation. "Let me reassure you the Buckster is expected to live many more years. Provided he surrender his stressful involvement in his company, Chisholm Lakeland Development Corporation. He asked his sons, Mark and I, to take over. With the knowledge of council, my brother and I immediately sent out feelers for a trustee to manage Dad's company during my term as mayor. We have yet to receive any interest in the post."

He paused and tried to gauge the crowd. Everyone waited, trusting him. Oh God, they trusted him. His throat tightened with appreciation for the people of his town. How long would their trust last?

"While Mark and I were going through the files in preparation for the trustee, we found an active offer to purchase a parcel of land on Mill Lake owned by Dad's corporation. The buyer, BDC, is a well-known multi-national conglomerate. On the surface, all is good. One contract replaces another and the town is solvent. However, BDC has a nasty habit of undermining and hollowing out the downtown business center of whatever town grants it permission to build. These displaced businesses are run by the families of Clarence Bay."

Murmurs from the savvier members of the crowd rippled around the hall.

He leaned over the podium as if to whisper a secret. "Let me tell you, our eyes almost fell out of our heads at the number of zeroes in the offer." He straightened. "This offer has a problem apart from the reputation of the conglomerate. It's in direct opposition to the portion of my mandate saying 'keep it small.'"

Second point done.

"So, folks, we have two contracts before us."

He held out his left hand. "Althorp's broken contract which will cost the town a pile of money."

He held out his right hand. "And BDC's offer which will pay for breaking the contract but has a considerable downside. With my eyes on those contracts and my promise to you, I've come up with a solution to deal with the broken contract and re-affirm my mandate—our mandate—to keep Clarence Bay a prosperous small town."

He brought his cupped hands together in front of himself, about ten centimetres apart. He hauled in a deep breath to steady his twitching nerves, sorted his pages.

"I declined BDC's outrageous offer and successfully negotiated with Althorp to accept the land at Mill Lake as a substitute for the lost land on Georgian Bay. Clarence Bay is off the hook for a multi-million-dollar fee."

"Well done, Ryan," somebody shouted. A smattering of applause supported the evaluation.

"The good news doesn't end there. Instead of an exclusive resort for summer people, Clarence Bay will get a mixed-income eco-friendly development for year-round residents. The development will respect the environment and support a vibrant downtown core. The increased tax base will provide public services like buses and lifeguards. The Mill Lake development will supply interesting, challenging, long-term employment to keep our kids at home. Clarence Bay will be at the forefront of planning strategies for the twenty-first century."

Third point covered. The applause was so reassuring; Ryan

barely heard the growing rumblings. But he heard it.

"My promise to you is three-fold: clear, clean, and small. I'm before you now to make it clear that council knows everything of which I speak today. They know it all. However, to belie the appearance of dirty dealing behind closed doors, to avoid even a hint of scandal, to function within the law as CEO of our family company—I resigned the mayor's seat *before* I opened negotiations with Althorp."

So many wheels spun in so many heads, the hall sounded like an iron foundry. The applause started small and grew in volume. Pockets of troubling silence remained, as expected. On the whole, the people were receptive and reassuring.

"I thank you all for your continued support and look forward to Clarence Bay becoming the best place to live in Canada."

Ryan drew a huge cleansing breath and his numb hands fell to his sides. Paul stepped forward and slung his arm over Ryan's shoulder to urge his frozen stance into motion. People approached with words of understanding and sympathy for his choice between the devil and the deep blue bay.

If only his Dad reacted the same way.

Beep, beep, beep, beep. Cathy pushed the Cancel button before the line connected for the long-distance number. What a coward. But, she desperately needed to talk to somebody. *Dio mio,* the whole my-aunt-is-my-mother thing had fractured her sense of self. The only person she wanted to talk to was the only person likely to hang up on her. Ryan. She missed him with an unexpected intensity, missed his touch, his intelligence, his kindness. No one else had such deep insight into her relationships with Yola and Lucia. No one else could help her put herself back together again.

She reached for the phone, for Ryan.

"Mom, Mom, Dad's gonna be on TV!" Hayley ran into Cathy's home office jolting her away from her supposed study of complex budget sheets.

Leo? On Canadian TV?

Cathy blinked, not quite comprehending her daughter.

Oh, duh, Ryan.

Hayley hauled Cathy out of her chair and down the hall to the front parlour. A commercial played soundlessly on the television. Hayley cuddled up to her grandmother.

"Hi, Mamma. You're back early." For the first time her tongue didn't stumble over the name. Mamma noticed. Her smile trembled and firmed as Cathy bent to kiss her mother's cheek.

"*Si,* Leo had a business appointment with Giancarlo. I didn't want to bother them, so I came to join you three for supper."

"Helen went out, but there's lasagne in the oven."

"Mmm, I know, it smells delicious."

Cathy pointed at the television. "Do you have any idea what this is about?"

"Not a bit."

"Hayley? Did your dad say anything to you?"

"Nope. The guy said something about it just before the stupid commercial."

The ads ended and the anchorman for the northern Ontario regional station smiled into the camera. A small map with a pin stuck in Clarence Bay showed to the man's left. "In a surprise development, Ryan Chisholm, the newly-elected mayor of Clarence Bay, has resigned his close-fought seat after a mere four months in office. Reporter Tara Shearing spoke with Chisholm this afternoon. Tara..."

A whippet of a woman with a faux-serious expression said something or other. Cathy didn't hear the hand-off for the disbelieving din in her ears. The camera switched to Ryan, his handsome face occupying the screen in living colour. He smiled and her knees wobbled with a shock of longing. She collapsed onto the couch beside Hayley.

"Dad's on TV. Look!" Hayley bounced with excitement. "Hi, Dad!" she shouted, muffling Ryan's first words. Mamma hushed her.

"...complex and difficult decision." His voice resonated in her heart and sent shivers down her spine. Damn, she missed him so much.

She listened, dumbfounded, as Ryan stated his actions and detailed their reasons.

The endangered rattler. Eww.

His father's heart attack and subsequent surgery. Ryan, Mark, and Nana Jean must be still so worried. Ryan had even declined the invitation to Mamma's wedding because of Bucky.

The offer from an unidentified conglomerate. Big Deal Corporation?

The land substitution. Brilliant solution. Clarence Bay will truly benefit from his actions.

The conflict of interest and his resignation. Oh no. After he'd campaigned so hard. Please don't mention Hayley's mistake.

A compelling story. A veritable hero.

"No, I'm no hero," Ryan replied to the reporter. "I'm a man who wants to keep his promise to his town in whatever way circumstances permit."

"A noble sentiment. Thank you for being with us, Ryan."

"You're welcome." Ryan looked directly into the camera, directly into Cathy's stuttering heart.

Tara finished up and handed back to the anchorman. The rest of the news was an unintelligible babble as Cathy mulled over the implications to Ryan. Wonder what his father thought about the whole thing?

And then it hit her. It began as a small involuntary contraction in her belly, rumbled through her chest, pulled her mouth up one side of her face. With a gasp, she sucked it back, held it in. Surrendered. She fell back into couch while great, gasping, soul-freeing gales of laughter burst from her. Tears soon joined to finish the cleansing of her heart.

"Caterina, what is it? Is something wrong?"

"Mom, what's so funny?"

When she could finally speak again, she said to her family, "No, Mamma, there's nothing wrong. I thought *we* had scandals in the family, but they were never *this* big."

CHAPTER 18

Third Time Lucky

"You are the dumbest business man I have ever met! Why did you give up the BDC contract?"

Ryan wanted to cover his ears and hum loudly to block out another repetition of his dad's lecture. Instead, he paced to the other end of Mark's family room.

"You know all the answers to all the questions. Now calm down. You don't want another heart attack, do you?" Mark said in a futile attempt to halt his father's tirade.

"Fat lot you care! Why did I ever expect you to be any good at running my company? You two are gonna kill me with your stupid ideas."

"Enough!" Ryan shouted.

Surprised, his father stopped, mouth ajar. He snapped his jaw shut and drew himself up as tall as he could while seated in a recliner. "What did you say?"

Once upon a time, the gesture and the glare had scared Ryan witless. Now that he'd started, he would finish. "I said I've had enough. And so has Mark. During the year I worked for you, I saw enough shady deals and sleight-of-hand contracts to make me sick. You negotiated with your cronies for the most money you could make. Regardless of what happened to those around you or the town you were born in and lived in your whole life. I ran for mayor to stop what amounted to a land racket."

"Did you not benefit from those deals? Did I not give you two everything you wanted as kids?"

"Sure, we had a comfortable life, fun at camps, hockey equipment and tons of other things. We knew we had it good and we're grateful. But the end does not justify the means."

"Did you think I was in business for any other reason than to make money? I'm no candy-assed philanthropist."

"Philanthropy is a good thing. The strong among us are obliged to help the weak—"

"They'll suck you dry."

Ryan slashed the air with his hand. "All this is immaterial. You resigned as CEO and gave the job to me. I hoped for your support in running great-grandfather's company. I must have been dreaming in Technicolor. As agreed, the company is mine, to run as I see fit. As agreed, you will *not* interfere."

"Well, practically giving the land away is sure as hell not what I would do."

"No, it isn't. But newsflash, Dad, I'm not you. For a while, I thought I might be and it scared me shitless. I refuse to define myself by not being you. I am me. No more, no less. Just me. Take it or leave it."

His dad gaped at him for long minutes. Unexpectedly, he turned to Mark, "Are you with him on this?"

"Completely. The town will be better off. You know Ryan won't destroy the company."

His dad slumped in the recliner, his face grey with fatigue, and absently rubbed the top edge of the scar peeking between the unbuttoned collar of his shirt. Finally he raised his head, looked Ryan in the eye. "Okay, son. I'd rather live than fight. Do it your way."

Tension slid off Ryan's back like a ton of bricks clattering off a scaffold. He simply nodded, limp and empty from the argument. "Thanks, Dad. You won't regret it."

"On one condition," Dad scowled at him, prepared for another slap down. Ryan's shoulders climbed back up around his ears.

"You bring your daughter home if you want to distract me from what you're up to." Geez, Ryan's shoulders were like a pair of yoyos—up, down, up, down, tense, relax.

"Hayley will be here for March break. You do what you can to get stronger for her."

The stubborn old goat glared at him. "I meant permanently."

"No. I won't take her away from her mother."

"I want to spend time with my granddaughter before I kick the bucket."

"The guilt trip will only move the bucket around so I can puke in it. Someone will be disappointed. If not you, then Cathy."

"Your ex-whatever is more important than your old man?"

"Yes, absolutely. Cathy is the most important one of all."

The words rang with a truth that damn neared bust his heart with joy.

Of course, Cathy was the most important person to him. He had never stopped loving her, longing for her. And, now, dammit, he was going to do something about it and not take no for an answer.

A huge grin splitting his face, he rushed across the room and planted a kiss on his stunned father's thinning hair. "Dad, you're a freaking genius and I'm a total idiot."

Ryan tore out of the house and into his truck.

Ryan huddled into his leather coat as he strode briskly along the sidewalk. He paused to assess the big red brick house with a million-dollar view of High Park in Toronto. Festive streamers and balloons were visible through every brightly-lit window on the main floor. A group of people came from the opposite direction and entered the house, spilling party sounds across the daring spears of spring bulbs.

Damn, he'd forgotten Hayley's excitement over some huge shindig. Like he summoned her with the thought, Hayley popped out of the door and ran down the steps into his arms.

"Daddy! Daddy!" Her unadulterated happiness lifted his soul.

Would Cathy respond the same way? Of course she would. He hoped.

"Hey, honey." He kissed her cheek and carried her up the stairs and into the warm house. The second he put her down, she spun to bell her skirt around her legs.

"See my party dress. Isn't it pretty?"

"It's almost as pretty as you are, Hayley-girl."

He hugged his little girl close, revelling again in her very existence. She wrapped her skinny arms around his waist and nuzzled his chest.

"You smell nice, Daddy. Is that for Mom?"

He tapped her nose. "Do you think she'll like it?"

She tucked her hands under her chin and batted her

eyelashes. "She'll swoon over you."

Ryan was still laughing as she took his coat like a proper hostess and jammed it into the overstuffed closet like an average kid.

"C'mon in. Everybody's here for the rehearsal dinner."

His heart fell to his feet and he tripped over the darn thing, stumbled a few steps, and caught his balance. "Is your mom getting married?"

"Mom?" She tilted her head at him just like her mother. "No way! Not Mom. Nonna!"

"That's right. Zia Yola's getting married to Leo." He still had a hard time thinking of the lady by any other name.

"Poor Dad. You forgot you were invited because of Grandpa and having to quit as mayor, didn't you?" She took his hand with sympathy in her eyes. "But now he's lots better, so you came anyway."

He squeezed her hand and gave her a reassuring smile. "You are one smart little girl. I guess I did forget. And Grandpa's doing much better."

Hayley tugged him through the open doors and into the light and laughter. The pretty cocktail dresses and dark suits made him conscious of his pale yellow shirt, dress slacks, and loafers.

"I'm not dressed for a party."

"Don't worry about your clothes, Dad. Mom will be so happy to see you, she won't care."

He dropped his hand from the front of his shirt. "Will she? Be happy?"

"Totally. C'mon, this way." Like a tugboat with a tanker, she dragged him inexorably through the crowded front parlour and into the massive kitchen. People milled about the island and spilled out the French doors into the back yard where heaters kept the temperature bearable.

Brilliant red captured his gaze immediately. Cathy stood in a group, her back to him. On the circuitous route over, he absorbed the view of her curvy butt and slender waist in a knockout red dress. Her dark hair was a pouf of curls twisted with a few red ribbons. Hayley went to her, touched her arm and Cathy turned.

Smoky sexy eyes and full red lips rounded in joyful surprise. Her joy leapt across the room and settled in Ryan's heart. A huge smile split her face.

And vanished.

His heart just stopped. Simply stopped.

At her touch, an incredibly handsome older Italian man turned to face him, his tailored suit driving home the fact that Ryan had come to the ball dressed in rags.

A younger, taller version of the older man approached Ryan. He blinked back the sensation of seeing double, then triple, then... Oh God, there were five of them?

"Ryan! How perfect to see you here." Zia Yola stepped from between Version Two and Version Three. Her smile lit her eyes. She looked years younger, trim and happy as she wrapped him in a hug and a cloud of perfume. "You were the one person missing from the festivities. Come and meet my *fidanzato,* my fiancé. You will like him as he already likes you."

He didn't resist her urging him to Cathy and the older man. The quad squad followed closely. The expression on Cathy's face gave Ryan the odd sensation of being led to his doom.

Zia Yola released him and tucked her arm into the older man's elbow. "This is my Leo. Leo this is Ryan Chisholm."

The older man beamed at him and grasped his hand. "So this is my Hayley's father. I am pleased to finally meet you, though I have a bone to pick with you."

Ryan turned, scanning the five Italians, seeing the resemblance in the nose, the jaw line, the set of the head on neck and shoulders. Of course, Cathy's family.

Cathy slid between Zia Yola and Leo and tucked a hand into the crook of each elbow. "Allow me to formally introduce you to my parents." She turned proudly to Zia Yola. "Mamma you already know. This is my father, Leo Giacometti." She kissed her father's cheek. Cathy waved to the five men crowding Ryan's back. "These are his sons by his first wife." She rattled of a list of names sounding like an Italian menu.

Hayley bounded over to Zia Yola's side. "And I'm their real granddaughter."

The wall of men tightened close behind him. Five hands landed heavily on his shoulders, bending his knees. "And we want to know why you haven't married our Caterina yet," said Version One with menace in his voice.

Ryan straightened under the weight of those hands—and shrugged them off. He locked gazes with his sweet Cathy. "Because she keeps saying no. But for some reason I still keep asking."

She cracked a huge smile and practically ran into his arms.

He swept her up and spun her around, clearing the space around them, before putting her gently back on her feet. She felt so damn good against him. He wanted to hold her there for the rest of their lives. She took his face in her soft hands, held him until he went still, until his breath stalled in his tight dry throat. Brown eyes glittering with wicked intent, she rose on tiptoe and kissed him. Not caring who watched, he pulled her closer yet, kissing her back until she softly whimpered.

"Hey, *sorella,* I suggest you get a room," Version Four interrupted.

She broke the kiss. "Shut up, Ilario," she said while still looking up at Ryan. Tears of joy shimmered in her beautiful eyes.

"Just wait until the town hears this!" Ryan laughed.

Cathy rolled her eyes and stepped back. But only a tiny step, as that was all that Ryan would allow. Not that she was complaining. "Oh, please, do we have to talk to the town? The gossip must be horrific."

He shook his head, his beautiful grey eyes twinkling down at her. "The gossips are beside themselves with indecision. They just don't know which scandal is the juiciest. They debate it endlessly amongst themselves, while I just go about my business."

"And now, folks," he addressed her grinning family over his shoulder as he gently, firmly, tugged her away from them. "Cathy and I really need to talk—alone." In the hallway, he headed up the stairs, towing her along. "Which room is yours?"

Nerves chattering, knees clattering, Cathy directed him up to the third floor. She scanned her room as they entered and scooped up the strapless bra she'd chosen not to wear this evening. She felt his eyes on her hands as she folded it and put it away. She lifted her gaze and caught a sneaking disappointment in his eyes.

A gust of laughter drifted up the stairs. Ryan closed and locked the door. Silence settled over the room. Then he was across the floor, his hands around her waist, his mouth on hers, swallowing her gasp, pulling her flush against his responsive body.

Long minutes later, he released her. "I needed that so much. I missed you so much." Ryan said.

Cathy was still worried though. "Downstairs, you said the gossips in Clarence Bay left you alone. Is that true? What did they say when they found out about me and Mamma?"

"Everybody adores Zia Yola—what do you call her by the way?"

"For a while I called her Zia Mamma, but now I call my mother Mamma. Hayley switched to Nonna in the blink of an eye."

He nodded. "Anyway, the whole town adores your mother, just like they adore your daughter. They've forgiven me for abandoning the mayor's office because—well, because I gave them the small town they wanted—no matter the means. What they will never forgive is—"

"If you have anything to do with me and my scandalous secrets?" She lifted her brow in a teasing question.

"You're just jealous because my scandal is bigger than yours," he teased her back.

"Mine involved generations."

"Mine involved a whole town."

She laughed with a bow of surrender. "You win, Ryan. The floor is yours."

He bowed with a cheeky grin. "Thank you. The good gossipy folks of Clarence Bay will never forgive me if I don't tell them all about...Yola's wedding in full and glorious detail."

Cathy's arms dropped to her sides. "You're kidding."

"Nope. The folks of Clarence Bay are a romantic lot, in love with love. Romance flourishes on the grapevine—more than any other gossip. They'll be delighted Yola is getting a reward for all her years of sacrifice."

Cathy couldn't recall any incidents from her youth that would refute his view of his town. Although plenty of examples sprang to her mind from last summer, when an adult perspective had altered her perceptions. Sure, there were people like the Carleton-Grants, but there were many more like Melody and her parents, and Emma and her brother.

"Now, the next thing you can do to make the town sigh with happiness—is to make me the happiest man in the world." He reached into his pocket, dropped to one knee, took her hand and kissed it. He turned his hand to reveal a ring in Streight's distinctive textured black box. He grinned at her tiny gasp of approval. "I've loved you since grade three. I loved you when you left me, both times. Despite all that, I still love you. Cathy, will you marry me?"

One large and two smaller diamonds winked at Cathy then scampered away with her heart. He'd laid to rest all of her objections. There was only one supporting argument. She loved him. From a tousled boy to a mature responsible man, she'd loved him all her life. "Yes."

He blinked as if he didn't quite believe her. "Really?"

"Yes, really."

Grinning, she waggled the fingers of her left hand to remind him of his duty. Chuckling, he slid the ring on and sealed it in place with a kiss.

"I love you, my silly man."

"Silly? Silly! I'll show you silly." He rose to his feet, scooped her up, tumbled her to the bed, and followed her down to the quilted softness. She squealed in delight, opened her arms and her heart to his love. Gazing up into his handsome face and gorgeous grey eyes, she memorized the moment. His sandy curls embraced her fingertips as she cupped the back of his head and drew his mouth down to hers. She opened her mouth to his caressing tongue.

He groaned and deepened the kiss, tightened his hug until she gasped for breath. He released her only enough to rain kisses over her face and neck, nibble on her shoulders.

Desperate for the feel of his skin, she tugged his shirt from his slacks and burrowed under the soft cotton. Smooth skin over firm muscle delighted her hands. "Too long, too long since I touched you."

"Never so long again." He spread his knees over her hips, rose up, and shucked off his shirt.

She lifted herself to press her breasts against his tanned chest, kissing and caressing and nibbling. A breeze down her back, told her he'd found the zipper and put it to good use. Shoving the dress to her waist, he cupped her breasts. Almost folding himself in half, he bent to kiss her nipples.

She halted him by clasping his wrists.

"What?" he groaned.

She stroked his erection through his slacks. His hips jerked forward, thrusting into her grip. She tugged at the fabric covering him. "These need to go."

"Yes ma'am." He leapt off the bed and got naked in three seconds flat, stripping off trousers, underwear, socks and shoes in a single movement.

"Nice trick." She reached out and stroked his hard silky

length, tearing a rough gasp from his belly. "Now come here." His body went rigid under her exploring fingers, unbending briefly to spread his legs for her caresses. He jerked hard enough to fall over when her questing hit the magic spot. Amazed he was still upright, she tested his limit and mouthed the tip of him. He leapt away, huffing and puffing, he bent over with his hands on his knees, to regain control.

She gave herself a smug little smile for a job well done.

Moments later, he lifted his head. His face and chest were flushed, his eyes dark and glittering.

"Pleased with yourself?"

"Uh huh." She licked her bottom lip.

"Well, now it's my turn to make you crazy." He prowled towards her. Her nipples peaked in anticipation. He laid her back on the bed, captured her wrists in his hands and pressed them down into the mattress. He kissed her mouth and only her mouth. Not a single other bit of her did he touch with any bit of him. He kissed her until her breasts begged for his hands on her. Arching up, she was just a tiny distance too far away. Without warning, he tweaked one straining nipple and she flew into orgasm. He slid a big hand up her quivering thigh and pressed the heel of his hand into her throbbing core. She cried out and convulsed on a massive aftershock. He kept up the rhythmic pressure until she went limp.

"Now who's pleased?"

She gave him a feeble smile. "Still me and not you."

He threw back his head and rocked the rafters with a shout of laughter.

"We'll see about that."

Ryan rolled her over and slid the zipper of her dress all the way down, laying kisses on her spine as he went. She obligingly lifted her hips to allow him to slip the dress down her silk-clad legs and off. Dragging out the anticipation of grabbing her gorgeous bare ass, he laid her sexy red dress over a chair. She lay sprawled across the bed on her stomach, faking sleep.

He grinned, crossed his arms over his chest. To remove, or not to remove, the red shoes. He examined them for function. Ah, they just slipped off. Easy does it. Mustn't disturb the sleeping princess. Yet. Her shoes plopped quietly to the thick carpet.

His good fortune struck him mute. The beautiful woman on the bed was his, all his. Finally all his. From the tumble of dark curls and red ribbons, down the long sweep of her spine, over the curve of her luscious ass to her excellent legs sleek in thigh-high stockings, he looked his fill of her.

Hmm, where to begin his delectable feast? While he pondered, she turned her head towards him and peeked up at him through the thickness of her lashes. She smiled coyly. His heart hammered in his chest with love. Her eyes drifted shut, granting him permission to eat at will. His cock bobbed with excitement.

"You know, I have always loved your ass," he said to warn her. She still jumped then wriggled in pleasure when he trailed fingers down her spine, over the fine curve and dipped between her thighs. Her hips thrust down into the bed. He bent and licked where her legs creased into her butt. Her woman's scent, hot and sweet, drove him a little mad. Mad enough to bite the juicy curve. She squealed and he soothed the faint mark with tongue and lips. Lifting her hips, she invited and tempted him to touch her. He accepted the invitation with a slow soft slide of his fingers between her sexy folds. She moaned into the pillow. He played among her curls, until his hips kept rhythm with hers. He withdrew his hand and laid it over the base of her spine, quieting her and himself.

Enough of this distance.

He retrieved a condom from his trousers, gasped at the cool glide of latex over his hot cock. He stripped off her stockings, teasing her with nips and licks, leaving no square millimeter untouched.

"Turn over." Demand? Request? He didn't care.

She rolled in a luscious sweep of flesh, lifted her arms, opened her legs.

Controlling the urge to pounce on her, take her, and pump like a madman, he eased his weight onto her welcoming curves, moaning at contact with her soft flesh. Smiling down into her lovely face, he savoured her beneath him then lifted his hips and entered her in one easy thrust. Slick wet heat surrounded him, stole his breath, and gave it to her. She wrapped her legs around him, locked her ankles in the small of his back, sliding him deep, sliding him home. They groaned in satisfaction.

She started a strong rhythm and he followed her, adored her, loved her until the rhythm broke into wave upon wave of soul-shattering, soul-healing ecstasy. Inert, he laid atop her until she gasped for breath. He rolled off her like a dead man, spooned around her like a lover.

He puffed a straying ribbon away from his mouth. "Now that would be a real scandal," he declared.

"What?" she murmured already half-asleep.

"Not sharing this for the rest of our lives."

Epilogue

Later that fall

"Here's the photos from our wedding," Cathy said.

Ryan looked up from ending his call. Cathy plopped a large box on his conference table, circled his desk, and made herself comfortable in his lap. He wrapped his arms around her waist, holding her securely.

"You do know that employee fraternization is against company policy."

"Not for the CFO. Not if she just happens to be the wife of the CEO. She's feeling very deprived."

"Deprived? You want a bigger house, a fancier car, more clothes?"

"No. I want something only you can give me."

He placed a gentle hand over her tummy and gave her a charming lopsided grin. "You have our baby in your belly. What more do you want?"

"A kiss." She pouted playfully. "I haven't had one since

breakfast. And that's simply unacceptable." She toyed with the buttons on his shirt.

"Well, I can't have an unhappy CFO," he murmured and kissed her the way she liked best—soft and pliant building to passionate and breathless. She sighed and leaned against his shoulder.

"Happy now?"

She wiggled her butt into his burgeoning erection. "Very. Hayley's happy, too. She told me at breakfast she can't wait to play with her new baby."

"*Her* new baby?"

She giggled and rolled her eyes. "I know. She's gone all protective now. Told me Lindsey said to stay away from second-hand smoke."

"Yeah, Lindsey calls herself an expert with all her younger brothers. Declared she's going to be a paediatrician when she grows up."

Her face blanked for a moment, an unusual expression for his very sharp executive. Her hand cupped her right side. A bright joy lit her face.

"The baby moved!" She grabbed his hand and planted it on her little belly. They sat frozen for some time, but apparently, the little guy had gone to sleep. Regret filled him. He wished he'd been with Cathy to share her joys and trials with Hayley. He sighed the sadness away and patted the snoozing baby. This time would be different.

"It's only three months, so you'll have plenty of chances to feel him kicking. Come see the pictures." She kissed his cheek, climbed from his lap and pulled him over to the conference table where she'd left the large white box of their finished wedding photos.

From the top layer, Cathy took a large framed photo of Mamma glowing in deep golden-rose silk and Papà in a charcoal suit. Over a year since their wedding and their joy shone like a new-minted loonie. Cathy ran a finger over their beloved faces, an answering smile warming her heart.

"They're so happy. Reunited after all those years." Ryan said, his hands gripping her thickening waist.

Another photo showed Hayley in her flowered pale-pink and rose dress coming down the aisle, grinning broadly. A family photo, crammed with faces of all ages, caught at her throat and easy tears brimmed in her eyes. From a family of three women, they'd grown to a sprawling family of four generations in Canada alone. From a skinny stem to great big tree, Hayley had said. Plus, there were countless relatives waiting to meet them in Italy next summer.

She said a silent prayer for Lucia and Antonio—hoping they were happy with the way their family had grown. Cathy's resentment had faded with understanding. Her aunt and uncle had done the best they knew how for a young girl in a desperate situation. It was better to accept and learn from others rather than wasting emotional energy on the unchangeable past.

Another photo was the classic wedding party shot. Cathy and Ryan stood between Melody, Emma and Meg on one side, and Mark, Paul and Asher on the other. Every last of one of them were grinning until their faces hurt.

"Thank you again for asking Meg to be in the wedding party. She was afraid you'd hate her forever after she lied about me being her husband."

"I admit, she did give me a few sick moments, but she

apologized, and she's family..."

Cathy lifted the photo closer. "Emma's so sad." She showed her husband.

"You're right."

"She's worried about her grandmother. Myra's hasn't been doing well for months and now she's failing badly."

He shook his head. "Poor Emma's had so many losses in her life. It's her time for happiness."

"We'll have to see what we can do for her."

The final photo showed Cathy in her bridal gown of palest golden-rose. At her side, Ryan stood proud and manly in his dark tux.

"You brought tears to my eyes when you came down the aisle. You're so beautiful." Ryan nuzzled her neck. His hot breath fanned goose bumps down her back. She lowered the photo and tilted her head to let him closer, humming her approval when he slid her shirt from her shoulder and nibbled on the exposed skin.

"I thought you were adorable the way you choked on your vows," she teased

He stopped kissing and leaned his forehead on her bare shoulder. "Oh, God, don't remind me. I blubbered like a baby." She giggled at the heat of his blush against her skin.

Turning in his strong arms, she cupped his beautiful face. "I will treasure the memory forever." She stood on tiptoe and pressed a kiss to his soft generous mouth—a kiss holding the promise of an open loving future completely above scandal.

Meet Joan

Joan Leacott is skilled in many arts: sewing, knitting, crochet, cross-stitch, painting, and piano. The skill favoured by her husband and son is cooking, especially pumpkin pie.

She spends her winters in Toronto, Canada attending piano classes, melting in the hot yoga studio, and writing.

Her summers are spent on the shores of Georgian Bay relaxing on the deck with a romance novel and a glass of wine. After she's done her laps in the bay, she settles down to write more multi-generational stories of people living and loving in today's world.

Joan loves to hear from her readers.

Connect with Joan via her website at **www.JoanLeacott.ca.** Read personal posts, sign up for her newsletter, and link to Joan on Facebook.

See you on the streets of Clarence Bay!

Other Books by Joan Leacott

Coming Winter 2013

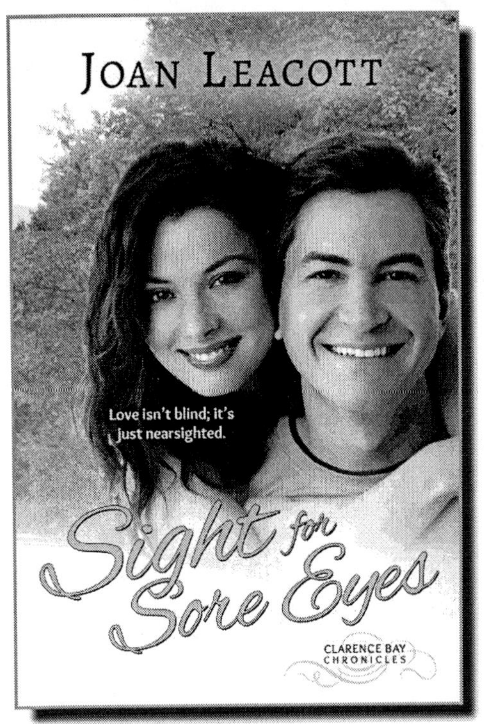

Love isn't blind; it's just nearsighted.

Emma Finn has had enough of life-altering changes. Stability is all she wants right now, no matter how boring.

Ophthalmologist Asher Stockdale wants her to dust off her old dream of globe-trotting photographer, no matter the cost to his new dream of home, family and small-town life.

Carpenter ants, cream pies, and a pair of scheming seniors help Emma and Asher to see what really lies before their eyes.